THE FIXER

Steve Bunce has worked as a journalist and broadcaster since 1985. He has been at five Olympic Games and reported on over fifty fights in Las Vegas. As well as being a regular columnist in *Boxing Monthly*, he also contributes to *The Independent*. He has a monthly boxing show on BBC 5 Live and a weekly sports chat show on BBC London.

THE FIXER

STEVE BUNCE

MAINSTREAM
PUBLISHING

EDINBURGH AND LONDON

First published in Great Britain in 2010 by
MAINSTREAM PUBLISHING COMPANY
(EDINBURGH) LTD
7 Albany Street
Edinburgh EH1 3UG

ISBN 9781845965624

The Fixer is a work of fiction. Well-known figures from the boxing
world appear, but for the most part their actions and conversations
are fictitious. All other characters and descriptions of events are
products of the author's imagination and any resemblance to
actual persons or places is entirely coincidental

A catalogue record for this book is available
from the British Library

Typeset in Champion and Concorde

Printed in Great Britain by
Clays Ltd, St Ives plc

1 3 5 7 9 10 8 6 4 2

LONDON: A BRAVERY PROBLEM

Peter Close lost most of his fights. He had just lost for the ninth time in a row and it showed. It was not the longest losing streak in the history of the ring, but it was nothing to brag about. It looked like a child had drawn a pair of cartoon goggles on his face. One eye was black, a general term that always does the trick when talking about damage to an eye, and one was closed. Blood stuck to six dark stitches on his bottom lip. A red tissue dropped from his nose. He was not a bad fighter or father or husband; he was just a bit too brave for his own health. And in professional boxing that made him stupid. He was a nice guy with a bravery problem.

Ray Lester walked from the desk with a tall drink in one hand and a pack of frozen peas in the other. He took another look at the fighter and shook his head. He shook his head a lot. He gave the peas to the man and took a long sip of the drink before he sat down on a worn black leather recliner. It was gone midnight and Lester could still smell the fight on the man. It was the stale and familiar smell of blood and sweat and grease and dirt and smoke. It was the smell of the poor. The rat-arsed kid in school had had the same poor smell. The man on the sofa also smelled of defeat. That was an old smell, a memory smell. Lester wondered, and not for the first time, why it was that so few boxers take a shower after their fights? They leave the ring, get back to the changing-room and wipe the blood and snot from their face and chest. They spray their armpits and gel their hair, but that's it for the evening. They are dressed and ready for the out. *Dirty sods, to tell the truth.*

A few hours earlier at the Wembley Conference Centre, Close had been dropped and stopped in three rounds. It was his 43rd defeat in 52 fights. He was a journeyman from the old school. He was just a good loser. He lost fights for a living and was a necessary and kosher part of the boxing business. Close was an idiot in boxing terms because he still fought like a winner. Lester had tried to talk sense into him countless times and it was a waste. How do you tell a man to forget his pride and to just lose when he still thinks he can win? Where's the dignity in the noble old game?

Lester had known Close for a long time. He had known Close before the fighter had stopped caring about the defeats on his record and that was a lot of fights ago. Lester had booked him for this latest night's work. In fact, Lester had booked him for most of his recent fights. Lester had also refused a lot of fights and turned down decent money for several late-notice jobs. But not everybody said no and that was a problem in boxing. Lester cared about Close and liked him as a man, but business in the boxing business is most definitely strictly business. There is no love and no heart and that is why Lester booked Close for fights that the pair of them knew the fighter had no chance of winning. Business. It is a mistake to look for too much glory in the fight game and, to be honest, it can be dangerous.

The way Lester approached a deal was easy: he wanted to make sure that everybody made the most amount of money for the least amount of risk. He had to make sure that Close never got seriously hurt. From where Lester was sitting, it looked like he had failed miserably. But it was impossible to book Close in a fight where he had a chance of winning and make any dough. Close, when he wasn't dribbling through stitches, was aware of the conflict in the job he had chosen. He knew that if he wanted to win a fight, he had to take a drop in pay and fight in obscurity on dinner shows at venues that time had forgotten and the money had missed.

But boxing is a harsh professional sport on both sides of the ropes. It was also hard for Lester to get a living from writing about boxing. Those days were long gone. The paper business had been in the shitter for a few years. There were simply not enough names to keep the editors happy and not enough editors prepared to miss a lunch with a football agent, or a man working for the agent, to listen to a boxing story. There had been a slight improvement in interest of late and the writing caper was thankfully starting to get as popular as it had been in the '90s, when Naseem Hamed, Lennox Lewis, Nigel Benn, Steve Collins, Michael Watson, Frank Bruno and Chris Eubank dominated. It had been a decade of conflict followed by years of avoidance. To make ends meet, Lester booked a few fighters for one or two promoters and picked up a few quid on the side. He was doing what reporters from other sports had been doing for years. It worked, and during the last few years the extra money from the work with fighters and promoters had taken over from the other money. It was not, strictly speaking, a legal arrangement, but it was comfortable and easy for all involved. Some of the old writers – men from the glory days – shook their silver-haired heads in disgust. Bent money in professional sport. *Shirley not.*

In theory, Lester needed a licence from the men who ran the sport, but that was too much like hard work. And saying that they ran the sport was stretching the truth. Promoters ran the sport. Where was the harm in Lester nicking a few quid? Lester helped fighters get a living. It was also especially important to Lester that all of the men he helped had reached out to him.

Lester was not a whore. There are too many of them in the boxing business. Lester worked with men he had known for a long time, and he liked to think that there was a degree of mutual understanding and respect. Not exactly bosom buddies, but something different. He was probably deluding himself and he probably knew it. Trust and respect are elusive in the boxing world; the moment one man takes a pound note from another man, the barriers and rules tend to crash down.

Lester was not a fool. He knew who did and who didn't respect him. Close had respect for Lester and that is what made each beating, each cut and stitch, hard for Lester to stomach.

Lester was not a pimp. He wasn't out there in the shadows after fights, telling beaten fighters he could get them more money. Lester knew that a guy with his eye sliced open and his ribs taped together would believe any type of shit in the hours after a fight. It was easy to turn a fighter's sore head in the hours and days following a loss. A fighter would sell his child for revenge at that moment; he is always low then, cursing the idiots who helped to get him bashed up. He is looking for somebody who will help him blame other people, a voice that understands his warped reasoning. What he needs is a meal and a bunk-up, but too often what he finds is a smile on a snake.

Never forget: it is never a fighter's fault when he loses. Sure, it is a glorious delusion, but there is always an excuse somewhere and a reason. If a beaten fighter can find an ear, he will bend it all night. He will bend it until it sizzles with indignation and bullshit. Boxing's pimps fit the role sweetly and, with their gentle assurances and a fine line in cobblers, they hook fighters with their sleazy lies. Lester told himself he was not like that, but he did often wonder. Looking at Close's face would make a mackerel think. Boxing is a lonely planet for anybody unlucky enough to have a conscience. Ray Lester was not a bad man, but he had his moments.

The fight was supposed to be an easy payday, if there is ever such a thing at the level that Mr Close called home. Close would lose – that was a given – but if he'd used his brain he wouldn't have got hurt. Simple, just move for a round, stay away from the kid's left hook and the short right and, if it was getting a bit warm after a few rounds, the corner would pull him out. Bish, bosh, bang. Straight business. It was the way things worked; it was not too brave, but it was sensible. On any Friday or Saturday night in Britain, a dozen boxers lose the same way: they lose because they have no chance of winning. They are not in fixed fights; they are involved in business deals in the ring – simple transactions in a sport sick of defending itself. There are no fixed fights. It's true, there are some tossers working in the media who are convinced the sport is crooked. There is no need to pay somebody to jump on the floor when TV companies and worried managers are scared of letting prospects fight anybody with a pulse for the first three years of their careers.

The New York agent Johnny Bos joked about a pulse, but not much of a pulse, being the only prerequisite for an opponent. A matchmaker finds a fighter like Close and he is booked. Close then becomes part of the building process for a prospect. It's a beautiful way to do simple business; there is no need for fixed fights and gangsters and investigations. It's not football; boxing is a straight business. It's certainly not horse racing. The posh and country and racing mob look well with a little velvet on their collars and the same smooth touch in their nicely rounded voices. Looks and accent can be a pain; too many people in the boxing business hurt their sport when they open their mouths. If you want bad dreams, look at the fatalities at the Grand National each year.

'So, tell me what happened one more time,' Lester asked.

Close put the peas on the coffee table and dabbed at a bit of blood and spit that was trickling down his chin. His eyes were wet. Lester had only seen him look this bad once or twice before and he had been paid far more for those fights. The beating he'd taken against Justin Juuko at the Elephant two years earlier was worth every penny of the six grand he'd walked away with. The Ugandan was vicious, the best that Close had ever met, and it was not pleasant watching from ringside. Lester had taken his percentage reluctantly that night. But he had still taken it. This latest fight was for just 1,800 quid, and in Lester's mind that was not enough for what he was looking at. It was like Close had been given a partial facelift. A bad one at that – and a cheap one.

'Before the fwight, the skinny geezer from the board told me I had to win. He told me that if I lost the fwight I would lose my licence.'

It was as Lester expected. Stupid interference, and there was no need for it. He knew the men in charge at the British Boxing Board of Control, and the skinny geezer in particular. The fella was walking and talking way above his cheap suit. Sadly, he didn't know any better. He never would. He was an egg in the business and he would remain an egg no matter how many years he sat at ringside. He had been a pain in the arse for a couple of years – a danger, because he sometimes forgot the sport was a business, to tell the truth. The board's inspector had known the strength of the fight, known it was just another payday, another undercard mismatch. There was certainly no reason to scare Close and give him reason to take a hiding. The men in the blazers had the option and the power to veto the fight and tell the matchmaker to find another body; they could stop it, but there was no reason to get involved. If they started to get too busy, they would have to stop dozens of fights each week. It was, Lester knew, a pop at him, a cheap little dig. But the problem with cheap little digs is that they can go both ways.

Lester knew that the fella in question had been in Berlin a year earlier at a European title fight and he had been given a brass. It was not a big deal, and he was a grown man, but it left him open. The promoter in Germany had a favour in his pocket for future fights and now Lester had reason to bring it up. The man was arrogant.

When the Close fight was offered, it had taken Lester about two seconds to grab it firmly by the balls. He knew Close was giving weight away to the prospect, the house fighter with an unbeaten record of eleven, including nine knockouts. There would only be one winner, but that was how Close made his money. It was also how Lester nicked his little bit.

Lester also knew the prospect was not living right and would run out of gas and ideas after a few rounds. His days as a prospect would continue. He was not a smart fighter, but he thought he was and that made him *two smart* in Lester's book. In the boxing world, being *two smart* is not good. *One smart* is cool but *two smart* is dangerous. Simple, simple boxing axiom.

All Close had to do was float, hold a bit and get to about round three unmarked. Lester told him not to get involved and not to go toe-to-toe with the young banger. It's called surviving. If he followed the plan, used his brain, he would be able to glide easily to a loss on points. Basically, Close was in a lose–lose situation. And he would win both ways if he listened. What was the problem? The Berlin whore-lover from the board had just shown Lester his ring by pulling Close over and telling him that he had to win. Lester would stick it right up him at the right moment. The poor man was exposed and had just bent over and touched his toes. Dummy.

The fight was a nice and tidy bit of business. *What do people expect for a 50-quid ticket?* There were probably eleven or twelve fights on the card and so what if a few of the fights had only one possible outcome. Well, more like ten of the eleven, or eleven of the twelve, to be brutally honest. Not every fight can be 50–50. Racing is no better for mixing the good with the bad and the fast with the so obviously lame. Most races include a donkey or two with even less chance of victory than a bad pro, but that had never stopped doughnut punters from backing them. What the hell was that moron from the board doing even opening his mouth? The idiot – he could have got somebody hurt.

'So, why didn't Curly pull you out after a round or two?'

Lester knew the answer; he could guess exactly what had happened.

Curly, as he was known, was the trainer of Close and a lot of other fighters who Lester had an interest in. It suited everybody. Curly Smith had never been very brave in the corner, unlike a lot of the younger trainers who were coming through. Curly hated a beating and that is why Lester had put Close with him in 2004. A good trainer could save a fighter a lot of years by being careful, while a brave one could end a career early. Often, in the boxing ring, the two bravest people are the referee and one of the trainers. And there are times when the referee is scared to make a decision and call off a fight. If that happens, a brave trainer can get a kid killed or seriously hurt. But Curly was a good man. A raving poof but a good man, and in boxing that made him a rarity on two counts.

It was odd for Lester to miss a night at the fights, but he had been waiting for a call from Don King's matchmaker to confirm a fight for one of his heavyweights, Billy Effra. The call had come at just about the same time as Close was getting his face moved around by eight ounces of red leather. Six years earlier Effra had been a genuine heavyweight contender, but an attack of pacifism and a savage brawl with the fridge had reduced him to a half-decent name for hire and a big lump. He was not quite shadow-boxing in Close's no-chance saloon, but he was not a million miles from its door. King's man had the right news: Effra had his fight in South Africa on good money. Lester had quickly shifted the story to about ten of the Sunday papers. A simple night's work. It would be news for the morning and Billy was a nice kid; he certainly needed a break. The win over Mike Green had been a lot of defeats ago and memories never pay bills.

Lester had been busy on the phones for over an hour. No need to write, no need for a laptop, just bang it straight down the line to copy. Bosh, bosh and always a bit of a chuckle. New copytaker and the same nannies with just a bit of spin. A simple little routine with a new top and tail. It was reporting the way the old boys had done it and it was the only way he understood.

'Billy could still be the future of heavyweight boxing in Europe, according to King,' Lester repeated. All the papers had that little beauty because that was the story.

'Don has not seen such natural power in a veteran since . . . George Foreman's comeback, comma, end quotes,' claimed King's press officer, comma, Bobby Goodman.' A few papers had this version and one or two had a mixed-up version. The story was filed and it was the truth now in paper-midnight-land. It was not uncommon to vary the source of the invented quote, as long as it was complimentary and made sense. That was the rule – well, it was Ray Lester's rule and he had been taught by the boxing scribe-masters.

Yeah, it was a bit strong, but when the order is ten pars, what do people expect? Surely not the truth. And what was it that the legendary Wally Bartleman had said to Mickey Duff all those years ago on the streets of Soho when they bumped into each other? Duff had a copy of the *Evening Standard* in his hands and was reading something that Bartleman had scribbled at dawn that morning. Bartleman had been telling boxing tales in the paper since the end of the war. He was part of a triangle of war veterans writing about boxing in the London papers. George Whiting and Reg Gutteridge completed the triangle. They were three tough old bastards, but they knew their boxing. Duff was livid that day. 'Wally, this is cobblers. This is wrong. That fight ain't made. It won't get made. Why would I make it?' Duff had said. Old Wally had cleared the phlegm from his throat and put a calming hand on Duff's shoulder. 'Mickey, what do you expect for threepence, the fucking truth?' Wally loved that story. Lester had been Wally's apprentice, serving at his wooden leg for years. All gone now. Duff, too.

Lester adored the tale and others from the lips of men who operated before technology and the kids in editorial chairs sucked the heart out of boxing coverage. In Lester's mind, the Effra yarn had followed the principles of scrupulous journalism that he had picked up at the creaky, wooden knees of veterans like Bartleman and Gutteridge. They were men who knew their sources better than the sources knew themselves. Interviews were for a crisis, quick nannies were for the morning paper and the truth was for the wife. Lovely little set of rules, and please don't point that fucking Dictaphone this way. Lester had heard something similar to that a good few times.

So it had been a good night at the papers. There had been hundreds like it before and it still felt real getting a few words in a national. It had also been a nice night's work at Wembley. Lester had a bit of the two Americans in with Richard Milton – gone in four – and Sean Wayne – gone in one. And he had Closey.

Lester had missed being at the fights. He knew staying at home was a risk and he knew he had made a mistake when he opened his door to Close. The face was harsh evidence. Had he been at Wembley, he would have spoken to Curly and grabbed Close's ear before the fight. He would also have grabbed the man from the board and stuck a Berlin reminder right up his arse.

But the night was not yet over. In a few hours' time in Las Vegas he had his Colombian flyweight in a winning fight on a King undercard at the MGM. If Pablo Pérez won, which he would, he had a slot in South Africa on the Effra undercard against one of the seemingly endless stream of African flyweights. There had been a 20-year conveyor belt of dead-eyed boys with the telltale dry skin that suggested they all lost too much weight too quickly. They were six foot tall and barely tipped the scales at eight stone: fearsome flyweights and health hazards. It was not right. Lester had heard too many stories of weight-drained injured fighters. It was the anonymous injured that would one day hurt the sport in sub-Saharan Africa: victims of too many rounds and not enough care.

The fight in South Africa would be for a bogus title, a belt that was worth nothing in America but could be used in parts of Europe and Africa. Boxing belts were reduced to the market value of the territory. There was a fight for a version of the world title every week. Some weeks six or more world title fights could take place and every single one of them would slip under the radar somewhere else in the boxing world. There was a time in 2004 when Britain had 20 world champions, holding world title belts from five different sanctioning bodies. It was out of control, but the promoters, the fans and the TV executives accepted it. Lester abused the soft so-called world title fights to make money. Thankfully, the darkest days of the mutual deceit were over. The fans deserved better and the strange list of bad fighters with glittering belts had been erased. There were now good champions holding proper belts. But a lot of damage had been done.

Lester had his eye on a Danish flyweight that Torben Hansen had been wrapping in cotton wool for about two years. The Danish kid sold a lot of tickets, but he was simply not strong enough for top-level fighters. Pablo could beat him, but first he had to win in Vegas and then in South Africa. A lot of the matchmaking in boxing was a long game and Lester had played it dozens of times. He knew it would take a few months to convince Torben to accept the job, but the shrewd Danish veteran would inevitably take the fight. And when he did, the money would be good. Hansen had a lot of money because of his TV deals throughout Scandinavia, where he had been exclusive since Thor was shitting his nappies. The trouble was that nobody could win in Denmark over 12 rounds. Little Pablo would lose if it went the full 12, but he would not get hurt, that was for sure. It had 12 written all over it. Hansen was an old-fashioned but decent boxing man and it was always a pleasure to do business with him. He was a species in decline.

Close was sitting in front of Lester, serving as a reminder of what could and often did go wrong. Lester drifted back and fixed his eyes on the state of Close's face.

'So, go on.'

Lester waited, pushed back and got comfortable in the chair.

'I told Curly not to pull me out. I told him I had to fwight.'

Lester knew that was coming, too. It was hard work sometimes. Very hard work. Lester got up and went to the kitchen for his phone and a new drink. He came back into the flat's living room and dialled Smith on the phone. Lester knew that Curly would be at the Victoria, one of the oldest and dullest casinos in London. The place had carpets that had crystallised from years of abuse. Curly was there after each fight, doing a few quid on the tables and eating. Lester knew Curly had been seeing a croupier there for over 20 years; he needed to relax, unwind and he liked the Vic.

A Saturday night could be busy for a trainer like Curly. He might have five boys on, and one or two of them could be in swing fights, and that meant about six hours of constantly being prepared. Swing fights were a necessary pain for young fighters. A boxer had to be ready to 'swing' into action at any point during the night and could be gloved and ready from 5.30 until midnight, hoping that one or two of the other fights ended early. If there was a quick stoppage, the swing fight would go on. If, on the other hand, all the fights went the distance, there was a chance the swing fight would not take place. The fighters would still get paid. And some fighters like being the swing fighter.

It was a hard night's work for Curly. Lester had often seen the trainer walk away from a venue like a punch-drunk fighter, his heels scraping on the pavement and his eyes blank. It's not easy to be a good trainer. It takes a lot of effort and concentration on the night. Anyone, by the way, can be a bad trainer. Any mutt.

'Curly. Ray. Yeah, I know. He's here now. So why did you listen to him?'

Lester looked over at Close and pointed to the peas and then pointed to his eye. Close picked the peas up and put them against his head. The pack was defrosting and water rolled down Close's cheek. A beaten fighter can look a bit sad.

'Curly, Curly, listen, listen, silly bollocks. I know what he said, but that makes no difference. When was the last time he said something that made sense? He's in a right state. OK, all right. Speak in the morning.'

Lester put the phone down and looked over at Close.

'What's he say?'

Lester ignored him and pushed back in the chair and clicked a button that silently initiated a gentle vibrating sensation at the base of his spine. He closed his eyes and let his mind drift. He could hear the low hum of the machine inside the chair and remembered another night when he had listened to the sound. It was with the late Phil Martin up in Moss Side. That was when Lester first got the idea of the chair. It must have been 15 years ago, when he was doing a bit of work with Martin at Champs' Camp. The pair of them had stood in silence when Martin turned the chair on. The gentle buzzing noise tickled Martin, whose eyes would glaze with comfort. Looking back, Lester realised that Phil must have known he was close to death. Billy Graham and the fighters in the gym had no idea.

Phil's gym in Moss Side was a hard place for any fighter to learn the business and the streets outside the door were at the time the most lethal in Europe. There was a bloody handprint on the wall by the entrance at one point. It was a chilling reminder. Graffito of death. It had been one of the last desperate grabs of a 16 year old as he fell along the wall with his stomach leaking life onto the streets. He was shot, he died and the handprint of his death remained. Inside the gym, Martin was in control and he feared nobody. At the end of each session, he would walk up to his office and his mood would change. He would put on a video of a fight – any fight, because the quality was shit – and lounge back in his favourite possession: a black leather recliner with gadgets all over and a gentle humming purr from somewhere inside the padding. It was the trainer's secret: Phil and a buzzing leather chair in a room high above the streets, watching his boxers win and lose and planning a future.

Enzo Calzaghe often talks about delivering his fighters a dream.

15

Phil did that too. His high room was a private little pleasure dome. He was gazing into a future that he sadly never got to see. The chair didn't help when the cancer arrived. When it comes with a death mission, the hardest bastard in the world – a nut swinging a crowbar – has only tears to show for his fight. *Fuck you, cancer.* He died very quickly. It was a funeral service Lester would never forget and one he would never want to repeat. His story of the life and death of Phil Martin in the *Sunday Times* was the finest thing Lester had ever written. Not like the shite he had been turning out during the last few years. *Well, most of the time, to tell the truth.*

When Lester opened his eyes, Close was still looking at him. He knew that the fighter should quit, but he also knew he had to keep going because of the house and the kids. It was the same old story. He had tried to retire him slowly and get him into a gym to work with fighters. It never worked. He was hopeless as a trainer. Most fighters are unable to make the switch in the gym. It takes a few years for the desire to fade before a boxer can teach another boxer. And it takes a lot of years before a boxer becomes a trainer. What was it Billy Webster had said all those years ago, back at the Fitzroy Lodge gym? And he was right. Webster had taken Lester to one side and told him never to put the gloves on once he had taken them off. A horribly simple but ignored boxing truth. Webster had got it right. 'When you are a trainer, you have to stop being a fighter.'

In Lester's opinion, a retired fighter needed a few years to get the fight out of his blood, and even then life away from the neon lights and the hurt needed to be taken one day at a time. Boxing was a fix and a lot of fighters had it bad. Simply walking away was never enough, never a real option. Boxers Anonymous was a nice idea. That is why old boxers like the company of old boxers, and why a lot of fighters go out of control when they quit. Close was a lost cause, but he was Lester's cause.

'This is what we are going to do. I'm going to speak to the fella at the board, straighten that prick out, and I'm going to get you some easy wins up with Johnny in the Midlands. Then when Frankie Gavin goes pro after the Olympics I'm going to get you little Frankie at late notice for six grand.' It was a retirement plan. Lester took another look at Close and decided that he would not take another penny from him. If the Gavin fight could be made – or one similar – he would tell Close that it was over.

It was exactly what Close wanted to hear and he looked happy for a man in his state. It was gone one in the morning, his face had stopped aching and six grand was nearly on the table. You could close your eyes and smell six grand – money started to smell when there was about three grand on the table. It was possible to smell it the moment you walked into a room. It's a filthy, old smell even when it is new.

Close could tell Tracey about the money when he got home. He could tell her when she woke up in the morning, saw his face and banned him from taking the kids to school for a week. She did that each time he came home from a fight with a face like mince. He hated creeping in when he was bashed up, but there was no alternative. Tracey would go potty and had even whacked him on the odd occasion. Even she found it easy to hit him. He had been at her dad's third wedding with both eyes nearly closed, a constant drizzle of pus oozing from the corner of his left eyebrow. She had kicked him out of the pictures. Odd, because there were some stunning uglies on the day. Tracey's old man had about 22 years on his new wife, but she had about nine stone on him. They shared about the same amount of teeth, but she had more tattoos. The marriage never lasted – it was evens on the day that they would see midnight in a merry embrace. The odds were understandably shorter on her knocking him out. Lester had loved the wedding.

Close knew the plan would make it a bit easier for him to go home. In his mind, he was going back with a six-grand promise, and the money would make him look a bit better. The money was necessary camouflage for his stupidity in the ring a few hours earlier. He was smiling. He could feel the gelt and might now just swerve the sofa. And on the promise of six large, he might possibly pull off a rare post-fight legover. Close's punch-shot eyes glazed for a second.

Lester put his drink down and stood up.

'Have you eaten? Come on, we'll go to Vincenzo's.'

LONDON: FOOD AND THE FIGHTER

They took a cab from the flat to the club. It was just a short journey but walking the streets with a man who looked like Close at that moment was never a good idea. It is amazing how many people want to have a fight with somebody who has been in a fight – even if he is holding a pack of peas to his swollen features. It had happened a lot to Lester and he knew better than to walk at night in busy streets full of drunks with a beaten and bloody fighter.

Picking a fight with a boxer is a common mistake. A drunk at one in the morning is a brave hombre. Fighters can fight, and no matter how tired or bashed up they are they can still fight. It's what they do for a living. Even the tiniest little boxer with cuts and bruises can still hurt any civilian. It's just the way it is. Lester had seen a lot of citizens find out the painful way. Boxers get hit in the face thousands of times during their careers in gym rings and prize rings. It's a pain thing.

At the club, Tragic was on the door. He took one look at Close's face and gave Lester the unpleasant eye. It was true that Tragic liked fighters on his premises, but he liked them without bruises and without blood. It was not a good idea to have a man who looked like Close inside a restaurant. Any restaurant – even a kebab shop – would probably turn him away. Tragic's place was not a late-night kebab shop.

'Fucking 'ell, you gonna have to sit downstairs in the fuckin' corner,' Tragic told them. Evidently, the maître d' job at the Savoy had been filled.

It was dark in Tragic's basement, but the food was always good. The club was called Vincenzo's because the original owner had been called Vincenzo, though he had been gone for a thousand years. The upstairs was a mix of media people and 'Willesden warriors', the name Tragic used to describe the builders and plumbers he packed in each weekend. They were builders and plumbers who didn't really want people to know they were builders and plumbers.

They all had dough. There were far too many plumbers for it to be hip and far too many media luvvies for it to be real. It was just a legal spieler with good vine leaves, and at 1.30 in the morning that is rare in any city. Athens is the one exception, but try and find a decent plumber in the ancient city. Exactly. The wine list was also beautiful: bottles hidden in hessian from lost vineyards.

The dirty basement with its sticky dance floor and purple walls belonged to another time. Actually, it was the time a paintbrush had last licked the walls. Lester had been part of that other time and had spent a lot of years in the basement. He had also lost a lot of years in the basement and one or two others just like it. They all looked the same in the middle of the night.

The two waiters had been serving kleftiko off the arm since God was a boy and they were real good. Archie and Vangelis had worked for the original Vincenzo. Tragic had kept them on and they ran the place below the stairs. Lester had even heard a rumour that they owned the place. It was hard to disprove and very easy to believe.

At the weekend, there was music. That's Greek music. A bouzouki player called Monopoly finished his night in the gloom of Vincenzo's basement. Lester knew that Monopoly had done his stint earlier that evening at various plate-smashing bullshit gaffs on Charlotte Street. At about two, he would show up. He drove a cab in the week and that is why people called him Monopoly. Every street had a price. But he was a Greek and a natural philosopher – he smoked slowly and talked cobblers – and at the heart of his universe was the bouzouki. It was all that Monopoly cared about. And he had a touch of the John Coltranes if anybody laughed. He was a very serious man, very intense, and would abuse anybody drunk or silly enough to ask him for 'Zorba the Greek'. 'Fucking wankers. It's a great book, the cunts, but the film is a fucking bullshit.' Lester had sat and listened many nights to Monopoly.

It was a relaxing place to be and Lester liked it. He liked it a lot. After 20 minutes, Tragic joined them. He would not eat. In nearly 20 years, Lester had never seen an ounce of food pass Tragic's lips. Not even a grape. He had seen plenty go up his hooter, but nothing in his mouth except Scotch.

'So, what did he do? Forget to duck?' Tragic pointed at Close. He laughed. Nobody else did.

The simple answer was yes. Yeah, he forgot to duck about 60 times in his last fight and perhaps another thousand or so times in other fights. The truth about Close, and the dozens of fighters like him in rings up and down the country, is that they know how to lose, but they still believe they can win. That was the difference between a bum and a fighter like Close.

A bum knows he will lose and that is all he understands. Close always thought he could win and that had been the problem a few hours earlier. A bum just comes and falls over. Bums give good losers like Close a bad name.

Close could fight – he had been a fair amateur – but as a professional he had been hopelessly overmatched in almost every fight at the start of his career. If he'd been a greyhound, he would have met the brain spike a long, long time ago. If he'd been a horse, he would have been a burger in Belgium. He never really had a chance in the real meat factory. He could get lucky, but that was unlikely. What he could do, if he used his head, was fiddle and survive and frustrate. Lester helped him use his brain. If he had done tonight, he would have heard the last bell a few hours earlier and then could have been ready for another late-notice job. Lester liked the late jobs because of the money. Fighters like Close liked late jobs for the same reason.

The way he looked at the moment he would struggle to get out for two months, and if the board steward was serious it could be a lot longer. Lester knew it was not going to be easy moving the minds at the board.

'Trag, leave me alone. He knew what he had to do and he never listened. It's called fucking genius disease. He's too brave for his own good.'

This seemed to satisfy Tragic and he stood up and left.

Close never said a word; he was struggling with his food. It was a complicated act getting the food over his sore lips and the stitches and anywhere near his mouth. It was not pretty to watch.

It was gone two when Lester's phone went. It was a rare night indeed when Lester had a mobile phone in his pocket. He hated the things and went weeks and weeks without using one. He picked up any messages and used a proper phone for proper calls. It was not too late for a call on a Saturday night, and it could be America. It was a bit early for little Pablo's result.

It was not America. It was Mickey Boyd.

'Micko, what can I do for you?'

Boyd was on his way back to Essex after a meal. He had probably eaten at Luigi's. The usual suspects would have been with him. A few old faces, but no unwelcome ones, if you exclude the writers. Boydy always had a few writers with him, just so he could have a scream-up. He'd blast them and then top their glasses up with chilled Meursault or something similarly cold, dry and expensive. Then he would give them another blast about their lousy profession and how they had no idea about the boxing business. Then he would reach for the ice bucket to top up their glasses one more time. It was his liquid therapy. 'It's impossible to give those pricks indigestion,' he would say after the last writer had left.

Lester would have been there, crunching crab and lobster and testing his gout at Boyd's elbow, had he not been at home waiting for King's man to reach him. Boyd was one of the top promoters in the country, but the main man was still Frank Warren. Lester did a lot of business with Boyd; it was not an exclusive arrangement and that annoyed Boyd, but it suited Lester and, to be honest, most things annoyed Boyd.

'Raymondo, did you speak to King? Did he say if anything was happening in Vegas?'

Lester had been with Boyd at three the day before in the promoter's box inside Stamford Bridge. It was still a khazi, as far as he was concerned, even with the Russian's money. He hated the whole area – the little football outpost in the posh streets. He had broken scampi for 30 minutes with Boyd, a few of his old friends and some of his daughters and sons. Nice kids, to tell the truth. He had watched Chelsea go two-up against Sunderland or some other team in a few easy minutes. Just before half-time, Boyd had touched Lester on the shoulder and that meant the match was over. It was a relief. Lester excused himself and walked to the back of the box with Boyd. They chatted for a few minutes; Lester told him about the King deal with Effra and one or two other pieces of information. None of it was news to Boyd, but they still talked. Boyd reached into the pocket of his suede jacket, which was hanging by the toilet, and pulled out an envelope. He gave it to Lester and turned without saying a word. Not a fucking word. He could be a cold bastard.

It always ended that way. Lester opened the toilet, went in and locked it before counting the cash. It was all fifties and it was all there. Five grand in total. It was Lester's lump for helping to get the two Americans and it was not bad money for a few calls. Ten minutes later, Lester was walking away from the ground. It's never a problem getting a black cab outside Chelsea. People raved about the location, but it left Ray cold. Too many collars turned up.

Lester had left the Bridge with a bit of bridge building to do. Boyd worked with King when they could find a figure they both agreed on, but it was never easy. The truth is their main skill was finding a figure, a sum that made cash common sense to everybody. Beyond the kissing and the hugging, they hated each other. Their rivalry was often very good for the sport and was always very good for Lester. They did share one thing: they hated Lester but knew he was often the best middleman for them, which was a normal way to do business in the boxing game. There were other men in the fixing game, both on the streets and in the offices of the sanctioning bodies and the television companies with the money, but Lester was the best there was.

Boyd had talked to Lester about a few fights and it was obvious that he needed to do some business with King. There were three fighters in particular under King's care who Boyd wanted. Everybody involved knew that King was not bothered about the trio and that was where Lester could do some damage. The three could fight but couldn't a sell a ticket; they had quality but no pull and that meant they would always be available at the right price. Lester would try and find the right price. It was simple business and he would, and could, take care of it – in Atlantic City, at the Championship Boxing Association's annual conference.

It was at the conferences held by the different sanctioning bodies each year that most of the big business was done. All the champions and their people would arrive for the three-day event of buffets and handshaking. There was a gala dinner, but the real purpose, as far as Lester could work out, was fixing up fights. Simple. The people in charge of one fighter spoke to the people in charge of another fighter over an informal cocktail. Lester filled in the gaps.

Lester would spend a few days at the CBA's event in Atlantic City after the Ricky Hatton and 'Pretty Boy' Floyd Mayweather fight in Las Vegas on the Saturday. He had some business to take care of in the background of the big fight. There was always business in Vegas.

King, as expected, was holding out and nobody in the history of boxing could hold out like King. His bids and counter-bids were like time capsules. He made them and then he just went away and forgot about them. It was hard to match him at the table, difficult to ignore him when he wanted you, but nearly impossible to do a deal with him if he knew you wanted something he had. That is the key to dealing with anybody in boxing – force the person on the other side of the table to make the first move. Nix the weakness of the eager. King never put a foot wrong, but Lester had a few ideas and he knew King would offload the three boxers without breaking Boyd's balls.

'I spoke to Wally, not Don, and he never said a word about anything. The usual, but nothing different. Why, what have you heard?'

'Nothing, nothing. Just curious. Your two septics never let you down tonight, son. All did what they were supposed to do, unlike that other nutcase. He decided to have a war with May.'

'I know, he's with me now at Vincenzo's, trying to suck a kebab through a straw. I'd let him say hello, but he can't move his jaw because of the hiding your ref let him take.'

Lester knew Boyd would ignore his comment. He was right.

'Forget that. You know May's got four stitches and a bruised knuckle? I'm telling you, Ray, I'm gonna have to stop using Closey if he keeps trying to win.'

I will tell him, thought Lester. We can't have fighters trying to win. Terrible state of affairs.

'Ray, I almost forgot. There was a good sort at Wembley looking for you. A right good blonde sort. A Northern lot.'

Lester waited for the punchline. There wasn't one. Boyd just said goodnight and the phone died.

A blonde sort? It was a bit of a mystery, but it was probably just another PR woman or TV producer with a great idea for boxing. It was always a great idea and there was never any cash. It was the same every single time that a blonde with a clipboard came knocking with an idea. They always landed at Lester's door. Lester had worked his way in and out of blonde women from TV and PR companies a long time ago. They were all wasters and they never had a penny worth having.

He went back to the meal. Close was starting to drowse, but he had slowly eaten his way through kalamari, moussaka, a steak and six lumps of ice cream. He'd done 50 quid in food. The night was nearly over when Tragic appeared and sat down next to Lester.

'Ray, you want some?' Tragic asked. Lester knew it was coming. It had been that way for too long.

'No, Trag. I'm having a break, son. Can you just grab us a cab?'

Lester had not had a single line of cocaine in over six months and he felt better for it. He had not been calling it on for two years, but friends never notice. Most coke users consider it a betrayal of some sort if one of the gang does a U-turn in prang alley. Lester had worked hard at pulling away and attempted at all times to play it down and not make a big issue of it. He was not on a crusade and he certainly didn't want a single coked-out friend losing his mind over it. He had seen that happen and it wasn't pleasant when pranganoia kicked in. Tragic was cool, always had been, but others would make a fuss if they worked out that Lester had stopped; Tragic didn't give a fuck, but there were people who would panic.

After Lester settled the bill, he slid into the back of an old silver Mercedes. The African driver seemed a bit concerned about Close's face and kept looking in the mirror, even when the fighter started to gently snore as the car pulled away.

The first stop was the early morning paper pitch at Paddington station. Lester jumped out and picked up every early Sunday edition. He liked to grab the first editions because the version that came through the door in the morning was often very different. He knew by then some of his Effra copy would have been replaced by live boxing from the night before. At Paddington, he could get to see the full Effra copy in all the papers and he needed that for billing.

It took less than ten minutes to get back to Lester's flat. He gave the driver a score and woke Close to tell him that it had been taken care of. The fighter went straight back to sleep. It had been a long night for both of them.

The phone rang as he was going through the door. Little Pablo had knocked out a Mexican in two rounds and that meant it was Carnival City next. Lester could sleep. It was 4.03, according to the clock, and he was ready for the drop.

LONDON: TOO EARLY TO THINK

At a few minutes to nine, Lester woke up. A second after he turned over, the doorbell went. He left it to ring. It went again. It had to be the paperboy; he was a nuisance. It went again. Then there was a serious kick. Lester jumped up, found a pair of underpants and walked down the stairs. The bell went again and he was fuming.

'Just leave 'em,' he shouted as he opened the door.

Lester was about to tell the kid *for the fiftieth fucking time, just leave the poxy papers*, but it was not the kid. It was certainly not the paperboy. It was a woman of about 25. She was blonde and most definitely a good lot. The blonde from the boxing, he thought. She looked down at his pants. She was smiling and she had in her hands all the papers. She was gorgeous.

'The lad gave me these. Sorry. Have I got you up?' she said.

There was a slight accent, perhaps Manchester, but nothing too strong.

'You are Ray Lester, aren't you? Can I come in? I need your help.'

Could she? Why not? He took the papers from her, positioned them over his pants and invited her upstairs. She went first, skipping up two or three at a time. A second or two later, they stood at the top of the stairs.

'Shall I put the kettle on?' The voice, it was close to Manchester.

He managed a nod and looked at the kitchen. She smiled and turned and he went to the bedroom to put some strides on. When he got back, she was looking for coffee. He was just looking at her.

'It's in there.'

She turned, but there was no laughter in her face or her eyes. Oh shit. Lester knew she was close to tears.

'Was it you last night at Wembley?' he asked.

She nodded and then she did cry.

After a minute or so, she started to talk. 'I've lost me dad.' It was all she could say for about ten minutes.

Lester had her in his arms; he could feel her tears soaking his shirt.

'Darling, do I know your dad?'

She was still crying, but she stepped back, her bum resting on the sink. She moved her head. The tears were hanging onto her lips and her nose. She kept shaking her head and one tear left her nose and landed on the back of Lester's hand. The girl was suffering. He moved her to the living room, sat her on the sofa and kept his hand on her shoulder as she sobbed. *This is typical, the best-looking woman I've ever had in the flat and I don't know her name and she can't stop crying.* She reached up and touched his arm.

'I'm fine now. I'm fine. Sorry about that, Ray. My dad is missing and I need you to help me find him.'

'I don't even know you, love. I don't know your dad.'

She took a deep breath and sat up. 'You do know him. His name is Eddie, Eddie Lights. He lives in Las Vegas, but he once lived in Blackpool with me mum. He's me dad. I've never seen him, but I speak to him. And I was meant to go and see him next week. But about a month ago he vanished . . .' She was crying again.

'Easy, kid, easy.' He just held her tight, his shirt wet and her shoulders moving.

Eddie Lights. Sal's boy. The man with the electric suit. What a slippery old bastard. Lester had known him for about 15 years and Eddie had never mentioned a daughter or a wife. He had never even mentioned Blackpool. He'd said he was from Manchester.

Eddie Lights of Las Vegas. The crooner. The keeper of a thousand tales. The provider of the best sorts and best coke in town. The legend. Eddie Lights. Lester *did* know him. He knew him very well. Everybody in the boxing business, and a few other trades, knew Eddie. He was Mr Vegas, the facilitator. A fixer of all problems. And now his daughter had a problem.

'Sure, I know Eddie. We'll give him a call. I see him all the time. He's probably just out of town, at a fight somewhere. Relax, we'll get hold of him.'

She was shaking her head and trying to take deep breaths. Her face was soaking from the tears. He stepped back.

'I've tried everything, called all the numbers, but I just can't get him. I'm really scared. Ray, please help us find me dad.'

She was crying again, and Lester moved across and put his arm around her back. She moved her face to his chest and he could feel the tears. She was sobbing.

'Please, please help me find me dad.'

Lester sat there with the blonde in his arms, rocking her gently as she cried. He was wet, but he liked the feeling. Her body was hard, fit. She smelled nice against his body. He just held her, feeling her breathing against his wet chest. He would help her, no problem.

Getting hold of Eddie would be easy. Lester was off to Vegas in a week or so for the Hatton fight. Perhaps the sort could go with him? That would be cool. He knew the way Eddie operated and he was probably shacked up with a young bird in Florida. A waitress lost in a dream. It would be a doddle to get hold of him.

'I can do that, sweetheart. Don't worry, I'll find him for you.'

Finding Eddie Lights: how hard could that be?

LAS VEGAS: THE FLIGHT, THE FANS AND THE PEST

The girl at his door had been on Lester's mind. Her missing dad was proving to be an elusive old bastard. Lester had tried a dozen times and a lot of different people. There was no sign, no word. He would be in Las Vegas in about 12 hours and then he could start a ground search.

Moving through the airport had been surprisingly easy. It had been busy with Ricky Hatton fans and the other travelling lonely. The chorus of dumb approval was everywhere. 'There's only one Ricky Hatton. One Ricky Hatton.' They had been singing the same tune since the January fight against the hapless and one-dimensional Juan Urango. It had set the tone for a British invasion and nobody wanted to be left behind. Some people were talking about 30,000 fans making the journey. It certainly looked that way. Lester kept his nut down.

Ray had used a bit of guile and a few air miles to get a big seat up the front. It had cleared him out of miles, but he was not planning on too many more trips. He could still hear the singing masses when the plane left the runway and he knew then that he was in the right place up the front. It would be a long ten hours and the looks on the faces of the men and women in charge confirmed his fears. At the back, it was a party, open invite.

The seatbelt sign went off and Ray settled down for the flight to McCarran Airport. The joyful introduction of direct flights to Las Vegas had made the haul bearable. It had also made it even easier for bad gamblers, sex tourists and fight fans to make the hop. It was a bewildering pilgrimage that came to an end when the plane slipped out of the desert sky and into the streets of Las Vegas. It always felt like it was about to pull up short outside a store or in a casino car park. The place was lit and sprawling, and the runways at the airport were lost inside the neon lines of urban spread. Ray relaxed – had one drink down – then he heard the curtain divide being pulled over.

He was hoping that nobody would disturb him. It was a foolish hope. The flight was mad busy with Hatton's fight faithful. Heathrow's fighting choristers had jumped the big bird to the City of Pleasure and they were unlikely to rest. The umpteenth of a million chants of 'Hatton Wonderland' drifted down the plane. The first of 16 pints at 8 a.m. had simply improved the lungs of the hopeful. Hatton fights were events, and Hatton against Floyd 'Money' Mayweather was arguably the biggest event in British boxing history. It was also one of the top-ten most lucrative fights ever to grace the Strip. It had taken over $14 million at the gate on the first day of sales. But the real figure paid for the 14,000 tickets by the fans probably nudged the $14 million official takings to about $40 million. It was crazy business. Ricky had cracked it and he deserved every single penny. Ray could hear the noise at the back of the plane and he knew ten hours of laughing and shouting when he heard it. The fans were not Ray's problem. Vegas would take the edge off some and ruin a few others, but most of the 30,000 would get back on planes wet-eyed, poorer and happier. It was the Vegas way.

The curtain clicked back closed. Ray waited. He had seen somebody he knew when he was checking in. He had seen the old man moaning and then arguing. He had realised there was very little chance of a pleasant trip the moment he saw the geezer shouting and pointing his finger at the woman behind the desk. He had a bad feeling.

When the seatbelt sign pinged off, it had taken the man, a real pest, less than three minutes to walk forward and take the empty seat next to Ray. It was Solly Mantle. A terrible man in many ways, a ponce in every way.

'Raymond, Raymond. A pleasure to see such a friendly face.'

'Solly, what a shock. Sit down, relax a bit.'

'I was back there,' Solly added for no reason, gesturing with his hand to the curtain.

'It's not getting any better in the cheap seats, Solly. You should know that by now.'

The old man was comfortable before Ray had finished his greeting. He was always comfortable inside the thickest skin in the boxing business. As an extra precaution against abuse he wore a coat that absorbed insults – a kind of magic robe for arseholes. Boxing was a business with a lot of thick-skinned men, both old and young, and to have the thickest of thick skin was an achievement. An honour to insult, a pleasure to witness.

Solly had been involved with fighters and fights for about 50 years. Ray had never really liked him and Solly, as was his way, had never liked Ray. The only good thing about Solly – who, incidentally, was known as 'Solly the Brolly' from his days selling umbrellas at Brick Lane – was his inability to conceal his contempt. He could do good business with a man, but he would still treat the man like he hated him, like the man was fresh dog shit stuck between the toes of a child. He was the king of effortless disdain and bile. There was not a lot more to him. Now he was just an old man living with splendid memories and his own hate. His nastiness was all the more impressive because he was genuinely not bothered what people thought of him.

Ray had fallen out with him many times. It was easy to do. Once it had turned physical, at the Savoy, in a khazi, during a break at the Boxing Writers' dinner. Ray had dragged Solly, who was drunk at the time, from in front of a piss pot into a cubicle. But by the time Solly had stumbled back and fallen over, spraying his stinking brown piss all over the place, the anger in Ray had vanished. He left Solly that night sitting on the toilet seat, still dribbling his own piss. Ray had been lucky to get out with a dry trouser leg and, to be honest, slapping the old fella was a bad move. Solly had never once mentioned the incident. Not once. And when the night was over Solly seemed to go out of his way to shake Ray's hand. He was a shameless man with the ability to be horrible.

When Ray was starting out as a straight boxing writer, Solly had been a pain in the arse. He had tried everything to stop Ray getting a living. That was simply Solly's charm, the way he worked. He had been deeply unpleasant, but he was old now and he was a bit sad. Over the years, Ray had slowly started to look at the fight genius, which is what Solly had been, in a different light. His opinion of the veteran was no longer clouded by anger. Ray had mellowed with age and was finally showing a bit of wisdom. He liked Solly more each time he listened to the parade of champions in the old-timer's spiel. It was also true that he saw less and less of him. Ray figured it was hard to dislike a man with a permanent smear of food on his chin and a memory packed with the gaps where fighters and great fights lived. Or once lived. Ray knew Solly suffered because the memories were inside his head somewhere, but he was unable to call them up on demand. It must be like reaching for something in a dream that edges away with each lunge and slips further back into the dark lights with each desperate grab. Perhaps they haunted his sleep and then fell out of vision when he opened his eyes.

Mantle was from a different time on planet boxing, a time Ray had just been squeezed into. But Solly was stuck there. Ray also knew that the man sitting next to him would never consider him anything other than a mug. The old man was on medication for one or other debilitating ailment and he often acted clueless – it was not always an act.

There had also been the time a good few years back when Solly had come close to getting Ray sacked from the *Daily Torygraph*. He had accused Ray of several things and banned him from a lot of shows. Even if the accusations were true – *and some were a bit close, to tell the truth* – there was no need for Solly, a wealthy individual in his own right, to try to ruin a young reporter's career. It was vindictiveness, and unnecessary, but Solly had also been wound up at the time by a few of the veteran writers on the scene. Many of the typewriter relics had died and the others were dribbling somewhere. It was bullshit aggro then, and it is the same now, but at the time Ray was crushed. It hurt in all ways.

The ban cost him a flat. The paperwork was complete, but the sale had to be scrapped when the money from Solly's shows stopped coming in. Ray was considered a risk and a few doors closed – closed a bit too sharpish for his liking. The money dried up and the flat had to be kicked into touch. It was £33,000 at the time and one-bedroom flats in the same street shift for £390,000 now. The ban stayed in place for over three years, but it was not the boxing that Ray regretted losing – it was not missing a few house fighters bashing up fat Mexicans that caused Ray the grief – it was losing out on the flat that hurt most of all.

Still, it was a long time ago and Ray had pushed most of it out of his mind. Most, not all, and whenever he was in Finsbury Park and anywhere near the little flat he felt a tug inside. Solly, bless him, had simply forgotten.

Once, at a terrible show in Basildon, when a young Chris Eubank was fighting a nobody, Solly had shared a car back to central London with Ray. For about an hour, the old man had not realised that Ray was the third man wedged into the back of the two-seater car. It was clearly a difficult time for Solly and he seemed dangerously out of touch. Ray had thought he was close to death. Pat Brodie, a man with a few secrets of his own, had been driving and he had nearly crashed the old Porsche a dozen times because of the dialogue. In all fairness, the Brodie Man didn't need any excuses to nearly crash a car. Any car, at any time, in his hands was in danger of leaving the road. He was lethal behind a steering wheel. Since that night in the Essex wastelands, Solly's medication had been increased and he was a lot better now. There were still reports of bizarre sightings, but in general he made sense when he spoke. The Brodie Man remained a hazard on any road at any time.

Over the years, Solly the Brolly had put together some great deals and had made a lot of money. It was his love of a pound note and his ability to make bitter enemies meet and find a deal that justified the respect. His hand had touched many legendary fights and for that alone he deserved his position. He was for real in the increasingly plastic world of boxing. He had cut his teeth in the matchmaking game of the 1940s and 1950s, when a good night at a small hall wouldn't often generate enough money for a decent supper. He had to follow the graft back then and try and spring a meal for nish in Soho after a fight. Often he would be the last-seat-kid, ligger number 13, at a long table. If he was pushed aside and ignored, he would end up at the Westminster Hotel with brown sauce, a pie, a slice of apple tart and a tea. That was then, and it had left him reluctant to buy another human a bite to eat.

He was also a multimillionaire, but it never made him happy. It was that ugly millionaire story, the unhappy one. He had homes in Florida, Spain and a luxury flat in London's West End.

He was not yet dead in the business and still had his claws in a few fighters. Well, the truth was that he stuck his name in the frame with a few fighters. And there were certainly some fools in boxing's outposts, tourists in the trade, who liked to use Solly for advice – none of it free. They were managers and promoters who knew the right names but would never know the game. They had the words, the look and often a fighter that bought them a degree of acceptance, but away from boxing they ran gift shops, hotels or restaurants. They ran their civilian businesses well, but boxing is not part of the normal world. Solly made them all feel part of the business, but the reality was that they all had real jobs and boxing for them was a passion. It was a hobby, not their life. There were too many people like that and they got in the way because occasionally they found a real good fighter. That was when the trouble started. They always wanted too much and knew too little. It was Bob Arum who once called them 'boxing tourists'. It was a perfect fit for the posers. And Uncle Bob should know; he became the king of the boxing tourists when he quit the legal world and fell in love with the ignoble art in the '70s. In just a couple of years, he went from being Bobby Kennedy's sidekick to breaking bread with Don King in Zaire. *Only in America, baby*, as King howls.

Ray knew that Solly's best work was never spoken about in public. He had done some deals that would remain secret. He had been responsible for putting fights together involving managers and promoters who found it impossible to breathe the same air. Often he hated both sides. 'Listen, they hate each other. To me, they're just two people I have to talk to. That's the way to do business, the boxing way. Why make it difficult and make friends with these people?'

He had a rare talent for bringing enemies to the same table and that was because it was impossible to insult him. In Solly's rheumy eyes, nobody should ever fall out if there is a few quid to be made. He brokered some angry meetings. He had been clumped a few times. And, in truth, there was a lot of hate in boxing, but with Solly it was always business because hate was easy and sold for nothing. He was not Ray's speed, and he never would be, but he was always worth a few minutes on the ear. He had far less power in the boxing world now, but he could still be a cunning and evil old man. He could still pull one or two moves out of the bag. Even at his age, with a mind that required a pill to give it a kick-start each morning, he was not finished.

'So, Raymond, how are we? Anybody travelling with us? Any of the boys?'

'I'm fine and no, it's just me up here. I have no idea what's going on back there.'

Solly was comfy in the chair next to Ray. A stewardess gave them both a stern look. Solly was not up the front of the plane and she knew it. She also knew that it was difficult to move old men like Solly. People like him – rich, tight bastards – never turned left on a plane unless somebody else was forking out the money. He never went up the front if he was paying for his own ticket, even if it was a long, long trip. He was at the back and the stewardess had seen him slide through the curtain. It was hard to miss him. Ray smiled back at her. What could either of them do? She didn't smile at Ray. Solly was wealthy, greedy and unwelcome and his face never flickered. He had the ability to glaze over and ignore scorn. The special coat again. The poor woman was wasting her time if she imagined for one second that Solly would feel uncomfortable and shift his arse. Ray knew he would need a lot of encouragement to leave.

'I was thinking about the fight and wasn't sure what to do, but, fuck it, I thought, I've got the money, why shouldn't I spend it?'

'Well, I did expect to see you, to tell you the truth. I had a sneaking feeling you would show up here at some point.'

'It's not a bad flight,' added the old man, taking a look for the first time at his surroundings. He nodded his approval. 'It's nice. Very nice.'

Solly motioned to the stewardess and when she arrived he ordered champagne. She was about to say something, but Solly had turned to Ray. This was the way Solly had treated people all his life. Nobody can ever remember him saying 'Thank you' or 'Please'. He just ordered. He ordered, he never paid. Somebody had once told Ray that it was just Solly's way. 'No, in any language it's called acting like a prick,' Ray had replied. And he was right.

'This fight's not easy for the little shit. It's not easy.'

Straight to the boxing. It was hard to work out if Solly was talking about Mayweather or Hatton. It could have been both, as both were either 'shits' or 'kids' in boxing language.

'It's never easy at this level. But you know what you're going to get.'

'Nah, I don't agree. It's about nerves and staying calm and that means you never know what you're going to get. Trust me.'

Ray knew the World Boxing Council welterweight title fight

between the holder, Mayweather Jnr, and Hatton was not a straight fight to bet. If Ricky climbed in the ring with his brain, then he could make it difficult. The sensible money was on Mayweather, but the odds were crap. The gamblers were looking to take numbers, gain edges, and about 30,000 travelling British fans would help their search. The clever moneymen on the British jets could hide behind the mug punters. Everybody with a boxing pulse knew it was not an easy night for either of the boxers in the ring, but it was a nightmare for proper gamblers on the safe side of the ropes.

Solly, in addition to his many flaws, liked to state the obvious and imagine he was spreading wisdom. It was something that a lot of boxing people did, especially the older journalists. Ray had given up complaining long ago and would just sit back and listen. It was often a repetition of the biased, 'Nobody moved like Ali.' Well, nobody will ever give you a serious argument over that, but somebody might tell you that Sugar Ray Leonard was sweet on his feet or that Julio César Chávez made cutting a ring down his personal scientific offering to the sport. Sure, Ali could move, but please find something else. Anyway, this kid Mayweather could do a few things. And he could do them all very, very well.

The drinks arrived. The quarter bottles wet and glistening, with two champagne flutes. Solly grabbed both and put one in the inside pocket of his jacket. The other he opened and poured. He took a long drink, poured some more and put down the empty bottle.

'Raymond, Raymond. This kid has always been able to fight. But he has been protected, and people forget that. I'm on big with Hatton. That's why I'm here.'

Simple money in Las Vegas went on late and went on the short end. Solly would keep his hand out of his pocket until close to the first bell. He would act like the gambler he was and not make mug bets at the wet end of an empty glass.

'I hear there's plenty of money going down.'

'It's too early now. It'll get real busy, a friend told me.'

Solly always had a friend and the friend was always telling him.

Ray had heard that some real gamblers, proper people in Las Vegas, had placed a lot of money on the outcome of the fight. Ray had also heard a lot of late money was flowing into town for Hatton. And it wasn't just the British punters sending $20 to the vaults in hope. Mind you, 30,000 Hatton fans dropping $20 or more was a fair amount of lost cash.

Solly loved to gamble, and even when the odds were bad he always found an extra bit of action for his cash. It was easier to do business with a cash man in town. In Vegas, the extra point, even a slither of an extra point, could make the difference. Men like Solly found that edge all the time, but they had to put their dough on the table and leave it there the longest. Luck? No chance. It was balls and sweet knowledge in gambling.

Solly had heard about Mayweather and women and the fights with his dad. The usual stuff: Little Floyd could fight, but he lived a bad life. Well, so the stories went. However, there was another side and Ray had seen it plenty of times. Floyd did have some problems, but he was the product of a home built on lies and syringes. He was still at war with his father, but they existed in the same town and crossed paths. They talked, worked together for a day or so and then fell out.

Jay Hain had shown Ray the other side of Mayweather. In the gym, nobody could live with him. It was insane at times, and always in private, and often at two in the morning. Ray had been struggling as the days went by to find a way for Hatton to win. He was sticking faithful, but struggling. It was down to mindset – Floyd had to get it wrong and Ricky had to get it right.

Solly had not shocked Ray on the plane. There had been a lot of conversations in the last week or so since the girl had arrived at Ray's door and Solly's name had popped up a few times. One hundred thousand US dollars had also been mentioned; that was real money for one man in one fight, even in Las Vegas. Solly always bet proper money. It was not a weakness; it was his only disease. Solly had no connection with the two boxers, so the only reason to be in Vegas for the fight was to collect or pay out the money.

Ray knew Solly's money would be wire transferred to Los Angeles and delivered from there. The old man never flew with cash. Solly always bet cash because in Vegas cash still breathes. Ray had heard a big gambler once talk about feeling the pulse of the wad in his pocket. Ray also knew Solly, like a lot of real British gamblers, would not use a Las Vegas bank. And carrying cash in excess of ten large was not an option with modern customs and their tools. It is a lot safer now, but there was a time when customs took cash from professional gamblers on an irritating and regular basis. Sure, it was easier now to move money around, but old habits die slow. There were too many sets of eyes and ears in Vegas banks and too many desperate people. It was the same at the airport.

Vegas had a filthy criminal side where armed shakedown artists operated in every parking lot next to every bank. The city had always been more than doped-up white tigers, perfect tits and penthouse suites with basketball courts. Too many of America's skilled and unskilled reached the end of their journey when the lights welcomed them to Las Vegas. It was in many ways the most professional city in the world because there were no amateurs in any of the thriving industries. Best cooks, cleaners, beggars and drivers. Best thieves, whores, con men and stick-up artists. All part of America's daily exodus to dreamland. It was a city where bad business turned good, for illegal and legal, but there were rules for everybody to understand.

People learned quickly that the major casinos were to be left to the serious grifters. Men and women on the inside. They also learned that casino security was mostly lethal. There were many shadowy men working the security detail in Las Vegas and essentially they were mercenaries – part of the same silent war machine that exists in Iraq and other conflict zones, both on and off the axis of evil. There were billions at stake in each and every casino and an old fat fella with a little gun was not going to stop the organised criminals. The threat of vicious force by a group of former US Navy Seals or Special Operations soldiers was the final wall against crime. It was a very real and evil wall.

The private security operatives were all over the city, though most visitors would never see them. Away from the dozen or so neon cash cows of the Strip, there remained an endless army of victims to find. It was a city highly charged with crime. The one remaining local paper ran the low-key obits of dealers and stick-up artists. The streets of death, where a boy or girl went to Jesus just about every single day, played on the nightly news. These streets are just minutes from the lights, but 60 seconds is a long time after dark. The intersections are often left sloshing in the dumb blood of the young, their death puddles silver under the night lights and clearly visible as stains on the sidewalk behind the thin blue lines of police tape. It was not Vegas as the men who ran Vegas wanted anybody to see it, but it was real and it was regular. It was a part of America that was not protected by the anonymous men on the payrolls at a casino.

In the crack houses of Naked City, the hot bed rents had not changed in years and life and death was a blur. The area is next to downtown, where the motels and flops slowly decay each year. It would be hard to find a happy Las Vegas story in the dim glow in that leftover town. But it's just a few minutes in a cab – that 60 seconds of change again – from Naked City to the quarter-mile-long stretch of dark water that fronts the Bellagio, with its 1,200 multicoloured fountains that bring the glittering sea to life each night. The jets reach 250 feet into the desert sky and there is music from the world's finest sound system. It is a light show by the lake, in front of a hotel where half a billion dollars' worth of nineteenth-century art is on display. It is just a few minutes from the ten-buck fuck shops where skinny whores with crack sores will suck your cock for a tiny crystal release.

Ray knew only too well which parts of the town never got to be illuminated by the distant neon of the dream Strip. Too many fighters ended up out there as blank-eyed sentinels – lost and lonely. It wasn't their fault. The streets were nasty, the people broken and mean. Vegas was two cities, and the one away from the casinos was vicious and unforgiving. Ray had seen too much of it too many times. The city under neon that everybody knew was packed with smiling dreamers, but it could also be ruthless. It was, after all, fondly referred to as Sin City. But that was more an image than a reality for the millions who parted with their cash in legal ways each and every day. If a man wanted to act like a fool and get in deep with hookers and coke dealers, this was his place. If, in his fried mind, he wanted to believe that he was a player each time he sat at a card table, then that man would be broken in Las Vegas. He would be left desolate and bewildered by his bad luck but welcomed back like the prodigal son as soon as he found a new wad of living green. He was a light bulb on the scene until the cash ran low and the credit ended. Bing and out. If a man wanted to drink, look at women and gamble a few dollars here and there to feel like a player, then he was the safest man in the west. Just don't piss on the carpet or insult the people taking your money. More importantly, don't run out of money. Never run out of green, my son.

Ray often thought it was the safest city in the world for straights. Solly, however, was not straight and he insulted everybody. And it had cost him. The senile old boxing man had had been using a limo firm in Los Angeles for years to deliver his money. A secretary at the firm would collect the money from the bank on Wiltshire and it would be sent to Vegas in a little bag. It would be placed neatly on the seat next to the driver. It was never a car, always a limo. The driver always received the same tip. A crisp ten-dollar bill. Just a ten for his work. Solly was from a time when a ten spot was a lot of cash for any kid grafting at any job. In Solly's world, a ten was still 15 per cent of any meal. Any meal, not that he ever got near to picking up the cheque. The guy could calculate multiple points in his head on several bets, but when it came to correct tipping he liked to stab everybody in the pocket.

One afternoon in 1989 the limo only made it as far as Indio, just the other side of Palm Springs. The dark side, in many ways. The money and the driver vanished, the car was left in the parking lot at the Boys' Club. That night there was just the limo and a metal basketball hoop in the car park. There was not a lot left of the limo by the time it was light. The police figured the bag left with the driver.

The night the money failed to arrive, Solly had had an envelope pushed under his door at Caesars Palace. He always stayed at Caesars. There was a note inside the envelope and it said 'Fuck You'. It was written on a ten-dollar bill. Solly told the story. And he had added a punchline over the years. He insisted that the fighter he was in town to back – so he claimed – had lost big and therefore he had made ten bucks because his money was saved from the bad bet.

'The *schvartze* driver did me a good turn. The only time that ever happened in 50 years of boxing.' He was lying. Too many people had told Ray he'd cried like a baby the night the money went missing. Some said he even bought a few drinks, which seemed a bit strong. Still, Ray did mix with liars.

Solly was a throwback, an unmitigated racist, and away from his insults the only language he knew was the lexicon of the fight game. He existed – and had done so for half a century – inside a mental ring surrounded by fighters and fight people talking endlessly about money. He loved it inside his boxing prison. He talked about fights he had arranged and some he had not made. To Solly, it made no difference because he claimed that he was involved even when he was not. He also claimed a percentage of whatever any fight generated. Any fight, mind. Ray had to listen, and not for the first time. It was boxing-tale time at 26,000 feet.

Solly raised his fingers every 15 minutes, never moving his head, and called over the stewardess. He kept ordering, two at time. One for the pocket and one for the glass. Ray had watched a lot of boxing writers do the same thing over the years. There was a time when it was not uncommon to be in a writer's room in Las Vegas or Atlantic City and see 20 or more miniatures lined up on a table. Some even took them back to the UK. It reminded Ray of a time when glass miniatures were considered a bit swanky.

Ray had never got over one party, which had taken place about 15 years earlier at the home of a senior boxing writer. Solly was there. The house was a classic suburban semi in Barnes. The party was legendary for two reasons. First, all the spirits were courtesy of first-class travel on British Airways. Second, and more importantly, there had been a VIP section in the fella's lounge! A woman's red scarf had been stretched across the door. Entry to the sanctum beyond the scarf was restricted to the writer's supposed VIP guests. On a table in the special room there were dozens and dozens of miniatures lined up next to a bowl of Twiglets. What a pompous fool that man was. Still, he had a daughter and she was a fearsome old slapper. Trish, Trina, Tina – who cares? Ray had taken her for a walk, out beyond the koi carp pond, and ended up giving her one behind a garden shed. It was a good memory.

Ray listened, which was about all he could do. He was not sure about asking if Solly had seen Eddie Lights. He thought about asking Solly if he had heard from Eddie lately. It was not an easy thing to ask. Ray wanted to keep the search away from too many ears. Men like Solly traded snippets like currency, twisting a word for barter, and Ray had a feeling about Eddie. It was not a good feeling. But he asked anyway.

'Sol, you spoken to Eddie lately?'

'Lights? Nah, never liked him. He's a thieving prick and he could never sing. Not one note. Why would I speak to him?'

Solly shrugged his shoulders and just kept on talking. It was doubtful the old man would remember the question. Eddie Lights was outside Solly's little world. If Eddie had been laying off bets and offering points above the sports book, then Solly would have led Ray right to him. Or if Eddie owed Solly any money – possibly, with a few sunk, the chance of a tear over a lost few quid – it would have fired a spark of memory in the old man's watery, blank eyes. Equally, if Solly owed Eddie any money, it would have lit his oyster eyes up. In the gloom of the first-class cabin, the eyes looked like they belonged to a man close to death. They were eyes backing away from life.

Solly had never taken Eddie for a lot of money – he always remembered the ones he'd won. He had started to wipe clean the defeats years earlier when his memory worked without the assistance of a chemist. Ray had only fleeced him once and it had taken a lot of effort to get people to come in late on a bet – a bet Ray knew was easy money, and one that Solly, because of his arrogance, refused to realise was a lost cause. It was a stinking bad bet and Solly, for once, was blind. Ray walked with 20 grand – and 20 grand in 1992 was a lump. But it was not good money. It nearly ruined everything for Ray.

The tales rolled without a break. Solly had never lost a bet, never made a bad fight and had never been played for a sucker. He was perfect at all times in the boxing business. He had a lot of familiar lies and he told them all very well. Ray knew of a dozen good fighters with serious complaints about the veteran. The fighters had been with Solly and they were convinced they had received the short end on fights. Ray knew that several of them were right, but it was in the past. It had all happened a long time ago. Solly dismissed all of the claims and, amazingly, a lot of Solly's old fighters still smiled when they saw him. He was the last of the old-fashioned cigar-chewing mistress-slepping father figures from the fight game. There were one or two fruitcakes who wanted to kill him, but they had thankfully drifted away from the business. Though it didn't mean that one day they wouldn't kill him.

Ray knew just how close Solly had come to being dead a few years earlier. One of Solly's fighters was in a halfway house in Swindon. He was from London, but it was no longer safe for him to be an ex-fighter with demons on the streets of Hackney. It's tough enough for any kid with an empty head, but his skull was swimming with hate. Revenge is a wicked trophy to carry, and it's also a fantasy that can be visited day after day in medicated isolation. The kid had failed at boxing and that made life away from the ring dangerous. Boxing had been his life for too long and too many people had told him that it would be his life forever. After a bit of fame in the ring, he was a dismal nobody on the street, a malaise that ruined a lot of retirements. Ray had been to see him and he was a sick and mentally unstable man. A living threat with killing on his tongue. He came so close to killing Solly. Ray knew because he had stopped the murder.

Solly was starting to feel the booze and Ray was starting to hit the wall of understanding. The old-timer's tales were getting more and more personal. He was putting together a list of the men who had denied him money because they were idiots; basically, everybody who had no idea about boxing and had ruined the sport. He was swearing, red in the face, and at his best, to be honest. But he was not really suitable for the big seat area and one or two people were looking over. The list of fools and pricks was long. Ray knew he was in another version of it and probably near the top.

Solly's credentials for self-deception were impeccable, and as he slurred his words and cursed his former partners, it was possible to feel pity for him. His personal life was awful, his marriage was finally over and he spent his days in loneliness making phone calls to people who didn't really want to speak to him. Not now, anyway. Ray knew how that felt.

After an hour the stewardess decided to get rid of him. Solly had done about 12 bottles and, like a dirty old dog, had taken to farting. He was drunk, his pockets were clanking and she wanted him gone before the food arrived. Ray wanted him gone before the food arrived, too. She asked Solly to move and it took him a few minutes to realise what was happening. He asked for another two drinks. She said no. He got up and just left. He never said goodbye to Ray or thanked her; he just left noisily after grabbing the first-class toiletry bag from the seat in front. That would be a present for somebody, thought Ray.

* * *

Ray was relieved when the old man took his anger and funk with him back to the singing section. It was no surprise that Solly had not been in contact with Eddie. Ray knew the answer before he'd even asked the question. What was far more alarming was that nobody Ray had called in the days before the flight had had any idea where Eddie was. Not one person had a word or a clue about Eddie's vanishing. Ray had spoken to a few well-connected people, some of the best facilitators in Vegas, men who knew where people were and why they were there, even if the man wanted to be invisible.

Since Eddie's daughter's visit, Ray had been thinking a lot about the singer's absence. He knew Eddie, knew he would not just go missing without leaving word. Not before a fight like Mayweather and Hatton. It was big and that meant money to Eddie. Each time he picked up the phone he'd had a feeling inside that the person on the other end would say 'No' the moment he asked them if they had seen Eddie. He knew enough to be careful and never asked about Eddie directly when he made the calls. Thankfully there had been no odd or slightly disturbing silences when he had mentioned Eddie. Ray was convinced he'd not sensed that anything was wrong. It just felt a bit weird. He had tried all the direct numbers. All dead. The phones rang or the message machines were full. Eddie had never returned any of the left messages.

Nobody in Las Vegas had let on that there was a problem with Eddie. Not a problem? Well, where is he then? No problem, they all said, but at the same time Eddie had just walked off the radar in a Napolito shirt and a pair of Gucci shades. That, Ray knew, was not right.

Ray had blanks from the MGM, the Mandalay Bay and the gyms. Eddie Lights was out of circulation. It started to play on his mind because Eddie was getting old. Perhaps he was ill. The poor old sod could have drowned in his jacuzzi trying to remove a hooker's bikini with his tongue.

Ray remembered a long night a few years back after the first Tyson and Bruno fight. He had ended up with Eddie and a few others in the hot tub out at the house. Warm night, stars, water and brasses. Bosh, as it was back then. There had been a few women. At dawn, Eddie had asked for five notes each from everybody. It had been an expensive night. The coke was shit and the three whores had spent most of the time talking to Dan Marks. They had been convinced that Big Dan could help reverse them into Hollywood. Big Dan, it has to be said, wasted little time reversing into each of them as the night dragged slow and bright behind the coke glow. Big Dan, if the brutal truth be allowed to break out like a rash, had a name but no power. He had the teeth, but no real personality. Still, nobody told the dozy tarts that they were grafting for zippo with a flubber. The public still liked him, but people in TV considered him a suntanned fool. He had become a TV star when a straight back, a huge schlong, a set of pure white teeth and the ability to read an autocue were absolutely all that mattered. He also knew people in Vegas and that helped. Still, it was one of those nights. There had been many nights like it. Ray had plunged a monkey on absolute bollocks. Not now. That was over, Ray told himself each time he checked in for Vegas. No more long nights. Ray had found out that 4 a.m. is 4 a.m. the world over. It's always dark and it's always lonely. And his wallet is always just a bit lighter there.

Ray was starting to get concerned. If Eddie was ill, the daughter would get on the next plane. Ray would sort the whole thing out, get her a ticket and pick her up. She was a good sort. Get her on a plane, find Eddie, take her out, have a meal. It was a nice idea. As soon as he checked in at the MGM, he would grab hold of Jay and get a car to Eddie's house. Sure, find Eddie and then call the daughter. One, two. Easy. Simple. Find Eddie frozen and bloated in the tub with his arse burnt red from the sun and a pale pink thong clenched grimly in his white teeth. Not a pleasant image. Not pleasant, but at the same time it was one that he could not rule out.

LAS VEGAS: HOME OF JAY AND HIS FRIENDS

Ray spotted Jay's man the moment he came through the gate. He knew he would be there. He was a kid called Chip Montgomery. He had been a promising young lightweight 15 years earlier. He had built a nine and zero record in Ohio. He beat losers and looked good. One night Don King had seen him at a show in Akron and invited him to Vegas. Chip had shared a room with Moses Komakech for a while. They were just two more gym rats in the boxing city. He moved out when Komakech started to lose control.

Komakech was the first black African ever to win an Olympic gold medal in the boxing ring, but he had trouble adjusting to life in Vegas. American fighters have trouble adjusting to life in Las Vegas. For Ugandan fighters, there is next to no chance of adapting to the life. He needed help and Vegas is not a city known for its little helpers.

There are only two things that matter to any young boxer and Komakech was unhappy because he never liked the food and the women scared him. It was 1991, he had the gold medal, he had the talent, but he was like a lost little boy. Vegas is a savage, dark forest for the lonely and nobody is lonelier than a boy fighter from a foreign land. There is only so much solace in getting hit for a living. Komakech was a wreck waiting for disaster.

Komakech died after a routine fight, a fight he should have won. Chip had left the mad Ugandan's apartment a month or two earlier. He left the morning he found Komakech naked in the kitchen, sitting in the fridge. The door was open and the food was all over the floor like tiny islands in a sea of milk. He was wearing a headguard and singing 'Like a Virgin'. Poor Komakech had lost it. In the ring, he was still winning, but there was no life behind his eyes. Everybody close to the fighter knew that a pick-up waitress had cleaned out most of his money. She had worked on his innocence, ruined his mind and told him she was saving herself for the right man. The right man was anybody with about $100 to spare, but poor Moses of Kampala never worked that out. The right man had been through the shitbag a couple of hundred times. She took names and cash and poor Moses' little heart. There was nobody to save him. In the gyms, he still looked sharp. He was nasty in sparring and his people were happy with their product. She helped keep him nasty.

Komakech's brain exploded in the final fight. He never regained consciousness and he died in hospital from a massive series of clots. There were crocodile tears at his bedside, but nobody really cared. His family couldn't make the trip. There was no money for flights and he went too fast. The virgin waitress never visited him after the first night. Ray heard she had left the bed in the intensive care unit with Moses' clothing and wallet. She was gone. So was Komakech, and so was his money.

There are a thousand boxing tales like it in Las Vegas because it is a place without pity in the fight game. Ray wondered where poor Moses' gold medal was. He doubted it was with his desolate mother back in Kampala. That would be a fairy-tale ending, a long shot in the dead fighter's life. The whore won.

Chip had two quick wins in Vegas and then Dr Flip Homansky, the ringside doctor of a thousand fights and nights, called King one day with bad news. Chip was totally blind in one eye. The fighter had known all along, but what else was he going to do? He was twenty-three, he had never known his father, one brother was dead and two others were crack addicts back in Cleveland. King gave him $10,000 in cash. Don had no reason to be generous. Chip sent $8,000 to his mother. He knew that she would give it to his brothers, probably go with them when they scored. Mothers often do that with their addicted children. Jay – that's Jay 'the Big Soul' Hain from the Muhammad Ali days – gave him a job at the MGM. Chip had been close to Jay's action ever since. Jay was, Ray knew, one of life's great men.

Chip was always there for Ray. He met him again and again. They walked to the baggage hall from the gate. The Hatton faithful had landed. They were singing. It would be a big weekend.

At the airport, the slot machines were humming their clanking tune, their tinny melody of welcome. A din for the dumb. The familiar voices of the men and women Vegas adored came from the loudspeakers above the moving walkway. It was show time: show time in Las Vegas for the dreamers. The brightly lit signs were reassuring, the glow warming. Vegas is the only place on earth that grows so fast but changes so little.

Each year Ray saw the same faces; the same people smiling from the garish posters that covered every inch of wall in the arrival area. The truth was that the faces on the walls were getting younger. Ray had heard that models – good models, not shaved-twat-in-your-face models – have tiny bits of surgery over a period so that it is more difficult to spot the work in their pictures. It looked like the Vegas stars had had the same idea. Damn, it was probably a Vegas invention. There was the familiar fat Italian fella with a lobster the size of a goat. Ray had seen his smiling face for nearly 20 years. He had often thought about finding Fat Boy with Huge Lobster in his Podgy Fingers. Nice idea for a story, a way to make a little bit extra on the next trip. He made a note in his head: invent the fat fuck. He would be unrecognisable now and he was certainly not one of the Vegas beautiful people. He was probably dead with a heart clogged to bursting from grease and eating lobsters the size of large Shetland ponies.

Mostly the walls at the airport advertised the shows. In Vegas, nothing was bigger than the white tiger boys, Siegfried and Roy at the Mirage. The two old queens from Germany had once performed their magic tricks as a warm-up for a long-since-forgotten chorus line. Most people under 40 think a chorus line is a coke trick.

They were gone now, the two German queens with their big white cats. They had worked with Eddie back then. Eddie said they were lovely men. They had not aged because in Vegas the plastic worked. It worked across the counter and it worked in the operating rooms. Boy, did the plastic work. Onstage, they had made planes appear and vanish, and they could make six-foot-tall beautiful white tigers walk from under their cloaks. It was the 'hey presto' life. Bang, there's a white tiger. Bosh, there's a double-decker. Bish, I'm going to be 40 forever. Fuck it, it's Vegas.

But then one night it went wrong for our magical men. A white tiger went off script with a vengeance and chewed on the neck of his friend. Roy – or was it Siegfried? – was supper that night and the show fell dark. It was not a laughing matter: the skinny little magic idol came close to death. The pictures of the magician in a wheelchair were disturbing. He lived, but a life without magic was hardly a life. The tiger was innocent, by the way. It was simply being protective. Well, that's what the press release said.

The airport walls were lined with pictures of the rogue's gallery of performers who came to Vegas to die slowly in the heat. Or to have their head bitten clean off by a wild animal in a theatre packed to the rafters with fat people. Tickets, by the way, start at about 250 bucks a pop.

Fake adulation was critical because the place slowly ground down ambition and desire. Killed it off quick; sucked it out like laughter marrow and replaced it with a complacency that thankfully got confused with quality. The petty gamblers returned again and again to pay for the life because they believed in the fantasy. For most people – the normal people – the Vegas life started as soon as they felt the heat and heard the coins dropping. The airport, in other words. But there was also that other equally pitiless Las Vegas and that was through the same airport doors. There were no pony-sized lobsters in that retreat.

The men and women were smiling in all of the posters but, then again, surgery had probably locked their jaws in permanent joy. They were all Vegas people, entertainers with gleaming ivory in place of teeth. The regular entertainers played Vegas halls for every fat cent that rolled down from the skies and landed flush in the pots that the casino pitmen called the drop. It was all about the drop.

It was still Las Vegas, and it would always be Las Vegas. It was no longer on the edge of the desert because it was now at the very centre of a crazed place where lights spread out like mystical beanstalks across the dark desert floor. It was impossible to hate the place, but only a player could love it.

Ray was a player. But it was nothing to brag about.

The car pulled clear of the traffic and turned straight for the MGM. Ray had once walked from the MGM after a night. He had suffered a terrible loss at a sickening time and there was no money involved. It was another time when day avoided night and became day again. No breakfast – it was one of those nights – but it was a lot more than just one of those nights. In the past, he had been wide awake at 6 a.m., ruined by 9 a.m. and suffered for a week many, many times. That morning was different. Ray had emerged and nearly fallen over from the sun. He had started to walk, dragging his bag-on-wheels down the kerbs and in front of amazed motorists on his way to the terminal building. He arrived at the airport 40 minutes later, his suit soaking. Jay was standing there, coffee in one hand. Big Soul was waiting like a true friend. He had not met Jay for breakfast; he had avoided him and left without saying goodbye. That was a violation of their friendship.

That had been a bad night. It was all part of the loss. It had been Ray's darkest time. And the dawn delivered no relief.

Earlier that same morning, Jay had received a call at home from hotel security. It was from a guy called Duke, a nice guy, a fight fan, and he told Jay about the visits at two and four in the morning to Ray's room by a known narcotics dealer. Ray was pleased to see Jay. He was a friend and there are very few of them in Las Vegas.

Ray had lost big, but not at the tables. Ray never dropped a penny at the tables. That was the night that changed it all for Ray. The feeling of utter and total despair as he walked out that morning had nothing to do with money or gambling. Since then it had only been about business with Ray. He returned from that trip to an empty house and it stayed empty.

He tried to close the mental blind on the story as the car moved through the streets, but the shuttle from the airport never failed to open the memory. The empty house. It was a different house now, but it was still empty.

Chip took the direct route from the airport and avoided the new tunnel that added both dollars and miles to the journey. The green beast that is the MGM grew like a glistening inflatable in the sun at the far edge of a heat haze that was lifting heavily from the road. Ray had stayed at the MGM since it opened its doors. Before that he had liked the Flamingo. The Flamingo had an old Vegas feel to it, a civilised feel.

Eddie Lights had stayed at the original MGM when he had first arrived in Las Vegas. It turned to cinder after a bad fire one hot afternoon. Eddie wore a fur coat back then. 'It's made from rat,' Eddie had said.

Ray would never grow tired of the story, even if Eddie had told him a dozen times. His voice was less Manchester and more Caesars Palace on each retelling. Not many had made that same journey in style. Eddie certainly had. And Little Ricky was doing a good job of making the switch. Two wins in Vegas and then Mayweather.

'We all had fur coats on,' Eddie would say. 'Three of us and the fucking bear. All dressed for Siberia, packed like sardines in the smallest cab ever in Vegas history. Fucking guy had a Mini. I swear he had a Mini.'

Ray remembered the names, but he struggled with the faces. Les Savoire and Rumping Bear. Tony Bullion, the man who could hold a perfect note. And Eddie Lights. It was 1977. Their small cab dropped them at the MGM. There was no booking for them; no room at the inn for three British entertainers and a stuffed ventriloquist's bear. They were unknown, drunk and came close to being asked to leave. They could hardly stand and it was left to the bear to do all the talking. Rumping, as he was known, was asking every single woman who came near them if he could touch her tits. The first woman behind the jump had started off smiling, determined in a Las Vegas way to help the three British gentlemen. The bear had her in tears after about two minutes. She was not laughing. Her replacement lasted just a bit longer. It was not a great start to their Las Vegas tour.

The three suites they had boasted about on the plane were not waiting for them. There was no pink champagne for the trio. They rented a room with two beds just seconds before security evicted them. Savoire immediately claimed he needed one of the two beds because he had to sleep with the bear.

'Forget that shit, I told Les. Let me sleep with the fucking bear, I've always liked him!'

People loved the story. Eddie was a good talker.

They slept with a lot of things for about two weeks, but then it started to get serious because only Savoire was working and the money he was clearing was just enough to pay for the room. They even tried a comedy act in the fur coats called The Four Furkas. It failed. They called it the Four Bears. It failed. Three weeks went by. Their money was low. They were all failing. The coats were in hock, but they were still in Las Vegas, chasing the pot. It's a contagious ailment. When they lost the coats, their dreams were in danger. It's a terrible item, a pawn ticket. It is nothing and everything. It has details of your failings and no hope for your redemption.

Eddie did manage to get a spot by the main buffet in the Sands. It was only a small bar, but it had a loyal following – a clientele of players having just one last drink to end the night. The stage, which was so small Eddie dubbed it 'the Tray', was at the back in the gloom. Eddie was right; nobody could see him. He was behind the cleaners and so far to the back of the bar that he was lost from view. All people could see was the suit, the suit of lights. He was like a discarded and moving chandelier.

During the first 30 minutes each morning, the vacuum cleaners drowned out most of his voice. 'What a gaff! They couldn't see me, they couldn't hear me, but they loved my backing band, The Hoovers. I was killing them. Killing them!'

Las Vegas was different back then. A singer could still find work by walking from bar to bar. Eddie crooned over breakfast from nine until noon.

The first day that Bullion and Savoire had gone to watch him they had all ended up in tears. It was a proper laugh and they had stopped laughing in Vegas. The next day they took two lamps from the room and put them on tables at the front of the stage. He had a captive following of weary crossover waitresses and waiters. He was a diversion, a comma in their casino lives. A bright point in the dark of their day. Even the cleaners started to keep it down when he was on the Tray. Word was spreading. He never played to fewer than 30 and he never took a request.

'I had integrity. Anyway, I sung the arse off my set every day.'

One day Sal Lazarro heard him. Sal finished a double Dewar's most mornings in a soft red leather chair at one or other of the anonymous little bars. He was going to work, not taking the edge off a night. Somebody told him about the Englishman. He pulled a chair from a table, adjusted his cobblers as he sat, ordered two fingers of Dewar's and listened. He heard Eddie and he liked it. It was the day it changed for Eddie Lights. His life would never be the same again. It was a true story.

* * *

The car bumped hard on the bottom of the ramp at the MGM and then slowly moved under the gold-and-green canopy. Chip was out before Ray could get his hand on the door. A valet was in the driving seat before Ray was out. Las Vegas could move fast when it had to. Chip had the bags from the car and was waving to a bellman. Ray recognised the man. Another invisible fighter.

'Take Mr Lester's bag to the VIP. Mr Hain's expecting him,' Chip told the ex-fighter. He grabbed the bags in silence, never once looking up at either Ray or Chip.

Ray was still fumbling for a ten, but the man was gone with the bags. Chip saw Ray trying to locate his cash in his jacket pockets and shook his head. 'Mr Lester, man, you know better than that. You in our town now. You know Mr Hain don't ever let you pay.'

Inside the lobby at the MGM, the screens above the check-in and check-out desks were showing clips of Mayweather's knockouts and Hatton's sickening body shots. It was a gruesome loop. They were impressive, very impressive endings. They each talked. Ray could see how hard it was for people to like Mayweather. Or how easy it was to dislike him.

Ray had first seen Mayweather in the prelims at the Atlanta Games. He was a spoilt boy, a quality fighter and he seemed to enjoy being nasty. There were too many young fighters with a bad attitude and, unlike Floyd, there was nowhere near enough talent fighting in America. In many ways, it was their stupidity, their inarticulate speech, that had helped Hatton become a massive dollar player and media attraction in just one year of Vegas fights. He had a personality, he made a few jokes and he travelled without an entourage. Little Floyd loved his entourage but was slowly winning people over with the smile. He'd been on the ballroom dancing caper.

Ray lumped Floyd with the Philly middle Bernard Hopkins. They had two lives and they both worked hard to keep one in the shadows. Hopkins went out of his way to keep private what good he was doing. They each smiled when people called them arrogant. They enjoyed being misunderstood.

Floyd was on his own now and he was building avenues back to a life he had left when he was a child. It had been a troubled life. When he was one, his father had used him as a human shield after his uncle on his mother's side arrived with a shotgun and a demand for money. The uncle adjusted his sights and shot Floyd Snr in the leg. 'My dad was a hustler and my mother was an addict,' the kid admitted. His dad was sent down for trafficking crack and his mother went further into the zero.

Floyd grew fast in gyms, learning the old skills the old way. The Atlanta Olympics came and went and the teenager left with a medal. That was over ten years, five world titles and a few hundred million dollars ago. It was also before the problems with his dad, the fights with the mothers of his kids and the battle for his image.

The Hatton fight was about a new Floyd, in many ways. He was the real American kid. Not quite apple pie, but an inspiring tale. It was a hard sell next to Hatton's blunt jokes, but it was starting to work. American fight fans were being introduced to a Floyd they would love. It was a boy with a classic American tale to tell, and in the weeks before the Hatton fight he was telling it. He was winning hearts with the real tragedy of his early years. And the sequin outfits from the dance show helped.

He also had his mum back with him. He called her his wife, the only woman he needed. 'Why should I fight my whole life and then watch some woman get rich from me? That ain't happening.' She was from a time before jewel-encrusted playthings littered his house. A time before he trousered $20 million for his fights. A time when he was just a snotty-nosed kid. She was an ideal counter to the money mayhem that drains the decency out of too many modern fighters. She was the right person to have in any wealthy boxer's carnival of vultures. Lennox Lewis always had Violet, his mum, by his side and she kept his life straight. Big Len loved sweet Violet.

LAS VEGAS: FIGHT PEOPLE IN A FIGHT CITY

A ring had replaced the circle of seats in the middle of the MGM's foyer. The screens were on and way back somewhere in the fog of the casino the people were singing. They still smoke when they play in Vegas. The lobby was full with flag-draped hordes from Britain. Ray had to stand and take it all in. It was special.

There were still enough of the usual Vegas suspects walking from the din of the casino floor to the calm of the white-tiled lobby. The lobby was far enough away and the money clanking had started to fade. This was all about the noise of the fans and their continuous anthems. Each time Ray walked through the double glass doors into the MGM's lobby he knew nothing would have changed. Only now it looked like it was under siege.

From inside the 20 or so doors, the view over the tables and machines stretched until it vanished into a slow blur of smoke and air conditioning. He missed that first neon hit. All the colours inside the casino world had the brightness of life filtered out of them by the lighting. It was eternal day inside the casino, but it was not a bright day. That helped the cash palaces on the Strip to collect their toll from the visitors. The noise and light tricked people into believing that sleep was a hazard in Vegas, that they would be missing out if they ever closed their eyes. Hatton's 30,000 fans needed very little persuading to avoid their beds. The truth was that nothing ever really happened. And if it did, the people on the casino floors would never know about it. Las Vegas had blips, but it had created its own life a long time ago and like the temperature and the lights it was always the same.

Jay had told Ray that Vegas belonged to about a dozen people and that they ran the entire empire from just a few mysterious locations. They worked from hideaways reinforced by walls lined with 50 years of gold and cash and secrets. And a lot of blood. Ray liked the image of a modern Aladdin's cave buried in the desert, perhaps under one of the new casinos. There was a lot happening below the surface in Las Vegas – there were rumours of hundreds of miles of connected tunnels. Nice tales. Beneath the desert there were a lot of shallow graves from the early days. Well, that was the story. There was another story about the two-lane highways for golf trolleys that connect all the casinos on the Strip. Nice tales.

It was a strange place at night. Ray had been out in the desert in the blackness. There was a disturbing calm. Ray would always remember the way a torch softens the hard earth in the dark. It can make the scorched earth look like calm water. Out in the desert, the city twinkles like a thousand prawn ships on a moonless sea. Standing in the blackness and looking at the lights is like wearing an enormous pair of binoculars and staring at the sky.

Jay had once taken Ray to the extraordinary house that the Avon millions had built. It was a nondescript five- or six-bedroom place that was now directly behind where the MGM's amusement park had been, but it had once been two or three miles from the nearest casino. When the casino business started to expand in the late '80s, the Strip had drifted south like a concrete neon tsunami and it now surrounded the house. Jay had often talked about the house and, to be honest, when he took Ray there in a white Merc that Tom Jones had given him, Ray was disappointed. Inside, it was empty. A foul-smelling shell, and it was cold. Jay had pushed a light switch in one of the halls and Ray had heard a distant humming. When Jay opened a door next to the switch, it led to another door that was metal. He pushed a series of numbers on a keypad and the door opened. It was a lift, about six-foot deep. The pair stepped in.

After ten seconds, the lift stopped with a thud and the door opened. There was an enormous underground room. In fact, it was more like a warehouse. Directly in front of Ray was a cottage. The tiny home was about 100 feet long. Its front doors were open. There was a hallway, and beyond that Ray could see a chandelier hanging above a dining table. To the left of the cottage, there was a rock pool with a diving board, and to the right there was a putting green. The whole area was perhaps 200 feet long and 150 feet wide. The ceiling was about 30 feet high. It was the house that the Avon millions built. It existed. It was not Vegas myth.

An old black woman in a nurse's outfit appeared from a room and walked into the hallway. She smiled at the pair of them and walked out and by the side of house, next to the pool, where there was another much smaller cottage. Jay walked from the lift and towards the entrance to the cottage. The entire floor was covered with fake grass. The four walls had been painted and were now living murals. On one wall was a view of Los Angeles, on another a collection of scenes from New Zealand, and on a third a ski resort somewhere. The back wall had been painted from the memory of the Avon heiress. It was a simple scene. There was a farmhouse and a small home in gentle hills. Ray realised that it was the same cottage.

The rich old girl had the house built in the early '60s: a place of safety and sanctuary. Her wall was full of images from a childhood spent in a distant and peaceful farming town. It was what she wanted to look at when the Cold War ended in a nuclear attack. The home was the ultimate bunker for millionaire paranoids and the city of Las Vegas was its only possible location.

The walls of the cottage were covered in the oddest of artefacts. There were icons from Russian churches, the necklace worn by Elizabeth Taylor in *Cleopatra*, pictures of Muhammad Ali and letters of thanks from dozens of men in the movie business. In the middle of the dining area, a shrunken old man was sitting at a table tapping away at a small manual typewriter. He was the husband of the dead heiress. A gentle man in every way.

That had been the first time Ray had met him. The last time had been more recently, perhaps a year ago, when Tyson had been in the dining area. Jay and Ray had arrived and watched from a distance as Tyson smiled and stroked the old man's arm. He did that a lot. The boxer had been sitting there in silence, listening to tales of Havana before the revolution or of meals in the Avon heiress's New York City apartment with various presidents. Tyson had ignored Jay and Ray that day. It was not the first time Ray had seen the other Tyson, the one away from the lights and expectations of controversy, away from an entourage of any kind. The boxer had been on his own in the cottage with the old man. One of the fighter's sons was outside in the pool being watched by the nurse and off to one side was Crocodile, for so long Tyson's faithful servant. Crocodile was cursing because none of his mobiles worked in the underground house. The Croc cursed a lot and the nurse kept firing him looks of pity. She was a wise old woman and knew enough not to bother with anger in the company of men like Croc. It never could change a man packed with rage.

Tyson had left that afternoon with a small wooden statue. It was a carved gift of an African warrior holding a spear in one hand and wearing a boxing glove on the other fist. Ali had given it to the old man after he had returned from beating George Foreman in Zaire. Jay watched Tyson walk away with it.

'I saw the guy carve that for Muhammad. It took him a few minutes. Muhammad gave him one hundred bucks. The guy was in tears. The guy came to the house during the wait in Zaire.' The wait had been for Foreman's cut eye to heal.

Ray had seen the statue a few months later in Tyson's den in the fighter's house on the edge of Vegas. During his life, he had given away new Bentleys and diamond watches worth a million dollars, but it is unlikely that he would ever part with the statue.

But that was a long time ago. It is a forgotten Tyson from a lost day in a life he no longer had control over. The Avon man was now dead, Crocodile was gone and the house had been sold. Jay had mentioned that the new owners had pulled down the shell house, dug up the cottage and filled in the amazing home's hole.

But Ray had also heard that it was still there.

Las Vegas was always good for a conflicting tale or two.

Jay was waiting at the door of the VIP lounge. His suit was classic Vegas: dark and cut to shine. His golden tie was hidden under the collar that every wise guy was now wearing. His ring glistened, the ring Ali had given him for being part of the inner circle. He was Mr Vegas.

'You're late, goddamn it.'

It was usual for Jay to be a miserable sod. He pushed back through the door, called a waiter and ordered a water and a coffee for himself and pointed at Ray.

'Vodka. Cranberry, if it's fresh. Or lime juice if it's not. Thanks.'

Jay sat down in one of the two leather chairs in front of a VIP desk. Behind the desk was a blonde girl. Her MGM badge said *Tiffany from La Jolla, CA*. He grabbed her hand, rubbing her fingers. She smiled like she knew she had to, but she had a look on her painted face that also said she hated having her hand touched by every creep with 50 bucks and access to a line of credit that resembled a date of birth. Each time it happened she was reminded why she hated Vegas. But, in truth, she probably never needed reminding. 'Oh, Mr Hain. You know I can't do that,' she said.

Ray sat down next to Jay and she glanced over. It was just a glance, less than a flicker, the type of look a doctor would struggle to find life in. There was nothing there. A fucking cash android. She was not blushing. Jay had pawed her hand a dozen times each day during the last year or so. She found Ray a mini-suite and sent him a plastic smile when he slipped her a fifty. She vanished the folded note in a blur. Just another magician. It fell from her fingers to her bag on the floor and by the time it landed she had forgotten the face that had given it to her. She had a memory for forgetting faces and names. She didn't look beyond the tip of the table after Ray had stood up. No *Thank you* and certainly no *Goodbye*. There wasn't even a remote moment of thanks in her eyes, which she had obviously plucked from a dead Barbie. It was probably the look a condemned man has when the torture ends and the bullet is due – due, or on its way. She was what the men in suits, the men with too many years and far too much influence in the city, liked to call a Vegas Bitch, or VB for short.

It was a name that fit so perfectly a life that only the knowing wanted to live. She was unpleasant. The city of her choice had been her finishing school. She had her cold plan clear in her skull and she was taking deep breaths to survive each day. She was banking the money daily and counting down to a time when she would be able to look in the mirror and smile. Ray knew and had heard the story many, many times. Lap dancers, hookers, waitresses. All the women serving in Las Vegas had their escape plan. Ray was too polite to tell most of them they would never use the parachute.

'Ray, page me when you're in the room. I gotta go and see somebody.'

Then Jay was gone.

Ray stopped at the shop and picked up the local papers. The phone booths were packed with fans and fixers and dealers and players. There was a lot of action going on. The coke was flowing. Everybody was pissed. Pissed and happy. It was obvious what type of shit was going down. Ray had heard that there had been an endless party since the Monday, when the fans had started to drift in. He nodded at a few familiar faces and said hello to a couple of American writers. People were talking about the weigh-in and Hatton's behaviour. He had run his finger across his throat. It seemed odd, not like Hatton. Little Floyd had been cool. Hatton most definitely had not.

The phone was ringing when he got to the room. A bag was on the bed and another was hanging up. The bagman would be back. Ray moved round the king-size bed and picked the phone up. It was Jay.

'Ray. VIP lounge, now.'

Ray never had the chance to answer. There was a knock on the door. It was the fighter, the bellman. Ray told him to wait and he went to get a bit of cash. He only had twenties. The guy took it, nodded, but never said a word. That was fifty at the check-in and twenty for the bags and not even a *Thank you*. Not even a word of recognition. Ray knew that respect in Vegas started at about a ton. He would have to do fifty with Mickey at the cab rank, and fifty with Sanchez at breakfast just to get him near the front of both the lines. There was a chance that nothing would work because of the fans. Vegas was being pushed by Hatton's people and new rules were being set. Ray knew three days in Vegas could cost $500 in tips. He also knew that for the next 48 hours the guidebook was obsolete. There was a feeding frenzy down below. Jay would comp him the room and not take a cent, so it all worked out in the end. It all worked wonderfully in the end, but it was still a lot of money and times were lean. He knew it was simply the Vegas way, but it was a bad time in the gelt department.

Jay was talking to Budd Schulberg and his young son, Adam, when Ray entered the VIP lounge again. Budd was on a comp. He'd won an Oscar for *On the Waterfront*, for fuck's sake. The man was 94 or something and should never have had to buy a drink again. Adam had a beer, Budd an apple juice and Jay a coffee. Budd was talking about the first time he saw Mayweather and how the kid had reminded him a bit of Henry Armstrong. Only Budd could get away with making comparisons like that. He had been the old man of the ring for longer than most other writers had been on the planet. He had been there so many times. Jay had tickets for Budd and Adam to watch something or other and they left for whatever show it was he had managed to find tickets for.

Jay sat down. He looked tired. He was not a young man. He had to be nearly 70, or even older. He had watched Ali win the Olympic gold in Rome. He had met the fighter a few times after that and during the champ's exile in the late '60s he had gone to work with him. Jay had been the fighter's business manager. Everybody knew him as the Mechanic. He made it happen everywhere they went. When it was all over and everybody limped back from the Bahamas after the last defeat, Jay ended up in Vegas. That was over 20 years ago – over 20 years since Trevor Berbick's fists provided the end that everybody feared but nobody could prevent. He was still the facilitator. Binion's, Maxim's, New York, New York and the MGM. Jay had been an executive host at all of them. He was the quintessential executive host. Ray had known him for about fifteen years and had tried for the last ten to get a documentary commissioned. Big Soul was Mr Vegas.

'Let's walk.'

At poker tables in the middle of the floor, Jay patted people on the back and nodded and shook hands. The diehards were playing through the noise and the occupation.

'You ever seen it like this?' Jay was shaking his head.

This was his routine, but with Hatton's army in place it all seemed crazy. The casino had been taken over. Jay's shifts could last 24 hours and go for days on end if he had the right people in town. Hatton's fans were unlikely to pop up in the Griffin Book, but they could deliver other problems. The fans were not grifters in any of the banned casino dark arts. There was too much laughter and singing for anybody to count cards. But there was a bit of an edge. England shirts, drunks arm in arm and songs: guilty. And Ray had heard talk of a football amnesty. There was something in the air and Ray had seen it many times outside or near grounds. He also knew that some top boys had put themselves in charge of a variety of ventures. Mickey Pockets had given him the heads-up. Ray also knew that extra security had been drafted in.

Jay's unofficial office was the Brown Derby, the steak house that had started in Hollywood in the 1930s. They went straight to the back booth. A phone arrived and was plugged in and at the same time his iced water and coffee was placed on the table. Ray asked for a vodka and cranberry. Jay had tipped two people before Ray's drink arrived. The singing was off in the distance.

'They been up three fucking days and nights. Same song? Same motherfucking song. You believe that? They sure love the kid.'

Jay picked up the house phone and let the reception know where he was. He pulled out his two mobiles and his bleeper and started to crunch ice. Ray had finished his first drink before his old friend spoke.

'You got something to ask me, right?'

Ray knew Jay would know. There are few secrets in Vegas and Jay knew all of them. Ray knew his friend would know he was looking for Eddie. It had been a mistake not reaching out directly to him. A big mistake, and now it was way too late.

'Yeah, I have. I was going to call, but I figured I would be here and we could have a chat face to face.'

Jay raised his hand. His rings glistened. 'Bullshit.'

Ray had been telling lies and they both knew it. Ray had not called because it was impossible to get away with a lie when speaking to the Vegas veteran. If he had called and asked Jay something about the fight and then suddenly switched to asking about Eddie, he knew it would have been an insult. Ray knew that and so did Jay.

'Don't bullshit me, Ray. I heard from Rich and Michael at the Rio and they all told me the same thing: you're looking for Eddie Lights. You call those little faggot bastards. You call them, but you never called me to ask. Why is that? You spoke to Susan about the room and never asked for me. That's disrespectful and insulting. What's wrong with you?'

Ray had finished his second drink and, with the travel and the time difference, he was feeling a bit light. He needed some food.

'I'm sorry about that, Jay. I just, ergh, never called because I'm not really looking for him. Well, I am, but nobody is paying me. This is not a job, there's no dough for anybody. His daughter came to me and asked me to help her find her dad. That's all I know. And I figured I could ask you when I got here. I didn't even know he had a daughter.'

It was a clumsy attempt to make a heavy moment light. Jay never moved.

'Ray, how long I known you now? Ten years? More maybe. I always helped you, never gave you a bad time. Never told you wrong was right. Never sold you out, right? So I'm gonna tell you something real simple now: forget Eddie Lights. Forget that fuck.'

Ray was stunned, and before he could open his mouth Jay raised his pudgy fingers from the table. A second later a woman called Sherry appeared. Well, that is what it said on her badge, but there were far too many Sherrys in Vegas for all to be real. She worked in the boxing office at the MGM. She passed Jay an envelope, said 'Hi' to Ray and walked away. Jay opened the envelope and counted 15 ringside seats before putting them back and sliding the envelope into one of his inside pockets. Ray knew to be quiet when his friend was working. People in Vegas like their business to be their business.

'Ray, this conversation is over before it started. You know what I'm saying, don't you? I'm saying Eddie Lights is gone. He's gone, it's over. Now, let's eat some food.'

After the food, which as usual was poor, Ray left the Brown Derby. Eddie's name was not mentioned again during the meal. Jay said it was over and to him it was. Ray had left Jay in the Brown Derby deep in conversation and food. His phones would start to ring at about midnight, the time when gamblers started to run short and Jay had to vouch for them at the cage. Some he would go with and agree to extended lines, others he would leave dead in front of the cage, stunned in an upright crucifixion at the end of a long friendship. Old friends in tears; Ray had seen that. But Jay would just shrug. He knew too much about deception and desperation to worry.

He understood the way a gambler worked. He had spent a lot of time with Stu Ungar. Sad little Stuey, a Vegas legend. Jay was inside their heads and never wrong on a call. He fronted many times for Stu and they split a lot of money, but near the end he would not part with a dollar for coffee. There were times when the man behind the shades never had a dollar. He died that way, a great and lost genius of the tables. Poor little Stuey was skint and lonely at the end.

With Jay, it was an art. The art of knowing when to say no, and that is why he was the best at his job in the city. He never gambled, he watched. He watched and said no to men who could not say no.

Ray took a cab to Caesars. He was still looking. He had to. He got out of the cab under the Forum shops at Caesars and seconds later was at the bar in Spago. He was surrounded now by smarter Hatton fans working the cocktail lounges where drinks were nearly a score a bang and there was half a chance the women were real. At Spago, there were often gorgeous women and nothing was for hire. Well, that was the theory, because they could still knock the bollocks out of a normal man's wallet.

Ray was looking for a former journalist called Mike Marley who had for a time worked as King's press officer. Marley always knew what was happening in Vegas, but he was not in Spago. It was probably a bit pricey for the fight man. He was not on the barge at Caesars. Ray jumped into another cab to the Mandalay Bay. The recent run of big fights there had created a couple of unofficial boxing watering holes. They were both empty of real fight people but rammed with Hatton's boys and girls. Ray wondered where they were all going to be when the first bell sounded. There were officially only 3,000 tickets available to British fans and about 20,000 on closed circuit. Would they even leave the bars?

The vodka gaff at the Mandalay was wet from melting sculptures and he was happy to escape without having to stay. He hated the Mandalay Bay because it attracted the stupid to gawp. The fans there had booed Oscar De La Hoya and Felix Trinidad after two rounds because they were not hitting each other. How could a place that attracted punters like that call itself the Home of Boxing? It was a disgrace. Still, the hotel was nice enough.

LAS VEGAS: NOT THE NEON BIT

It was gone midnight when Ray sat back in another cab and gave directions to the driver for the Diamond Room. The Diamond was run by Jimmy, a one-time player from Detroit, and the place was always open. It was also where Stacey Bright liked to hang out. It was always a safe haven from the fans, the singing and the casino life: an escape from the permanent glow. There were other times when 40,000 paramilitary faithful were in town for their annual death convention and they were also certainly best avoided. The armed Jesus boys could be scary because they had the Lord on their side.

The cab stopped in the car park at the Diamond Room 20 minutes later and Ray gave the guy thirty. He pulled away without saying thanks or offering a cent in change; the fare was $24. No thanks Vegas. Ray had done about 30 bucks earlier on cabs. It was a money trip.

Stacey was at the bar steadily feeding a 21 machine with quarters. Behind the bar a short woman called Debby with cheerleader legs and the rest of the set-up was pouring a beer. All the women at Jimmy's wore shorts. Even the ugly, fat ones. Debby was not one of the ugly, fat ones. She had been at the Diamond for many years, but there was still a lot of life in her eyes. Stacey turned and smiled, but there was something wrong with his face. He stood up and the pair embraced, and Stacey performed a short step to turn Ray so that he was facing the door that he had just come through. Boxers use the move all the time to turn each other in corners.

'Hey, Deb, get my friend a beer and send some more over to Jimmy and his friends.'

Stacey had been a decent fighter, he was a good promoter and he knew Vegas better than most. He could be noisy, a legacy from his years with King, but he had ordered the drinks in a whisper, which was not like him.

Before Stacey pulled off the little turn, Ray had noticed on the other side of the bar a group of men sitting at two tables. There were four of them and Ray only recognised Jimmy. He had on his trademark crushed-velvet tracksuit, the red one with the white piping. It was an important piece of leisurewear for men from back east and Jimmy was from back east. The others had on leather coats and were facing away from the bar. They looked like Jimmy's friends. Ray knew enough to know that they looked like men from back east. That's where Jimmy's friends came from. They arrived with their history and it was never good. They were mostly dangerous men.

As soon as Debby ducked away to get the drinks, Stacey walked to the other end of the bar and out of Jimmy's vision. He stopped smiling. He was still holding Ray's elbow and there was sweat above his eyes.

'Ray, you got about ten seconds to get the fuck outta here before those guys with Jimmy come looking for you. No, don't speak. Just listen. They heard you were looking for Eddie and now they're looking for you. Now, go. And don't look back.'

Eddie again.

'What the fuck's going on? I can't leave. I'm not in a car. Where can I go? There's no chance of a taxi outside, it's the middle of nowhere in the middle of the poxy night and every cab is packed with Hatton fans.'

Debby arrived with the drinks. Stacey smiled and placed a hand on Ray's shoulder, pulling him closer. Ray knew it was serious, knew the men on the other side of the bar were involved before Stacey had opened his mouth. He just knew.

'OK, about two blocks up is Rodeo Girls 2. You know it? Find somewhere to hide. There are some shops there. Find a shadow or something. Don't move, you hear. I'll be over in about 30 minutes. You understand? Now, just go.'

Ray walked, never looked back and didn't breathe until he was outside. It had suddenly turned cold, just like so many winter nights in Vegas. December is deceptive but always cold once the sun dips. Ray hesitated for a second and then took off across the car park. He knew he was running for some reason but was short on answers. He had no idea what was happening. He just kept running. Five minutes later, he was behind the lap dancing club.

Rodeo Girls 2 was cheap but not as cheap as some of the other clubs on the edges of the city. It was a lot better than the pits hidden in industrial lots where flesh cost less than a beer.

West Charleston was empty; the street was dark and silent. There was the distant echo of faraway voices. Surely it was not Hatton's chorus of approval filling the night sky? Ray looked out from the doorway of a doughnut shop and studied the traffic. It was the only place for him to wait because there was no cover behind the club. If he pitched up at the back wall, one of the bouncers would be on him in a second for lurking too close to the product. Every few minutes the back door at the Rodeo opened and bare-legged women in sweatshirts stepped out to smoke a cigarette or pull slowly for relief from the butt of a joint. From the waist up, they looked more like mums at a soccer match than dancers on the dull highway scratching a living on a sticky wooden platform with a few hundred dollars wetly stuck to their G-strings. He could hear their voices but not their words. A few punters left the Rodeo and took a piss on the side wall.

It was closer to an hour later when Ray spotted Stacey's silver Mercedes. It was moving real slow up West Charleston from Jimmy's place. It turned off and into the strip joint's car park and then it stopped. Ray could hear the engine's gentle purr somewhere above his heart beating. If Stacey was panicked, then Ray was nervous. He had tried not to dwell too much on what might have happened during the wait. He knew it was shit serious.

Stacey moved between empty cars, took a slow sweep of the car park that served both the Rodeo and the ten or so shops that made up the mall. He then parked right by the road under the Rodeo's neon sign. The lights in the car went off, but the doors stayed closed. Ray could not be sure, but it looked like Stacey had slumped forward in the seat. Ray thought he might have to wait a bit longer in the shadow of the doughnut shop doorway and he was right.

A few minutes later, a Lexus pulled into the Rodeo's car park. It cruised slowly by Stacey's car. Ray could see that there were two men inside the car. He caught the shine of the neon sign as it bounced off the driver's black leather sleeve. They were two of the men from the Diamond Room. He had seen enough of them before Stacey had twisted him away from their line of vision to recognise them. Ray was sweating now. This was no longer funny. He heard Jay in his head: 'He's gone.'

Ray knew exactly what that meant and right now he was about as scared as he had ever been. Vegas was not a good place to get into trouble. It was too easy to die and he knew that all too well.

The Lexus moved between the dozen or so parked cars and then pulled up next to the Rodeo's entrance. Both men stepped out. They looked like what they so obviously were: two bad men heading for a flat beer in a dimly lit room of fake tits. The driver pointed his keys at the car and the noise of the electronic locking system shook Ray. The car's back lights came on and flashed off. The pair were looking over at Stacey's car just 20 feet to their right. If they went over, they would find Stacey and then what? Ray knew that if they started to walk towards the car, he would have to shout or do something. He had no choice. He could not just stand back and let the two of them find Stacey curled up on the floor of his car with the lights out. Ray had no idea what was really going on, but he knew enough to know that it was not Stacey's problem. He would have to break cover from the doughnut shop and that was a particularly scary thought. There was no guarantee that his voice would support his bravery. He had to hope that the men in leather would think that the empty car meant that Stacey was inside the club with him. He had to assume they were looking for him and Stacey. What else? That would have been Debby. She meant no harm and she had no reason to be silent.

The pair were still looking hard at the car when the back door of the Rodeo opened and two women stepped out. There was a quick blast of old-school disco from the stage inside. The girls were smiling and laughing as they lit up smokes. Ray looked at them, and when he looked back the men were gone. In the same second, he saw Stacey's car suddenly screech forward and race at him without lights. The two women looked on in total silence. They knew enough not to see anything. Stacey stopped at the kerb right in front of Ray and the window on the driver's side went down.

'Get in!'

Ray didn't need to be asked twice. A few minutes later they were lost in the streets that link the soulless communities that surround the brightly lit miles of Casino City. Ray had no idea where they were going and Stacey was not talking. Thankfully, there was no sign of the Lexus.

'You at the MGM, right?'

Ray nodded. Ten minutes later the car pulled up by the service entrance for the old MGM theme park. The theme park had been slowly dismantled when casino executives realised that nobody wanted kids in Las Vegas. It was a nice idea. The back street was empty at night but served as a highway for workers during daylight hours.

'Ray, you gotta get out of town.'

'What's happening here?'

Stacey looked over. He shrugged. 'Ray, you know what's going on. You're playing fucking detective all over town, looking for Eddie. You ain't the only one looking, you know what I mean?'

Ray did. He did now. 'Why? What's it with Eddie? I've asked a few questions, nothing serious, and now I'm dodging through car parks like a thief. What the fuck has Eddie done?'

'I don't know. I really don't, but I just know those guys were asking about you because you been asking all over town about Eddie. That's all I know and now I'm in the middle of this shit and I have no idea what the hell's going down.'

It was the first time Ray had heard fear in Stacey's voice. He sounded very different, very low. He was scared, and all scared people had the same voice.

'Stace, I've only been in town five hours. This is crazy. Tell me it ain't happening.'

'Look, if you need somewhere to stay, I know some people in Henderson that could put you up. You know this ain't a game, right? Those guys were serious people. You know what they are? This is no TV *Sopranos* gangster bullshit. Even Jimmy stopped smiling when they came through the door. The little guy was a cold fucker.'

Ray sat back and closed his eyes. This was not right. Jay with his arse in his hands, Stacey frightened, Jimmy losing his smile and a car of goons wearing leather coats.

'Thanks, Stace, but Jay never puts my name down so I should be cool here. Anyway, I'm out of town on Sunday morning. I'll keep my head down at the fight and then I'm gone. It's going to be chaos in there.'

'You're crazy to go to the fight. Man, they'll just pick you up there and God knows what guys like that will do. Ray, go tonight. Get a car and go to LA. Forget the fight, just who you gotta see? What's so important? Hatton's gonna get his arse kicked. Leave now before your boy gets beat.'

'What's going on here? What has Eddie done?'

An MGM security car cruised by and slowed to a stop 50 feet from them. Stacey looked up, eased the Merc into a silent gear and moved away.

'I'm gonna drop you by the villa. You know how to get in from there?'

Ray nodded.

A few minutes later Stacey was pulling away from the kerb and Ray was alone by the side entrance next to the exclusive high-rollers' villa. He knew he could get from the entrance to his room without going near the main lifts and the reception area. He knew a route that avoided the tables and avoided the diehards with their oxygen tanks and running noses on the casino floor. He sometimes even used it when the floor was empty. He could hear the singing. It was everywhere.

He entered, turned left and went through the group meeting point to the lifts that once served the hotel which had been consumed under the construction of the MGM. The old hotel was now encased in glass and was part of the MGM. The rooms were tiny. He spent a week at a fight in the '90s on the floor in one of the rooms. He took the lift to the second floor and walked down the tiny corridor to the main lifts. All the lifts stopped at the second floor and he found the bank of four that went to his floor. He needed sleep and some answers. The lift opened and amazingly it was empty, but the floor had dozens of stashed glasses. He could smell the shit perfume, body odour and smoke. He stepped in and pushed 19. On the 19th floor, the door opened with the familiar ping and he edged out slowly. There were another dozen or so discarded cocktail glasses on the floor by the bins. The fans were drinking the place dry.

Ray moved from the lift concourse to the landing and looked down the long rows of rooms. A room service waiter was at the bottom of one row, but the other two were empty. The moment he started to walk a door opened near the ice machine. He froze, his legs went stiff and he could feel the sweat on his back. He was waiting for the pain.

'Everything OK with you tonight, sir?'

He turned and smiled at a security officer, then mouthed, 'Yes.' He wasn't sure a sound came out.

The guard walked by and started to move down Ray's row. Ray followed about ten feet behind him. At 19-321, Ray stopped and fumbled for his card. He eventually got the door open and stepped inside. The room was freezing cold. The bedside clock was fixed at 3.11 a.m. and the phone's red message light was buzzing. Ray ignored the light and crawled into bed.

LAS VEGAS: SUNNY EGGS TO START THE DAY

The phone went before eight. It was Jay. He would know all about the visit to Jimmy's place because information was his business. Fifteen minutes later, Ray joined him in the Brown Derby.

It was early, but the fans had not been to bed and the lobby and the areas near the lifts were full of confused and weary people. It was like they had nowhere to go and were in no hurry to get there. They stood in noisy clusters, talking bollocks, just happy to be at a big fight in Vegas. There was pride on their faces. They were content, knowing that the first bell was getting closer. Time seemed to move more quickly if they sang and held a beer. Ray spoke to a few who he recognised and heard a tale or two about no tickets and bars being closed. Mostly people were just trying to focus and speak. It was the third or fourth or often the fifth day of constant boozing for many of them. And they had called it on long before the planes took off. They would sleep like babies on the way home.

Ray ordered coffee and smiled at Jay's silence. He knew.

Jay finished murdering a few eggs between hefty slurps of his own black coffee.

'Ray, what the hell were you doing out at Jimmy's last night?'

There was no need for Ray to answer. He didn't have an answer.

'What did I tell you? The fuck I tell you? What did I say? I said forget about that fuck Eddie Lights. And then ten minutes later you're out at the fucking wise guy saloon asking questions. Now, listen. You listen. Eddie is gone. That's the end of it.'

A waitress came to take the plates and Jay gave her $5. He waited until she had gone before continuing. There was food on his chin and his tie.

'I'm trying to straighten it out with Jimmy, but even he doesn't want to get involved.'

Jay looked over and shook his head.

'Ray, tell me one thing, and don't even try and bullshit me. Why are you looking for Eddie?'

'I told you already and it's the truth. His daughter came to me last week or the week before and asked me to find her dad. That's it. I shouldn't even be bothering. There's nothing in it for me. I'm just playing good Samaritan.'

'No, you're just playing a dumb schmuck and the type of arsehole who could end up very fucking hurt. Dead hurt. That motherfucker hurts.'

Jay got up and walked over to another table. Ray looked over to see that Michael Buffer and his latest young wife had just sat down. It was fight day and Jay always had a lot of business. His men were in town and he was fixing and facilitating many, many extras.

Ray's food arrived and Jay never returned. After 20 minutes, Ray left, tried to pay and was told 'Mr Hain has taken care of your check, sir.' He left a ten. It was taken in silence. He knew it would be.

Ray went to see little Scotty in the press room about accreditation. He still had some business to take care of. He was not going to run. Jay would sort it out. Ray had to make a few calls and little Scotty let him use one of the phones on the main desk. The press centre was the busiest Ray had ever seen. Along two of the walls, over a hundred radio stations from all across America had set up their broadcast tables and they all seemed to be on air. The noise was friction, a kind of mad white sound, with voices stopping and starting. Ray had never seen it this frantic, and that included all the big Tyson nights. There was a raised platform in the middle with room for 50 cameras, a press conference area with nearly 300 chairs and the press conference stage with 20 positions. There were a dozen or so groups of journalists milling and taking advantage of the free breakfast from the buffet on the far side. Ray worked the room for a few minutes. He had business.

Most of the journalists in the press centre were the younger ones, many from the online boxing sites. They ate off plastic plates all the time and stayed in motels way off the Strip. Ray had done that often enough when orders for copy ran dry and the days and nights ran long. He was not a great fan of the new writers. There were exceptions, but Ray thought the passage from nowhere to ringside was too easy. He recognised they had the same type of dumb idealism that had once gripped him by the knackers, but that was long before the plans and dreams had been slowly sucked out of him. They were passionate about things that didn't matter. Boxing had taken a dreadful toll on his hopes during the nearly 20 years that he had been inside the business. Pity for the dream boys. He'd seen a play called that once a long time ago. It was a rotten play but a nice phrase and it was ideal for the new young writers. They were dream boys.

He wanted to just go back to his room and leave. Jay's coldness and Stacey's fear were enough. He had also seen the men. It was not a myth or a joke or a threat. It was real. Men in leather coats were looking for him in Las Vegas and he had decided to stay. He knew it was wrong, stupid. It was difficult to act normal, but he had business in town.

He called Richard Steele, the former referee, to talk about two young kids who Steele had just signed. One of them could fight and he had been born in Scotland. He also called Faye down at Colonel Miller's gym. She was fine and thanked him for the T-shirts he had sent. He called Gordy Oak over at Caesars to talk about the vintage programmes. He arranged to see Oak and Steele at the fight.

Nobody he spoke to gave Hatton a chance. He could still hear the singing off in the depths of the casino. It formed an odd backdrop of defiance as Steele and Oak condemned the British idol. It was still early in the day, but the crowd was relentless, filling every gap and corner of the MGM with hope. The booze supply was, Ray heard, under threat.

Ray returned to the room. He took a long route, using mirrors to check for men watching his back. He met more familiar faces. They all believed in Hatton's right to win. 'He deserves it,' many said. Odd, because right and wrong and good and bad and justice and injustice had nothing to do with boxing at this level. Don King had it right when he said 'In boxing, you get what you negotiate and not what you deserve.' That was it, really. A simple assessment of a business that was not even as complex as prostitution. No pity, you see. There was no emotional involvement at this level. The man with the most money could get the most. No poetry, no beauty; just cash, and all of it legal. It helped if a boxer could fight a bit. Hatton could and Mayweather could and they were both about to get what they deserved in the ring. Hatton about $30 million and Mayweather perhaps as much as $40 million.

Ray walked another mirror-heavy stroll, avoiding his own eyes as much as possible. This time he arrived at the spa area for a steam and sauna. A few hours in the steam was the best way to get through a day at the MGM; the best way to wipe away the memory of the men looking for him. He figured that he would be safe in one of the thin white gowns that everybody wore in the spa, safe deep in the heat of a naked steam and invisible on the third tiled tier of a room that was boiling his body like a cooker. He took up position, hidden away behind the steam.

It was nearly four when he started to make his way back to his room. He had to walk through a wall of fans waiting for the doors to open. It took thirty minutes for the three-minute walk. He felt safe. They were Hatton's people and it was clear that the estimates of just 3,000 British fans inside the MGM Grand Garden were way off. This was a takeover, an invasion of believers. Hatton was boxing's biggest attraction.

At the lifts, Ray could hear the band, the Yorkshire brass band. They were playing in one of the lifts. Just going up and down, playing like lunatics. The noise was deafening. *The Sun* had paid for them to come out, to perform and to make people smile. It was mayhem. People arm in arm, crying and singing and drinking. Thousands and thousands of Hatton fans. It was devotion – fanatical devotion to just one man, and it made no difference that his cause that night looked lost. He pulled himself free and entered an empty lift. The silence left his ears ringing.

Once again, the walk down the long corridor twisted his gut. In the room, the red light was still buzzing. He ignored it again. Ray hated messages. He only had an hour or two to kill. He tried to push Eddie Lights out of his mind, but it was not easy. There was something wrong. Something seriously wrong? He kept coming back to the tears of the woman who had arrived at his door. Where did her tears fit into the scene outside the Diamond Room? In the Diamond, and outside, behind the strip joint, he had felt a very real fear.

All that mattered now was that he got through the night and out in one piece the following morning. He could talk to the woman about the events when he got home. And Eddie – well, if he showed up, good. If not, so what?

At six, he went downstairs and shifted and nudged and pushed his way to the MGM Grand Garden's entrance. The casino was finally starting to look like it had before the fans arrived. There was space and the hustlers were taking up positions. The white women were walking the same loops and the black women were parked on seats, playing with melting ice. The pimps and pushers had filled the gaps. They had probably been there the whole time, but with thousands of fans packing the bars it had been impossible to see. It looked like the dregs of a Tyson crowd. Men swilling from Cristal bottles and women silent and staring – going to the toilet three at a time to report back. There was the old menace back on the floor and the singing had finally finished. The boxing boys were at the fights and Tyson's faithful were in the bars.

Before his exile, the fallen heavyweight idol had attracted the same crowd whenever he fought at the MGM. The fans ran riot when he bit off Evander Holyfield's ear. Guns went off that night, tables were overturned and security prowled through the debris, their hands hovering over their holsters. It was a vision of war in a city. The lights in the casino finally changed during the battle for order. It was like walking into a hotel bathroom: flicking the light and killing the darkness. The mist was removed and replaced by real light.

The drop took a killer hit that night, bigger than any planned heist. The MGM closed until the carnage had been cleared, and when that was done most of the punters had moved on through the heat and neon of the pavements and were losing money elsewhere. Thousands of high- and low-rollers walked out into the night and away from the anger and danger and talk of death. It made casino folk cry to see their money walking out the doors still in the pockets of their punters. It was impossible to get them back once they had walked through the door. Extra security was employed for all fights after Tyson v. Holyfield and now moving around on fight day and night required patience. Since that night, Ray had often used the tunnels.

It was still early by Vegas fight-crowd standards but already the only people outside were the ones without tickets. It was tense at the entrance and there was a build-up of security. The big men on the casino payroll had stopped smiling at the chorus boys. At the ticket barrier, Ray pulled his pass out and put it round his neck. He drifted through the thinning crowd and made his way slowly to the press area at ringside. It was full. Three hours before the bell and the Grand Garden was full. Ray had never seen that. He could feel it. The walk from the back of the Garden to the ringside press area was heavy. The noise, the noise. The drums and the heat. It was December, but it was hot.

In the ring, two local kids were fighting and it looked like they could sense the enormous watching wall. Vegas shows were often terrible until the main event, but still promoters like Arum and King insisted on putting 12 or more fights on. Tonight the crowd was not from Vegas. They had paid their money and they wanted to see a few fights. The pair in the ring were in fight five and it was not yet 6.30. The early start allowed for the main event to be broadcast at a reasonable time on the East Coast, but the night would be all over by nine and the fans would reverse into the casino and start to empty their pockets. The art was keeping the thousands from jumping cabs and taking walkways. The drop was crucial. And keeping all the high-rollers was critical. The Hatton and Mayweather crowd was spending, and had been spending like never before. It had been a dream week at the bank for the casinos.

Ray watched the young black kid in the ring. He had once been a quality amateur and Ray had seen him at the Ali Cup in Louisville a few years earlier. He had lost his way as a pro – a common enough problem – and he had also lost his unbeaten run after five or six easy wins. He was still trained by Keith Clay and Tel Bennett. It was an odd pairing because they had worked with Eddie Futch for years and having losers was not part of their long-term plan. They had worked in recent years with some good fighters and there had been hope. Ray was watching the end of that hope. They knew what they were doing as trainers, and liked doing it with winners, but it looked like they had found out that it is often easier to get a living with losers.

The bell sounded to end round three and the kid – Ray couldn't remember his name – walked back to Clay with his head down. There was a shattered look on his face. Ray had been offered a chance to work with the kid a year or so earlier on a Stacey show at the Rio. Faye down at Colonel Miller's gym had told him the kid was a bad liver, liked dumb people and loved stupid girls. Mrs Miller knew about the way kids lived; she knew better than any of their trainers and most of the parents. Not that many of Mrs Miller's fighters had too many parents. Ray had been a bit concerned that Stacey was trying to sell 50 per cent of such a hot fighter. The kid had won, but he had not looked good against a bum. Ray could see the start of the end that night and it looked like he was now witness to the kid's final act as a contender.

The next time out the kid was matched in an even fight and he lost. Stacey was working like a nutcase to try and shift bits of the kid. Ray knew that there had been some interest from a New York promoter called Leo Dinos. It was obvious that Dinos had asked for the kid to be tested before investing any of his money, which was a move that suggested Dinos was learning. Dinos never got involved with Stacey's kid, but the word was that he was backing enough losers on his own and paying far too many ordinary fighters too much money. He would learn, Ray thought, but it would not be easy and it would not be cheap. Dinos owned a dozen dry cleaner's in Brooklyn and Staten Island and he always looked sharp. Well pressed, to tell the truth.

Ray sat down just in time to watch the Mexican catch Clay's boy with a short left on the temple. It was only round four and Ray knew the fight was over. The kid beat the count at 8 and the Vegas ref – it looked like Randall Smith – let it continue.

The bravest referees in the world operate in Vegas. It is a dangerous place for an overmatched fighter to go and lose.

Three punches later, he was down again. His eyes were clear, but his head was shot. That is the way it works when a fighter gets caught with a good shot on the temple. It also looked like losing too much weight far too quickly had just beaten another fighter. It was happening all of the time, at every single show Ray sat down to watch. Losing weight too quickly could ruin a prospect's career. It could also kill him. And that was a fact that many in the fight game ignored.

Odd business boxing, very strange. Journeymen and losers never have to worry about weight because they are seldom in fights where making weight is an issue. It is the protected kids, the house fighters, who put their lives in jeopardy to make weight by fighting drained. It was a risk and one that Ray hated trainers to take. It was disturbing that too many trainers had no idea about the risk, no idea about the statistics. They operated in oblivion of the lethal dangers of losing too much weight.

He had been at too many death and near-death fights not to have a healthy respect for dehydration and its evil role in a boxer's suffering. Clay and Bennett helped the kid back to the corner. He looked sick. He would never fight for a title, even if he moved up a weight.

Leon Smith, that was his name, and he had fought over 200 times as an amateur. He was about 28. Only the Cubans and the Germans – the East Germans, when they had been about – could have that many fights as amateurs and then make the transition to the professional ranks. The Americans could never make it. They sparred too hard and their lives were too difficult and dangerous. The American kids never had the right type of rest. The Cubans sparred hard, but a lot of their rounds were technical and their struggles were different and, importantly, they rotated the squad.

The Cuban fighters had real breaks; the American kids burnt themselves out during long amateur careers proving absolutely nothing to each other in dirty gyms. They fought for compliments against each other in obscure gyms every night. They were fighting for stupid bragging rights and their idiot coaches stood watching, nodding their heads in misplaced appreciation at rounds that were ridiculously savage. There were too many fools in the game, and a lot of journalists believe the only way boxers can improve is by tearing lumps out of each other in gym wars. It's wrong. The business was packed full of stupid bastards who had no idea what they were watching.

Ray was looking at all corners, all the seats just back from the ring. He was doing a headcount for risk. He knew the men would be there.

The fights continued and the noise never dropped. Ray had to put Eddie on hold in his head and went off to find Oak. He found Trevor Beattie instead. The ad man was part of a group tucked away in great seats. Trev told him that they had been in place from the start. Each fight, every round. That was what fight people did. It showed respect. He moved on and soon found Oak. He spotted the sickly looking man at the back of the press area.

Oak was a serious autograph hunter and memorabilia expert. The story was that he was a wealthy kid, a hotel baron's son, according to one rumour. Ray had met him many years ago and the pair had developed a good relationship, even if Ray hated to shake his damp hand. Ray sent boxing programmes, signed pictures and any other boxing junk to Oak and the spindly American then sold them for peanuts. The real business was the deal in reverse. A US banker's draft for $10,000 was burning a hole in Ray's pocket – it was for Oak. For them, it was strictly business. The pair spoke briefly, the money was exchanged and they parted without touching. That suited Ray and Oak never noticed. Nobody ever shook his hand for fun.

Moist, as Ray called him, was happy with Ray's turnover. It kept him in the business and that was all that mattered to him. Oak had a lot of quality boxing products under licence and Ray was his sole European agent for a few of the items. They went nuts for Kronk stuff in Scandinavia. The Kronk was the little boiler-room gym in the basement of a community centre in Detroit and there was something truly mystical about the sweatbox. It had been home to dozens of world champions. Tommy Hearns was perhaps the most famous son from the basement gym and there had been a conveyor belt of fighters and world champions in the '80s all trying to grab a piece of the Hearns magic. There was enough soul in the building for Errol Christie to train there. It had finally closed its door after a losing battle against cuts and dereliction. It was now a dead fort at the heart of a community in name only.

It was tricky at times because of all the fake stuff flooding in and killing the auctions. The market was slowing up and people were getting wise. A month or so before the fight two con men had been sent down in Manchester for peddling fraud memorabilia and the snide problem was not even close to going away. Ray had seen more snide gear than real gear in the last few years.

Oak knew nothing about the boxing game and that was a bonus. He was straight in that sense and he just arranged sales on behalf of various hotels, fighters and promoters.

Ray was back in his seat with his pocket empty for the last 30 minutes of waiting. The crowd had not dropped the noise.

It was not a pretty fight to watch. It was not the fight people expected. Hatton got it all wrong. He lost it somewhere and everybody had a theory about when exactly it all started to go wrong. In the end, his bravery was a hopeless tool against Mayweather's artistry. It finished in round ten, with the final image of the night being the Manchester kid stretched out with his face swollen from Mayweather's fists. His eyes are closed, but he's not unconscious.

The picture is the sorry story of the fight. It delivers the last hope with an emotional impact that is in equal parts bravery and stupidity, the final image of a lost cause from a long week. The fans kept soaring, kept hollering their approval, but even their lungs fell silent in the minute after the fight ended. There was no anger or outrage or riot. Some predictions had been bad, but nothing had gone wrong on the safe side of the ropes. The damage was in the neon square and it was not nice.

'I must've slipped,' Hatton joked at the end, but there was no smiling in his red eyes. He was still suffering from the punches that had cut him and sent him down. He was made to suffer in the ring, and it was the type of suffering that only the very best prizefighters ever get to experience. It's the end of something inside – the end of a life they have been living away from all thoughts of defeat. It is a fantasy life because everybody loses. It's not just about confidence; it has to do with what goes on inside a fighter's head. They believe they will never lose and the hurt is staggering for an unbeaten fighter because he blurs the lines and pushes reality to one side. Fighters like Hatton simply can't understand defeats, they can't sense the loss, and when it arrives it causes turmoil. Hatton would lose sleep to tears in the weeks that followed and that was obvious late that night.

Hatton's fight never went right. He moved like a fool, captive to Mayweather's taunts. Perhaps Mayweather is that good – so good he can make even exceptional fighters like Hatton move to his deadly dance. Ray doubted it. Hatton had had a bad, bad night and he knew it. But knowing it and dealing with it are two different things in a fighter's mind.

In all the weeks of talks and planning and watching DVDs of the American, there was never a moment when anybody in Hatton's team considered Mayweather's power. It was not an option; it was not something they worried about. If Hatton was going to lose, then it would be on points. Wrong and wrong.

Mayweather had done his job in the days and weeks before the bell. When Hatton had swiped his finger across his throat in front of thousands of delirious fans at the weigh-in, he had set in motion his own downfall. His heart was sunk too deep in victory and his mind was lost. Mayweather balanced his children on his lap, kissed his mother's head and hugged his people in the last hours. Hatton was ready to knock down walls and that is easy to do without a brain. Mayweather had his own heart in check.

In rounds one and two and three, Hatton was competitive. He shaded a couple, but he was using train lines, straight lines, and not altering predictable mistakes. His lead shots fell short and instead of adjusting his feet he lunged with another miss or two. Mayweather was moving a fraction, keeping out of distance and measuring for later. He was using the big ring with stealth. Hatton was like a boy on a sponsored run at times. In round four, Mayweather hurt Hatton with straight rights and a left hook. All of the punches came in from slightly different angles and all were impossible to stop. Hatton needed to be told that rushing in was a disaster. He needed to start using his brain against Mayweather's brain. Hatton was making Mayweather look like a tactical genius.

Hatton did keep the pressure on and he won round five on all three scorecards, but that was it. Mayweather sat and listened at the end of round five. The fight was close at that point, but inside the ring there was a story unfolding that had nothing to do with the jottings of the designated judges. Mayweather was in control and boxing people feared the worst. They sat back at the start of round six and watched a masterclass to the end – some watched through their fingers.

Hatton lost a point for hitting the back of Mayweather's head. There was nothing else available. It continued like that with the frustration mounting. There were quick single shots that stopped Hatton still like he had been frozen. There was a second between punches and then Mayweather was gone. Where was Hatton's movement? Where was the promised subtlety? There was nothing but guts and pain. The crowd loved it, but they knew. The brass band played.

The fight was sinking into a vortex of ruined desires. It's a terribly British moment and it hurt because Hatton was better than the kid in the ring, better than the Hatton getting beaten in front of the world's eyes. Forget the money, at that point. It was cruel, but it couldn't be reversed. It wasn't Rocky in the MGM ring.

Round eight was hell. A 10–8 round without a knockdown. The ref was anxious, the noise increased in despair and still Hatton followed the same pitiless lines to slaughter. He walked onto fists that were gone before his flesh turned red. It was just heart now and Mayweather was in no hurry to end his night of glory. Nine was bad and ten was the end. A short hook – a check hook, Mayweather calls it – sent Hatton head first into the padded corner post. He sprang back on legs that were folding under his resistance and collapsed.

Hatton got up – everybody knew he would, that is why they were there. They knew he would never let them down. Never. And he had not let them down in the ring – he had let himself down by fighting a dumb fight, but not the thousands and thousands of fans. He could never let them down. It's a pact they have with the kid. They love him and he loves them back. It's a personal and unique bond; the envy of the sporting world. It's Hatton fever.

Hatton got up and the ref looked hard into his eyes and let it continue. Mayweather landed a few more punches and the ref ended it. Hatton was over again, falling under the outstretched arm of the referee. His eyes were closed, but he was not out. Was he feeling for the first time the sickening sensation of total loss? It was possible. Maybe he wanted to vanish right there, fall through the canvas, find a tunnel and appear in a bar in Spain.

It was over for him. Was that a tear on his cheek mixed with his blood? A puddle would have formed if he was left long enough. There were also tears at ringside. It had been that type of fight, that type of night.

The crowd applauded the winner. Hatton's people were gracious, standing and shouting and holding up thumbs in respect to Mayweather. Ricky was surrounded by people. They were cutting his gloves away and wiping his face clean. All of his people looked exhausted. Mayweather looked stunned for the first time ever in the ring. The ring filled and it was impossible to see the fighters.

Ray was still standing. He knew he now had to leave. The post-fight was not for him. He was due out of town and due there soon.

LAS VEGAS: FIGHT-OVER TIME

Ray Lester starts to move down the aisle and away from his seat. It is a hard walk because of all the wires on the floor and the writers smashing out their reports. He nearly slips before reaching the end of the row. There he stops. He can hear Solly Mantle moaning at security and behind Solly, near the seats that moments before had been occupied by a few basketball players, Ray caught sight of Jimmy and the three men from the previous night. They were not looking his way. They were standing talking to Jay. Nobody was laughing. On second thoughts, perhaps they had seen him and Jay was trying to facilitate Ray's survival. They were perhaps 15 feet away.

Ray could hear Solly hollering about his obscured view, but his eyes and ears were on the other men. He dipped his head slightly and moved swiftly to join a group of Nevada Commission officials as they were leaving. He nodded at one he had met before, a hopelessly dapper referee, and stuck close to the little group. He knew once he reached the end of the tunnel under the stands there were several ways to get back to the casino floor without mixing with too many fight people. The hidden doors to the secret highways under the casinos were concealed, but Jay had often taken him into the connecting passageways and tunnels. He just wanted to get out, get away and get on the plane to Atlantic City.

Ray ducked behind a wall near the long bar that served the trays that balanced on the shoulders of waitresses all night. He found the door he was looking for. No sign, no hint. It led to a staircase and at the bottom of the stairs was a stark concrete room, its walls lined with lockers. The ringside punters were at his side and he knew he was in front of Jay and the others. He tried to move in shadows, just to be safe. There was an open door out of the room and it led into the main tunnel connecting the MGM's Grand Garden arena with the rest of the hotel. On both sides of the tunnel there were several golf trolleys with their drivers standing against them, holding up signs. Ray recognised a lot of the names, but he felt comfortable that nobody knew who he was.

It was chaos in the tunnel and that suited Ray just fine. High-rollers with their skinny women shouted for their drivers and personal fixers. Most were on their way to the exit under the villa where the card rooms were discreet and the cash piles serious. Ray had no trouble moving through the crowd and down the slight incline of the main stretch. He was part of the fleeing crowd of waitresses and low-key hotel workers. He was walking with women who were counting up in silence hundreds and hundreds of dollars in tips. They had been smiling and showing their tits all night long, serving the ringside guests with booze from the first bell until the last. Now it was no longer business time, even if they were still showing their tits in their ugly costumes. There were tits all over the place, but nobody was smiling. It was the Vegas end of a long night. Smiling was over. They had finished being polite for the night. It was just the cash count now.

About ten minutes later, just before the tunnel narrowed and split, Ray opened a door. He went up a few steps and through another door and emerged next to the New York Deli by the sports book. The casino floor was so full it looked impregnable. They were still singing. He went straight to the bar inside Giant Wok and ordered a Stoli and cranberry with a Pale Ale chaser. He took one more drink, a big double, before moving off. He figured the main lift area would be too dangerous for him, so once again he used the old lifts and walked along the row of rooms to the second-floor concourse. This time when the lift arrived it was packed. He squeezed in, looked at nobody. Everybody was a refugee from the fight.

On the19th floor, a few other people got out. Nobody was wearing a black leather coat and certainly not a short padded one. They were all fight fans, with just one white hooker in the group. She was not with them. She didn't have to hesitate on the landing like some of the fans. They had no idea where their rooms were and they had been in town three days. She knew exactly where her room was, even though she had never been in it. Ray smiled at her, she smiled back. She walked about ten feet across the landing that connected the long hallways and then turned, walked back and gave him a card with her mobile number on it.

'You call if you get lonely, baby.'

Ray thanked her, smiled again and watched her walk off. He was at his door a minute later. He put his ear to the frame and listened. Nothing. Not a sound. He had pulled it off. He slid his card in and then out, and pushed the door open.

How easy was that?

All the lights were on. A man in a leather coat was sitting on the window ledge that framed the far end of the room. That was all Ray caught in a flash of movement. It was his only look. Before he could speak he was moving forward and moving fast. A hand had come out of the bathroom and grabbed him by the elbow, launching him stumbling into his own room. He felt something hit him across his back and he fell forward. He was winded, not hurt, and as he caught his feet to avoid falling over, his shins hit the metal edge of the bed and he went down heavily across the king-size quilt. The guy in the window laughed. Ray tried to push his hands down to steady his drop and lift his head up, but a hand yanked at the back of his shirt and he was standing again. He fell back against the wall. He tried to get his breathing in order and sneak a look at the man who had pulled him into the room. It was a big gorilla of the very oldest school. The man in the window was a lot smaller. He looked tiny. It was Jimmy's friends.

'Who the fuck are you two?'

Ray had to act tough.

The man who had pulled him into the room with such violent ease moved to his side and out of his line of vision. Ray assumed he had been whacked on the back with his laptop. It had been on the bed and now it was gone. That was a bit of a liberty, he thought. It was new.

'Ray. It is Ray, right?'

The big guy with the laptop nudged Ray in the back.

'Yeah, so what?'

'Ray, I've heard good things about you. Jimmy, the Hain guy, the black dude Stenson . . .'

'It's Stacey, not Stenson.'

'Yeah, right. Stacey, the fancy nigger, smooth talker. All good things, but the one thing that none of those motherfuckers can tell me is why you're looking for Eddie Lights. Not one reason. And another thing that makes me curious. Why are you running away from me?'

The guy was anywhere between 30 and 40 and slight. Ray could tell from years of hanging around with fighters that he was lean – lean and probably very fit. He had on a dark open-neck shirt, shiny slacks, black loafers and a tight-fitting leather jacket with padding in all the right places. His hair was black and short and Ray could smell his cologne. He looked like a lot of men Ray had met – and that was not a coincidence because he was like a lot of men Ray met in Vegas and New York and Atlantic City. The man had the look. Ray had known for a long time that lethal men seldom arrive in combat boots with guns in their belts. This man had the ability to be nasty and the ability to blend into any half-wise crowd. In other words, he was invisible in casino land.

'They say you're a good guy, a guy to be trusted. A straight guy. And what is it you say in London? A nice bloke? That's it: a nice bloke.'

Ray nodded.

The bruise on his shins from the collision with the bed's metal rail was starting to ache. Ray was actually starting to ache all over because being thrown around and smashed over the back with a laptop was not really sensible exercise for an unfit man of 40.

The guy in the window frame stood up. He was a lot shorter than Ray had guessed – not a lot over five foot, and Ray was six foot two – but Ray was at a disadvantage in the increasingly absurd struggle because it was a struggle he had no reason to fight. His heart was not in it. It was not personal yet.

The laptop was a handy weapon, but the real weapons filled the padding inside their coats. The lump was a little less than six foot, but he was carrying a lot of weight across his neck and back. All three men stood on different sides of the king-size bed.

'Ray, I'm a nice guy, too.'

Then window man looked at the lump. He was about 25 with the telltale tiny eyes of a steroid freak. Tiny eyes, tiny cock, no fucking brain and lethal. It was a modern phenomenon. He also had regulation clothes: casual wool shirt, dark slacks and the ubiquitous black leather coat. He was dangerous because he was stupid. Ray could tell that he could be a very dangerous man, but he also knew that he was only as bad as the instructions given to him. The trouble was the midget silhouetted against the window didn't look short of unpleasant ideas.

'Now, we have a problem and your name keeps coming up. As I said, a lot of people are telling me how much of a nice guy you are. So I figured I'd find out if it's true – and get to the bottom of our problem.'

'We don't have a problem. We have a misunderstanding, a case of one and one making three.'

'That's a good start. You admit that we have something in common. I like that. Ray, I like that a lot.'

He listened, he smiled and he sat back down. He was only an inch or so shorter when he sat.

Ray stood up straight and was about to tell his story.

'No. Stop, Ray. I have to stop you because we do have a problem, trust me. Now, tell me all that you know about Eddie Lights. Everything, or I'm going get Chris to stick that laptop right up your ass. What is it Larry Holmes said that time? Yeah, that's it. Where the sun don't shine.'

Ray told them what he knew. He told them what he had been telling people since landing in Vegas. As he was talking, he tried to make sense of it all. Eddie had clearly pissed off some serious people. But why? The short guy never spoke; he just smiled and nodded, as Ray told the story. Ray kept back the bit about meeting the daughter. He claimed that she had called. He didn't want them to know he had a face to go with the info. That little lie aside, he told the truth and nothing but the truth.

'So that's it? Why'dya run from Jimmy's? You see, I hear you're a straight guy and then you take off. It ain't nice.'

There was nothing Ray could do. There was no way that he could drop Stacey in the shit. No way. His Vegas friend had risked enough.

'I didn't know you were such reasonable men. If I'd known, I would have stayed, had a drink.'

'Ray, no jokes. The people I'm helping don't find any of this funny. None of it. And I agree with them. This is no joke. '

'Sorry.'

'That's OK. I'm gonna let it slide. Now, Ray, I know we're going to have to talk again and I just hope that you've not been lying to me. To both of us, actually.'

The man in the window stood up. He looked over at the jacked-up eyes of the steroid monster as the pair walked to the door. The beast paused by the bathroom, went in and dropped the laptop into the toilet. Ray heard the splash and knew it was the machine down the khazi. The splash was followed by the noise of the flush handle being jerked and the water rolling. Ray was not in a hurry to look. He was still standing staring out of the window when the door closed. He was still there ten minutes later. Still there 20 minutes later, and sweating. He looked at the clock. It was not even midnight.

He also noticed that the message light was no longer buzzing on the phone. The night was over, but Ray knew he would not sleep. He pulled his clothes together, packed away his suit and then went and fished the laptop out of the toilet. It didn't look good.

It was not even 1 a.m. He had a few decisions to make and one was easy: he would leave right now. Just go. The MGM was buzzing and nobody would notice his skip. Anyway, the people he had been avoiding had found him. His party was over.

He left a message for Jay, knowing that it would be impossible to reach him until about 4 a.m. He wanted to avoid him and he knew this time was Jay's busiest of the day and night. It was show time for the losers and Jay was their only salvation. In the field of play downstairs, the game was in full swing.

Ray planned a route away from the MGM that avoided the main entrance and kept him well out of Jay's possible vision. To be honest, the rules had changed since the invasion of Hatton's fans, but it was pointless taking any risks. It took him about a second to get it straight in his head. He closed the door on his room at 1.04 a.m. He was leaving Las Vegas and at that moment he hoped he was never coming back. Ray had made the same promise too many times. But this was different. Fuck Vegas forever.

The lift going down was empty. He changed at the second, pulled the suit bag high on his shoulder, dipping his head at the same time, and strode down the now familiar thin corridor of old rooms. The suit bag obscured his face, but it was too late to try to go unseen. He had been found and now he just wanted to vanish. He took the smaller lift at the end of the rooms and was soon on the street by the hidden entrance to the villa. A dark limo was waiting outside the gate. It was starting to get a bit cooler, a typical desert night was settling. By four, he knew it would be cold. Freezing outside, but blistering with play inside.

Ray walked by the side of the MGM, walked in front of the entrance on the Strip and took the escalator up to the pedestrian bridge that connected the MGM with the New York, New York casino on the other side. Nothing was moving on the Strip; the car lights were not a blur because traffic was sitting still. It was a Saturday night, a fight night, and the Strip was packed with cars. What was it all about? Ray swore that he was never coming back.

The doors at New York, New York swished open as Ray approached. He had both bags in his hands and he was now carrying them low because he didn't want anybody to see him leaving in such a hurry. If he was spotted, it would just look like he was walking across the casino floor. The place was solid with Hatton's people. There had been a total takeover. He went down the escalator and into the main part of the casino. New York, New York was, and always had been, a tacky little number. The door to the taxis was just before the check-in, the line about 50 deep. He kept his head down, got out a dollar and waited his time. Things moved quickly.

'Where to buddy? The airport?'

Ray caught himself. He looked up at the taxi boy, slipped him the dollar. 'Rodeo 2.'

The car pulled up, taxi boy hollered 'Rodeo 2' at the driver and pulled open the door. Ray sat down in the back as the cab pulled out. He told the guy to turn it round and take him to the Hard Rock. The guy was not happy, but Ray touched his shoulder and dropped a twenty onto his lap. It was a five-bucks journey, but nobody thanked him. Nobody was smiling in Vegas.

Ray slipped inside at the Hard Rock. There were no machines and just a few Hatton stragglers. It looked almost normal. He found a bar and shouted for a vodka. He could smell his fear and sweat. It was too close to going seriously wrong for his liking. Under normal circumstances, it was easy to feel relaxed at the Hard Rock, but he was not there under normal circumstances. He was still sweating.

He had a few vodkas and at 3 a.m. he went outside and grabbed a cab to the airport.

Nothing made any sense. He was somehow involved in somebody else's play and that was not a bright move. He was not making a penny helping the blonde. It was just not right. His back ached, a lump had thrown him across the room, his laptop had been thrown in piss and a midget with a gun under his coat had threatened him and all his pals in Las Vegas. Nice going for a favour.

'Fuck this,' he said a bit too loud.

The search for Eddie Lights had now turned personal.

ATLANTIC CITY: THE OTHER GAMBLING PARADISE

The flight was on time.

Ray was already asleep when the plane's white slipstream left behind the desert city of Las Vegas, its bright lights finally flickering, fading and falling dark.

It was the end of the night and the start of another hot day. But inside any building in Las Vegas there was the same heat, the same colour of glowing murkiness. It was a city of few shadows.

Three hours later Ray woke. Amazingly, his sleep had been peaceful, his head calm up in the clouds. He put it down to exhaustion because when he opened his eyes clear memories of the previous evening came flashing back. He ordered a coffee and started to put together a plan. Should he ring the daughter and call off the search, or dig just a bit deeper? Ray was a man not easily put off the scent, but he needed to know he was doing the right thing. His back was still sore from the whack with the laptop – getting clobbered by a big, dumb lump was not what he considered fun.

It was clear to Ray that Eddie had gone seriously on the missing list and under the radar. Had he gone on his own, or was he led there with a towel over his head, tape across his mouth and the last bit of fear a man ever feels in his gut? Ray knew Eddie was well connected and that meant it was serious. In fact, Eddie was very well connected, which meant it was very serious.

The two men last night in his room – the men he had first caught a glimpse of in Jimmy's bar – were real. Running through the car park was also very real, as was hiding for an hour in a doorway watching strippers smoke. Jay's insistence that Ray walk away had been serious, perhaps the most ominous warning of all. So, clearly, Eddie had done something to piss off the wrong type of people. Had he taken something that wasn't his? Maybe he had turned over and started to give up names. The choices were not good.

Ray wanted to believe that Eddie had upset somebody and that perhaps it could be sorted. Perhaps, though Ray knew it could not be ironed out. That much was crystal fucking clear for anybody and everybody to see. It was a mess. And Ray was bang in the middle of it.

If Eddie had walked away from the life – his life – and started to talk, for whatever reason, it would be fatal. However, if Eddie had flipped, the people looking for him would not have been in the bar off the Strip or at the fight. Eddie would be gone – gone for good somewhere remote. Or dead already somewhere in the silent night. If that were the case, nobody, certainly not connected people, would be looking for him because he would never be found. And the men would not have left a trail for the police. The police would have been looking for the searchers and asking questions. No, Eddie had not turned. There was simply too much interest. So Eddie must have ripped off the wrong people. He was not a snitch; this whole situation was about money. Ray and the daughter were just innocent witnesses.

The flight continued smoothly. The food came and went without any fuss. Ray checked for something he had missed, a detail he had omitted the first time. He knew he had to get his head in order before arriving in Atlantic City. He had serious boxing business to take care of there. Eddie Lights would have to be shifted from his mind and that was not easy.

The men who built the casino haven of Atlantic City had failed to build a proper airport, which was tricky, considering the place held delusions of being an international resort. There is a tiny strip for the largest of players to land the smallest of planes, but everybody else has to land in Philadelphia and ride a cab. Sure, there are helicopters, but Atlantic City is really a limo place, a limo city by the sea. It could give Vegas a run for its limo quota, it really could. People had died trying to acquire a licence to run a limo service in Atlantic City. Too many people. The brief and bloody limo war had been truly savage.

There was nobody waiting for Ray in Philly. He went straight through, careful to look for any unwanted greeters.

Getting a cab at Philadelphia airport is not a problem. Getting one that does not have an anti-puke plastic cover over the seats is a lot harder. The cars smell and they are uncomfortable. And the drivers are miserable. They always sit down low over the wheel. From the lumpy back seat, they are nearly invisible. The driver steering Ray's cab never looked back, never said a word when Ray asked for the Hilton in Atlantic City. Ray had no idea if the driver was male, female, black or white. He sensed the driver was a man. It was probably just the smell.

Ray sat back and enjoyed the sticky plastic seat covering as the Olds rocked out from the kerb. The car driver struggled with the gears but had no problem locating the potholes. The crosses and identity cards, and what looked like a garter belt, that formed a formidable hanging mobile from the mirror shook violently each time the driver nosed the car into a trough. It was never comfortable sitting in the back seat of a car with springs that had stopped working.

Once, in Atlantic City, funnily enough, Ray had been in the back of a police car after a Mike Tyson fight. It was the late '80s and Ray was keen to write a story about the big city after a big fight. There was a lump of hair and flesh and blood on the seat with him. It was smeared across the back and it was still damp.

'It's from a ghetto pony,' the driver had assured him.

The cop had one of those late, long laughs that certain cops have to let you know what they have just said is a joke. It was a bad joke. A ghetto pony in Atlantic City was a wild dog that roamed the deadland between the boardwalk hotels and the two projects. They prowled in hungry and vicious packs.

There were a lot of empty lots in Atlantic City. The dream that the place would spread back from the ocean, a gleaming metropolis of apartments and designer shops, had died many, many years before. The local residents had waited for the growth, hopeful that their tenements would be destroyed to help the expansion. They had waited and waited for their new homes and their compensation. And most were still waiting.

The ride with the Atlantic City police was ancient history, when Ray was a different type of journalist. He had cared back then. It had been a good story, a good idea to drive the streets of Atlantic City after a big fight to take a closer look at the midnight people: a police-eye view of the streets after dark. It had ended up being a long and pretty dull night, with the police baiting bored kids on the corners of the two projects.

In many ways, it was early reality TV, but there were no cameras. Ray had missed the moment. Who would have wanted to watch a bunch of cops cruising the mean streets of an American city, rousting the losers and squaring off with the bad guys after domestic squabbles? It was 1988 and it was just another one of those things Ray hadn't realised would appeal. There were other ideas, simple ideas, that had been transformed into hours and hours of crap TV: life in a gym, life on the force, life on the game, life on a corner; an endless list of windows on different worlds, worlds Ray had stepped into and out of for over 20 years. It was too late now. Every man and his dog went there now.

The route out of Philadelphia was one of Ray's favourite American drives. The raised freeway split open the city. The docks spilled out to the right in black-and-white desolation. There were hundreds of ships rotting on the dank and still water. The old vessels sat in the contours of the filthy water that coiled through the badlands of south-east Philly like an evil snake. It was easy to see from the raised freeway. On the left, the old city and its tiny streets looked like a garden of brick flowers. It had a movie quality. The ships looked like old pictures of Pearl Harbor. They were monochrome and dead. The little houses were brash, with harsh strokes of worn-out colour, and they stretched to the edge of the city's business and financial centre. The colour came to a sudden end when the glass from the business district started.

Also, down below, way under the freeway's thunderous shadow, in another part of South Philly, were the taverns, bars and clubs. Ray had been in a few of them. Lively places. He had heard tales about a lot of the others. He went over the names in his head. The 9mm Bar, the Pushcart Saloon, the Mars. The Mars bar had always tickled him.

The city started to thin as the cab moved across the rivers, over the bridges and away from the urban sprawl. One of the bridges was called the Walt Whitman, but Ray had no idea which it was. The cab and its silent driver nosed through the traffic and out of the slums. Less than 15 minutes after leaving the airport, Ray was in the country. It was green and it stayed that way all the way to the shore. The swamps started to take over as the ocean approached.

Lovely ride.

After 30 minutes of driving, the first signs appear on the highway, launching a sales pitch for the weak dreams of Atlantic City. They rise from the swamps on either side of the blacktop and break the monotony of the flat ground. They offer money at the slots for just a bit of your time. *New Slot Thrills at Harrah's.*

'Slot' and 'Thrills'? How? Thrills?

The money signs try to suck in the punters with their hollow guarantee against failing. They blend easily with the giant billboards carrying the images of the fallen idols of the stage. Some of the singers and dancers had nowhere else to fall after they had dropped and crashed; in Atlantic City, though, ghosts can live. Their bright faces fill every inch of their raised banners and turn each poster grotesque with the desperation of the faded. The men and women have the swollen tan faces of botox victims, but still they smile down. They are all part of the performing loop that starts and ends in Las Vegas. Atlantic City is a pitstop, a place where stages ache.

Hundreds of men and women throughout the history of entertainment have had their faces fixed on one of the signs littering the highway to Atlantic City. For many, it is the final moveable feast of their careers. Men with tans and teeth from tusks, women with highly flammable hair and voices that now need a lot of help. The surgeons can only work on the outside, arranging smiling faces after endless hours under a scalpel. When the voice starts to go, then it really is the end of the road for the old masters. The road to Atlantic City is one of the bleakest roads in America. It is a boulevard of failure. Ray loved it.

Far off, behind the signs, the skyline changes and the hotels appear. An executive at a casino once told Ray that the resorts in Atlantic City and Las Vegas were 'dream factories'. It was the wrong thing to say to Ray at the wrong time. He had fixed the tanned fool with a smile and told his X-ray-thin, fey wife that she looked like a Siamese cat. It was meant as an insult, but, with hindsight, she had probably taken it as a compliment. It had been a bad trip. There had been a lot like it. The man and his wife didn't take offence. Skin needs to be thick in the casino industry, even if the wives' veins are visible beneath their stretched faces. The faces look thin and translucent and hard in the bedroom mirrors of rich women.

The Jersey shore gets ever closer on the road into town. There is nothing but the hope of a destination, and then the first street people shuffle into vision. The homeless push their trolleys with care on their endless daily journeys.

Then the city abruptly arrives. The Hilton is at one end of the city and the Borgata and its cranes are at the north end. Ray had read somewhere that Steve Wynn had created 5,000 jobs at the Borgata when he had finally built and invested in Atlantic City. Perhaps it was on a sign out in the swamp during one of his journeys to the glittering shore. There were so many signs and so much to take in. It was a case of fact in, fact out and just keep driving.

It was the same Steve Wynn who beat Don King and all the others in the boxing business to put on the Evander Holyfield–Buster Douglas fight. He had to go to court and it was messy. The fight took place in a temporary ring behind the Mirage in Vegas. October 1990 – a good time for getting high and wasting a life. The traditional thinking is that Wynn did his cobblers that night. He was paying the two fighters a total of $32 million. Douglas, the lazy slob, fell to earth with a fat thud when Holyfield landed for the first time in round three. Douglas walked away from Vegas with $24 million after just seven minutes and ten seconds in the ring. Wynn's Boy Friday, Mike Trainer, had called Douglas a 'piece of junk' and 'a dog'.

For Ray, it had been a great pleasure to cover the fight, like so many from that period. It was almost one of the last proper Vegas events. Since that night the place had become increasingly corporate and plastic. There had been a lot of old-fashioned boxing fans in the seats for Holyfield–Douglas and they had died away over the years. Who can blame any of them for their flight?

Wynn had indulged Douglas in the months before the fight. He had flown the new champion all over the place in the Mirage's private jet. Johnny Tocco, the real veteran, who had worked with Liston, talked about the sweet treatment and shook his ancient head. 'Buster was riding all over Vegas in a limo with Wynn and eating like a dog.' On fight night, he looked swollen.

Wynn had moved Douglas into a penthouse with its own sauna. It was an attempt to get the increasingly fat fighter to drop some weight. Only the silly rich ever get to see the penthouse suites at the golden Mirage. Douglas was both silly and rich. On the first day, Buster famously ordered 98 bucks' worth of hamburgers from the phone inside the sauna. He sat there, dripping sweat and eating onion rings.

The penthouse suites are stylish and not like the high-roller suites, which have cheap glitz and kitsch and seem to come with a bimbo tit-deep in a jumbo jacuzzi. Ray had a theory that every chair and sofa in every decent suite in Vegas was soiled with spunk and he never once put his naked arse down anywhere in the open. Never.

The penthouse at the Mirage and the Villa apartments at the MGM are where the real players stay. Real players are anonymous, even when they sit at a Vegas table, and they prefer a secluded spot to put down their heads, if they decide to sleep. There are exceptions: men so odd that they gamble and pull their hair out on the $10 roulette tables and at the same time drop 200 large on a single dumb bet at the sports book. They have millions but demand a free paper. They want to walk and wait with the punters in the line for the 99-cent buffet. Very strange.

When the fight was over, Wynn didn't want to pay. He suggested that only the winner should be paid. He was hurt by Buster's collapse. The ex-champion left the hotel in a hurry. Poor old Buster Douglas woke up one day with the belt by his pillow and the sound of dolphins splashing in the special pool outside his back gate; the next, he was being booted out of town like a traitor to the dollar. No doubt the fat fool had ordered a few dozen sausages to start the day the right way, not realising he was about to get clocked out of the dream factory in disgrace.

He was not the first and he will not be the last fighter to fall from high in a hurry; however, his downfall remains the most spectacular in the sport's history. That night in the ring he fought without conviction or brain. He lost, and the dolphins played out of earshot the following morning. He never came close to hearing them ever again. When the sums were done, the cash was counted and the dust had settled, it was said that Wynn dropped about $2 million. Not bad, considering the publicity the fight still generates.

Douglas had knocked out Mike Tyson a few months earlier but then fell in love with his fridge and weighed 14 pounds more for the Holyfield fight. That was not the whole story, though. His decline could not only be measured in pounds or a few extra inches round his stomach; his decline was in his head. He turned soft and safe the moment the cheques started to land in his account. He was virgin rich and desperate for experience. Everybody called Douglas a coward and a bum the night he went down against Holyfield, caught cold by a perfect counter on a bad night under the stars. The greatest minds in boxing lined up to give him stick. Don King and Eddie Futch led the abuse and outlined the obvious, but they only opened their mouths after Douglas was dropped and counted clean out.

Ray had been surprised that Futch had joined in – was mildly upset that the legendary tactician had only looked as far as the evidence available in the ring. The referee, Mills Lane, didn't help matters when he claimed Douglas was not unconscious during the count and could have climbed up. There was no need for Lane to blab.

King had not been directly involved with the promotion, but he had received his end. Don had been paid something like $4 million for doing nothing.

Poor old Buster. Ray had liked him, liked him a lot. A year or so later, Buster had cried like a baby when Ray had gone to Florida to interview him. There were excuses in Las Vegas, but none in Miami.

'I fucked up, it's that simple,' Buster told Ray.

There is a tragic image of Douglas, captured the morning after his sad collapse. It was Ray's old friend, Mick Brennan, who took it. Mick was always in places at the right time at fights. He could sense despair. In the picture, Douglas is on his own in the Mirage lobby surrounded by several large and expensive suitcases. There is not a friend or ponce in sight. His face is still puffy from the food and Holyfield's fists. His tailored suit is bulging with his excess flesh. He looks disgraced, distressed and ashamed, but he still has some of the gaudy prizes from his spoils as champion. He is wearing a nasty pair of shiny loafers, cut in the style known as the pimp's pump. He is also wearing a pair of his own monogrammed socks. His line of Buster clothing never saw the shelves, but that morning he had on the socks. Ray guessed Buster truly believed that sometimes in the dirty world of sport socks make the man.

But Ray never needed a photograph to remember a bad moment. A few seconds before the photo was taken, Ray had walked in front of Buster and had seen his tired eyes fixed on the distant fields of the casino floor. There was something like longing in that look. He must have known that he would never be back. Ray had paused on his way to coffee and watched the fighter from behind a cluster of plastic palms. He noticed that Buster was already starting to become invisible to most of the people who walked in front of him. Buster was finished: his time had come and gone. He had helped to speed up its passing by letting his mind go flabby in comfort.

It is hard to understand the destructive qualities of fighters. A man can work all his life to get close to the glory and the cash. He can come back from terrible beatings, push his body for years in gyms and have wars in the training ring for the type of money that no sensible person would accept. Small-end money, they call it. And then, with the first parts of the money and fame in place, a fighter can fall apart as sudden as a heart attack. The list of the lost is long in boxing and expanding each and every year. Boxers and boxing people never seem to learn the lessons of the men who have crumbled with nothing. Or, in Buster's case, vanished with millions.

Ray had been in Tokyo to watch Buster beat Tyson. That had been one of the great nights, without any doubts. Buster had taken a terrible hiding in some rounds and survived a sickening knockdown. He had broken Tyson's fragile heart. He had stood toe-to-toe with the greatest heavyweight of his generation, and arguably one of the best of all time. Buster had triumphed. He was brilliant in Tokyo. The night Buster went down against Holyfield, Ray had to remind a lot of people of the Tokyo fight. It was heated at times with the short-memory boys.

The fight against Holyfield was a brutish night for Buster, but it was just the start of his fall. A few years after the Holyfield fight, Buster nearly died when his love affair with the fridge and buffets led to diabetes and he collapsed into a coma. He survived and actually made a comeback as a fat wreck, a sad imitation of the former fighter. He was a freak, even by the pliable standards of modern boxing.

The new Buster, hopeless as he was, wobbled into a comeback and managed to convince some in the game that he was still a contender and could still be a player in the right fight. He had beaten Tyson and beaten a diabetic coma, and that looked good on any fighter's CV. So it was obvious that a long-overdue rematch with Tyson made a lot of sense. A rematch was needed, certainly from a cash perspective, but Buster's obesity and Tyson's conviction for rape made the sequel to the Tokyo bash a fight too far. It was simply a few years too early. There was always the chance that it would eventually happen. Both men would make a lot of money. The slug for the poster was beautiful: Never too late to forgive or to fight. There had been a rape and a coma between the bells, but a rematch was still out there. Thank you very much and make that $69.99 for the pay-per-view.

Buster fell back into obscurity when the fight failed to happen. The Wynn millions kept him happy. Happy and fat, and to this day the 33–1 against underdog who first exposed Tyson's heart problems in the ring one afternoon long ago in Tokyo is still hunting for marlin in Florida. Who cares about falling and rotting like a dead elephant against Holyfield one night in Las Vegas? Certainly not Buster.

Wynn had kept on moving and put in place the Borgata, the largest hotel in Atlantic City, but his time in boxing was over. Losing money and then falling out of love with the sport can happen to anybody when they glimpse boxing's dark side for the first time. Tourists, as Arum called people like Wynn, quit early once their love affair with the sport starts to cool. People in the middle of the game, deep in the beast of the sport, just get stronger and more unpleasant each time they are screwed by the business. They have the ability to somehow scrub up clean in the filthy slipstream that others leave behind and for some reason they enjoy it.

Ray had sat with Tyson one frozen afternoon in Denmark and talked about Buster's fall. Tyson had wiped a tear away. He's never off target when he sits and reflects on a life, any life, in the ring. He has been to every filthy hole that a life in boxing can offer. Tyson travels in the black night without a torch.

Tyson and Douglas are just two names on the heavyweight list of men who never really knew when to quit.

In many ways Vegas, and to a lesser extent Atlantic City, is like a dumping ground, a final resting place for the surrendered dreams of ruined fighters long past their best. It's a nice place for a fighter to die.

Sonny Liston, the big ugly bear of legend, is buried in a plot by the airport in Las Vegas, his simple grave nearly anonymous in the middle of a hundred dead children. Just Sonny, the hired Mob man, and dead kids. He loved kids and now they surround him. He has a simple grave that is lost in a burial field of teddy bears and toys. It is the most heartbreaking scene in Las Vegas, a place of genuine sadness and pity. The big ugly bear now watches over dead babies. He had been ignored for two decades until a few Europeans started to take an interest in the great man. Today, his stone is at the heart of a thousand pilgrimages each week.

It is thought that more fighters have died in Las Vegas than in any other city in the world. Atlantic City is probably second on the list. Ray knew the graveyard in Las Vegas well, but not the one on the edge of the swamp in AC.

It was 65 bucks for the cab and it pulled away from the kerb the moment Ray closed the door. There was no thank you. Ray was left with just a barely legible receipt in his hand. A bellhop approached. Ray didn't recognise him, so shook his head.

The AC Hilton was easy to get around, unlike a lot of casino hotels. Ray went through the revolving door and quickly realised the front desk had moved. A small bar on the left of the revolving door was also gone. It is not uncommon in the casino world for check-in desks, bars, the gym or even pools to move. Some switch location overnight. The beach at the MGM in Vegas closed one day, washed away by the desire to build a luxury block for the casino's real punters. Within months, the Villas, with their top-secret rooms, appeared on the spot where kids had once played on a sandy beach at the MGM. Like it, the idea of a family Vegas never stood a chance. It was all part of a misguided and serious effort in the '90s to get the wife and kids to Vegas. The pool went and the theme park behind the MGM was cut in half. A very adult pool complex, with the emphasis on European charm, was built out back in the shadow of the green beast of a hotel. The new European pools in Vegas cost 50 bucks. That's 50 bucks to look at a topless woman in a tight G-string posing as a ripe-titted French teenage girl. It's a fucking magic show. An illusion in the sun, and just make sure you leave your old woman at home.

The family idea was dead at the MGM. Most people never even knew a beach had been there. What dummy imagined it could become a bucket-and-spade paradise? In Atlantic City, far less effort had gone into making the gambling city a family resort. No fake sands, clowns or puppet theatres.

Ray found the new reception and used his Diamond Hilton executive card to get a decent room, a mini suite on the 15th floor with panoramic views of the ocean. He pulled out his clothes and then had a look at the laptop. It wouldn't fire up; it was finished. It had been a nice buy and was less than a month old.

The view from the window was generous, with the empty beach stretching both ways and the waves breaking in slow motion against the sand. The AC Hilton is at the south end of the boardwalk, the last hotel on the wooden strip, and off in the distance, in the middle of the main hotel cluster, is the ugly pier. It was still obscured by some morning mist when Ray looked out. Atlantic City had been on the verge of a renaissance for 15 years. It was in a constant state of rumour – that it was about to *finally kick Vegas's arse*. It was always about to happen. Just promises and lies, but people had died for a lot less in casino America.

The truth was that the battered shopfronts on the boardwalk were mostly empty and had been empty during a decade of neglect. The ones that were open were filthy and ragged and sold old pizza, souvenirs and boxes of Salt Water Taffy. The only businesses to survive the blasts from the ocean and a drop in punters (who sensibly tried to stay inside as much as possible) were the one- and two-dollar palm-reading booths. They were shops really, but people called them booths, for some odd reason.

The booths had simple glass fronts that were split into two, a window on one side, a door on the other. A thick curtain, a cast-off from a motel stock sale, was draped across the window and the door had the simplest of Open and Closed signs hanging from a rubber sucker. It was all that was ever needed. Some of the fellas called the shops 'Open and Closed'. There was often a bell rigged above the door – a proper bell, not an electronic version. It clanked loudly and alerted the palm reader that somebody was in the booth looking for a reading. She was never working when the door was Open. She only worked when the sign on the door read 'Closed' and it was locked.

When she was busy, the curtain was pulled across the entire front window. There was a small room at the front and usually it was packed with toys, a TV and a video. A young, or possibly even an old, Russian woman took care of your dollar or two and then led you to another curtain at the back of the room. Inside the tented cubicle were two seats, a low table, a crystal ball and a large kitchen roll. It was a bit more than a dollar back there and there was often no palm reading or crystal-ball gazing. Punters seldom placed a single in her palm.

The palmists often stood in their doorways, watching their kids playing on bicycles or with doll's prams on the boardwalk. Ray had seen their faces before, on trips to Moscow and Kiev for fights. If it rained, or when the cutting wind from the Atlantic whipped across the boardwalk, the kids watched Disney videos at the front of the shops. If their mum was busy, they went next door. It always reminded Ray of Mumbai, with its street kids who made him smile. Mumbai was a happy memory. A great trip. The last one before the final weekend. The laughs got lost when the gloom fell.

It was still early and a chill was in the air when Ray stepped through a back door at the AC Hilton and out onto the boardwalk. The sudden noise of the surf and the wind replaced the steady hum of the casino floor, where the tinny tinkle of glittering machines never ceased to be irritating.

Out on the boardwalk in the sun, the palm shops were starting to open. A few of the kids were out. Ray could feel that old renaissance in his bones as he walked from the Hilton to the Championship Boxing Association's annual convention at the Boardwalk Hall. Yep, the renaissance is just about here, he thought. He noticed a sign offering a 99-cent special for Sanitation Workers in the window of a particularly filthy restaurant. *One hot dog or a slice of pizza and a beer*. The Sanitation Workers of America had obviously held their conference in Atlantic City recently. Perhaps they were still in town. What a thought: 10,000 shit experts all in one khazi.

Ray continued walking, watching the boardwalk slowly come to life. In each doorway or down each of the ramps that led to the streets, there seemed to be somebody pushing a shopping cart or carrying a bag stuffed with their temporary residence. The tourists had not yet surfaced. A poster was clipped to the wall at the Convention Hall: Atlantic City Salutes the Sanitation Workers of the USA. But the Toilet Men of America were not foremost in his mind. He still ached from the meeting the night before.

It had been a long time since he had been hit and pushed about. Had they been button men, proper players or just messengers, Ray wondered. He suspected the man in the bolero-style leather coat, the short little fucker, was a very dangerous man. A killer? Yep, probably. It added an edge to Ray's considerations. The fat-necked boy with the squinty eyes was trouble because he was stupid and loyal. Being a hired hand, a mercenary muscle boy, required loyalty and stupidity in equal measure and the big lump in Ray's room the night before had that jacked-to-the-eyes scary steroid stare. He was a fucking moron, but one with a lot of power.

He let the two men slip from his mind and tried to put them, with Eddie, in another place. He had other things to think about. There would be no shortage of scumbags and con artists around during the remainder of Ray's day. They would all help Ray to put Vegas and what had happened there behind him for a bit.

The registration for the conference was simple. Ray had a short wait for his photo ID, with its small chain. He put the pass in a jacket pocket and went in search of a coffee. He spoke to a few people, bottom feeders and autograph hunters. Ray had strict and simple business at the conference. He was in Atlantic City looking after the interests of three promoters and about a dozen of their boxers. Each of the fighters had slim claims on a future fight for the CBA title. Slim was always enough. Ray was there to push their claims to challenge for a belt. In the modern business, a belt was a belt and the CBA had done well, especially in Europe, during a lively decade.

Ray had been instrumental in persuading the British Boxing Board of Control to sanction CBA fights in Britain back in the '90s. It was a time of expansion and without the introduction of the CBA and the WBO the fight game in Britain would have struggled to satisfy the demands of television. By 1995, Nigel Benn, Chris Eubank and Naseem Hamed were all pulling in over ten million viewers on terrestrial television, fighting for the various gaudy baubles.

It had gone wrong when too many sanctioning bodies had managed to secure fights in Britain. Sanctioning bodies were opening up all over the place . . . a lawyer's office in Miami, a politician's retirement home in Phoenix, above a flower shop in Bethnal Green. It was impossible to invent the carnage. There was one ludicrous time when no fewer than four British fighters held a version of the world light-welterweight title. It was a joke, a comedy Ray had stopped defending. He had also stopped laughing.

There were simply too many belts in the modern business. Ray had a WBO version – a mini one for being the WBO's Boxing Writer of the Year a few years back. He also had one from the International Boxing Organisation and World Boxing Union. 'I'm the unified champion of the writing game.' It was a giggle at the time, but the ironic worth of the belts had waned over the years and Ray no longer had them hanging up over his bed; they were now arranged in the toilet back at the flat.

The CBA conference had a few planned meetings, plus the gala evening meal. Ray would swerve all of the official functions and operate in the bars and restaurants at Bally's. And, if all went well, at night he would pull away and eat at one of the two quality Italian restaurants, Fellini's and Franco's. The food was always good, the company entertaining. The restaurants were both set back from the boardwalk and that suited Ray. They were quiet and a man could do a deal in peace there. Then, with the deal done, Ray would relax. It was by no means a bold plan, but Ray knew it would not run smoothly. It never did. However, first he had to find the right people and start doing what he had to do.

Nothing felt right – and it was not just his back. Eddie Lights, missing person: the disappearing little fucker was taking control of his mind.

Breakfast was a simple affair at Bally's. Ray knew it would be the best place to start looking. He found Pepe Santander in the coffee shop. Santander was with Dan Majesty. It was not an official meeting, not one of the scheduled events at the conference, but Ray knew that in the time it took for a few eggs to get tossed in grease the two men could plan and plot a dozen fights. Ray needed to speak with both of them, but not at the same time.

Santander had been an official with the International Boxing Federation and briefly at the World Boxing Association. Most people assumed he was from Puerto Rico, but he was born in Newark. His father was a Spanish sailor and his mother a teacher. It was his story, his life, so he could invent it if he wanted to. But Ray knew it was true because in the beginning he had often stayed with Santander.

Ray also knew that Santander had a heavy and steady crack habit. A quick look at Santander's swollen fingers betrayed his passion for the pipe and his nights tipping lids in the darkest of lonely places. He had been a good friend once.

Nothing happened in New Jersey or New York rings without Santander knowing about it and knowing why it happened. He was often credited with being the man who delivered the bag to Jersey Joe Walcott, the former heavyweight champion who ended his life as a dupe for boxing's various factions in Atlantic City. Santander, the bag man. Ray knew it was nearly correct. Santander would just shrug whenever the latest crusading journalist crossed his path and accused him of being a sleazeball. It happened often. 'Joe was an old man,' he once told Ray. 'He never had nothing. At the end, we gave him something.'

It was inevitable that the story about the old heavyweight champion would break and nobody was shocked. Why would they be? The fixers from the '50s had ended up serving time on Alcatraz for arranging bad fights. When boxing went bad, it went bad in a certain style.

Boxing officials in New Jersey had been working a bit too closely with promoters and the promoters had become far too friendly with the local sanctioning body. The rest is predictable history. They formed a nice circle for the boys to dance in. There were simply too many imported Jaguars, too many men in fur coats in the middle of July and too many bad fights with average fighters. It was like the scene in *Goodfellas* after the Lufthansa heist – everybody spending and nobody thinking. It was a wild time with too many people out of control; the bars at hotels before fights started to look and sound like cartoon saloons in a modern frontier town. Thankfully, the sheriff never came in for a drink. His beige uniform would have clashed with the white fox furs and crimson-toed shoes.

Walcott lost his job with the boxing commission. Most people knew he'd lost his mind 30 years earlier in great fights with Rocky Marciano and others. Sweet Jersey Joe could fight and when sad old Jersey Joe was implicated, nobody held it against him. He had been paid peanuts for fights that are part of boxing's history and will never be forgotten. He was a great little fighter – so what if he got carried away with the cash that was on offer. There were cash and cocaine and hookers everywhere. He made a few bucks at a time when Atlantic City was the first and last stop for every get-rich-quick cowboy and gangster in a trashy wonderland of greed. For a time, Jersey Joe was the head honcho of the top sport in the top resort. It was a pretty tight position for an old man with a lot of memories.

The resort of Atlantic City was out of control and every law-enforcement agency in America was lining up to swing into town and take the credit for pushing the latest Sodom into the sea and watch as it floated off into oblivion. Artie Schulman, an executive host at the Mirage in Las Vegas, once told Ray that Atlantic City in the '80s was like Havana before Fidel Castro. 'That bum Castro fucked up the party good and proper.' Artie could spin a yarn.

One of Artie's favourite tales from the Fall of Havana days was his memory of the night Marilyn Monroe sorted him out. In 20-odd years of going to Vegas, Ray had met a dozen men who claimed to have been sorted out by Norma Jeane. Bless her heart, some were lying. Artie had told the tale with a bit of soul and that was because he had style. He was a grifter from the old school and he remained a relic to the bitter end. He was what the chaps called a 'lovely man'. Some of the more dramatic fellas added 'a beautiful person'. That *is* praise.

The old man was potless when he died, so Ray was told. Ray had thrown in a grand for the funeral only to find that his girlfriend at the time, a waitress 43 years younger, was sitting on Artie's cash. Ray found out a year later that she had copped for all the dough, which was considered fair in Vegas. It was not a city for real lovers. Forget that little baby of deception. Ray also found out (and this pissed him off no end) that the board at the Mirage had taken care of Artie's funeral. The discovery meant that Ray had parted with a grand for nothing – he had been conned.

Now, Ray knew a long time before the kid released the album that a grand most definitely didn't come for free. The weasel behind the dirty trick, a lowlife pornographer from the '60s called Layson Filo, had grabbed the grand from Ray. Filo was still in Vegas to this day. Filthy Filo had never really been part of boxing society; over the years, he'd used an old friendship with Artie to stay near the edges of the life. There had been times when he would deliver somebody who was prepared to lose a few dollars at a table. Never much to scream about. Filo was also one of the men who moved in the shadow of poker genius Ungar, but he was never a backer of the genial boy behind the shades. He was a leech, a blood and cash sucker.

When sweet old Artie died, Filo, the old prick, worked quite a bit of cash from a lot of concerned people. He was well over 70 at the time Artie died, which had been about ten years earlier. His age was his only defence because old men often get a break from fatal violence. Had he been 60, he would never have made 61. Jay had made sure that Filo never worked in or near a casino again. It was the only type of death that people like Layson Filo feared. It put an end to a life with the players that he had enjoyed for 40 years. Ray had forgotten about that grand. It had been the only time in Ray's life that a grand really had come and gone for free. *Too many had gone, to tell the truth.*

Walcott took his tumble from corrupt office at a time when Atlantic City was pushing its own limits. It was a hard fall for the granite man of a dozen ring wars and he went down like a baby. It had been a deadly time at the very start of the '80s. There were a lot of deceased men from those early years and a lot of people had been willing to spend obscene amounts of cash to get established. The shysters, the comedians and the tricksters provided comic relief for the hit men and mobsters. The place was a fucking zoo. The gambling commission was under pressure and hanging on by the skin of its teeth. The licence to become a gambling resort had been introduced in 1976, but by 1980 the violence looked like ruining the prospects of another New Year celebration. The place was kept sane by tales of such outrageous craziness that they had to be true. Ray loved every second of every trip he'd made to AC back then.

One night Marv Pelozzi took Ray to one of the triple-X motels that lined the streets away from the boardwalk. Pelozzi was an odd soul even back then. A few years after Ray went with him to the motel, he just walked away from the life to live as a cross-dresser in New York's Greenwich Village. He had been a player in Atlantic City and had for a few years run a worn-out Vegas hotel and casino with his brother. Since Marv's departure for Bloome, the brother, a vicious idiot called Marty, had become one of the most unstable human beings with a firearm Ray had ever had the misfortune to meet. He was unstable without the gun and with it he crossed every boundary of acceptable lunacy. How Marty had not been killed or convicted during the last five or so years was one of life's great mysteries. The man was nuts. Fucking mad. His younger brother had loved him a lot.

Marv had asked Ray to go with him to a sleazy motel to help him move something. It was a slow night a few days before a fight and Ray had gone with Marv without a second thought. Ray assumed that Marv had a couple of hookers waiting and he was looking for somebody to spread the cost. That was not a problem. It could be fun, so Ray went up the stairs and approached the room on the second floor with a light and expectant step. At the door Marv had warned Ray to cover his nose and then he had put the key in the lock. Ray had quickly grabbed his hand and stopped him.

'What d'ya mean "cover my nose"? Fuck me, Marv, you're having a laugh, son. I'm going. I'm off, boy.'

Ray had turned, walked down the steps and hurried back to the bar in Fellini's. It was a paranoid time and Ray, so he was told, looked ill when he walked in. An hour and six or so vodkas later, Marv came through the door. He was laughing and there was pigeon shit on his shoulder and splattered on one of his thighs.

'Wha'dya think I had in the fucking room? I had a dozen pigeons. Crapping all over the place. They're called Birmingham Tumblers or some shit. I had to get them for that crazy old guy Cus D'Amato. He's got a new kid, a heavyweight. Tyson. You seen him fight? I hear he's fucking untouchable. I wanted you to help me move 'em.'

They had stayed in Fellini's drinking late that night. Nothing unusual. Pigeons, smelly pigeons, and not a dead body in sight.

There was even one bar that nailed the shoes of dead men to the ceiling. Nobody ever asked how the owner came to have the shoes. Who cared?

There was Saul Kane's My Way lounge. Kane had a slogan: *Hang out with the Mob at the My Way lounge.* It was hard to invent the place. Kane was a Mafia groupie and bail bondsman. The place eventually blew up. Ray was sure Saul was dead now, alongside Frankie Sindone, Frankie 'Fat Frank' Naponegro and Alfredo Salerno. All good Catholic boys. Ray had met them all at some point before a bullet or two had ploughed through their faces or ears or mouths and lodged in their brains. Ray had met a lot of these guys in the early '80s when Atlantic City had been his favourite destination in the world. They were all dead, or so it seemed. So perhaps was Eddie Lights. Ray had been with Eddie several times in Atlantic City. Eddie had always been very busy there.

It had been during this time, in the middle of the wars, that Ray had been driven late one night to the Friendly Tavern in South Philly. It was anything but friendly. Eddie had been there that night, off in the corner with somebody whose face Ray never saw. It was not a glimpse he needed. He had forgotten about that night. That had been a scary night. Philadelphia was a really scary place. And not a lot had changed, Ray thought. What had Eddie been doing here? Ray remembered Eddie had barely acknowledged him that night. It had been a strange one, so long ago. It reminded Ray how connected Eddie had been.

Ray sat having a coffee, watching Santander and Majesty and running his eyes over the heads of a few other familiar faces. What had made him think of that night in South Philly and Mad Marv and Filthy Filo and the rest of yesterday's men? Eddie Lights was in there with all of them as part of a thousand forgotten nights. Ray could not get him out of his mind. Eddie had been part of Ray's trips to fights for a very long time.

After the Walcott scandal, Santander had circled the business for a time, fixing a few fights for some people in Miami, providing a body for a fight in Vegas. He was never far away from fights involving Latin boxers, but it is unlikely that anybody ever printed a card for him. He was just there, lurking in the background, instantly available, with a reliable name for a challenger. His role with all the sanctioning bodies was unofficial. It was the usual story, but his mark was all over a dozen fights or more each year. To be honest, most promoters would struggle without men like Santander to do their dirty work. He was an agent, shaker and mixer. 'Pepe Satan', Don King called him, but even King used him when he had to come up with a reliable name and come up with it fast to keep the TV guys happy. The Latin TV market was one of boxing's booming areas.

Ray finished the coffee, put three singles on the counter and stood to leave. Santander watched Ray walk forward and then pushed back his chair. He got up and started to walk over. He was still wiping his mouth when they shook hands.

'Raymondo, good to see you. Give me a minute and I'll be with you. Just a minute. Go grab another coffee.'

Ray nodded and made to turn back to the counter. He had not realised Majesty had seen him come in and sit down.

'Hey, Ray.'

'Dan, how are you?'

'I'm fine, baby. Real fine. And you?'

Ray just shrugged and turned.

'That bad, eh? I hear you're looking for Eddie.'

Majesty had a sharp voice – and a sharper mind. Ray knew he would know about Eddie. Majesty knew everything that mattered in boxing. He was the fixer's fixer, the main facilitator in a business that existed in a secret world. He was a genius at survival. Shameless survival. He had survived and remained with Lennox Lewis after the culls. He was still in the frame, copping for his dough and appearing at fight after fight long after his previous allies had been dropped. Majesty was good, real good. He was probably Ray's main rival for scraps of trade, leaks and info.

'Who told you that?'

Ray knew it was the wrong thing to say. He should have just kept his mouth shut and walked away. He knew straight away that Majesty would notice the tone, the edge in his voice.

'Easy, whoa. OK, Ray, go get a coffee. I was only asking because I hear things. I hear a lot of things. Eddie's name came up last week out in Sacramento at the Chávez fight. I just hear a name, it's nothing to me. I hear his name, I hear your name. Nothing. I just hear.'

Majesty shrugged and raised his palms in an exaggerated gesture of innocence, then glanced at Santander for backing. Ray walked to their table and touched the back of a chair. Santander nodded and Ray sat down. Majesty offered his hand. Ray shook it. A waitress breezed over and filled a cup with coffee.

'I was out at Mayweather and Hatton last night and I asked a few people if they had seen Eddie. No big deal. And before that I made a few calls to make sure he was in town for the fight. Me and about 30,000 other Brits. I was just gonna grab some lunch with him before the fight.'

Ray was a decent liar.

'How was it?'

'Mayweather did a good job . . .'

'No, not the fucking fight. I know what the fight was like. The lunch, how was the lunch with Eddie?'

'He was out of town.'

Majesty smiled. He speared a piece of bright orange melon and held it up. He looked the piece of fruit over.

Majesty was an odd kiddy. Away from the business, he spent all his time, and most of his money, keeping the Bronx zoo open. Most people thought it was a joke, a line that he used to put people off guard, but Ray knew it was the truth. In 1997, when Naseem Hamed beat Kevin Kelley at the Garden, Ray had gone up to see the place. Majesty had given him a tour. It was a weird day. Majesty loved every bit of it. Ray had left him in the reptile house and returned to the city to do an interview. Majesty in with the snakes . . . It was perfect.

'How can anything from nature be this colour?'

All three studied the piece of fruit.

Santander seemed uneasy and that was odd for him. Very odd. Ray finished his coffee and pushed back in the chair.

'Anyway, I'll leave you two to finish what you're doing.'

'Ray, where you staying?' It was Majesty again.

'The Hilton.'

Ray knew that was a mistake even before he stood up. He was getting edgy, he needed to calm down and not let this Lights situation make him act too stupid. He sat back at the counter, thought about an early vodka to calm him but settled for more coffee.

Fifteen minutes later Santander came over to the counter. Majesty was just behind, but he was leaving. Ray waved at Majesty as he headed out the door.

'Raymondo.'

Santander looked a little scared. No, he looked a lot scared. Ray had noticed the fear earlier and had ignored it. Now he knew that it had nothing to do with the usual demands on Johnny Nobody to defend his CBA belt; Santander had no problems with boxing dilemmas.

They were simple to fix. That is how he made his money. The same way that Ray and Majesty made their money. It was not boxing that was on Santander's mind and Ray knew that before his old friend sat down on the stall next to him and started shaking his head.

'Pepe, drop the drama-queen bollocks and tell me what the problem is.'

Santander turned to face Ray. His eyes were clear and bright with fear. 'Not here. Come on, let's go. Let's walk. Meet me outside Starbucks in front of Bally's in ten minutes.'

The beach in Atlantic City is often ignored by visitors. It is the wrong side of the wooden boardwalk for most of the people who arrive in town on a bus with their pockets stuffed to bulging with coins. It is also on the wrong side for most of the derelicts who prosper along the railings that separate the boardwalk from the sand and the sea. The people who live on the street need buildings for shelter. And there are no tourists on the beach to ask for cash.

The boardwalk is a barrier that controls the movement of the punters and tourists and at the same time keeps most people out of the sand. Every 100 feet or so, there is a gap in the railing and a slope that leads to the beach and the sea. The problem is that often every ten feet or so on the busy part of the boardwalk there is a street ghost hanging onto the railing either singing or dribbling. The talented ones can do both. The really talented ones can dance.

The street people in Atlantic City are getting younger and scarier. Many wear combat jackets from the first Gulf conflict.

The people on the boardwalk like to stay as close to the railing as possible. It is their place. The beach is also their place. It's their place, and they don't go there to paddle. There are spots hidden from view behind some of the sand dunes where a crack pipe can be fired up without anybody knowing. *More people go onto the beach at night than during the day and they ain't checking on turtle eggs.*

When it is dark, it is possible to stand for just a few minutes at the railing and hear people making love or howling in madness at the night sky. Their moans and groans slip in under the wind and the steady growl of the Atlantic Ocean. During the day, even during a hot day, the beach is mostly empty.

Ray had only ever seen one person in the water in over 20 years of visits and that was Carol. Sweet and dirty and disabled Carol. Her boyfriend, an old black man of about 80, took her to the ocean to wash her. Lee was his name. Early most mornings he would struggle to push the wheelchair through the sand to the water's edge. Carol had been a singer, but her voice went in the '70s, before the heroin needle had destroyed her limbs. When Ray first met her, she had stumps for arms and legs. She spent most of her time in a supermarket trolley, banging away on a small keyboard that was fixed to the handle by grubby bits of rope. Lee would tap dance next to her and the pair collected a lot of money. Even by the gruesome standards of Atlantic City they were extreme and that helped their show. People found it hard to resist paying for their revulsion with some small change before having a little gawp. It was a cheap way to clear your conscience.

Carol had had a child once. A sad but true tale. The authorities in nearby Woodbridge had tried to take the baby away from her. They lost in court at the first attempt. She had had two arms at the time, but her legs had already been removed, sacrificed to the brief joy of her relentless needle play. She had a major habit. Heroin, pure and simple and often. She kept the kid and the habit, but the arms eventually went. It was a small price to pay, she joked.

Eventually, the authorities came for the kid again. At the time, Carol was living in an old school bus and that was only possible because a lot of people helped her. One or two freaks helped themselves to Carol and there was a rumour of a film, but enough people cared about her to help her live. Lee was not on the scene then. Carol lost the kid for a time but somehow managed to win custody through the courts once again. It was a celebrated case, a case that pushed the boundaries. Could a woman without arms, legs or a job look after a baby? After winning, she was pushed outside the court with the two-year-old girl on her lap. She kissed her little girl, cried some and gave the child to her solicitor. All this was played out on the steps at the court in Trenton. She had fought for the right to be a mother; it was the principle, she had told Ray. On the steps of the court that afternoon, she gave the child away.

'I had to prove I could be a good mom and by giving my baby away I finally acted like a good mom.'

She made her way to Atlantic City that same afternoon. That was back in the early '80s. She died there about ten years later. A car hit her wheelchair one morning as she left the boardwalk and the beach. Lee was knocked out by the collision and Carol was killed. She was thrown from the chair, the blanket covering what was left of her naked body blown away, and she landed in the doorway of a liquor store.

'Man, she looked like a skinned dog. I weeped for my baby when I sawed her,' Lee told Ray some months later.

That was a long time ago. She had died just before or just after a Holyfield fight, or perhaps it was a Whitaker fight. Ray couldn't be totally sure. Fights had started to blur in his memory. There had been just too many over the years.

Sweet Carol was another lost soul who had not been in Ray's head for a long time. The Atlantic City trip was turning into a depressing stay with far too many dead people and fuck-ups drifting in and out of his thoughts. It was only morning coffee.

There were very few people on the boardwalk when Ray walked through the dark-glass exit at Bally's and adjusted his eyes to a sun that was now even brighter and higher in a perfect blue sky. It was also cold. Ray thought AC looked beautiful in harsh frozen blues and greys. Often the tourists in their purple and yellow leisurewear charged down the boardwalk in Atlantic City like animals, without seeing the beauty. There were a lot of fat people in gambling cities.

Ray looked to the right and saw Santander hovering in front of the coffee shop. Santander nodded and walked towards the beach, where there was an opening in the railing.

Ray followed him and stopped at the end of the wooden slope. The sand looked dirty in the glare of the sun and the fight fixer was nudging a lump under its surface with the pointed toe of his olive-coloured shoes. His foot finally revealed a shoe, a child's sandal. He turned, looked above Ray's head at the hotels.

'You gotta get out of town. Go now, Ray. It's Eddie, man. You gotta go and go quick.'

It was getting to be an annoying request.

ATLANTIC CITY: STILL UGLY WHEN THE LIGHTS GO OUT

Five hours later Ray's conference was over. He was finished with the convention for another year. He had managed to meet with most of the people on his list over a long day and all the promoters he worked for back in Europe and in Australia would be happy with what he had started to put in place. The future fights he had discussed all made cash common sense. As far as he could tell, he had put in place six or seven fights and moved about ten boxers up the CBA ratings. Considering the circumstances, it was a good day's work.

It was not hard to move a fighter up and down the ratings of any of the sanctioning bodies. Ray had done it dozens of times. The CBA had set a high standard for rankings in 2001, when they had famously put a dead man in at number 8 of the super middleweights. It had been a great story. The man moved up when he died, stayed for a month or so and then, after dipping a place or two, made a comeback. He moved as high as three and was looking good for a title shot. It was beautiful to watch the kid's progress.

Ray had reluctantly broken the story when the dead fighter appeared on a shortlist for Welshman John Hunter, who was no stranger to meeting and beating dead bodies in title defences. At the time, the guy had been gone for seven months. To be honest, he wasn't much of a fighter when he was alive.

The CBA president had told Ray, 'He was a promising fighter.' They had both laughed at the situation. What else could the boss do? The CBA had seriously put their house in order since that early shambles.

Ray found Hugo Mendez of the CBA at the conference and grabbed a quick lunch with him. It had been a rough old affair in one of the many buffet holes that work as steaming lures to get the punters in. There was always too much crushed ice, too many scarlet-coloured fruits and prawns the size of small kittens. The pair found a room and Ray sat down with the slick lawyer for an hour.

Ray had Hugo's word on the Hunter and Gerd Seldorf fight. It was a mandatory and nobody really wanted to put it on, which meant Ray could tell Mickey Boyd, Hunter's promoter, to bid sensibly because his German rival, Hans Kurthoff, had no interest in wasting a TV date on a fight that his man couldn't win. Boydy knew the German would lose, but he wanted to know just how little to bid. Ray had been in the middle of a reverse auction like this several times. Anybody can win a bid to stage a fight, but it takes skills to win it for the right money. Ray's feeling during the sit-down with Hugo was that everybody was telling the truth for the right reason and that reason was cash.

Simple business boxing. Nice business.

Ray had done some work for Kurthoff and he had provided a lot of the bums that had built Seldorf's 28 and 0 record. The Germans liked to put their men in with losers who were guaranteed to fall over. Their modern business was constructed safely around the principles of discipline and mismatches.

Seldorf could fight a bit, but not a lot, and he was ugly to watch. After a decade of Henry Maske and Sven Ottke in dozens of dreadful world title fights, the German public wanted a bit of excitement and Seldorf was not the right man. He was cut from the traditional cloth of clever, sensible and protected fighters. He was boring.

The sealed purse bids were due in ten days and Boydy had been pulling his hair out trying to find a figure that would guarantee his fighter home advantage against the awkward and towering Seldorf. Ray would make the call later to let Boydy have the news – the good news – that he wouldn't have to waste too much of his money.

Purse bids had been a speciality of Ray's over the years and his last-minute flights to Mexico City or San Juan had always provided him with a few laughs and a few quid. In Ray's opinion, they were a totally pointless exercise and a waste of time. The ancient ritual required a man from each of the bidding camps to fly to the main office of the sanctioning body. In the office, or a nearby restaurant, the representative would formally hand over an envelope to the president of the sanctioning body. In the envelope was a figure, an amount in cash, which one of the promoters was prepared to pay for the two fighters to meet. It was that simple, and in theory the open process eliminated illegality. Well, that was the idea behind it.

'Transparency, transparency.' It was a favourite word of the World Boxing Council's José Sulaimán, president of the Mexico City-based organisation for over 30 years. Perhaps the Mexican translation was different.

The highest bid won – it was a simple and archaic way to do business. But then boxing was full of ancient rituals. There would be a hushed silence for a few seconds as the president or the highest available official sliced opened the envelope to reveal the secret bid. After all the envelopes had been opened and the winner declared, the representatives of the various bidding promoters would go back to the airport and get on a plane home. Often a counter deal was arranged in a private room if the amount was too high or too low. Nobody – certainly not a promoter – wanted to be left holding his arse with a bid two or three times higher than his nearest rival. Green promoters made dreadful financial errors by bidding too much. Ray had once done Mexico City twice in six days and he had fallen short both times; he had known he would before he guided his lips to his first Bloody Mary in the lounge at Heathrow.

He often made the trip with what he called 'dead envelopes'. Ray had flown several times with two envelopes; once, he had made the journey to Caracas with three sealed bids for just one fight. He had no idea what he was offering. On that occasion, all three of his bids had fallen short of the winning offer.

Ray had been knocked on that trip by a little tosser with no idea. The tourist had invested a bit of money in boxing and had had a bit of luck with a fighter. The fella decided to bid for a fight but was so far short that everybody had a chuckle. The prick had started to move away from the sport by the time Ray arrived home, though, and had refused to pay the money he owed for Ray's services. It wasn't a lot, just a grand or twelve hundred.

It was a dumb ritual, but losing a purse bid for a promoter without a deal in place was not good business and that is why Ray had to get on a plane so often. He liked to see the envelopes being opened and the men who sent him took his word.

If the Hunter fight took place in Germany, there was a good chance he would be pushed and a close fight would be a disaster. There had been a lot of bad decisions and bad refereeing in Germany; it was turning into a tricky place for anybody to fight and win. The Sven Ottke and Robin Reid clash in late 2003 was a shocking disgrace. Reid had looked a clear winner, but the referee never helped him and after the fight the three men at ringside went against him. It was robbery, plain and simple.

Boydy was desperate not to put Hunter under pressure and fighting in Germany was pressure. Hunter also had a divorce on the go and a young dancer in tow, and his contract was up for renewal after the Seldorf fight. He was not that bright and, as Ray had seen on several occasions, he was easily spooked. Boydy had to win the right to stage the fight because he knew there was a good chance Hunter would lose his mind in a foreign ring – lose his mind in a fight that was on paper a walkover.

In Atlantic City, Ray had Hugo's word that Boydy was going to win and that he was not going to have to break the bank to make it happen. Ray calculated that he had saved Boydy 100 grand and a lot of aggro.

Ray was also offered a fight for little Pablo Perez against a flyweight from Thailand for the CBA's vacant title. Ray knew the CBA had never managed to worm its way into the Asian market, but a recent deal with a casino and resort near Phuket had opened a door for it. He also knew that Thai flyweights were never easy to beat. He had a route planned for little Pablo and it made a lot more sense to avoid Thai flyweights. It always made sense to avoid Thai fighters in Thailand.

'Hugo, thank you. I'll see you next week at Wembley?'

'Yes, Ray, yes.'

'I'm sure Mick's sorted you out, but you know you only have to call.'

Sure, Hugo knew he could call and on occasion he did. It was usually at about four in the morning when something unexpected had come up. It was not easy putting a fighter and his retinue on a plane for a title fight. There was always a request from somebody for some late money, or an extra room for a mistress, or an extra plane ticket, and it was down to Hugo to try to make right a bad situation.

The CBA received a sanctioning fee from championship fights and Hugo did his diplomatic best to make sure that as many fights as possible for the CBA bauble took place. He would always call Ray for his advice and that meant the CBA boss calling from his home in San Juan and getting Ray out of bed in the middle of the night. Ray had to pick every call up, no matter what time, and that was a pain when there was a problem.

It had been a draining day at the end of two hectic days of travel. Ray still ached from the assault at the MGM. It had been a disaster in Vegas. Thankfully, it had picked up in Atlantic City, but he was still clearly in the middle of something he had no right to be in. Santander's fearful look that morning had convinced him that opening his door to the woman had been a mistake.

Santander had told Ray straight that he was in danger. They had stood in the damp sand and he had said to Ray not to look for or ask about Eddie Lights.

'Ray, give up on Eddie. He's gone and you don't have to go with him.'

'What's he done? Pepe, is he dead?'

'Ray, just forget about it. Stop asking. Drop it. Go, and go now.'

'I've only asked a few people. Actually, I'm not bothered whether I see him or not, I don't give a toss. But why are you so worried?'

'I had a call from Vegas and they told me to tell you to keep moving.'

It was Stacey. Ray knew that Santander and Stacey were real close.

'All I've done is ask about him.'

'Yeah, and you're just looking for a lunch partner. Don't bullshit me, Ray. You're looking for him and so are some other people.'

Santander stopped and looked along the boardwalk. His eyes were tight and sweat was starting to appear on his brow. He needed his pipe, but that was not the only reason for his anxiety. 'Now, I don't know these other people, and I don't wanna know these other people. You know what I'm saying?'

'Yeah, well I do fucking know about the other people. I met them on my last night in Vegas. So what? I've not done anything and I don't know what Eddie has supposedly done.'

Ray looked out over Santander's shoulder at the edge of the ocean. The man was very uptight.

'You just gotta go. You gotta get out of town before they find you again, man.'

It was no longer funny, but Ray had to laugh and he was not sure why. None of it made sense.

'Pepe, I've been thinking about this shit since I arrived in Vegas. Now, I reckon that if Eddie was dead, nobody would be looking for him, right?'

Santander nodded.

'OK. Now, if he had turned, then nobody would be looking for him because the Feds would have him under lock and key. If that was the case, then nobody would be chasing me all over the poxy place.'

Another nod.

'So I think he's alive and on the missing list. I think he's seriously pissed somebody off and that's why the two nutcases have been running after me. I'm innocent of anything and for some reason I'm in the middle of Eddie's bullshit. It just ain't right.'

Santander nodded for a final time and moved up the slope before turning back.

'Pepe, what the fuck has Eddie done?'

'Forget it. I don't wanna see you again until this is over. Just fucking go home, man.'

ATLANTIC CITY: STILL NO ANSWERS

By Ray's simple reasoning, only money or drugs were left as possible options for the interest in the old crooner. Eddie obviously had something that somebody wanted. The old rogue was not short of a few quid, but Ray couldn't get his head round the idea that money was at the bottom of the deadly manhunt. If it was cash, then how much had been taken to justify the chaos that Ray had stumbled in and out of since letting the woman into his flat? It would have to be a serious amount of gelt. Nobody had mentioned the police, so that meant the problem was internal, a feud of some sort. All the right people, the proper people knew, but there was no suggestion the old bill were involved. It was strictly business. But still nothing added up. Ray refused to accept it was just about money.

Eddie was not a mug; he was a connected man and respected. Had he backed a big loser, put too much money out and found himself short? That was unlikely; it wasn't Eddie's style. There was one other thing. Perhaps it was personal. Now that, in Eddie's world, was serious. Perhaps it was a bit of both: money and a personal insult. Nasty combination.

The desperation in Santander's voice had shaken Ray.

'Pepe, what the fuck has Eddie done?'

'Forget it. I don't wanna see you again until this is over. Just fucking go home, man.'

Ray had watched Santander walk back onto the boardwalk and head off to Bally's entrance. He never looked back and Ray never moved. He remained on the sand with the vibration from the gently breaking waves settling on his back every few seconds. Eventually, he had left the beach and gone to work. The little game was wearing a bit thin.

All day Ray had looked in mirrors for people he didn't want to see. When the day inside Bally's at the convention was over, and before 1,000 hungry-eyed guests descended on the banqueting hall, Ray had slipped away. It was getting dark and cold and the sun had come and gone on the shore. The readers of men's palms had their lights on and bulky shawls covered their skinny shoulders. Their kids were gone; the palm trade was about to get busy.

By the time Ray slipped through the back doors of the Hilton, he was ready for a steam and a beer. It was night and he was whacked.

He knew the red light would be flashing on the phone the moment he opened the door to his room. He half-expected the leather coat boys to be relaxing on his bed, drinking a cocktail through a couple of pink straws. Thankfully, the only thing that assaulted him when he opened the door was the icy air conditioning and the distant smell of a smoker. The boys were not with him yet, but he knew they would be coming.

He decided to listen to his messages. There was just one and he was expecting it. He knew the caller before he heard the first words.

'*Message one, recorded today at 9.04 a.m.*: "Ray. Pick the phone up, babe. What about a cell? I called you out in Wages a few times. You know where I'm at. I'll see you."'

It was from a man called Rube. *The* Rube, to be precise.

Ray had known the Rube a long time. When they were first introduced, Ray was told Rube was an ex-fighter. It's not uncommon for people in the boxing business to pass as an ex-fighter and over the years the fiction becomes blurred fact. Ray had taken Rube's boxing past at face value but realised Rube had never been in the ring. His disability was from birth. The Rube had never walked, let alone had a pair of gloves on. He had no legs and was in a wheelchair. Ray had never asked Rube for the truth because there was no need; the Rube had given Ray another type of the truth on so many things and so often that Ray no longer cared about Rube's identity. It had been, Ray now believed, the Rube who had sought Ray out all those years ago. Ray had been running a bit too wild when Rube appeared and plucked him clean out of a particularly messy affair. Ray had stopped thanking him, but he would never forget. When a man saves you from a bullet, it tends to remain in your brain. Rube saved Ray's life. It was that simple.

The Rube knew Eddie well and they shared some history, though Ray had started to forget the details. The man in the wheelchair knew a lot of people with both influence and ignorance in equal measure and he knew all the lost souls that lived the life in Vegas or Atlantic City. He spoke of Vegas like he had a map of the place in his head, but he had never even been there.

Nobody waited for Rube to arrive because he never went to people. He had a few places where he met people in Atlantic City and that was about it with him. No fixed abode, just a place for a meet – a bar or restaurant where the Rube was safe and men could talk.

It was rumoured that Rube's brothers were major drug dealers in Philly or New York and the Rube was often grabbed by the Atlantic City PD if there was a black killing. He had nothing to do with any black killings in that sense; it was all just a game. Rube operated at a much higher level and the police knew it. He was not close to the random and brainless shootings or crack murders that piled dead bodies each week in a heap of numbers and stunted baby faces; anybody could pay a few hundred bucks to buy a bit of personal slaughter. Rube had been held and never charged so often that he'd forced the police department to put in disabled toilets, special lifts and a larger interrogation room long before it was policy. Over the years, Ray had heard too many rumours.

Ray had no idea where Rube lived, but he knew where he would be and knew what time. He had a bit over two hours to kill, so he went down for a steam. It was a a simple way for Ray to unwind. All the attendants were new and that was cool with Ray. They had big ears and big mouths. A lot of business could be done in the spas at casino hotels. The little wooden sauna that was part of the complex at Caesars on the Strip was once dubbed the 'closer' because so many big fights had been made inside its four small walls. It was gone now, like a lot of the traditional spas.

The Hilton's enormous sauna had an old feel to it. Big steam with tiled steps as wide as seats. The complex was never clean, but the grime was part of the appeal. The heavy marble showers were against the wall at one end of the tiled area and they were all empty when Ray walked down the few steps. The spa's white sandals were about three sizes too small, but Ray was able to slap along without any problem. The tub was up a few steps, but Ray generally avoided the shared hot water of a spa's jacuzzi. Too many hot-water wankers and that was a fact.

There was just one other white robe on the pegs outside the steam. Nobody was visible in the white heat of the steam as Ray went in and sat on the top tier. A minute later the door opened and through the steam Ray could just make out one of the attendants from the front desk. He had a plastic cup of cranberry and a towel folded and packed with ice. The kid stepped up and gave both to Ray. He never said a word.

'Get me a towel, son,' somebody said from the end of Ray's tier. Ray couldn't see the man through the swirling steam. It was hot and anonymous and that is why a lot of business could be done in the wet heat.

An hour passed, with Ray wandering in and out of the steam, the sauna and the showers. He let Eddie and the problem drift for a bit as he soaked his balls with frozen towels and warmed his sore back on scalding wooden sauna slats. When he finally put his robe back on, he realised it was not his robe. In the pocket was a $100 chip from the casino. Ray kept it when he left an hour or so later.

Ray was back on the street at ten after a couple of drinks in the Hilton's anonymous Ship bar. Two vodkas, quick and cold. This time he missed the boardwalk and went out on Boston, turned right and walked three blocks in the direction of the Flame. At the back of the Tropicana, he was stopped by a couple of security guards. They formed a thin barrier between a large truck and the doors at the rear of the casino.

'Hold it there, please, sir. White tiger coming through.'

Ray didn't say a word, He just watched as a cage was wheeled from the back of the truck. The tiger was beautiful and sleek and it paced slowly as it was pushed gently across the sidewalk and through the open door. White tigers were all over the place. Siegfried and Roy had a few, even Tyson had had one for a time. Every slick-haired magician could conjure one up from behind a silk curtain.

'Sir, thank you for waiting.'

At the next intersection, Ray turned left and the Flame was in front of him, on the corner, opposite the police station. The location always made Ray smile.

Rube was not at the end of the bar as normal; instead, he was all the way at the back of the bar next to the entrance to the kitchen. His wheelchair was against the wall, giving him a complete view of the whole place. Rube's eyeballs shifted easily across every inch of the place and moved with speed through the whites of his eyes. To his left and right were the Flame's booths, and above each table was a mini-jukebox. The Flame was a small step back into a fading world and the music helped. In each booth, there were framed pictures of local events, dignitaries and dead cops, and on the walls either side of the jukeboxes were mostly forgotten fighters.

Ray walked in, nodded at the barman and caught the song that was playing. He started to grin. Rube looked at him with silence in his eyes and nodded his head just a fraction as the song from the Flame's jukebox faded.

Rube was speaking as Ray approached.

'This is higher than the highest mountain, deeper than the deepest sea. You with me?'

Ray nodded. He knew the words, knew what the Rube was saying.

'So, who is it?'

'Brook, right?'

'That's right, Ray. Mr Brook Benton. Damn, he could sing.'

Ray took the seat to Rube's left. Another Brook Benton track was playing. Ray looked at Rube.

'What? I put the *Greatest Hits* on twice. Cost 12 bucks. But it's better than the shit-kicking music these cops play. They got some ugly ears. Even the brothers.'

A waitress came over and Ray ordered a large vodka and cranberry and a soda water for Rube. They listened to the next song, the one with Dinah Washington. There was no need to talk during a song like that. The drinks arrived and the songs – short, like they were 30 and 40 years ago – came and went. The vodka, which also came and went, was working. It always did after a steam. But it also seemed a bit short.

'You know Eddie loved Brook, right?'

First Jay and now Rube. That was it, no messing with the Rube. Ray knew Eddie had a thing for Benton's voice. And Ray knew that Rube was the one man in AC who would know what was happening.

There was a lot of knowing going on but not a lot of it was going on inside Ray's head.

Rube didn't have to ask what Ray was doing. He had been watching over Ray from a distance for many years. He had helped Ray too many times. Of course he was on top of the situation now.

Rube had brilliant white eyes. They never changed colour, no matter how late the hour. His nails were long, his fingers elegant like a pianist's. His hair was always short, his chin always shaved. Ray had stopped being intrigued by Rube about a thousand drinks ago; he was sensible enough to recognise an enigma when he met one and to just leave it at that.

'In 1986, it was Eddie hooked Brook up at the Sands. You knew that, right?'

Ray knew that.

'That was Eddie did that. And you know what Eddie did then, right? He found Keely Smith. You know that, right?'

Ray knew that, too.

'And you know why Eddie did that? It was because of Sinatra. You know that, right?'

Ray nodded each time. He knew the story.

Frank Sinatra had a thing for Keely Smith. He fell in love with her voice listening to her on the tiny stage in the lounge at the Sahara. Keely Smith and Louis Prima, her husband, and their band on a stage that was six foot by twelve. It was the '50s. The Rat Pack bullshit was in full flow and at the old Bingo Club Keely was tearing the city apart with a voice that nobody could get near. It was a voice to steal dreams any night. She was very special and each night the Vegas top-liners, all the big-name entertainers, would wind up in the lounge at the Sahara. It was a casino sound. Sinatra and his people loved it. They were real Vegas folk – no coins, no bullshit and no buffets. There were no tourists on the inside.

Twenty years later, Eddie had met her during his first weeks in Las Vegas. A dozen years after that, when she was at a low point, he'd reached out and put her back on the stage. She ran for over a decade. He had done the same for Brook Benton. Eddie had been a Benton fan all his singing life. He had used Ben Brook as his first stage name in the '60s. Eddie had told Ray that it was Sinatra who had asked him to find Brook and Keely some work. Eddie never refused Sinatra – or any of his friends – a favour. He was a lucky man and he never needed to be reminded. It was a rare story for Eddie to tell. He joked about the early days in Las Vegas and he dined out on tales of Vegas losers, but he seldom included the men who had made his world possible when he told his stories.

'It wasn't a favour,' Eddie once told Ray. 'It was a pleasure.'

That was that.

Rube closed his eyes and moved his head back. Ray could feel people approaching and hear them sit down at a booth just three booths away. They were not police. Rube looked over and then turned to Ray and moved a bit closer.

'Santander got you good this morning. His mouth's been working double-time. What he have to say that you never knew?'

Ray shook his head. Nothing new, was the truth. Ray had heard it all in Vegas.

'I figured that crackhead piece of shit never knew a thing. Boy can talk, talk too much most of the time.'

Rube had a short fuse for loose talkers.

'You don't know what's going down, right? I told our friends that, I told them, but they ain't listening.'

'I'm ready to know.'

'Ray, you ain't even close to ready. Not even close, my brother.'

Ray tried to speak, but Rube lifted his hand.

'No. Listen, because that is one thing that you can be good at. I'm gonna tell ya some things. And it could save your life. Your life, by the way, ain't worth too much at the moment. I heard the figure and I was shocked. Fine connected man like you with the complexion to make the right connections. It was a small price, brother, but it was real money.'

Rube sat back in his chair and closed his mouth and his eyes down once again. Ray could feel somebody approaching.

'Nice to see you, Mr Rube.'

Ray didn't turn around. He watched Rube watching the man walk away.

'Who was that?'

'He works at the Hilton. Nice kid. I knew his mom a long, long time ago. Nobody ever knew his pops.'

'Is he here because of me?'

'Yep. The men are about to go to your room, but that's not a problem. We got there just in time. They don't want to kill you. Not yet.'

'Can we sit down with them? Let me explain to them what's going on?'

'Ray, they're not really big listeners. You know what I'm saying? They're looking for Eddie and they think you know where he is. It's that simple.'

'I don't. I was looking for him. Well, a woman that I only met once asked me to find him. She said she was his daughter. I said yes and now this shit is happening. I have no personal involvement. I like Eddie, but I'm not ready to die finding him, for fuck's sake.'

'Good to hear. But with them it is personal. I know you don't have a clue, but I ain't the one chasing you all over America. What was that shit in the car park in Vegas? What the fuck was you thinking?'

'Rube, this is wrong. I know nothing.'

'Whoa, listen. You're running, I'm talking. That's the way it works when somebody knows nothing meets somebody knows something.'

Ray dropped his head. He knew.

Rube reached across and tapped him on the shoulder and pointed at a picture on the wall. 'Let me tell you a few things and then we gonna work it out. Trust me, Ray. Have I ever let you down?'

The picture was to the right of the jukebox and it looked like the first night at the Taj Mahal, or maybe the Hilton, or even the Tropicana. It looked like just another night during the glorious early days of AC. It was the type of picture Ray recognised from the offices of casino executives and boxing people all over the world: champagne glasses, dancing girls and men in tuxedos smiling as the mayor or senator or somebody in public office cut a piece of tape.

'What you see, Ray?'

The picture looked about 20 years old, perhaps a bit more. There were five guys that mattered. Forget the dignitary and the women – mayors and hookers come and go. 'Shit, that's Eddie and that's Michael the Boy. That's Little Nicky and Fat Frank. And the one with the short hair looks familiar. Yeah, he looks familiar.'

Rube adjusted his body in his wheelchair and pointed at the picture with one of his long, finely manicured nails.

'It's 1983. The first night at the Trop and, yeah, that's Eddie, that's right.'

Rube touched his nail against the glass and into Eddie's face. Next, the finger tapped silently against a smiling fat-faced man. He was dressed sharp even in black and white.

'That's Michael the Boy Lucio, correcto. Lovely man, nice to his family, but not a good enemy.'

Ray had been in Lucio's company a few times and had met him at a lot of fights over the years.

'Michael died in 1984. You knew that, right?'

There was no need for a nod, Rube wasn't asking.

'Nicky Raviolo. That's a fucked-up Italian name. Little Nicky. Man was fun, could last longer than any of the other fellas and he loved living the life.'

Rube ran a finger under Raviolo's chin, just about where the large velvet bow tie separated his body from his head.

'Nicky died in 1986. You knew that, right?'

No need to nod. Ray could remember Nicky Raviolo. Another dead and vicious wiseguy from the days and nights when Atlantic City was full of death. Rube moved his finger to the right of the picture and hit his nail with a crisp ping off the glass.

'Frankie "Fat Frank" Naponegro. Boy, that fat fucker could eat and be a real pain in the arse.'

Ray had been in Naponegro's bar in South Philly many times back when the road from the city to the shore was a race strip. There was never a wasted journey back then.

'Frank the pig died in 1989. You knew that, right?'

Rube tapped out their lives and deaths with his nail. He left his hand hovering over the fifth man in the group, the man Ray thought looked familiar.

'His name is Salvatore Leo. You heard of him, right?'

Ray nodded. Sure, he had heard of Sal Leo, but he had never met him. Well, he had never been introduced because Sal Leo liked to be anonymous. He was, so people said, invisible. He had the kind of Italian nickname that forced fat men to cross their bulky chests whenever it was mentioned. Very dramatic it was, too. Nobody had seen him in about 20 years. He had gone, left the life, but he was still talked about like a leader, a great leader.

'Salvatore Leo, the old man. The AC gent. I've never seen him. A bit before my time, to tell the truth, but I've heard a lot of stories,' added Ray.

Ray had heard all the stuff. The man behind the man behind Sonny Liston. Sal Leo's name was all over the place. He was a silent and private man. He worked with presidents and dictators and he walked with greats. He was like a folk hero to the made men on the East Coast. His one-man war in Detroit in the early '60s was still regarded as the dumbest, bravest and most amazing slaughter. Seven people died when Sal, travelling on his own, arrived in the Motor City to settle some business. His brother had been killed in Florida a month earlier. Miami's South Beach had always been a great place for connected men to be slain. He was shot in the face on the beach at night and left to the sand crabs. The crabs ate his brain before a Cuban exile looking for coins found the body. That was bad business because Joey Leo was not a dangerous man. He ran nightclubs in Miami, which was an easy way for a connected man to make a safe living. All you had to do was stick a pineapple in a glass. It was a business for soft family members, and Joey liked the sunshine and the cool people in Miami. Joey was no killer and everybody knew that; he had a flowered shirt and a smile for the family members who were sent to him.

The killing was wrong, but it happened. It was part of their job. But there was a little problem with Joey's death. One of the shooters took a ring from the dead man's little finger. That was not right. That was theft, common theft.

'We're not those type of men,' Sal had said when he found out about the ring.

He went to Miami to find the other type of men. The Cuban was in the frame for the ring, but he shit his pants when he was asked. The big fucker from Little Havana had been guilty before, but Sal liked his honesty. He lived.

Sal found out about the men behind the killing and then went to Detroit. He was there a night and a day. That was all it took. Three died in their homes, in their beds, before nine in the morning. Three never made it out of their cars. It was only six in the evening when

Sal found the last man. He was hiding in a hotel by the airport. He had a ticket for Los Angeles in his jacket pocket. Sal left him in the toilet, most of his head in the bath. He cut off a finger, but he never touched the ring the last man was wearing.

Ray kept looking at the picture. Fuck, he had a bad, bad feeling.

'You OK, Ray?'

'Just thinking. Eddie told me a story once. The story of the finger, Sal's trip to Detroit.'

'Yeah, I remember that. That was beautiful.'

Sal had been in control for a long time after the Detroit massacre. Then he left, simply walked away. Some said he was dead, but nobody knew for sure and after a few years people stopped asking. Ray had heard once that Rube worked for him. Ray had never even seen a picture of him before tonight. So why was he so familiar?

The nail tapped the glass three times, dancing with a ping off the smiling faces of Lucio, Raviolo and Naponegro. Ray looked at Rube.

'He's familiar because it is his son who is looking for you. You met him in Vegas, right? Slick motherfucker, with them eyes. Name's Little Sal and he can be real nasty. About the size of a mini-flyweight.'

That was it. That was the man in the leather bolero jacket. The neat and tidy button man. The son of Salvatore Leo had threatened to kill him, the son of the Butcher of Detroit.

The Rube tapped out a little beat on all of their heads one final time.

'You know these three men were all shot. Simple killings, hits, whatever the fuck you want to call it.'

Ray emptied the icy remains of an old drink and shook his head. There was suddenly a little humour in his eyes.

'Come on, Rube. I'm tired, man. I need to know some things.'

Rube's nail tapped again. Ray looked over. It was the mayor's head under the nail this time.

'His honour, the distinguished guest, the mayor. John something or other. Guy was on the serious take. Cocksucker was crooked and lived like he was clean. Dead, 1986.'

Ray could vaguely remember that death and the fuss it had caused. There were calls to put an end to most of the businesses in AC, but reform is never simple when the corrupt are involved and the dead mayor had his filthy hands, or at least a thumb, on most of the dirty money. It all calmed down after a week or so, when somebody obviously realised that if there was too much change a lot of the wives and mistresses would end up poor.

The Boy and Fat Frank and Little Nicky just died. When the three guys were shot, nobody wanted to close down all the bars and empty out the rubbish. The feeling was that they deserved their deaths and that was probably right. Like the mayor, they were certainly not innocent men. They lived expecting a bloody death.

The pair sat in silence for a few minutes and the Brook Benton loop continued.

'Eddie did them all.'

Ray never moved. Rube stopped tapping the picture and brought his hands down to his lap. Then he made the shape of a gun, clicked the trigger twice.

'Bang, bang, baby, you're dead. That was all Eddie's work.'

'No way. No way. I've known Eddie for years and he can't even act tough very well. I've never even seen him give anybody a slap. I've never seen a gun in his house or his cars. Never.'

'That's right. He never acts tough. What's he got to prove?'

Ray had met people with reputations and, Rube was right, they had nothing to prove. They were quiet men, family men, and they had their silence most of the time. Ray also knew that they had another look, a look that at times betrayed their craziness.

'Think about it, Ray. You ever seen anybody push him? You ever seen anybody bad mouth him or hold a grudge against him?'

Ray thought for a minute. It was true, but Eddie was just, well, Eddie. Full of stories. Always available. He was a singer from Blackpool. And not, it has to be said, the best singer from Blackpool. Ray was still shaking his head.

'What, you think he was some kind of angel? Don't you think that's strange now, Ray? C'mon, man, you're smart. He couldn't sing for shit and people gave him that much respect. Sure, he left everybody a big tip, but it takes more than that. It takes a lot more than that in Vegas. Don't you think that's just a bit strange? Eddie was the man, the top man, Mr Service. And don't look so fucking shocked.'

Ray kept staring at the picture. Rube let him look.

'Let me do this, then. Suppose he is everything you say he is, just suppose. So tell me what he did to cause all this trouble. Tell me where he is. Fuck, is he dead?'

'First we gotta back up a little. It's not a straight story. It was a guy called Yogi Merlino, Fat Yogi. A bum, but crazy with a trigger. He was Eddie's first. Eddie told me that Yogi refused to die, so he had to shoot him three times. Three times in the head. And it kinda stuck after that. There were a lot more and then this little gang came together.'

The name Yogi Merlino rang a bell somewhere, but Ray couldn't get the details straight in his head. Too many people with names like Merlino had died in AC's short history.

'So Eddie kills this geezer Merlino. Yogi, whatever the fuck his name was. Why did he kill him? Who ordered it?'

'Sal. Big Salvatore. He was with Eddie one night and Merlino arrived with three black dudes from New York. I have no idea what went down, but the next day Merlino was dead. Usual shit. Merlino went crazy with the crack money and delivered bad people. He was a risk.'

'No, this is wrong. I've been in Eddie's company hundreds of times and I've never seen a thing to suggest he was a killer.'

'Yeah, that's because they don't make a T-shirt with "I kill for cash" on it. Ray, what the fuck? Get wise. Eddie did them all and dozens of others. Why would I lie to you? Tell me.'

The Rube pointed once again at the picture and Ray just sat back. It was late. He had no idea what was going on. Eddie Lights a hit man? It was too crazy to even think about, but Rube would never lie.

'They had a good thing going, but it only lasted a few years. They were running wild. Between them they had an army on the streets. Here, and in Vegas. They were tight and that was all that mattered to them. They were the top crew, five chiefs, hundreds of soldiers. They had trust and you know how rare that is with these people.'

'No way. Eddie wasn't a chief. Even if he was this killer you're telling me about, he was not a chief. No way. No fucking way.'

'Have it your way, Ray. Eddie had power, man. You forgetting he was still known as Sinatra's man back then. He was loyal. He had influence.'

This time it was Ray's turn to study the picture. He looked at each of the faces of the dead men.

'Raymondo, it's true, baby. Their friendship was open, their business kept secret until The Boy tried to go solo on a massive shipment. It was the crack wars. You remember those dark days? His labs in the badlands went up in smoke. He blamed Sal for the destruction. He was probably right. But Eddie was picked to take care of business.'

The party was over. Ray wondered how long it was after the picture was taken that Eddie shot The Boy. Days, weeks? Damn, the same night?

'The same thing, more or less, happened with the two others. There was a lot of heat, a lot of fingers pointing. People with no brains but itchy fingers started talking. The problem was that the Feds were inside parts of their thing. They had informants everywhere, too many men had been turned. The juice had ruined their heads. Nobody was thinking straight at the end of a serious coke jones. Shit, you know that.'

The police and the FBI had used informants and undercover agents to bring AC under control. Nobody had control at the time, so they went in under deep cover to start the change. It worked. Ray remembered the paranoia from the '90s.

'In 1989, Sal was nearly taken down by the FBI. He and Eddie cooled it. Eddie had a legitimate face in Vegas at the time. The pair stopped doing business, nothing personal, they just stopped. Eddie was concerned about the FBI.'

'But Eddie never had that much money, Rube. He was never short, but he never had this type of money. Come on, Rube, this can't be right. There has to be a catch somewhere.'

'You're right. When Sal was nearly popped, the money vanished. I heard they lifted 25 million, but it could be more. It was all over the place – in Swiss banks, in bonds. But it all went into the night. Sal walked after a week in the hold. No charges, not a thing to hang the man for.'

'Why didn't Eddie simply take out Sal, if all the money had gone? If he's a stone-cold killer, why didn't he do him?'

'Eddie never would say. But I guess he knew his friend never had the money. We all heard the rumours about a deal. Freedom for the money. I always considered that Sal had saved both their souls. They were robbed by the law and then Sal vanished. Gone.'

The Rube paused and sipped on his soda water.

'Six weeks ago, Eddie arrived in town. He pulled me up to his room at the Hilton.'

'Why did he call you?'

'The same reason that you are here: information. If it happened, I've got the news. Ain't no secret. So Eddie sat down and told me that he wanted to go and see Sal. Could I set the meeting up?'

'Is that the first time they've tried to get back together?'

'For a fact, yes. I called people and set it up. Anyway, Eddie gets to sit with Sal.'

'What they talk about?'

'Who knows? Two old guys talking. I hear it goes well and then I start to hear about the dead bodies. Soon as I set it up, people start to die. It was like the old days for about a week. A guy I know in Jersey City was the first. He has contact with Sal and I had reached out to him. Another guy, I know him well, was driving Eddie and he's dead. A third man, another friend of mine, he's gone. Dead.'

'What? Eddie killed them all?'

'Not Eddie, not this time. Eddie is the reason they are all dead. The killer was Little Sal. Your man from Vegas.'

Ray knew where it was going. He had been right. It was personal. Sure, there was money, but this was about old friends and death and families.

Ray spoke. 'They all died because Eddie killed Sal, am I right?'

'Correct. Thirteen days ago.'

It made sense now. Ray's part in the death made no sense, but he now understood why he was in such high demand.'

'Why did he kill him? Was it the money? Why kill him now?'

'It's always the money, Ray. You know that. He emptied the safe and walked out of Sal's house with the cash.'

'How much?'

'A lot. You see, there was no FBI. He never bought any freedom back then. It was just a story. There was nothing like that and Eddie found out. Sal had just had enough of the life and he came up with the idea to quit and keep the money. He walked. And nobody is allowed to walk.'

'How much did Eddie get?'

'Over 20 million is what I hear. My guess is about half of that total.'

There was silence. Ray was stuck in the middle of deaths and missing millions. He was lucky to be breathing.

'Why did everybody believe Sal at the time?'

'There was no reason to not believe him. That's what Eddie told me. He said: He's gone, nobody will believe him now.'

Ray jumped forward in his seat, spilling the icy water that had formed in the bottom of his last vodka. Eddie was still alive.

'When . . . when did Eddie tell you that?'

'Three nights ago. He called. He told me about his meeting with Sal and he said that he was losing. "I'm losing," that's what he said. He never said any more.'

'Where is he now? C'mon, Rube, you must know.'

Rube looked over Ray's shoulder and motioned with his eyes. He then looked at Ray.

'I've no idea. He's gone and so are you.'

A young black kid approached and stood next to Ray. He let his left fist drift down and Rube raised his right hand and they touched knuckles.

'He the man, Mr Rube?'

'Reginald, yep, he the man.'

Rube started to wheel himself round Ray's legs.

'Ray, we got your stuff from the room. Well, most of it. We got your passport and ticket from the safe and most of your clothes. We left the laptop and enough stuff to make Little Sal believe you will be back. Right now, those two will be sitting and waiting for you to return. So what I've done is ask my friend here, Reginald, to take you back to Philly. You can get an earlier plane. I think there's one at four tomorrow. You cool with this?'

Ray never spoke; he just followed Rube to the door and outside onto the street. Reginald was sitting behind the wheel of a grey Oldsmobile. The back door opened and Ray slid in. Rube handed him his ticket and his passport.

'Ray, take care and speak soon.'

The car pulled away. It was 2.06 a.m.

Ray never looked back.

LONDON: HOME WHERE IT ALL STARTED

Ray always liked getting home after an American trip. The novelty of Las Vegas had worn thin over the years. He knew there would be a lot of messages when he got to the flat. He was in a needy business, and whenever he left the men he worked with for more than a few days, they fell apart; the perfect life for most people in the boxing world involved somebody else fixing things. Fixing everything, to be honest. Boxing people and boxers are very good at being dependent on others.

One way Ray had found to avoid their constant calls and complaints and problems was to leave the mobile behind. He did this all the time. Sure, it drove people nuts, but it helped keep Ray sane. His refusal to use his mobile on a regular basis had caused him a lot of problems over the years, but there was simply no way he was going to start using it all the time. If he kept his mobile on him at all times, he would be on 24-hour idiot alert, available to rescue any of the cranks from scrapes and on call to wake up fighters at 6 a.m. for a run. There were enough trainers with the ability to set an alarm and kick a fighter out of his smelly bed before dawn. That was most definitely not part of Ray's life. If he had a mobile, he would not have a life. Simple as that. Promoters and decent managers had enough lackeys and staff to take endless calls from fighters and their people.

As expected, the answer machine on the landline was full. He had no idea how to retrieve a message on his mobile. Not a clue, and even less desire to discover how.

There was also a pile of letters: a small and not particularly friendly batch – a few bills and a couple of small cheques. Nothing big. There was not a lot of outstanding money. It was a tight and lean time and there was nothing unusual about that. It was always tough with a pound note.

It was not even 9 a.m. when he sat down with a coffee and started to go through the phone messages. He had only been gone four days in total but he knew, what with the fight coming up on Saturday at

Wembley, there would be a lot of problem calls from men in need of a soft and gentle word to keep them happy. They needed their hands held and their nappies changed in the days and hours before most fights.

He stretched out in the leather recliner and prepared himself for the onslaught of the crazies. He was ready. He touched the button. The machine started.

'Ray, Jimmy boy here. Listen, mush, this fucking Ukwaianian is a nutcase. He's eating us out of house and home. Gi's a call, mate.'

The message had been left on Friday, the day he had flown to Las Vegas. It was from Jim Simpson, a trainer, grifter and gofer at the Eagle in Canning Town. Calling the Ukrainian a 'nutcase'. Now that was rich coming from Jimmy. He found rooms for cheap fighters in bad boozers and bad fighters in cheap boozers. He sold them tape for their hands at the gym and then drove them around, acting as a pirate cab. He got a living, he meant well and he had carried the bucket in thousands of fights. The 'Ukwaianian' was a decent fighter, a light middle called Sergei Dizakov. Ray had a bit of him but not enough for the grief the kid and his adviser had been giving him since they arrived from Kiev a month earlier. Keeping fighters was difficult, keeping foreign fighters was an art. Ray would get hold of Jimbo later, calm him down and find out what he really wanted. The kid would have to go. Or the fighter and his manager would have to take a real fight at realistic money.

'You left for Vegas already? Speak to me when you get back. And do us all a favour – use your poxy mobile.'

It was Mickey Boyd. Ray would call him first. He had good news for him. If he caught Boydy in the right mood, late in the evening when he was nearly arseholed and he'd done a few bottles of wine, the money would invariably improve.

'Ray, Simon here from the desk. We're looking for a contact number for George Foreman. Can you call? It's Friday afternoon, 2.30. Thanks.'

Ray had never met Simon, but he had been speaking to Simons and Keiths and Davids and Matts for years. They lived and worked on sports desks. This particular Simon probably needed Big George's number so that one of the named writers could go and listen to 60 minutes of schlock. No doubt Big George had another grill out and was available to talk. Ray had stopped helping sports desks when chefs had started writing fight reports. They could find their own number for Big George. Fuck 'em. Ray had heard Big George's spiel too many times. It was pointless trying to be a friend to everybody on a sports desk. They had such short memories.

'Ray? I came to see you a few days ago. Well, about ten days ago, I suppose. Can you give me a call? Thanks. Oh, by the way, my name's Carol.'

That solved one mystery. He had her name now. Ray pulled over a pad and turned a few pages until he found her number. He would call her, but he had no idea what he would tell her. Her voice had an extra edge, a lot more authority; she certainly didn't sound desperate. No tears this time. Ray wondered, not for the first time, if he would take her out. Well, he actually wondered if he would get his leg over and how quickly. And, sadly, if he was really that bothered. It was getting to that stage with women. It was more aggro than it was worth. He came to the conclusion he wasn't bothered, but, still, he had to call her and let her know some of what he knew.

'Ray, Johnno ain't gonna be any good for next Saturday. He's had a row with his ol' woman and he's vanished. Call me when you're back. We could use the other doughnut, Closey. I'm only joking, boy.'

Fighters and their handlers were like kids. They were grown men, big strong boys, but hopeless most of the time. They could find their way out of fights they were losing, their eyes cut, the pain mounting and blood everywhere, but the same men would crumble and fall into 50 tiny pieces when faced with the smallest of domestic problems. They married lunatics and that never helped keep them happy. How was that ever going to work? There were exceptions, so people said. Ray heard that all the time, but he had hardly met any of them. Perhaps a couple. Certainly one: Richie Woodhall. He was sorted, sorted and rare.

Ray had been home just ten minutes and had listened to five messages. He had a hungry eastern European deep in the East End surrounded by men who he would never trust. It had to be solved; it would be solved. On the other side of London, he had a halfway decent fighter called John Delaney who couldn't keep his prick in his pants. Both fighters needed protection from their own stupidity.

Ray thought Delaney was probably close to beyond help. He was twenty-two, had three kids with two women and was about to marry for the first time. Curly Smith, who had made the call, had warned Ray from the start to leave the kid alone. Ray listen? Not a chance. Delaney was a nice kid and he could fight a bit.

Message six.

'Ray, you're gonna have . . .'

Shit. He cut it off before Jimmy from the Eagle hit full flow and moaned his way to a breakdown. Perhaps he would tell Jimmy to poison Sergei's food and give him the shits for a day or two. Ray had performed that little culinary treat enough times with fighters, especially good fighters. It was a simple way to get an edge in a fight where an edge was needed. Not that there were too many fights like that in the modern British business. Bad rice was always a winner because dog food or a wayward cat turd could backfire. It is not illegal, but it ruins the gut. The first problem with a bad poison job was the danger of the fighter getting the flavour for the mix and that had happened. The second problem was hospital and an accurate diagnosis. The doctor would tell everybody that the fighter had been poisoned and that was never good for business. Rice was safe: bad rice knocked them over. Mexicans and Kenyans both ate rice and eastern Europeans treated it like a delicacy.

'You are a pain in the arse, Jim,' Ray said to himself and then pushed the button for number seven.

'Listen, this kid that DeMarco's fighting ain't any good, is he? Only he's been on the phone, silly bollocks Simpson, telling me the kid looks brilliant. Get back to me, Ray. See you, boy.'

It was Roy Strong, a small-hall promoter but a good man. His one fighter was a black Swedish middle called Roberto DeMarco. He could move a bit, the kid, but he couldn't break an egg. Roy's day job was running a tricky little hotel in Hounslow that was full each night and nobody was on holiday. Nobody went to Hounslow for the sun or the food.

Ray knew what had happened: Jimmy Simpson had tried to offload the hungry Ukrainian on Strong. Simpson, silly bollocks of the Thames, was unaware that Ray had matched the Ukrainian with DeMarco. Simpson had no doubt said the kid was the second coming of Sugar Ray Leonard and Strong, being a ruthless man with an enormous gap of confidence in his boxing knowledge, had bitten. Bosh! Strong was convinced Ray was trying to have him over. Now Strong was in a tight spot: he clearly wanted a bit of the Ukraine, but he didn't much fancy his man DeMarco in with him. Ray would have to sort this out. It was impossible to leave this mob for more than a few days. Two days at most. Strong was a decent listener and would understand when Ray called him back. Simpson never listened and would never understand, but that never made him a bad person.

'Ray, Ray. It's Dave here from the Sunday desk. Can you give me a call? We've got a tip that Tyson's gonna fight in Japan on a K-1 show. Thanks, Ray.'

That would have been easy money, a simple 30 pars of nonsense on Tyson's return to Tokyo for a mixed martial-arts fight. Ray had written that little baby a dozen times in two years. Still, no problem, it would come again and when it did Ray would bring out and dust off Koichu Hamada of the Japanese Boxing Authority. Hamada was a legend with a nanny, a controversial official and old friend of Tyson and other miscreants. Hamada was also non-existent. Ray had a spokesperson like him in Mexico and South Africa, two in Las Vegas and another, recently deceased, in New York. The obit for the New York guy, who Ray had christened Al Dyett about ten years earlier, even included a quote from Angelo Dundee. 'Al was a friend to boxers,' said Dundee. Dyett had had a heart attack one day in a cab. The cab driver had thrown him out, believing he was faking it to avoid the $7 fare. It was an outrage. It was an invention, but it was a nice story. Al's widow contacted the mayor. Five national papers ran with a mention of the passing of a New York training legend. 'Yonkers Al is Dead' one headline read. Dead Al had a finger on many greats. He was, if Ray was not mistaken, the man who invented the three-rhythm speed-ball routine. All complete and utter cobblers. Writing about sport could be a bad way to get a good living. And just to add to the legend of Al Dyett, cutsman to the greats, his name had started to pop up in copy from a bunch of other writers. What a liberty!

'Ray. Hi, I came to see you. Eddie's daughter, Eddie Lights. I've lost my phone, so I know you can't call me. I'll call you back. I hope your trip to Las Vegas went well. I'd love to go there. Hope

you've got some good news. Thanks again and see you soon.'

She was persistent. Ray would have to wait for her next call, and it was not a call he was looking forward to.

'Hello, this is Klaus from Dominance Promotions. Ray, I need to know how it was at the CBA convention. Can you call me? Hans sends his regards. Thank you.'

That would have to be the second call on Ray's list. Hans Kurthoff, nice enough fella, and he had helped Ray once, helped him when he was truly desperate.

The CBA convention seemed like so long ago, but it was less than 48 hours since he had been on the boardwalk. It was less than 48 hours since he had walked away from a crazy situation and returned to the normal world. Well, his boxing world.

After leaving Rube behind in the bar, Ray had sat in silence all the way to Philadelphia. He had no desire to speak. At the time, he didn't even want to think. He just wanted to get out and get away from whatever it was that he had fallen into.

The Rube had made arrangements for Ray to spend the remainder of the night and all of the next day in the hotel in Philadelphia's centre city area. It was a dark-carpet dump with bad lights and terrible room service, but it was fine for what Ray needed. It was a safe hideaway. The room smelled of tobacco and in the towels and sheets lurked the scent of dirty bodies. Ray just stretched out on the bed with his clothes on and stared out the window at a wall that was no more than 15 feet away. It was going to be a slow wait.

It had been easy to change the flight and bring it forward a day. He just hoped the rules held and nobody at British Airways released his new departure date and time. He left the room only two hours before the flight was due to leave. When it was time to go, he took a service elevator and went out a back door. He had paid cash for the room when he had arrived just after 3.30 in the morning and, according to the book, he was not due to check out until the following day. The Rube had registered him as Bennie Briscoe, arguably the finest Philly fighter in recent years until Bernard Hopkins emerged from prison to become an all-time great.

Mr Briscoe had checked in smoothly and stayed out of sight all day, which meant he would not be missed or remembered by any of the staff or guests. The 'Do Not Disturb' sign went on the door and stayed on the door. He certainly wouldn't miss the extra 300 notes that he'd had to leave as a guarantee. Using a card was never an option.

He was going home, leaving behind the mayhem that his few innocent questions had started. Nobody in Philly had seen him and in Atlantic City his vacant room had been cleared and his card charged. He had gone. The Rube had done a good job. He always did a good job and it was easy with help to vanish quickly.

But Ray was no closer to being able to help the woman, Eddie's daughter. Carol, as he now knew her. He had taken on her request that first morning believing it would be an easy touch. Now he knew Eddie was a hit man and that a little geezer in a leather coat was looking to shoot him – and probably Ray as well, if he had a spare bullet. Nice work, Ray thought.

It had been 17 days ago that she had arrived in tears with the papers, a lost little daddy's girl. She had mentioned ten days during the call, but Ray had checked and it was seventeen days. Perhaps he should have called her before leaving for Vegas and AC to let her know that he was off. He had told her at the time that he was going, but it was emotional and perhaps she had forgotten. He had legitimate business, fights to make. It had sounded like he was doing well and she had listened. He should have called before leaving.

Ray went into the kitchen and poured a fresh coffee and then went back to the messages. This time he headed for his chair. He pressed the 'Gentle' button. The silent motor started and he eased the chair back into a graceful recline. He reached forward and hit 'Play' again.

'Ray, I've got this kid. He's . . .'

No more cranks. The caller was Tony Southwick and he was in a blind hurry to become a boxing promoter. He was a decent businessman; he ran a plumbing firm, he had run a pub and he could move tickets. Southwick was entertaining in small ways and in even smaller doses. He was clueless but keen and each week he truly believed that he had found the next Naz, the next Lewis. Ray had been to see a lot of them and they were fine, decent amateurs but certainly not worth getting too excited over.

There were very few boxers in Britain who reached 16 without Ray having watched them at some point. It had happened, but it had been a long, long time ago. During the last 15 or so years, not one prospect had slipped under Ray's radar. Sadly, there was no way to guarantee that a brilliant 16 or 17 year old would be able to hold it together and progress to the paid ranks. There was a chance a kid of 16 would become a bum of 17. The kid would find the wrong friends. And if he didn't find them, they would find him. It was hard for a kid from a rough-arsed estate to stay clean for too many years. Temptation and violation tore away at a boy out on the street. The list of failures was long: stunning fighters who were blowing bubbles by the age of 21. Even more disturbing were the funerals. Ray had seen three kids, dead as men, placed in the earth and all were shy of their 30th birthdays. Three funerals in just over two years. The trio of fighters had won a total of ten national finals. They were kids when Ray had first met them and their baby faces had barely changed by the time their mothers broke down and cried in the damp funeral dirt. That's a scream you never want to hear.

'You don't know who this is, do you?'

Ray cut it off. It was Gary Mason, one-time British heavyweight champion and currently driving a cab. Or working in a hospital, wearing a jumper with a badge. Mason had a white Jamaican rapper. The singer was different and two of the tracks on his debut album had something. But what could Ray do? Nothing, to tell the truth. Mason had been calling for a month or so and Ray had been avoiding him for a month or so. Ray would have to give him a name to contact. Find him a name. It could be easy to set up a deal. The guy could sing and Mason was always good value. He could fight. He had been an extremely underestimated fighter. His brawl with Lennox Lewis at Wembley was a great fight until poor Gary's face started to swell. Mason's manager, Mickey Duff, did his dough that night. The old man thought Mason would win and went on big with several people. Duff obviously denied going on big.

'When you back? How my fighters doing?'

Boyd again and it sounded like a late night. He was pissed and had clearly slipped out for a night, away from his fourth wife. Ray moved on. He knew nights like that were good nights to find wife number five.

145

'Ray, this is happening all the time with Johnno. Does he want to fight or not? Call me, 'cos I'm getting fucking annoyed with this. And before you try, forget Closey. He's finished with us.'

Ray had been expecting the call. He knew that Boyd's matchmaker, Eric Puddle, would be on his case. He would make the call to Puddle and he put it at number three. It would take a second or two to iron out the problem. What did it matter anyway? It was an eight-round fight with nothing at stake, and there was certainly not enough money involved to get uptight over. If John Delaney couldn't fight Paul King, then Ray would suggest another name. King was unbeaten in about 12 and he could fight a bit. Ray knew about Kingy because he had delivered him to Boydy. He was a small light heavyweight and a big kid, with a mum that was a pain now and would be an even bigger pain in the future.

Mums, and not dads, had become the pests in the gyms. Single-parent syndrome had hit boxing and the mums were playing it hard and bad for their little boys. The mums of sons who could fight a bit were doing their best to ruin their careers. Dads were much easier to just fuck off and ignore but talking to a mum required a bit of skill. The best talkers in boxing were great liars, but they weren't necessarily diplomatic. Mums had to be handled with a bit of care because their little boys tended to react angrily if mummy arrived home in tears, having heard the facts of life from somebody at the gym. Ray liked to deal with mums himself and not leave potentially tricky chats to the trainers and matchmakers. There were a lot of old-fashioned men in boxing and talking to a mum about her little Johnny was never easy.

Kingy could fight the hungry Ukrainian, a small middleweight, but who on account of all his eating would be a lot bigger now. He was four and two officially, but Ray knew he had fought under another name a few times and gone unbeaten. His record was more like nine wins with two defeats, and both of those were wrong. Ray also knew that he was closer to 32 than the 24 he claimed. Perhaps he could get him beat and then offload him. Ray had never warmed to his adviser, a former vet from Switzerland called Hugo. Never liked him. What was a vet doing in the boxing business in the first place? And a Swiss vet? It made no sense, as Mantle always said whenever something new in planet boxing rocked his socks. Most of the last 20 years were new to Mantle, God bless him, but he could find truth and sense on the odd occasion. The odd sober occasion.

Ray had not yet bought into the idea that the former Soviet bloc countries were going to dominate boxing. The fighters lacked appeal and looked awful. The Berlin Wall had been down a long time, but outside of Germany nobody was desperate for an eastern European boxer. Some nicked a living as punchbags in British rings, but they were in decline. The boxing revolution had not yet taken place and even in Germany the fad was dying. The Klitschko brothers and Dariusz Michalczewski had enjoyed a good run, but now the German fans wanted German fighters. That was understandable. Also, the boxing regimes in the former Soviet republics were falling apart. If the boxing systems faded, then there would be a dramatic drop in world-class amateurs turning pro from the Eastern bloc. If the quality of the coaching and the support dropped off, then the Russians and Ukrainians would be about as dominant as Spanish and French fighters. They would be useless for decades, with a fighter every 20 years or so to keep the business going.

'Ray . . .'

Jimmy Simpson again. He could live on a mobile.

'Raymond, give me a call when you're back. I might need that brief again and pronto. See you, boy.'

It was little Billy Eden. He was a nice fella, a trainer of average fighters and a solid individual. Sadly, he was a hopeless human anywhere near a bird. He was constantly falling in and out of love and always with needy, desperate young mums. Billy lived in Hackney and there was no shortage of potential love jobs for him.

Now, Billy's real problem was not his old fella getting loose, but his reaction whenever he met a girl whose previous husband or boyfriend had treated her badly. Some of his women, it had to be said, rolled into Billy's life with two kids, a plastic bag of possessions and a battered face. Billy loved the whole package and that takes more than a little bit of bottle and heart. The new relationship would float along for a bit. The kids would start to look healthy again away from the chip-and-burger diet and that would satisfy the social services. The swelling and bruising on the little strumpet's face would go down and the sex would be fantastic. And then one night the dad of the kids would arrive. It always fucking happened just when things were going so well. Billy would calmly try and explain to the dad or boyfriend why he was not getting the girl and kids back. He would explain that the dad, boyfriend or husband was not going to get any money from the girl. Both of these reasonable arguments would be rejected. According to Billy, they always were. Billy, having fully exhausted the polite methods of persuasion, would go back inside the flat and tell the girl that he had to take care of some business. She would invariably be tucked up behind the sofa, sobbing and clutching her kids and the same plastic bag of shit that she had arrived with. She had invariably been through the same drama a few times. Billy had told Ray once that the kids would often not even cry during the aggro. 'The mums are only kids, most of 'em,' he'd said. 'Kids with kids. And – fucking wait for it – I then have some complete cunt at my door telling me that I owe him 500 quid. Yeah, that's about right.'

Billy had told the story a few times and Ray had listened. It was essentially the same tale. So, having left the fella at the door, Billy would calm down his new girlfriend and then walk back out, whack the geezer and drag him to a car. He wouldn't have to say a word. If the dad had arrived with a few other fellas, he would jump all over them. However, most back-up boys realised quickly that it was sensible to walk away when Billy walked out the door. He often had something in his hand.

Once Billy had the dad in the car, he would drive somewhere nice and remote. Then it got tricky. Ray had put him in contact with a good criminal brief a few times. It had been nasty more than once. Little Billy had a problem when he was pissed off. He had some anger issues. Ray would get hold of him and pass the number on again.

'*You there, boy?*'

Curly again.

'*Ray, Rebecca here from the Bannister show. Can you call me when you get this message?*'

What day was it? Wednesday. He was due on Bannister's late show on BBC Five Live at ten that night. It was three hours of topical discussion and the pay was piss-poor, but it was a good show to do. Becky was just giving him an early heads-up. He would make that call number four and organise a car for his pick-up.

'Ray, it's Philip at the business centre. I realise that you are probably away somewhere, but it's that time of the month again. I need to talk to you about transferring some money across and right now there's not a lot to play with.'

It was another call Ray had been expecting. Philip was his business manager at Lloyds and 'that time of the month' meant that Ray had to find the mortgage payment. It happened every month. This call would have to be placed at number two behind the first call to Boydy. It was a nuisance.

'Hello, Ray, it's Carol. Can you please call me?'

She had obviously found her phone. He would call her, get her at number three.

Final message. Twenty gone and all predictable, if a little complicated at times. There was just one left.

'They really call you Raymondo?'

Ray had been dreading hearing this voice.

'Hey, you're there, right, R-A-Y-M-O-N-D-O? OK, that was cute on the shore. But now we gotta talk. So call me. I'm at the Dorchester. I guess you know my name, right? Call me. It's Tuesday morning.'

Ray knew that Sal would find him. But was the big lump with him? How had he managed to get here so quickly, Ray wondered?

He had expected the call, but he had not expected Sal to be in town and breathing down his neck quite so fast. It was not even lunchtime. He must have left New York at about the same time Ray had jumped on the plane. He was very good and Ray knew it was just a matter of time before Sal got to him again. He wondered if there would be a knock at the door at any moment.

The phone went. Ray's head turned quickly and he looked at it. It rang again. And again. Ray picked it up.

'At last! Fresh from the seriously missing list.'

It was Boyd.

'All right, Mick. Sorry I never got hold of you. It was busy, very busy.'

'Busy? Busy? That ain't what I heard. I've had a dozen people on the line telling me tales. Running from gangsters, brasses, dead bodies, millions of dollars, dirty birds, lunatics, sleazebags and fucking hit men. It's better than crime fiction. What's going on?'

Ray told him a few things. He knew Boyd would have picked up something from Stacey, possibly Jay or Santander.

'So, where is he?' said Boyd, when Ray had finished.

'He's at the Dorchester.'

'What? Eddie's at the Dorchester?'

'No, the crank. Little Sal is there.'

'I know that, I've just left him. Lovely fella, Salvatore. His old man was a miserable old bastard, but Sal's a lovely fella.'

Ray had no idea if Boyd knew about the little crew that Big Sal and Eddie and the others had put together. Ray had to assume that Boyd knew something. He knew enough to bring up Sal's name with Eddie's. What else did he know? It was no great surprise that Little Sal had shown up and Boyd knew him. It was probably more a case of somebody knowing Sal and knowing Boyd and putting the two of them together. He could be wrong. It wouldn't be the first time a boxing promoter knew a bunch of gangsters and it certainly wouldn't be the last. It's easy to know people.

In fact, there was far less criminal activity in boxing than people liked to imagine. In many ways, it was convenient for boxing and crime to be lumped together by so many people. It was wrong, but an understandable mistake. The sport had an image problem going back 50 years or more, but not an organised crime problem. Even the top boys from the terraces behaved when they went to the fights. There was simply not enough money in the sport for modern criminals. Having fighters like those Ray had on his books, even the good ones, would not be enough to keep a man in fine clothes, coke and cars for a month. Sure, the faces came out for fights, and a lot of the faces were young and mean-looking – and they were getting younger and meaner – but their money had nothing to do with boxing. They just liked the sport. It was an association, certainly not an allegiance. The modern-day faces at ringside paid for their tickets.

Boydy had him on the spot and there was nothing Ray could think to say.

'Ray, eight tonight at Daphne's. That good?'

It was. Ray knew he would not be dining alone with Boyd.

'Mick, about the fighters.'

'Oh, fuck the fighters. See you tonight. And if that little prick

Eddie calls, find out where he is and tell him not to move and call me. See you later.'

First, Ray started with the calls. Looking at his list, there were important ones, but he decided to take the easy option instead. He knew he always handled the simple returns first. The fighting talk was simple. Forget the bank. And the bird. Opening the door and letting her in had been a mistake. This was no longer any fun, but he still cared whether Eddie was dead or not. So now he was involved.

Eddie was a good guy – a pain if he had too much to drink, and certainly a proper crank when he was on the gear a few years back. Like so few others, Eddie had recognised that the coke was not good for him and had walked away, left it on the glass. Ray simply could not accept that Eddie Lights had been killed. He was still struggling with Rube's assertion that he was a button man. He was a soppy old sod, silly as a sack most of the time, but not a killer. He just liked the life, with his pomade-drenched barnet, raging pinkie rings, triple handshakes and gleaming teeth. He was a sleek machine on the Vegas catwalk. Not a killer, Shirley.

LONDON: THE DAY JOB

Ray picked up the phone and started to work his way through the problems. He avoided the nasty ones, the calls he had to make. He called Simpson first. He was right – Jimbo had told Roy Strong about the Ukrainian and that, in turn, had created another problem for Ray. If only they could just relax for two minutes.

'I had to tell him. The fucking kid's giving me the creeps,' Simpson said.

Ray put Simpson away for a minute and called Roy. It took a bit of explaining, but Ray managed to calm him down and then he had him open to a suggestion.

'Roy, every fighter is a genius in the gym if the man telling the story wants something. You should know that. If the fella talking has nothing at stake, then the fighter is a bum. You know that, don't you?' It was a simple boxing maxim.

Thankfully, Roy knew it. Now, Ray had him. Perfect. He no longer thought he was being tricked. Believe it or not, there is a lot of trust in boxing and a lot of lies. Trust – not necessarily the truth – is strangely important.

Ray had once had a magical conversation with Mantle. They had been talking about a manager, a crooked manager.

'So what, you trust a man who is lying to you?' Ray had asked.

'Yeah, if you know he's being honest,' Solly had replied.

Ray knew exactly what he meant.

They agreed not to let Sergei fight Roy's black Swede and that certainly left Roy Strong a happy kiddie. They agreed another deal, an easier fight for Strong's man and a painless bit of business for Ray. He had to call Curly to ask about a kid called Derrick Maple. He was another pain, another lost cause that Ray had handed to Curly. For some unknown reason, he was in the gym and that was quite rare, Ray and Curly knew. If Maple was in the ring, it meant that trouble was on its way to the gym. Ray called Roy back and confirmed Derrick for Sweden the Black. It worked well and Ray nicked an extra 350 quid. That was cool.

Next up on the roster of fruitcakes was Eric Puddle. It was never easy calling Puddle, but that had more to do with his age than anything else. Basically, Eric considered everybody to be a mug loser and a know-nothing waste of space. Everybody. Ray offered Eric the services of Sergei instead of John Delaney. That went well for about a second.

'He's fucking enormous. I saw him at the Eagle on Sunday.'

'Eric, he's got big bones.'

'Big bones, my arse. He's a middleweight.'

'Eric, Kingy's a light-heavyweight. He's about a stone heavier.'

'Don't matter. Your kid's too big.'

It made no sense and total boxing sense. Ray had him. If Eric Puddle wanted to refuse a match, he always put an alternative forward and what he wanted here was a concession of some kind. Ray was ready. Puddle's fighter was nearly 13 stone and Ray's boy was under 12, but it was more than just the weight.

'Eric, listen. This is what I'm gonna do. I'm gonna to get him down to 11 stone 5. That OK?' Ray knew it would be good.

'That could work. Kingy can weigh in the night before, but I want that Ruskie on the scales on the day. Tell the board he can't get to the Friday weigh-in. Tell them his old mum in Moscow ain't well. Keep him off the scales the night before and we can make this work.'

It was one of the usual little moves and it made perfect business and cash sense. Ray knew that Kingy had sold a few tickets and nobody wanted a ticket-seller beaten. He would have to accept Puddle's offer, but it was not ideal. The British Boxing Board of Control had introduced weigh-ins for fighters the day before a contest back in the '90s, just after Brian Rock's death fight. The theory was sound, the practice deeply flawed. It allowed a boxer extra time to recover after losing weight and that was not a good development. It naturally led to boxers losing too much weight and foolishly believing that 24 hours was enough time to properly suck down enough liquid. It was not enough time. Many fighters often gained a stone or more before getting back in the ring. They were too often dehydrated and sluggish. They put their health at risk each time they dropped weight at the expense of liquid.

Ray would let Sergei come in at about 12 stone and then blame the scales, have a row with Puddle and then agree to take a cut in pay. Puddle would expect nothing less; that is why Kingy would end up being about 13 stone on the night. It's just a game. Sergei would be well over 12 stone and he knew enough to not get hurt against Kingy. If the fight was dropped to six rounds, there was no way Sergei could win. Kingy started too fast and Sergei started too slow.

After the boxing calls, it was time for the serious stuff. Ray reluctantly called the bank. The bank was not easy; the bank was never easy. However, he managed to persuade them to let him slide until Monday. At 10.30, he would need to be in the bank, telling them how much was due. Ray knew he would be picking up a grand or so on Saturday night for Sergei and a couple more for his work at the convention. The money would be enough to do the trick on Monday morning. He knew there were credit cards screaming to be paid and that would be the next problem. The flat was lovely, but the mortgage game was crippling him. Finding nearly three grand by the 15th of each and every month was knocking him all over the place.

He had to call and cancel the Bannister show and that went down like a lead balloon. It was, as Becky told him, the third time that he had pulled out in the last two months. There was nothing he could do, no way he could tell her the truth. They would call again, but he would probably be blacklisted for a few months.

With the bank off his back and the Bannister show tits up for a bit, it was time to try and nick a few quid. The old journo instincts kicked in and he talked to a few papers about Saturday's fight and, thankfully, picked up some orders. To be honest, John Hunter, who was the CBA's longest-reigning champion, was no longer doing good business for Ray with the papers. The orders were short and even with three pieces lined up there was no way they would make much of an impression on Monday morning when the bank opened. It had been a long time since newspapers mattered at the bank.

Hunter was due a real fight, like too many British boxers, and that is what Ray had hopefully helped set in place during his brief visit to Atlantic City. The Gerd Seldorf fight would be an easier sell to the papers – well, slightly easier – because it carried the increasingly tarnished recommendation that it was a mandatory defence. The problem was that European fighters are not sexy with papers. There were four heavyweight champions from former Soviet republics and they were being touted all over the place. It was a grim task by the devoted to try and sell modern heavyweight words. The public was not really interested in Ivan from the Steppes. Sports editors like noisy Yanks with a bit of previous or a Mexican who had turned pro at fourteen after six years of shining shoes in a slum. Gerd was studying to be an architect and it wasn't fanny, it was the truth – unlike the dozens of tabloid lines about British kids supposedly quitting university to fight.

Ray was putting off calling Carol.

It was gone four when he returned to the chair and dialled the number she had left. It rang once before the line came alive. He had only been going to let it ring twice. She had beaten him to quitting.

'Hello.'

It was her voice, the accent mostly Mancunian with just a bit of extra nose in there somewhere. She was somewhere very loud. He took a breath.

'Carol.'

'Yeah, who is it?'

'It's Ray. Ray Lester.'

'Sorry, Ray. Didn't get your voice at the start there, love. Sorry about that. Any news on me dad?'

He didn't have a plan. What a fool.

'Not really, darling. I, erm . . . well, it's hard to say really.'

'You never saw him, did you? Did anybody know where he was? Has anybody seen him?'

Ray didn't move his lips. Should he tell her what he knew and what he suspected, or should he let her wait a bit longer? He knew that Eddie Lights, her dad, could be dead. He also knew that Eddie would be dead the moment the people who were looking for him found him. How do you tell a scared little girl that her dad is about to get whacked for nicking $10 million or even $20 million? *That ain't easy, my brother, not by a long shot*. It's not something you can tell a stranger, so Ray kept his mouth shut. There was also no way he could share with her his gut feeling that her dad was still alive. If she had to hear it from his lips, she would end up in a garden of hope and there was no way he could rescue her if dad arrived dead.

'No, no news, but I'm still asking around and I'm sure there's a perfectly reasonable explanation for it all. Trust me.'

There it was again, that old trick: a stinking lie when the truth would have worked a treat. Brainless.

'Thanks, you're a love.'

'Where are you now? Blackpool?'

'No, I'm shopping near Oxford Circus at the moment. I'm staying at the Ibis, like you suggested when I came to see you. It's all right. It's clean and right by the station.'

He had forgotten that recommendation. It made a lot of sense to stay at the cheap French hotel.

'Would you like to get a drink tonight?' she said.

It caught him off guard. She was a good-looking woman, but surely her mind would be stuck on her dad. She had been in a bad way when she had arrived at his flat, but she sounded a lot different now, far more in control. Perhaps there would be a bonus for all the grief and aggro she had caused him. And if Eddie showed up dead in the future, he would have a clear conscience.

'I'm meeting a few people at eight. I might be done by about ten. Shall I call?'

'No, no need. Just come by and call the room. I'm in room 210. OK?'

'Yeah, fine. See you later.'

That was that, then. Boyd and little psycho Sal at eight, then Carol the Northern hornpot at ten. What a pleasant way to spend a Tuesday night. He hoped Boydy would help him remain clear of any blame for the missing millions. If that happened, he was sure he would be able to persuade Carol to let her dad vanish for another 20-odd years. Bang, I'm back to normal by midnight, Ray thought. Little Sal on board, a darling little shake-up with Miss Blackpool and then just a few cranks to control before Saturday's fight and the end of a busy ten days.

Ray knew it would not be that simple – it never was that simple when the problem appeared slight. This was a totally different situation. One man was dead and millions of dollars were missing. Plus his new laptop was ruined and he had left behind quite a few clothes in a hotel room in Atlantic City, including his favourite Tommy Bahama kosher Hawaiian shirt with the coconut husk buttons. The buttons had cost him $35. He had ordered them from a dealer in Honolulu. They had, according to their certificate of authenticity, been cut from a classic Duke Kahanamoku Aloha shirt. Ray had two original Dukes in his wardrobe. Now that particular Bahama beauty was gone because of Eddie Lights. Losing a shirt of that quality is never easy.

The phone went. It rang twice. Ray closed his eyes and dropped his head back. The flight was starting to get to him. It rang again, but the noise was fading. The caller would be one of the usual suspects from the boxing world with a problem that a gnat could solve. Jimbo with a moan; Roy with a plan; Tony Dreamland with an offer. Or it would be another loser from the sorry list of men Ray often made his money with. Some paid him and others he made money from in different ways. It rang again and again. Ray heard it ringing several more times, but at no point did he feel like picking it up. He was off for a few hours. The journey had taken its toll – as had the two days on the run for something he had not done.

The phone was ringing again when he opened his eyes. It was dark outside and cold inside. He looked over at the digital clock under the television. He had 30 minutes to get to Daphne's. The flat was central so that was easy; it was also why he owed so much bloody money each month. He ignored the phone and started to get ready. Something dark, simple and sombre would fit the bill for an evening with the dwarf hit man.

LONDON, AT NIGHT: FINE FOOD WITH A TINY NUTTER

Mickey Boyd and little Salvatore Leo were sitting opposite each other at one of the best tables. There was a wall on three sides of them and a lot of space on the exposed side. Two waiters hovered like cloth sentinels not six feet from the edge of their hands. Sal was facing the rest of the restaurant and started to stand before Ray had closed the front door. When he stood, there was not a lot of difference in his height.

By the time Ray reached the table, they were both standing and Sal had come round the table. He was six inches shorter than Boyd and that made him about five foot five in old money. He was slight in every way and wore the same black leather number that he'd had on in Las Vegas. The bolero look was seriously dated. His shoes looked like Action Man's dancing slippers and his sparkling diamond pinkie ring rounded off a tiny but grotesque caricature. There was no doubting the little fella was an unpleasant and nasty man.

'You're causing me a lot of trouble. You've become a big pain in my ass.' It was Sal's greeting. He was as unpleasant as Ray remembered.

The voice didn't go with the shoes or the ring or the manicured nails. It belonged to a New Jersey scumbag, a fat one with a filthy car, not this little gleaming rat in his tiny coat and toy shoes. Ray knew he wasn't in for a fun night. No handshakes, no small talk, just nods that were so obviously orders.

Sal was first to sit back down. Even Boydy looked lost for words, as he coughed and fumbled for a line. Boyd hadn't even looked Ray in the face.

Little Sal was cold on the eye. He had a silent mush, his hair was still his, but he had lost his smile. The waiter came over to the still and silent sea of their table and asked what Ray wanted to drink. Ray looked towards the ice bucket and knew it would be a good wine, so he stuck with that. Little Sal was fiddling with a butter knife, looking over the waiter's head. Ray knew Sal would speak as soon as the waiter left. He also knew it was the little man's night. And it was painfully obvious that Boydy had undergone a sense-of-humour bypass. He looked like he had dreadful wind and was stuck in a lift with a good sort. It was plain to see that far from being a curious observer with a role in the proceedings, Boydy was there under sufferance and that was not good. He had been made an emissary for the night, and in the promoter's unusual silence Ray realised this was far more serious than he could ever have imagined. For the third time in his life, Ray thought he could be killed. He'd been lucky the first and second times, and the recent scrapes in Las Vegas and AC had been as frightening. In Las Vegas, he had been out of control and had had no control. It was all too fast.

The waiter left. Ray sipped at his wine. It was good, dry and crisp, which was fine, as the fear had frozen his throat. He greedily necked the Meursault for all he was worth, but wine is a deceptive lubricant and its chill hit him hard between the ears.

'You know, I still don't know what you know, but I know that your fucking name keeps coming up. I go to Vegas and everybody tells me about you. I go to Atlantic City and you're everywhere.'

Sal picked up his water glass and took the tiniest of mouthfuls. It fitted perfectly with his features.

'I don't know what to do. I keep thinking, people tell me you're a good guy, a guy that a man can trust, then you fuck off and pull that little stunt on the shore. I know the crippled black motherfucker helped. And I'm thinking, why do people keep telling me you're a good guy? I ever do anything to you? I ever cause you a problem?'

Ray knew that mentioning the laptop would be unwise. He managed to shake his head, but it was hard. It was not a night for a comic to make a stand.

Sal suddenly jerked forward in his chair and plunged the butter knife into the table. It went through the pale pink tablecloth and stuck. Sal's little face was red, his eyes as black and still as Ray had ever seen on a human. They looked like they belonged to a dead eel. A tiny, deceased eel with a diamond pinkie ring.

'Sal, Sal, Sal.' It was Boyd. He reached out his right hand to put it on Sal's shoulder. Not too hard, Ray noticed; it was more like a reiki hover than a sumo slap. It was a sign at last that Boydy could talk. However, he looked ashen and wouldn't touch the tiny man.

'I've called this meeting to clear the air. I've known Ray for nearly 20 years. Longer maybe. And Sal, you know how I felt about the old man. Let's hear what Ray has to say. Let's calm down, have a drink and get to the bottom of this shit. We need to act reasonably. Sal, please, this is not Vegas, it's London, and we all need to calm down.'

Sal sat back and glared at Boyd before pulling the knife out and tossing it back onto the table.

'Start talking, arsehole.'

Sal's voice and Ray's cue.

Ray went through the story from the start. Boydy remembered the bird at the fight and that helped. Ray took them through the trip to Las Vegas. It was mostly correct in detail – he missed out a few names, but the story ran true. They ate and drank and Ray talked. It was well gone nine before Ray landed in Atlantic City. It was impossible to know if he was telling Sal the things he wanted to hear.

Sal never said a word. He nodded his head and once or twice he nearly smiled. Boydy kept ordering the wine. Ray could tell that he was not happy. He knew the feeling. Both of them were running against the corks and bombing the wine.

The Atlantic City story meant that Ray would have to drop Rube in the middle of the shit, but Sal had mentioned Rube before stabbing the table, so Ray figured it was safe. It was a betrayal, but he couldn't see another option. Rube would understand, Ray knew that. Ray started to plead for Rube's innocence. Sal stopped him.

'That little fuck in the wheelchair has nothing to do with this. I figured he helped move you. Other than that, he's not involved. I know that for a fact. He helped you, but he wouldn't help that other prick. That is fact.'

Another testament to the Rube's mystery: it seemed he could mess with anybody and wheel away without a scratch.

Ray continued with the Atlantic City end of the tale, but there was not much left to tell. It was gone ten by the time he came to the call from Carol, the daughter. Sal held out his hands. Ray took another gulp at his wine. He had done some damage to the grape, but Boydy looked worse. His face had a flushed, cartoon quality to it.

'Where is she?'

Fuck, this was it. Two hours of telling a story and this was what it was all about. Boydy never said a word. He didn't even let his eyes flicker on the table. He just sat back, leaving his manicured fingers on the edge of the tablecloth like an expectant pianist. This was it. Boydy was starting to tap. Gently, his fingers worked the cloth. Perhaps it was Morse code. Was he trying to help Ray? No, he was just anxious.

'I'm seeing her in the morning.'

A lie, but not bad. Not bad.

Sal stopped fiddling with the butter knife; it looked like a chopper in his dainty hands.

'She coming to you, you going to her? What?'

Ray closed his eyes. He had to tell. She was innocent and so was he. The three of them could get together and sort it out. It was the only way, the only way that made sense. The wine was making more sense and even before Ray had opened his mouth he knew it. Perhaps little legs would see that they were innocent the moment he spent any time with her. She would clear Ray and that would and should be it. What if the lump was outside? Her dad was the problem, not the daughter, and certainly not Ray. *If Eddie hadn't decided to pick up the gun again and walk away from an old friend with his millions, then this little scenario would never have developed. Eddie was the guilty one. Both Sal and Carol had lost a parent and that had to count for something.* Ray was down a laptop and a Hawaiian shirt.

'No, I'm going to meet her at her hotel at ten. Why don't you come with me and we can sort this out? She's not done anything wrong, she's like me.'

Great. Was he fucking mad? Ray tried to shake about a dozen fat glasses of wine from his brain, but it was obviously far too late. Even Boydy's jaw opened slightly.

'Stop, you're breaking my fucking heart. That's good, I'll go with you. We can all talk. What hotel?'

Ray pulled out a slip of paper – a folded sheet from a notepad he always had with him – and then a pen. He wrote down the Ibis address and handed it to Sal.

'What number?'

'210.'

Ray closed his eyes. Had he just signed a death warrant for a woman he didn't even know? *I've killed her.* It was a done deal in his head. He had given out the details before he had even thought about it. What a moron! What a drunk moron!

Sal reached across the table and picked up Ray's pen. He wrote down the number of Carol's room on the paper. Suddenly, he had a smile on his face. He was a nasty, cold little bastard.

'I'll see you there at ten, right?'

Sal was a happy man now.

Ray could barely nod. It was 11 and he was drained, totally wrecked. Boydy got the bill and they stood to leave. No backslapping or hugs, no laughs, just three silent men walking through a hushed restaurant. Diners had noticed. The men looked exactly like what they were. One or two in the restaurant would have known what they were looking at.

Boydy and Sal slid into the Bentley, which the driver made appear like magic at the restaurant door the moment they stepped outside. The night was over and they were gone. Boydy couldn't even look him in the eye at the close. The New Jersey arsehole never said goodbye. Boyd had been totally useless all night.

It was easy to get a cab in that part of London at that time of night, but not so easy to decide where to go.

Ray sat back in the cab. The night had happened in a slow instant.

'Where to, mate?'

Ray thought about Tragic's, but this was exactly the type of night that he had to avoid rattling his knuckles on Tragic's door. Showing up at the door would be dumb. He might well need some help to get through the night and he didn't want to end up getting hold of something. It felt good to realise that even with the death of an innocent woman hanging over him, he wasn't looking at spreading a gram of cheap and badly cut crap on a flat surface. That was something from dark nights in his head. And something was all that it was. No, he would never be a desperate late arrival at Tragic's door again.

'Hold on a second, son.'

Ray jumped out of the taxi and went back inside Daphne's.

It was 11.21 when the barman placed the house phone on the bar's stone surface. He dialled Carol's number. Three rings, four rings, and then it went to message machine. An automatic voice, not a real human.

'Carol, it's Ray. Look, I'm sorry about tonight, sorry about not coming by. I've got a friend who wants to meet you and I think he's got some info about your dad. I'm gonna come and see you at ten in the morning at the hotel. Call me back if that's no good, OK? I'm sorry. Take care.'

Ray thanked the barman and walked outside. The cab had gone, but that suited Ray because he needed a walk, he needed to clear his head. He could work on his conscience another time.

It was a pleasant stroll ruined. Ray had always liked wandering late at night in London. Regent's Park was his favourite – a dream at two in the morning – and if there was ice and snow on the floor he walked across the lakes. There was no snow and ice, but he would make the most of the walk. He went by South Kensington Tube, past the V&A to the edge of Hyde Park. He turned left, went along to Kensington High Street and narrowly avoided a final drink in Terry's old gaff. He had the option of walking the other way and finding Christian at the Wellington Club – it was an easy place to relax – but he decided against a last drink. Then he went past the place the nutty dentist had before Aids took him. He carried on, sobering up and clearing his head all the way to Notting Hill. Nothing really made sense. No change there – it was a theme with Eddie Lights.

He had stumbled with a smile into another person's nightmare chase. Men were dead, more were due to die. Hit men were popping up all over the place. People he had known for years were not the people he had known and he was in the middle of it all because a woman he had never met before had cried on his chest. Somewhere, somebody had over ten million in cash. Ray was also on a list of targets and less than an hour earlier had set the ultimate diddy killer on a girl whose heart was breaking.

The Rube's version was too much to take. Eddie a killer? But Ray knew it must be the truth. The Rube only dealt in the truth. The harsh and direct truth. But how had it happened? How had the man who crooned in the morning in a quiet bar in a faded Las Vegas hotel become the man Rube said he was? Eddie was pals with Savoire and Rumping Bear, not a fucking hit man. It was too much to take in. Too much to consider.

Ray kept going over what he knew, even if it made absolutely no sense. From the moment his bell had sounded that Sunday morning until the moment an hour or so earlier when Sal the skinny midget had slipped onto the cream leather seat in the back of Boyd's lilac Bentley, his life had come under siege. He had not yet made a penny from the search for Eddie Lights and it had cost him a good few quid and a lot of time. He'd also had to run like a crack dealer through a parking lot in a forgotten part of Las Vegas, then creep through tenement halls in a seedy hotel in Philadelphia where he was holed up like a fugitive. Ray was smiling. It was fucking insane.

It was nearly one in the morning when he stopped and looked up at his flat. He had a small, two-bedroom flat, but it was quality inside. It was a good street and good streets surrounded it. A lot of homes in Notting Hill had a pink Aga and a view of a council estate. That was a contrast in anybody's book. But not Ray's place. He could do without ever seeing a council estate again.

He felt fine now, sober, and with a few hours' kip, perhaps an early steam, he would be ready for the meet. It was not over yet.

He pulled out his key and stepped to the door.

'Raymondo.'

He knew the voice. Ray knew he wasn't dead.

'Raymondo. Well, say hello, then.'

Ray was right.

'Hey, you still got my $100 chip?'

Eddie Lights, the fucker. Ray hated comebacks.

LONDON, RAY'S FLAT: OLD FRIENDS, SAME PROBLEMS

The vodka was nearly gone. Eddie was draining it neat and smooth. Even under the dim light from the table lamp, Eddie looked old and weary, his face crumpled from years under the sun. The tan was gone, the cheeks had dropped and his teeth were no longer too white. He looked like what he was – it was that simple – and there was an even harsher truth to his appearance: his youth was gone forever. People who try to look young end up looking so old the moment the maintenance stops. Eddie's maintenance had clearly stopped.

Eddie also had the look of a faded gambler, which is not something that everybody can see. But Ray knew the look – a cross between condemned and exhausted, with a bit of coke fiend to turn the edge of the lips the wrong way. Nothing does it better. If Eddie had been a fighter, an old fighter, he would have looked like a loser, a loser 30 years after the last punches had sent him reeling. Ray had seen too many old men with that look. It was not a medical condition, but in the fight business it was known as being 'gone'. Eddie looked gone.

Eddie had always been comfortable inside the marathon hours of the casino neon that stretch out in an endless arc of gloom. Sooner or later all men looked just like Eddie Lights when they walked the golden and gaudy carpets of the casino acres. Women could look as bad, but cancer and skincare and surgery did more to change their look. Surgery disguised the decline of most Vegas women over the age of 25. It was impossible to determine a woman's age in Vegas once she had reached 30. It was easier with the men. A lot of the plastic boys were now pushing 70, with cracked and creaking jaws and dark claws for hands to hold the skinny palms of their trophy wives. But Eddie had an excuse. He had been a busy boy, far from the grooming rituals of his old friends. He was a long way from the spa at Caesars and the tanned geezers he steamed with most days.

Eddie's men had worn ties so sharp and suits so slick they'd had the look of marching mannequins. When they breezed with small steps alongside the green tables heaving with chips, it was impossible to ignore them. The Vegas veterans, the big players were angels in cut silk suits walking through their sparkling money heaven on strolls that ended at dawn. Eddie was the owner of a million respectful nods and a survivor from a time when respect was high end. It had mattered to Eddie and the men in Vegas just like him.

But Eddie had been away from his life. His hair was a bit longer than normal and his nails dirty. His clothes were an odd mix and, to tell the truth, it looked like he had been kipping in the clobber. His breath was foul. Ray had never seen him like this. Even his eyes looked borrowed from a rheumy geezer with a trolley and piss in his pants. He was – and it seemed outrageous to even suggest it – a mess. A right fucking state and the vodka wasn't helping.

'I had a wife. Did you know that?'

Ray shifted in his seat. They had been at the table in the flat for 30 minutes and this was where the conversation needed to go. It was the first mention of anything other than absent friends in Las Vegas and London. Ray had hardly said a word; he'd just nodded and laughed as the man in front of him, his old pal, Eddie Lights of Las Vegas, Sal's boy, the man who opened for Sinatra, had talked his way through a few inches of vodka. Eddie was in no rush to get to where the conversation had to go. He shifted his words from lost faces to forgotten faces and pushed for a laugh. It was not remotely funny to Ray. Eddie's smile slipped in and out of sad. Ray sat in silence mostly. He had far too many things to consider with every word that fell from Eddie's lips. There was far too much to go over for easy laughs. But now, Ray listened. The wife had been mentioned. Now the talk would change. It was kaput for the giggles. Ray would finally get some answers and that was exactly what he needed. Forget the morning.

'I was married once. In Blackpool, of all places. And I have a daughter. But you know that, don't you, son? You know. Sorry I never told you. Just one of those things.'

Bish, bash and fucking bosh. At last. Business.

Eddie dropped his eyes for a second. Moved the glass an inch, like a chess master in the endgame of a murderous session. Eddie had crossed the barrier. He would have to imagine Ray knew about everything; it was the only way he could think. Ray could see in Eddie's flat eyes that the bullshit for the night was over. Eddie suddenly looked like a man with a heavy heart. The tortured sparring was done and now they would talk. Now they would clear the air.

The clock slipped to 2 a.m. It had been a long night for Ray.

The silence stayed in place a little longer. There was not even the tumble of ice to set the scene for the next move. The empty glasses were frozen and piled heavy with smashed lemons. Eddie looked up, in no hurry to move the story forward. He was smiling the evening's first real smile. A laugh followed. Ray joined him. It was funny. The game was about to begin and not before time.

Ray knew it would be his turn to do most of the talking in a minute or two and that meant it would soon be his decision to tell the truth or lie his way to sunset: lie, or just shift the bits and pieces of truth about. The deception was not the problem, and the truth should have been easy, but at 2 a.m. odd things happen and Eddie had the track record to prove it.

Ray understood the man sitting in front of him and he knew that Eddie, like all the men he had spoken to, would not accept the truth at face value. What would Eddie believe? Ray had gone through it in his mind and he had to admit that his involvement was suspect at best and, to be honest, fucking odd at worst. No dough and no plan? It was not right.

The two men at the table shared the same morality. They knew each other, knew what the other was thinking. The daughter, the Vegas mob, the Atlantic City escape, the little prick in the restaurant. Now this. Ray was sick of it. He had nothing else to tell or add. He had enough problems without this extra juice running down his chin. What he didn't have was proof that he was not involved with the cash end of the carnage. It was somebody else's fiesta. Honest. But Ray knew it didn't sound right. There were questions – too many of them. Nobody had called him a liar, but nobody had believed him.

So, what were his reasons for getting involved? He didn't have a single poxy idea and that was what scared him most. It was always easier in any tight situation to be guilty and lying. The woman at his door had been a good-looking girl, but that was a slender excuse and, in the present troubled company, a potential insult.

'Raymondo, why don't you tell me what you think and what you know? Talk away, we been friends a long time. It's late and I've had enough of dead ponces and scheming pieces of shit. Do me a favour and treat me with respect. Tell me what you know.'

Eddie didn't look right and that only added to the menace. Ray put the odds at less than evens that he would be shot by 2.30. It nearly made him smile. Luckily, he had walked out on gambling a long time ago. Ray had kicked into touch his vices one by one and now this situation. It wasn't fair.

Ray started to talk, his brain bringing forward and rejecting words as he tumbled to the tale. It had to be smooth because he knew Eddie would know enough to see a lie. Eddie read liars like gamblers studied form. *Pace, big boy, gentle pace*, he told himself. They were two men from a world where liars prosper. The simple axiom for their lifestyle: if the lips are moving, then he is fucking lying.

'Well, one morning about two weeks ago a blonde girl arrived here, at the flat. It was a Sunday, about eight in the morning. To be honest, I was not very impressed.'

'How did she know where you lived?'

Ray had no idea. Still had no idea. It had never occurred to him. But he could see how it looked. He knew it was bad. The man on the other seat clearly wanted a better answer than the one that had just flashed through Ray's mind. *Oh Jesus, none of this was sounding right. There was too much money involved and too many kosher cranks to make it any fun. And one or two confirmed deceased. Let's not forget the dead, my son.* The sort had stitched him up from the get-go. It was a million miles from copacetic and Ray was desperate to get it back on track. He had to keep talking, but now he could hear the doubting voices of everybody he had spoken to since the knock on the door.

She knew because she had spoken to Boydy. He had given her the address at the fights that night. No, no way. He would have mentioned it when he called. Why give her the address? Did he even know the address? Think, think, think.

'I think she grafted on a secretary at one of the papers. But I don't know for sure.'

'Carry on. You're talking, I'm listening.'

'Well, what could I do? I invited her in. She told me a story about her dad. She said you were her old man.'

'It's odd, ain't it? This cunt arrives at your door early in the morning. You don't have a clue where she's come from. You've never seen her before in your life. You, being a clever guy an' all. Sure is fucking odd. You don't think something's wrong? Don't think, what's this bitch working? Tears, fucking story makes no sense. You let her in. What, you looking to fuck her? That's it. You just let her in? Make her coffee and promise to find her dad. Now, that is a fucked-up story, Raymondo.'

'Now, hold on a second, Eddie. I tried to call you then and there and I've tried a dozen times since. I had no idea that you'd pissed off into exile. I was on the blower non-stop trying to get to the bottom of it. I must a done a hundred quid's worth of calls to Vegas and a few other places. Anyway, what was in it for me other than getting my leg over?'

They both laughed. A proper laugh again, which was not such a bad thing.

'Ray, I don't know about all this. I have no idea, to be honest. But you have to admit that it's odd. What makes sense? Nothing. Not one bit of it. Sit in my Guccis, Raymondo, and tell me what you think. You start calling our friends, my friends. You start asking about me. What do you think I think?'

Ray went through the story. He told it with the knowledge gained from the many times people had listened and remained unmoved. They had listened in Vegas and Atlantic City and their eyes had told Ray that they thought he was a liar. He tweaked some items inside the tale. It was strange, but it was real. Why should he doubt the girl and her tears and her version of events? Eddie Lights was clearly, bless him, losing his mind. He was paranoid. He was acting like a nutcase, which was not surprising, considering the number of people he had topped and the amount of coke he had whacked up his snozzer over the years.

This was no way to spend the small hours. Ray had nearly lost a pinkie to the Butter-Knife Kid a few hours earlier and now he was telling the same story to another damaged man. The Vegas hobo at the table was not welcome. It was not good news.

'Who did you call? Who did you speak to? I know some of the names but tell me the rest. Every single one.'

Eddie knew everybody on the list and Ray suspected that some had lied to him. Ray grew to realise many had lied through their teeth. They had known all the time. Ray had been a fool, a dummy on a stupid search. Eddie nodded as Ray rattled off the names of the men he had called. Eddie sat in silence, moving the glass a fraction each second or two.

Ray continued. 'And then I went to Vegas.'

'You went to Vegas to find me. Raymondo, I'm touched.'

'No, well, not really. I was at the Hatton fight and I had some other business. I did ask a few people if they had seen you. I'd already spoken to a lot of the people I bumped into, but I kept asking about you.'

'Did you find me?'

It seemed to make Eddie laugh.

'Did I bollocks! No, I never even got close. You'd vanished, you old fucker.'

This time Ray laughed.

'So, tell me, who told you that I was gone?'

It was another end to the bullshit and oddly it changed the mood, lifted the atmosphere for a moment. There was a chance they could clear up the little mystery. They each smiled. Ray realised for the first time that Rubin might have been right. Eddie Lights could be the man Rubin had talked about and not the crooner and facilitator Ray had known for far too many years.

Ray continued, playing with time he had clearly run out of and ignoring Eddie's question. He was aware a careless word could end somewhere bad.

'Anyway, it was not going very well. Zippo. Nobody had seen you and one or two told me to just forget it. Forget you. Then, just what I needed, it started to go seriously fucking wrong. You gotta remember in the first place just why I'm looking for you. It's your daughter that set it all in motion and caused me all this aggro. It's fuck all to do with me. I was just trying to fix it.'

Eddie shook his head. He was a move or two in front and ticking Ray's truth against his truth. Ray told him about the trip out to Jimmy's Diamond Room. He told him about the men in leather coats and the leisure suits and the evil in the air. Eddie shrugged. Ray told him about the fear on Stacey's face. Eddie listened. Ray talked about being scared. Eddie missed that. He wasn't bothered if Ray was scared; Eddie was not a scared type of guy. Ray told him about the run through the car park, the strippers popping out the back for a snout and the arrival of the car. He told him about the race from the car park when the men went inside the nude clip joint. Eddie listened, occasionally smiling.

'You did all that because some blonde cunt shows up at your door. It is strange. So, what did Stacey say?'

'He told me to forget about you and leave. Leave right away.'

Eddie was not interested in the men. He clearly knew about them. Knew who they were. They were not Eddie's problem.

'Clever man. I'm seeing a pattern, Raymondo. So, then what happened?'

Ray had calmed down. He talked about the day of the fight and the night of the fight. Eddie didn't react when Ray told him about seeing the men at the fight. Ray tried to explain how difficult it was to get back to the room, but Eddie was smiling. He knew the tunnels under the casino floors. He knew the tiny silent lifts and the hidden exits that most visitors to Las Vegas never see or go through. Eddie always walked in and out of the secret walls. It had been his life.

'Anyway, I opened the door and bosh! Two of them. The little one and the greasy lump.'

Eddie sighed and smiled again, with a gentle shake of his head.

'You dummy.' Eddie was smiling now. 'Why didn't you ask Jay for a new room? That was stupid. Go on, what then?'

There was certainly no hurry, no speed to the story now. The vodka sat in its own spreading pool of water from the frosting that had covered it during its hours in the freezer. Eddie sat in total silence, but equally cold. Ray tried to recall the meeting of minds in his Vegas hotel room. The fear and frustration at having done nothing wrong had been real. He told it straight and kept his attempt to shake the pair to the facts – the separate cabs, the stop at the Hard Rock. He cut it short once he reached the airport and finished with his eyes closing on the plane.

'First up, Raymondo, there was no need to worry. If they'd wanted to kill you, you'd be dead. If they'd wanted to follow you, you'd have never seen them. They didn't have to follow you, they knew where you were going. They listened to your messages. They were not really looking for you, Casanova, so relax. They were looking for me and they thought you would lead them to me.'

'How do you know they listened to my messages?'

'I know because they followed you to Atlantic City. I'm guessing there was a message on the machine in the room. They played the message. Listen, they ain't that fucking smart. They needed you to continue acting like an idiot.'

Ray wasn't sure how fast to go from that point. Eddie knew too much. He was moves and moves in front of Ray. How did Eddie know he had gone from Las Vegas to Atlantic City? Eddie was sitting reading his mind.

'Let me explain, Raymondo. Somebody called you and left your travel details. Airline, hotel, somebody. I don't know who the fuck it was. "Hi, Ray. Flight to Atlantic City at blah, blah, blah." Sound possible? One of the fellas played your messages and was one step in front of you. It's not that clever. Trust me, these guys ain't that clever.'

'But how did you know I went to Atlantic City?'

'Ray, give me some credit. I'm not the schmuck in this conversation.'

Ray started to tell the story of his time in Atlantic City. He skipped over most of the waiting and the scheming at the conference. He moved quickly through the day and the evening steam at the Hilton. Eddie nodded, perhaps recognising that he was not part of Ray's busy day grafting at the conference. Eddie was patient and Ray talked his day slowly to an end.

In Atlantic City, there was just Rubin with a direct link to Eddie. The cheap talk at the conference was just that. People had heard one thing, imagined another and ended up curious. Ray forgot a thousand boxing conversations each day. He had to or he would go mad with the information inside his head. It seemed like months had passed since AC, not just hours.

He missed one thing – the $100 chip and the man lost in the swirling steam at the end of the tiled top row. It had been Eddie.

'You were watching over me. That was you in the steam. Why didn't you say something?'

'I did when I arrived. I said, "You still got my $100 chip?"'

'So, you know I met with Rube.' It was not a question and Eddie didn't answer.

Eddie and Rubin had known each other a long time. Rubin had been, Ray knew, the last person who had spoken to Eddie. It was Rubin who had told Ray the story. It was Rubin who had ended the mystery.

'So, what did Rubin say?'

Ray never answered.

'Ray, relax. I love you, man. Just tell me the truth and get the world off your back. Say the things you wanna say. I don't think you are lying to me, so don't start now. Let's get this shit gone now.'

'That's the problem, it ain't gonna just go away, is it? It's not like one of those poxy summer songs. I'm lumbered with this. I've got guns and nutcases all over the gaff. And there's nish in this for me. Not a penny. Not a centime. What the fuck have you done, Ed?'

'That's better, Raymondo. I knew you were upset. Now you've put your cards down and I like that, son.'

'Eddie, you obviously know what Rubin told me.'

They looked across the table at each other. Eddie looked fresher now than he had two hours earlier. He shrugged. It was what people called a wise guy shrug. It often accompanied a snippet of dialogue, like 'Hey, Angelo, they found that fat fuck Vinny the Wedge in his car – a skinny mocha smooth up his arse.' Then comes the shrug.

'What's the problem here, Ed? You think I'm involved in some way with whatever it is that you're doing? Well, I'm telling you that I'm not. I have no idea what all this is about. I have no desire to know. I'm stuck, as you've said, in the middle of this. And I don't have a good reason, a suitable excuse.'

'Other than the promise of a bunk-up.'

'Correct, other than a distant hope of a long-overdue legover.' Ray just shook his head.

'Rube told you a lot of things. And you don't need to believe any of them. It's your choice. Ray, look at me. Ray. That's better. I know you had nothing to do with any of this. But you are – I think we both agree – in for the ride now. You know what would have happened if I really thought you were in on the swindle, don't you? You know, right? Good, so let's start to get on top of this.'

Ray filled in some of the missing pieces from his final hours in Atlantic City for Eddie. He figured he knew about the men arriving at his room, the short stay in Philly and the journey home, but he told him all the same.

'There is something I don't think you know yet.'

'Let me guess . . . Little Sal's in London now and he's looking for me? Am I right? I can tell from your smile that I'm spot on.'

Ray knew he had to hold back the recent calls, the meet and the meal. If he knew and Eddie didn't, then he had an edge. Ray was sure Eddie had no idea there had been a meeting at the restaurant.

Eddie had stopped fidgeting and Ray was looking for a sign that the man in front of him knew that he was holding something back. Ray needed to avoid telling the whole story – to avoid telling Eddie that he had given his daughter's hotel and room number to a man who wanted to kill him and in all probability wanted to kill her. How else could he get round telling the whole truth?

'Boydy called me. You know, Mickey. He told me that a fella, a fella called Sal was in town and was interested to talk to me. I left it at that. I've been wondering what to do. I guess I'm going to have to meet with him. I told Boydy I would get back to him.'

It was a bad lie from a desperate man at exactly the right moment and Eddie reacted like he bought it. This way, Ray reasoned, he could make it look like he was still thinking about the situation. Ray knew it was a deliberate act of cowardice and stupidity from him. Ray also knew it was the act of a stupid coward. But a subtle shift had taken place because Ray was now leading Eddie into a new part of the story and hopefully away from the truth. It was a journey of continued deception Ray had to take Eddie on. But, for the first time all night, it also left Ray in charge and Eddie in the dark. Ray had no immediate bright ideas, but he was in front of Eddie in the story and that meant Eddie had to listen. In other words, Ray had the advantage to do a deal. In gambling terms, it was a strong hand. In both of their worlds, that meant power.

Eddie was on the back foot at that moment. Ray had only mentioned the suggestion of a meeting; there was nothing about the girl or the hotel, just a possible meeting with Sal he would have to arrange. Ray was playing the options game in his head. Getting out of the flat early in the morning was the only thing that made any sense. He needed to stick with his plan from the restaurant and that meant keeping Eddie away from any of the morning action.

He knew Eddie would not push him – not just yet, anyway. There was time. Eddie would play cool for the information, knowing it was coming and not wanting to appear desperate. Ray was sure he could pull it off when the morning came. He could slip away and hopefully find a solution.

'So, Ed, what's it all about?'

Ray had played his move perfectly. The timing was beautiful. Eddie sat back and blew out his cheeks, a sign the talking, the storytelling, was about to start. Ray was about to hear Eddie's version of events and there was a chance that somewhere in it enough truth would fall out to help Ray make sense of his position. He needed information for the early morning hotel confrontation. After all, it is nice to know why death is following your every move.

'It's not an easy story. Not easy. I've done my best to drop my history, you know that, but this has sucked me right back. It has changed me.'

Eddie cast his mind back two months earlier to a phone call from nowhere he had picked up late one night . . . or was it early one morning? He couldn't remember and didn't really care. Arseholes called all the time with a cash problem or another problem; the phone was never off. The phone light had gone on during one of those fat jacuzzi nights. Too many women and too much booze and coke and work and Vegas bullshit. Normal night in fucked-up paradise. A good time best forgotten. Eddie had no idea where it started, but when it was over he knew that his life would change and change quickly. The night's action was a blur before the dawn broke. The names of the punters and shitters he was relaxing with had slipped from his mind, but the call was different. It was not the usual middle-of-the-night distress call. Eddie had expected to hear the old hardship tale from a broken man at the pit window begging for a last grand he would never have again, but the call was from his daughter.

A silence disturbed and a life changed in one quick call. They had spoken for just a few minutes. Eddie couldn't remember if it was in the middle of the bubble-bursting action or after or before. He just knew that the stars were up in the flat sky and the lights in the distance, high above the Strip, glowed. Vegas was a beautiful place when the lights and the silence of the desert combined. That night there was just the laughter and the bubbles, and Eddie remembered taking a few seconds to gaze up at the sky, which on any dark Vegas night appears to sit about two feet above your head. It's an optical illusion that happens in deserts when the day is over. When darkness falls, the shimmering electric city is like a wall during a still night, the type of night when ice cubes can be heard in a glass two miles away. He stood in his robe and knew something had happened. It was the call. The call he had been waiting a long time for. Somewhere in his pool a man was laughing and a woman was groaning. Or was it the other way round? It was just hot-tub talk.

He found the piece of paper later the next day.

'I held the little strip with the number on it and went over the call again and again. My child – my little girl. Somehow I knew it was true. Just once, about 25 years ago, I had taken a call and a woman had screamed at me. I'm not sure, but I think it was my wife's mother. No, that's a lie. I know it was her. I was pretty wrecked at the time, but I remember her telling me about a child. "It's your child, you bastard," she kept hollering. I just put the phone under the bed. Fuck it, I told myself. It was a crank call, I was wasted and, anyway, fuck 'em all back in Blackpool. I never had a kid. I was in Vegas. I was a new man. Fuck the lot of them back in Blackpool.'

This time Eddie could not so easily avoid the call. He rang back. It was his daughter. He listened and he cried. She cried. He kept calling. He kept listening, as he was told about his wife and her illness. The cancer and the treatment. The remission and the need for rest and heat. The need for a few comforts after a lifetime of hardship. He listened with tears soaking his chest as he was told about the lack of money and the suffering. It was keeping him awake at night and he was measuring time by the calls. This went on for weeks. He wanted to do something. He wanted to see his daughter. He had to – it was that simple. He promised to buy the pair of them a house in Spain and put plenty of dough in their pockets. Straight cash, no mortgage. He was going to do the right thing at the late calling. He was going to change it all and put it right. He had spent his last 25 years putting things right for people he had never met. He had delivered change for people in bad situations. Now he had some personal business to deal with.

And that was when he started to have thoughts about walking

away from his life. Bad thoughts. He knew nobody could do it. It was not that type of life. Leaving was not allowed. Nobody ever wanted to leave. Leave? Why? Even in death the men he had been close to for 25 years stuck together, playing their roles until the sheet was pulled over their faces. Nobody retired. There was no retirement plan with the prospect of growing old gracefully. There was no pension for people like Eddie, not in his world. No such option. And that was just the way it was. The only way out was death and they all knew that. There was too much death. They all talked about it; it was often all they talked about. They were a morbid mob when the mood was wrong. He knew just how dangerous his thoughts were.

'After she first called, it was different. I looked in the mirror each morning, waiting to make the first call, and I swear I was getting younger! Ray, I was getting up at 6 a.m. The fuck was happening! That's when I go to bed! You know that. But I was getting up at six to call. I wanted out, right then. Out, fuck it. And I think some people started to notice. I was neglecting some things, turning away from one or two commitments. It was not cool. My friends are sensitive guys.'

Eddie had one trick to play. An old friend owed him some money. It was money that would not be easy to collect. He looked at Ray to make sure he was following clearly.

'It was an old, old friend and he was holding a large amount for me. You see, Ray, I've not got what people think I've got. Tell me, did you ever see me not pick up a bill? All I ever said in bars, restaurants and clubs was "Cheque, please!" I've kept more coke whores than anybody I know. Anybody. I mean that. I've schmoozed with and toasted pieces of shit and I've spent and spent and fucking spent.

'Jesus fucking Christ, Ray, I had my daughter on the phone, a little girl I'd never even seen, never knew about. Twenty-five years after walking away. She was mine and I'd turned my back on her. And now all she wanted from her dad was a few quid to buy a place to watch her mum die in the sun. To die in peace. And I couldn't find the fucking money. If I'd sold the Vegas gaff and pulled out some stashed gelt, I would have had about $400,000. That's fucking peanuts. A lifetime for less than half a million. And, let's be honest, not an ordinary life.'

Ray was stunned, but Eddie was right about paying. He covered everything for everybody. It had always been that way.

The calls continued and Eddie planned and plotted. He knew he needed a lot of cash to sever the ties and vanish because he would have to become invisible. He needed new everything and new cost heavy. It was a paranoid world he was trying to walk away from and that is why people had to stay. Stay or die or turn, and in many ways turning was the same as death. Turning wasn't an option.

The Feds had spoken to him because they speak to everybody. They are forever offering deals as part of their policy to break down the business. He had been pulled in on a parking violation and instead of two cops from metro there had been three Feds in the room with a wall full of pictures of men who were dead. It was a scrapbook Eddie kept in his head and it impressed him to see it mounted in such glory. It was crap and they had zilch. But it was shaking people up. In Vegas, all the fellas, certainly all his friends, had had the same conversation with the same men. It cranked up the paranoia and that was the aim. More than one or two people had been added to the scrapbook after their particular little chats were deemed to have developed a stage too far. Eddie breezed through on the car charge and was out in an hour or two.

He knew there are no happy endings in the witness protection programme. It's not an ending that anybody wants because it's not a life. It's a death for proper people, and a slow and boring one at that. Eddie had heard the stories of suicides and he had toasted each piece of news, each dead piece of shit. Toasted them and hoped that their deaths had been slow. To Eddie and his people, all the old friends were gone the moment they opened their mouths and left under blankets in the middle of the night. They departed for the dead life, cowering on the floor of a new FBI car. Eddie knew their hearts stopped beating when they turned and that they all regretted the moment. In Eddie's opinion, they were dead inside and he believed they knew it. It was why so many former wise guys in the witness protection programme tried to come back in some way. It was why they ruined their new life by dealing or stealing. They missed it. It was that simple.

'It's not prison; it's far worse, believe me, Ray. Most just eat their guns. They can't live like that. The Feds as friends? Come on.

Ordinary people? No fucking way. It just ain't happening and it was not the solution to my dilemma.'

Eddie told Ray that he had visited a few times with old friends. Middle of the night and middle of the day. The job was the same, the end was the same and, according to Eddie, they looked like they expected what Eddie was delivering. There was often no time for words. Once or twice the men had asked Eddie to take them out to the garage or the back of the garden so there wouldn't be a mess. Eddie never listened. They were not friends. They had no right to even talk to him. He arrived from nowhere and took care of business.

Ray didn't move. He was listening to a man he had known for many years – a fun guy, a former singer and a friend to every smart fella in Vegas – admit to killing men. How could Ray not have known? He was mystified at his total ignorance of his friend's real life. He never had a clue. To be honest, he believed that most of the stories he picked up when he was in Vegas or Atlantic City were just stories. Tall tales told by wannabes who would struggle to shit and think. Ray was convinced most of the killings he heard about were bogus. But he knew Eddie was not telling tales; this was real. All of it was just a bit too real for Ray.

'They killed people, Ray. Don't look so fucking shocked. They broke the hearts of good people and, forget the movie bullshit, because most of these scumbags went away on their own – they never took their wife or the three fat kids. No, did they fuck. They just upped and went. Now the wife, she's treated like a leper, the kids are frozen out. What type of future is that? And the rat bastard is living like a king somewhere. He's safe and he's got some young piece of cunt in his condo. But, trust me, he's not happy for long. There's not enough money, there's not enough action, and you know what he misses most? His pals. The same friends he has tried to put in jail forever. What a life, eh? But it's too late, too fucking late, and that's when he makes mistakes and that's when somebody finds him. Motherfucker. They all knew what they were doing. It's that simple. Business. So, anyway, I knew I needed a lot of money to go. And I had it – I just had to go and get it. Rube tell you about it?'

And he did go and get it. Eddie skipped the details, but Ray had heard that end from Rubin. He had landed in London at the same time as Ray. It was the morning of the night they were both trapped inside. London was an easy city to stay lost in and that was one of the reasons he had chosen the Ibis at Euston station for the meeting with his daughter. There was a chance – just a slim chance – that somebody would be waiting in Blackpool. It wasn't worth the risk. The Dorchester or the Grosvenor would be watched, no doubt about it. The Ibis was fine – a low-key hotel packed with cheap but clean tourists and bad travelling salesmen. Not a great bar and not a great restaurant. Simple rooms and easy people. No concierge desk, and that made any hotel an anonymous favourite. No cameras and just one security guard. It was right for the meeting. Eddie had found it, liked it and then vanished to wait for his little girl to arrive.

She was in town. Ray knew that. Eddie had gone over to see her. There had been tears and they had looked at pictures. Eddie and his wife on their wedding day on the Isle of Man. Eddie singing. Some newspaper cuttings.

'It was beautiful. Beautiful. I just held her and kissed her hair and head. It was worth everything. Everything that I've done to get back here. I was home, Ray. Home. You understand what I'm saying? We sat and she made me tea. There's no room service and I'd never been happier. We talked and talked. But she had a train to catch and I knew it was not smart to be on the station platform. I knew what I had to do. I left the bag with her. There was about $2 million in it. Left it with her. The plan is simple. It's going to work. They will leave Blackpool tomorrow, fly from Manchester and I will meet them in Spain by the end of the week. Simple. Anything wrong with that? You look a bit pale, Raymondo. Something I need to know?'

'Why did you leave the bag with her?'

'Why? I left it because I knew that Sal was in town, and he's good, and his people are good. I'm convinced she's safe – nobody knows she's there, right? So, even if they find me – and, believe me, they could be at your door any time now. Think about it. You're right in the middle here. I tell ya, I'd have been here a long time ago. So, if they get me, fuck it, but they don't get the money I was owed. That goes to my wife and my little girl. That's why she has the money. So, what's wrong, Ray? I can tell there's something you want to say. I'm right, I know I am.'

'I'm supposed to be seeing her in the morning.'

'Seeing my daughter? Where?'

'The Ibis.'

'Really? When did you arrange this?'

'Well, I've not actually spoken to her, but the plan is to go and see her in the morning. I left her a message.'

'She's gone, Ray. You're too late. You'll have to make other plans. I knew all you wanted to do was fuck her! She's my daughter, you little prick! She's gone to Blackpool and away from you – you're a bad influence!'

Ray smiled at the joke and kept his mouth shut. There was nothing he could say that wouldn't add to his problems. If he told Eddie that his daughter was in danger because he had given Sal her details, he would be dead in minutes. She could be dead right now and her blood would forever be on Ray's hands. Hopefully, she had gone to Blackpool with the money and her life. He was trying to work out what time it had been when he had last spoken to her. She could have gone; she could have changed her mind. But even if she was safe, there was still the Little Sal problem and the meeting. Ray had to vanish.

There had to be a way out of the darkness, a way to stop the killing and get his life back. There was the simple option of running, but he would have to return at some point. Eddie would not go away, Sal was not in a hurry to piss off anywhere and there would still be the missing money. Not to mention the slippery daughter.

'Ray, let's sleep. We can sort it all out in the morning.'

It was the one thing Ray had wanted to hear all night. Bed. But there wouldn't be any sleep: just a few hours to try and find a solution.

Eddie Lights was back and now the trouble would start.

LONDON: A BAD MORNING AGAIN

Ray had been dreaming again and that's when the banging started.

The blonde sort had been there, in tears, in the dream. He was going over it again and again: same salty tears on his cheek and the back of his hand. Her story fell into the rest of the dream. It started each time with her desperate kisses. He was naked and she was naked and she was telling him the story of her life and the daddy she had never hugged or kissed. Ray was listening to her and there was the noise again. The banging. She was back at the door. Banging, banging, banging.

No, it wasn't banging, not now, not this time. It wasn't her. She was in the dream, on the bed naked, not at his door. Not this dream. It's no longer a dream. It's the poxy phone. Check the clock: 7.31 a.m. Not even close to a dream.

It had been gone five when Ray closed the door and left Eddie to the futon bed. They had embraced and then Ray had walked to the bedroom and stretched out to go over all his available moves when it was light for real. He had to get out, keep Eddie happy and make the meeting in time. There was no chance of proper kipping, but at some point between the dark turning into light and the phone going crazy, he had dropped away into the old dream. It was one he liked. It was just like far too many other nights since she had walked into his life. He had been living inside the dream too often since her arrival. Perhaps she was a guilty replacement for what he'd chased too many times at 4 a.m.

She always came to visit during those dreaded few hours when there is nothing left anywhere, that time when all the 4 a.m. calls, the desperate last attempts to grab hold of some more coke, remain unanswered. It's over and the boredom starts to fight the grey morning. It's the final moment before the official end of the night. The birds are outside, mocking the end of a high, the end of another totally wasted night; the little fuckers out in the trees chirping their horrible chorus. It was into that melody of paranoia that the same blonde sort had been walking since she first arrived. Ray slept, expecting her each night, and she never let him down.

It was 7.32 a.m. and the phone was still screaming. He walked out of his room into the lounge. Eddie was looking at the phone and looking at him. It was light outside. No singing birds – too late for them to be taking the piss. Ray was fully clothed. Eddie nodded. Ray picked up the phone.

'Ray, Ray. We got a fucking big problem, boy.'

It was Boydy. And Ray never needed to be told there was a problem.

'She's dead.'

'Who's dead?'

'The sort in the hotel is dead. The daughter of that little singing prick is dead, that's fucking who.'

'How do you know?'

Eddie was up, hovering close to where Ray was standing.

'How do I know? I will tell you how I know. I'm there now. He's inside getting some more information, having a look through her stuff. But she's gone, son. We went to the room. Her room. He had some type of magic key that they have in Vegas. Simple, bosh! We were in and she was brown bread. Shot in the fucking eye. I didn't need that for breakfast and now little legs is looking to do exactly the same to you. Ray, you gotta talk to me before he comes out. Is Eddie with you? Tell me the truth, Ray, because this Sal fella is not right, son. He's not the full ticket. Your pal Eddie has done his brain in.'

'No, he's not with me. I told you, I've not seen him. I've been looking like crazy for him.' It was a lie for a lie. Boydy was not telling the truth.

Through the eye! An innocent woman shot through the eye because of his big mouth. Ray closed his eyes. *Think, think, think.* He was sure that Eddie had not been able to hear all of the conversation, but he would still have to lie. And then lie some more. And that was just to reach the Corn Flakes hour. Eddie would know that it was his dead daughter. There was no way he was going to be able to blag his way out of this phone call. How many dead women did Ray think Eddie would stomach before smelling a king-size rat? Answer: none. Correct. What about the money? Where was Eddie's money? How much was there? Dead daughter with two million or more was gone. What a start to the day!

'Ray, you still there? Get out of the flat. Get lost. I'll speak to you soon when I know what this mad little fucker is planning. And take that fucking mobile with you. Speak soon.'

Eddie was standing two feet in front of Ray. There was no escape. Eddie raised his hands by his sides. It was the simple 'What?' gesture this time. He wanted to know, he had to know, and he knew it was bad. Ray's face had been unable to conceal the shock. Ray felt a tear. He was crying, his cheeks wet and hot.

'Ed, I've gotta tell you something and I think it's my fault. No, I know it's my fault.'

Eddie turned his back and picked up an empty glass from the table. He went through to the kitchen and filled it with water. Ray tried to wipe the tears away with his hand. Eddie emptied two or three glasses of water and came back.

'So, tell me what's so bad. Talk.' And Ray had to.

'Everything that I've told you is the truth. Honest, trust me. The girl at the door, the Vegas aggro, the run from Atlantic City. This geezer Sal and his fat minder. All true. I didn't really know what was going on. I still don't know. I had no idea there was any money involved. Rube mentioned dough and you told me last night. But I wasn't chasing cash. It's cost me money. All true. I'm clean on this, Eddie, you gotta trust me. But . . .'

And there is always a 'but', they both thought at the same time.

'. . . but I need to tell you a couple of things. And, Ed, they ain't good. It's a fucking disaster, to be honest. First up, I met with Sal and Boydy. Last night. We went for a meal. That's where I'd been when I got back.'

Eddie nodded and raised his eyebrows, but there was nothing else on his face. Not anger. Certainly nothing sinister. And not a hint of surprise.

'You met with Salvatore. I bet that was a treat. He try and cut any of your fingers off? That's an old trick of his. Picked up from watching *The Godfather* too many times. Anyway, you were saying, you met with Sal and Boydy. Go on, Ray. Tell me the story.'

'He did try, as it goes, to cut my fingers off. He tried to spear me with a butter knife! He wanted to know about you. He wanted to know what I didn't know. Everybody wants to know what I don't know! Boydy was there to mediate, to act as the peace broker. There was nothing he could do. Sal told me he would kill me if he had to. I told him roughly the same story I've told you. The same story I'd told him at the MGM. The same story. And the reason it's the same story is simple: there is nothing else, that's it. My story.'

'But you changed it, didn't you? You never told me about last night's meet. The meal. You changed that part. Am I right? Now, I'm guessing there is more to come. You had to offer him something, right? I was out of the picture. You'd given up on finding me and never thought for a minute I'd find you! So, what did you give 'em? No, hold on, let me guess: the girl. Am I right?'

'Eddie, this is not a fucking game. Yes, I did give him the girl. I arranged to take him there today, this morning. I knew there had been a misunderstanding, or I thought there had been. I couldn't get hold of you. She was innocent, I was innocent and Sal would be able to see it. Boydy would be there—'

'Boydy's with him, you fucking idiot. Forget Boydy. He's not looking out for you, take it from me. So, what's happened now? Is it that she's dead? That was what the call was about, right? It was your pal Boydy.'

'Yeah, it was Boydy. She's dead. Your daughter is dead. Eddie, I'm so sorry. I'm so, so sorry. I know it's my fault and there's nothing I can do. He's killed her and I set it up.'

The tears fell from Ray's eyes. His cheeks were soaking. It was his end. Surely.

'Raymondo, nix the tears, big boy. He killed her because he was going to kill her. It was Sal and not you. He would have found her in the end. It's what men like him do. They find people, they get what they want and they kill people. It's very simple.'

'But why? Why kill her? Why not just take the money? You said it was there, so why not just take it? Why did he have to kill her? Why?'

Ray stopped talking and looked over at Eddie, who was sitting in one of the seats at the table, the same seat he had occupied since arriving at the flat. Then it occurred to Ray that there was an alternative. It was best left inside his head, but he realised then that it could have been Eddie who'd killed her. Could a man shoot his daughter in the eye? It was a question from a sick hell somewhere.

Eddie was grinning. 'Ray, listen to me. There was no money in the room. Give me a break. Who the fuck do you think I am? You think that little piece of shit can take me, can take my fucking money? Forget about it. Not a chance.'

'But you said you left it with her yesterday. You said it was just under two million in a bag.'

'I did leave it there and it was just under two million.'

Eddie stopped and dropped his head into his hands and delicately combed through his dirty hair. He peered up with an exhaustion now total across his ragged face.

'You're right, Ray. It's not good. They're on their way here right now. I would be. I'm guessing she was made to talk and I'm guessing she was singing like crazy because she truly believed her confession would spare her. No chance, amigo. She's dropped you right in the shit. Trust me on that one. I know a thing or two about women talking. They always talk – they want to.'

Eddie was in no hurry, even if time was running low. They had to get away from the flat. Eddie was right about Sal and Boydy. They would be on their way over – Ray knew it. Right now, he knew he had to go, had to leave the flat and put a bit of distance between him and Eddie.

He thought of Roy the Boy and remembered the little flop in Southend. He needed somewhere and he needed it quick, but Eddie was just sitting there, looking up at the ceiling, and that seemed wrong. His daughter was dead. The money wasn't there. Eddie was just sitting.

'So, where is the bag, where is the money? Why did you let them kill her? She's your daughter.'

'Relax, Raymondo. We've got about 15 minutes, maybe more. Sal was still inside the hotel, right?'

'Yeah.'

'Listen, don't worry about the money or the girl. I'm guessing Boydy panicked and ran to the car to phone you, right? Sal stayed in the room looking for clues. They were in her room, right? OK, so here's what they'll do. He'll find nothing. He'll come here and he'll find nothing and nobody here. We've got some time and I've got a few things to tell you.'

'The hotel's not that far away. They could be here any second!'

'Fuck that! Don't worry. And another thing: if your pal Boyd ain't working with Sal, then why didn't he call you before they showed up early for the meet? Think about it. He's stitched you up again. He's only getting busy because he's afraid he could be next. Ray, you're lucky to be breathing. Very lucky indeed.'

There was nothing Ray could think to say in reply. He sat down and Eddie started to smile and for the first time since he'd walked from the shadows he looked like the Eddie Ray knew. He still looked like shit, but there was something in his eyes now. He looked like the old Eddie, the greeter and facilitator of legend. The Vegas face.

'Well, it's like this, Ray. After I left the bag with her yesterday, I went to the lobby and was about to go through the doors, but I stopped and went back, had a piss and then took a seat in the bar. It's a soulless little place. Perfect, really, for what I needed. I sat there and I got to thinking, got to thinking clearly for perhaps the first time since I picked the phone up and spoke to my daughter that night two months ago. I just sat there, sipping tea and watching the world go by. It's not such a bad place. Nice kids work there and they left me alone. I read a paper or two and just kicked back. There was something bothering me. I've got a sense that way.'

Eddie fell silent. His eyes were closed.

'So the time drifted on. She never left for her train. People came and went. Some were workers, a few old birds were in and out in about 40 minutes. A lot of tourists – European mainly. And crap-looking salesmen. I reckoned the cheap fellas were sorting out the workers. I was watching it all. An hour went, and then two, and then three, and then something happened. I'm a patient man, Raymondo. I can sit for days in silence. It's what I've had to do. I watched this blonde woman walk in. She was familiar. At first I thought it was her, my daughter, and that somehow she had given me the slip – perhaps when I'd pissed at the start of the wait – but it wasn't her. No, this woman looked a bit like her, but she was different in so many ways. I could tell she was a player and in control. She was very, very different, but I knew straight away that she had something to do with everything. Don't ask me how, I just knew. I fucking knew it. She called the elevator and that's when I left and went up the back stairs, the ones by the toilet. And I was right. I knew it. I fucking knew it.

'I stood outside the door. I could hear them both laughing. I was stuck, Ray. I was stuck. It was bad. I knew it was bad. I had been set up and that never happens. I wanted to jump through the door and take care of it. Kill them both because I knew it was wrong. I didn't give a fuck at that point.

'But I didn't go in. No, I went back downstairs, ordered more tea and waited. I had some sums to do inside my head and only I could make the calculation.'

'Eddie, we've gotta go. We've gotta get out now.'

'Just a minute or two more. So, I waited and waited and then bingo. Out came the woman – the new one, not my daughter. Just one of the blondes. I knew it would be her. She had the bag. I could tell from 50 feet that the money was in it. She crossed over the street – the station's right there. I got up. She went through the back of the station. I followed. I watched her get on a Preston train. I went down and got on. It was the wrong move. I needed to do a bit more thinking, so I got off and it pulled away. She went back to Blackpool, that much I'm sure of. It was just gone ten and that's when I came here.'

'What now? What about your daughter? What about the money?'

'Well, it seems like the girl's dead and there's nothing we can do about that. The money's gone, but we can change that and we will. Right now I'm off to Blackpool. We have to make our way there separately. Yeah, you're coming with me. I'll see you at a gaff called Crow's tonight. Let's say about ten. You OK for money? You need any?'

Eddie stood up and went to the bathroom.

'Ray, you better get going.'

Then he closed the door and Ray heard the shower. What was he going to do? Stay and finish it with Sal and Boydy when they got to the flat? Wonderful! A bloodbath on his doorstep or, even better, a death or two in his kitchen. Ray had a shit decision to make: should he kick Eddie out, should he stay or should he go? It was easy and within a minute he was out the door, across the street and walking in the opposite direction to where Boydy would arrive from. Keep walking, he told himself, and stay calm. No running. The Tube was ten minutes away. Then he would get on the train and get over to the Eagle gym. He would find Roy – he'd be there – and get away to the safe house near Southend. He could leave Sal and Eddie to their own deaths. *Run as far away as possible from his doorstep of nonsense. Avoid everything and vanish for a time. Go on the missing.* If he stayed, he would be sucked in, and more deaths were a real possibility. *This little mob was fucking crazy.*

There was nothing to go over now, no mystery involved. He knew the story, could see the blood and smell the cash. Eddie Lights had found him. The bird that had found him was dead. The nutcase who had found him had killed the bird. Now Eddie and Sal, aka the dwarf shithead killer, could go and kill each other and leave him in peace. *Enough of this was enough for sure.* In a few days' time, he could emerge from the hideout and deal with any remaining problems. He had forgotten about Saturday's fights. They were the least of his worries.

SILVERTOWN: MORE GLORIOUS BOXING PEOPLE

'*Shit.*'

Ray said it too loud and everybody near him on the Docklands Light Railway looked up. He looked down. *He had called her!* He'd called the dead blonde and left messages and she had called him. The police would get the mobile phone and trace and track the number. This was a definite shit situation and it was going down right now. It was out of all control. Ray's name and voice were attached to the corpse. Simple as that.

Ray had been a step late from day one and he was stuck as the loser for a bit longer. Eddie was right about Ray's bad play. They were all right. He had been a fool from the jump. For all he knew, his flat was a death zone by now. The Old Bill could be on the phone, trying to get hold of him. He touched the phone in his jacket pocket and knew it was off. What a state of affairs to be in for a man who had not done a single thing wrong. The messages on the dead woman's phone were now an uninvited reminder of just how serious it all had become.

The train pulled into Canning Town and Ray walked off, knowing for sure that bad timing had been the difference all along. And he had very bad timing. He somehow needed to move a step ahead instead of trailing the money and the death and the fear. If he could get in front and move clear, he had half a chance. He needed to speak to a brief and get a good few quid in his pocket so that he could go under without leaving a money trail. In isolation, he could take a long and slow look at all of his options. The brief would do what he was paid for. There was a chance, and if Ray could monitor the fallout, an opening would appear.

The Eagle gym was the right place for him to be. It was not even 9.30 in the morning, but he knew it would still be busy. Too early for most of the real fighters, but fine for a lot of the others: the losers, miscreants, bad thieves, potless chancers and anybody else down on their uppers. There would always be somebody in the ring and that meant there would always be a chorus in the trenches that surrounded the four-roped pit. The men he needed to see would be there. They always were.

Outside the Eagle, there is a bronze statue of a fighter called Brian Rock, a local kid who trained at the Eagle and fought for a British title. He lost on the night, stopped on his feet but exhausted at York Hall, which is close by. He was just a baby of twenty-one, but ten years earlier he had boxed for the first time at the same venue. The area and the boxing had been his tragic little life. He'd seemed fine after the fight, when he'd left the ring and got dressed. He made it back to the tiny tidy flat he shared with his girlfriend in Silvertown. He put his head down on her pregnant belly to rest. By about one in the morning, he had a terrible headache. By two, he was being prepared for the operating table. By six, he was dead. The surgeons scraped the clot from the surface of his brain and did the best they could, but it was too late. The damage had been done in the ring the night before.

When Ray reached the hospital about nine that morning, the chief surgeon was still outside. Ray had met him a few times. A year or so earlier, he had saved another young amateur boxer who had collapsed at York Hall. Ray had been there that long night, walking through wards looking for the shocked eyes of a likely boxing family. Not his finest night on Fleet Street. It had been the same injury but a different outcome. The doctor had won the first time, but he lost the night he cut into little Brian's head.

The neurosurgeon knew he had been an hour late with the operation – head injuries are a cruel lottery against the clock. It really is that awful and arbitrary. At nine in the morning, still in his blood-soaked scrubs, he was outside in the wet. He was crying slowly in private. Ray had spent the day at the hospital with Roy, the girlfriend and her family. He had done his best to control the press, but it was hard when a boy died – very hard – because there is not one single positive to come from a dead fighter. It's best for everybody involved in the sport to just shut the hell up and not say anything stupid. There's nothing to be gained from trying to make a point when a dead fighter is still warm in a morgue. It's not the right time to defend the sport. Silence is the only thing that works on that first day. It's not a case of burying your head in the sand;

that's just wrong. It's just simply not the time to speak.

It's all too emotional for the boxing people, but for the press it's just another day. It's a good story for the press boys. A dead kid, a vicious sport, a pregnant girlfriend, a grieving opponent. It's a great day for the press.

Ray walked in front of the statue, kissed his fingertips and touched Brian's heart, then pushed the doors open and entered the Eagle gym.

The first part of the set-up was a simple little area with a kitchen, a work surface, a glass-fronted fridge and a couple of old birds behind the counter. It was pointless getting young ones in because they always ended up pregnant courtesy of a Latvian featherweight or a Congolese middleweight. There were six or seven tables with four or five chairs at each. The walls were covered with pictures and fight posters. Some were local and many were foreign. There was a list of the world champions who had been through the door and used the gym to prepare; it was a big list of quality fighters. In many ways, the Eagle was a unique outpost, a gym that time had forgotten in a part of London where boxing still mattered. Gyms like the Eagle had been shutting their doors for 20 years: the place bucked a trend.

The old fight town had drifted over the years, but Canning Town and Silvertown still held the tradition. It remained a place where people followed the fight game and kids boxed in the local clubs like their dads and granddads. Even at a time of vanished fathers, the kids still came through the boxing system, delivered nightly to the gym doors by mothers, uncles and grandparents. Kids from Somalia or Kosovans with death and suffering hidden in their eyes found the gyms. A lot of dads were gone for good and that didn't mean they were dead: prison, Spain, drugs – and any cocktail of the three – combined for the likely destination of absent dads. However, it had been a long, long time since a star had come from the streets. The East End needed a big Blond Bomber-style attraction.

Beyond the cafe area was a room packed with bags; every type of bag, dangling from every type of contraption, from old chains to stiff rubber belts. There were water bags and fat, low hooking bags; tall, skinny ones on speed swivels and floor-to-ceiling bags, and along one wall a half-dozen speedballs. There were even a few wall bags left over from the '80s, with their multicoloured circles for various shots. Relics from a lost technical time. The wall bags had once been treated like sacred objects.

The spare bits of wall were hidden by mirrors and more fight posters. There was a list of suggested sessions, which were mainly for the early morning and late evening crowd of white-collar warriors. It was big business taking the eager money of the converts from the suit-and-tie world. For them, there was the bullshit Rocky Marciano Bag Workout and a few other set-in-stone routines of absurdity. The Rocky workout consisted of six three-minute rounds of relentless hitting, including one three-minute round of right hands, or Big Suzies, as Marciano liked to call his equaliser. Ray had often seen little Billy Eden take the Rocky Bag class. Punters loved it and loved him and collapsed in grateful heaps when the 18-minute session came to an end. Billy would then throw a few trick uppercuts along the speedball wall in a blur. Billy had always been a quality thief, fast and tidy with his hands.

From the front door, Ray could see about ten people hitting the bags. He could also see the eyes and ears on one or two of the tables light up in recognition as soon as he slipped through the door.

There was nobody sitting down he needed to talk with. He kept his focus in a straight line to the distant ring. No matter what he did he had to avoid two hours of bollocks today and that meant being quick and possibly even rude.

It was early, but there were two half-decent-looking fighters inside the ropes. It felt like midnight at the back of the Eagle. The man he wanted to see was perched on the corner of the apron. A bell sounded and at that moment the man sitting on the ring looked up and caught Ray's eye. He raised his hand, meaning stop, and then he shifted his arse from the canvas and walked through the swinging bags in Ray's direction. The two fighters were still hitting each other in the ring. The man reached the cafe at the front and nodded to the woman behind the counter. Two teas were on their way.

'Outside. That OK, Sue?' It was.

Ray backed out the door and Roy the Boy joined him. As usual Ray had a bad feeling about what was going to be said. His gut twisted. They stood under the shadow. Roy kissed his fingers and touched little Brian's lips in an absurdly tender way. It was a grave mistake for any regular not to touch some part of Brian – everybody involved with the death fight had the right to touch the dead kid's bronze lips. It was an honour only available to those involved on the night. Ray always went for the heart.

'Some little prick put a cone on his head the other night. It's amazing. No respect. But luckily the boys were upstairs and heard the laughing. Mabuze, who's outside having a piss, takes a look over the edge and sees about five fellas sitting and eating kebabs on the wall. One of 'em, the fucking joker in the pack of cunts, slips a cone on Brian's head. It's about two in the morning.'

Roy paused as two women walked through the door, on their way to a Rocky Bag session, no doubt.

'Anyway, Mabuze's only a bantam and this little mob are big fuckers, so he calls back into the hut, looking for a bit of back-up. Now, it just so happens that I've got me new Jamaican cruiser up there. Denton, who had only just been told the story about little Brian. He's built like a brick fucking shithouse. He's a bodyguard for a Yardie boss. Only the Yardie gets himself shot, so Denton has to leave Kingston a bit lively and he ends up here with me. So, anyway. Long story short. They go down, the two of 'em, and bash the granny out of four of the fellas. A couple get away.

'Only that ain't the end of it. The Old Bill arrives the next morning. One of the mothers had been at the hospital all night with her little Johnny and she wanted to press charges! The kid wasn't so keen, so I'm told. Fucking liberty-taker – wanted to press charges. Having a laugh.'

Ray looked up onto the low roof and could just about see the flat roof of the hut. Well, Roy called it a hut, but it was more like a shed. The hut was a room with about ten bunks where Roy's overseas fighters lived. They could come and go by using the metal steps at the side and they could get into the top floor of the gym through a door at one end of the hut. It was not much to look at or live in, but Roy had only gathered together the truly desperate for the hut: a dirty dozen of boxers from some of the poorest and roughest khazies in the world. He had kids with nothing who had ended up with him after problems with immigration. Some had arrived as slave workers and Roy had rescued them. A few of them he had simply nicked off visiting managers and trainers who, in Roy's eyes, were abusing the boxers by knocking them and leaving them well short with the money. They were not all world-beaters, and quite a few were rubbish, but Roy and the men he worked with at the Eagle had a way of turning over a nice few quid for their fighters with the minimum of risk. He was often a bit braver than Ray liked to be when accepting fights for his men, but then again Ray was overcautious when he matched his losers.

Little Mabuze had been part of a South African world champion's team. He had been the chief sparring partner and boxed on the undercard when the champ defended his title one night at the ExCel Centre. Mabuze had given away a few pounds and lost without pain to a decent but protected house fighter. Simple business. Roy knew Mabuze had been paid a grand for the easy loss, which was a bit light to start with, but the same night he found out that the kid had only been given 110 quid. Mabuze, who was from a shanty town and had never lived anywhere with running water, was happy with the money. He was in London and he loved it. The people at the Eagle had looked after him. Roy was most definitely unimpressed with the money situation, so he found another 800 quid on Mabuze's manager the next day when the bus taking them all to the airport took a detour. Roy was the driver. Mabuze never got on the flight and the manager never came back.

'Anyway, forget that. How are you, Raymondo? You've been a busy little boy from what I'm hearing.'

Ray had told the tale so many times, but the events of the last 24 hours had changed it so drastically that it was now difficult to know where to start. Roy the Boy was a not a Jackanory merchant, so there was no need to drag it out; he was not looking for answers.

'You have no idea. Right now it's about to go crazy. I'm in a lot of shit and I was wondering if you've still got that place near Southend. I need to get there for a bit.'

The door opened and one of the women from the cafe came out with two teas. Roy took both, smiled and waited for the woman to vanish.

'Ray, I can't help you, boy. The place is gone. It's been gone a few years now. But if you need some money, I can help. Also I've got a pal in Aberdeen and there ain't no way that anybody is finding you there. Trust me on that one. It's just nutty jocks, dolphins and American oil men. It's the Wild West on a Saturday up there.'

'I'm fine for cash. But what have you heard, Roy?'

'Well, it's a bit tricky, to tell the truth. I've heard Boydy is desperate to find you. He's driving people fucking radio rental trying to get hold of you. He's been on the phone here for the last hour and he's called just about everybody I know. Now, one of those fuckers in there has probably called him since you walked through the door. I saw that slag Randall poncing a tea. He'd sell your name for a tenner, the dog. So you can either disappear, wait for him to get here or try and stay in front of him. I don't wanna know what you've done. It's none of my business. But my advice is stay in front: it's the only way. I've had it on my toes a few times and, trust me, it's the only way.'

Roy the Boy was right. Not running seemed like a mad idea. Eddie would be waiting for him in Blackpool and it was odds-on that Boydy and Little Sal would get there eventually. Assuming that nobody was dead in his flat. Nice thought. Going to Blackpool was ridiculous, but sticking his head down was not really the answer. It was not going to go away. The dead girl had his name and number on her mobile and that guaranteed it would not stop. Two weeks on cockles and take-away curry in Southend was not the cure for this little baby. It was just as well the flop was gone. Right now, it all seemed like an experiment in endurance.

Ray knew he had to stay in touch with the play and that meant getting to Blackpool. There was too much panic in his garden to start worrying about the problem now. He was involved and no longer an innocent. The dead girl was on his hands. Going to ground was not the solution.

'The man of the moment.'

It was Simpson, otherwise known as Soppy Bollocks, and a silent mooch called Stockwell. Simpson had on a dark suit and was carrying his leather gym bag. Simpson was a top hoister and that was the reason for the suit. It would be a good suit, too. He would always go to work dressed smart because thieves were supposed to look like junkies and not account executives. Stockwell was a cardboard South London spoof, all white trainers and fake Lacoste shirts. He never spoke, and nobody would listen if he did. Simpson liked him for his bottle and that, even at the Eagle, was respected.

'Jim, don't drive me mad about that Ukraine kid.'

'Forget him. He's vanished. I've not seen him for two days. But I'll tell ya what. I've just got off the blower with Boydy and he's going ape shit looking for you. What the fuck have you done, son?'

Roy laughed and Ray had to join him. The door to the gym opened and a trainer of good fighters called Chalky Jones stepped out. He was holding a mobile phone in his left hand. He winked at the group and put the phone back to his ear.

'That's better, Mickey. I couldn't hear you inside, all the bags and stuff. No, no, not seen him. I will, I will. I'll tell him if I bump into him. Any message? Yep, right. He's a total cunt. Fine, got it. If I see him, I'll tell him. I'm sure he'll be pleased to know.'

Jones put the phone in the pocket of his leather coat.

'Boydy?'

'Yep, second time today. You've pissed him off, Ray.'

'Is this to do with that geezer Eddie Lights out in Vegas?'

It was Simpson's question and everybody looked over at him.

'Easy, boys, it was just a question.'

Roy spoke first. 'Why do you ask?'

'Well, about two weeks ago I was with Boydy after the show at Wembley. I was in his office and he asked me if I'd ever met Eddie Lights. And I have. I think it was the second Lewis–Holyfield fight. He sorted everybody out. You were there, Roy. Nice fella. I told Boydy that and he said you wanted to find him. That was all. He's not mentioned the name since.'

'Simpson, you're a shit liar. "He's not mentioned the name since." Useless, you are. What did Boydy say about Eddie?'

There was a half-gesture of defiance and then Simpson laughed. He and Roy had known each other for over 20 years. They had done a bit of bird together, done a bit of work together. That was then and this was now. They were not as close, but that often happened. Best pals go into nick and come out a world apart. They can often become silent enemies for the rest of their days. Roy had sorted his life out and moved away from disorganised crime. He was a smart man now and had no need to be on the pavement working. Old men should never have to wear a balaclava. But Simpson would never change. Never. He was a grifter from the oldest of old schools. He couldn't help himself. He advertised his intentions with his silent partner Stockwell at his side.

'OK, you got me. Guilty. He did ask me a day or so ago if I'd seen this Eddie geezer anywhere. Like at the gym or a show somewhere. I thought it was odd, but I dropped it, forgot about it, and then today the phone goes mad and I put one and one together and came up with Raymondo and this Eddie. Simple. Everybody happy now?'

Simpson shrugged and went inside the gym. As he opened the door, one of the women from the cafe hollered out that there was a call for Roy. He followed Simpson in. Ray was left with Chalky and that was always awkward.

The pair had been close when Ray was starting out as a journalist. Ray had often kipped down on Chalky's sofa in Canning Town after long nights at amateur shows. They had fallen out over something Ray had written about Chalky's youngest son. Spencer Jones could fight a bit, but his heart wasn't really in it and Ray had said as much when the kid had lost in a Schoolboy final at 16. It had been a nasty situation – one Ray had regretted ever since, and one Chalky had never let him forget. Spencer was a man of 30 now and doing very well driving a cab. He was still a lovely kid. Ray had been at his wedding and Chalky had not said a word to him. Now they just about talked.

'I knew Eddie before he went to Vegas, did you know that?'

'No, I didn't, Chalk. How did you know him?'

'I worked in Blackpool in the summers. I've got some family near there. Place called Fleetwood, the same place Jane Couch comes from. Back then he was singing at a couple of clubs and I got to know him. Strange, though. He blanked me in Vegas when I met him. It happened a few times, actually. Just looked through me when I said hello. That's odd, innit?'

'What was he like back then?'

'He was always a bit full of himself. His wife was lovely. Good sort. Great woman. I always looked her up when I was in Blackpool. Nice daughter, too. I was gutted when I found out about the funeral. I woulda gone.'

'Funeral?'

'Yeah, about three or four years ago. Cancer. Quick, I'm told. I called the daughter when I found out. Carol her name is . . . Boydy asked me about Eddie. I told him about the wife. Told him she was dead.'

Ray was stunned.

'You sure the wife's dead? 100 per cent?'

'Kosher. Dead and buried.'

They stood in the shadow of the underpass in a moment of silence. Ray was trying to put the dead mum inside what Eddie had told him. What a liar the bird had been.

'Ray, I've got to ask you this, but why did you write that about Spencer? Why? It wasn't true. He loved being in the gym, he loved fighting.'

It had taken a lot of years for Chalky to ask the question. A lot of years and Ray had just waited and waited, knowing it was coming. This was not a good time, but Ray knew Chalky's anger had denied him the chance to explain since the day it had first appeared in the paper. There was no easy answer. Ray knew he had been right to say the kid was not, and had never been, in love with the sport. That he was sure about. But he was equally convinced that it was a stupid throwaway line and certainly not worth putting the kibosh on a friendship for. It was not his first and it would not be his last mistake. Ray regretted it each and every time his words caused him a problem or lost him a pal.

'Chalk, listen. I'm so sorry about that. I got it wrong. I hold my hands up. It's been a long time.'

It seemed to work. Chalk shrugged and stretched out his right hand. Ray shook it. There were tears in the trainer's eyes when he turned to go back through the door.

'Ray, hold on a second. Two things. I never told Boydy about the daughter and I know where she works. She works with my cousin's girl at a casino near the North Pier. I think it's the Grand, but it could be the Grosvenor. Anyway, whatever. It's the only one there. Good luck, and be careful.'

Ray thanked him and Chalky paused.

'That other thing. There was nothing you could do. You got to stop thinking that you coulda done something. It's not your fault.'

It was the first time Chalky had ever said a word about that night. Ray seldom had to answer questions about his loss: Chalky was not looking for a word in reply and he meant what he said.

Chalky smiled slowly and went back inside the gym. It had been a test and Ray had obviously given the right answer. He had also been given a lot of information, and that was legal and urgent currency. He knew where the daughter worked and that was an edge. A rare edge. He was in front of the people chasing him. He had something he could bargain with.

So, he was going to Blackpool. All he needed now was a taxi and that was another matter.

He walked away from the gym and up to the top of the flyover on the roundabout. He hit lucky inside ten minutes. The cab didn't have his light on, but he slowed when he saw Ray holding out his hand. It was that way in this part of London. Ray was lucky he was going in and not coming out: nothing stopped going that way any time of day or night.

'Euston.'

Not a word.

The cab lurched away and Ray sat back and pulled his mobile from his pocket. It was off. It was always off. He switched it on. The car pulled clear of the Canning Town roundabout and Canary Wharf glimmered over on his left. Ray had worked there 15 years earlier when it was just a single building and a few thousand dreams. An innocent time when mobiles weighed about five pounds and never worked.

Ray's phone showed he had six messages. He pushed the button. It was Boydy. Screaming. He clicked it forward. It was Boydy again. Screaming again. Ray was a decent listener, and often had to sit and listen to the wrong people telling the same old story. He could hear more messages and urgent screaming. He clicked it off and sat there with it on his lap as the cab swerved down the underground ramp into the tunnel.

He tapped the little black phone and remembered he had left a message on the dead girl's phone the night before. He opened the window and tossed the phone out. It clattered against the siding and split open before the window had closed again. Ray saw the driver take a nervous glance in his mirror.

'Didn't need that any more? What about if there's a problem?'

Ray had to laugh.

'It's too late. Too fucking late.'

BLACKPOOL: NO SUNSHINE BY THE BEACH

Not that time mattered to Ray any longer, but it was nearly four in the afternoon when he stepped off the Preston train. It had been a simple journey with constant naps. Now it was cold again and total darkness was not much more than an hour or so away.

He considered checking into the Hilton down on the front, but just as quickly changed his mind. It was too obvious. He had been dumb too long in his pursuit of Eddie Lights: it was time to start thinking with the light on. He decided to nix the room idea and go undercover in the penny arcades and along the front in the souvenir shops.

Blackpool was a great place to be anonymous, but even the sleaze parlours had eyes and ears and he wouldn't waste too much time inside any building. There was one place for Ray to go, where he knew there would be a friendly welcome. He also had to find the casino, but there was no point showing up there until nightfall and only then with a bit of cover and something that resembled a plan. Now he had to go invisible.

There was no way he could risk a cab. A big fella called Tommy Smiles had the cabs in Blackpool under his control and there was every chance Boydy had called ahead, called in a favour. They knew each other and Ray couldn't risk the pair being close. Forget wheels, it was city walk time.

Ray assumed that Eddie had been in town for two hours or maybe more. If Eddie had landed unmarked and breathing, there was every chance he was no longer separated from his money. Eddie had clearly been holding something back in the flat. Ray could see it in his eyes. Eddie knew more about the blonde and the vanished money than he was letting on, but he kept a secret very well. So, it was a sensible guess that if Eddie was back in his home town, he would be in the company of the girl with the money. Ray was trying not to think too hard about the dead blonde in London; when he did, his mind inevitably moved to potential dead blonde number two. Not a bad name for a band, but a disturbing addition to the Eddie Lights tale.

Ray knew he was already inside the police investigation. The one dead richard was his entry key to the Old Bill's latest game. She was gone and another one or two looked likely to journey into the darkness behind her. Ray was sure he was on a list of usual suspects, but that was better than being in the dead pool that was threatening to surround him.

It would be nice if he hooked up with Eddie at Crow's and had a laugh and then the pair shook hands at midnight and it was all over.

He was in Blackpool because Roy the Boy had persuaded him. He'd had the option of Aberdeen, a safe and quiet retreat where dolphins and surfers played innocently in the sea. There was great Italian food in Aberdeen and there were some nice people. But he knew – even before Roy started to make his case – that he would end up in Blackpool. He also knew there was no chance of getting together with Eddie, having a quick one and leaving. There were two other people out there and they would inevitably have something to say before the end of the night. Ray could feel it.

If he was right, Little Sal and Boydy would have probably pulled in and parked about an hour earlier. Where would they have gone to? Where would they have started their search? Ray had a couple of ideas, a couple of names above familiar faces. Boydy was a creature of his own habits, so he would drive right down the middle, and he was also a long way from home. It would be route one simply all over for him. Ray guessed he would be bashing the granny out of the mobile, reaching out to everybody he knew north of Archway. The calls to Ray would by now be frantic, but the phone was long dead and gone.

Boydy would make contact with Smiles, who was always at big shows in Manchester in comp ringside seats. He loved the game, but he was a tourist. A dozen years back he'd had a heavyweight that Boydy tried to look after and match with care. He needed a bouncer from Mothercare in the opposite corner to avoid tears at bedtime. The kid could fight a bit, but he could fuck and eat a lot better and he went down with heavyweight idol disease.

Old Tommy Smiles would no doubt be in the shake-up during the next few hours. The fat old bastard hadn't stopped smiling since his teeth surrendered to the Bulgarian full-cap job. From Plovdiv, with love. His super-size teeth gleaned in his newly set mouth; he was trapped forever in a permanent smile, like he was halfway through a very enjoyable dump. It would be easy to see him in the dark with his Day-Glo nashers. The taxi king of Blackpool would be part of the endgame, if Ray knew Boydy, and he most certainly did know him. He had known him too long and he had stopped liking him many, many years earlier. If Eddie was right about Boydy's involvement with Sal, then the feeling was both mutual and spiteful.

By the time Ray had walked through the tunnel from the station and had reached the street, there were four people in the Eddie Lights business in Blackpool.

It was getting darker and that would suit everybody. At the tunnel's steps, there was the usual gathering of street junkies on the edge of the city, hovering for the call that would send them off in a hurry to score. Ray knew Blackpool well enough to know it had a bad heroin problem. A transient nation of users swelled the population of the seaside resort for 12 months of the year. The tourist season was in conflict with addiction. The money had shifted: B&Bs were crumbling by the year; there was more cash now in smackheads than holiday folk.

Many of Blackpool's B&Bs of legend were now flop and junk houses at best. Forget the AA recommendations. And the new tourists were getting bolder: they had left the safety of their daily rate rooms to clog the alleys with their filthy tools. There were shooting and smoking galleries down around the beach and on the boulevard walkways, the same walkways people, decent people, had been strolling along for fifty years during their seven-day breaks from the world. Now, they pushed charred bottle tops, syringes and darkened foil out of their paths with their toes. Times had changed for the fish-and-chip mob: their Blackpool was not the same. Cheap foreign holidays had sucked the soul out of the city.

The truth was a disgrace. The place had simply been abused. Caps from water bottles littered the slopes that connected the street to the still grand but wasted promenades. They were the constant detritus of a junk fix and always seemed to be left as an innocent-looking reminder of the dark trade. The pensioners only took the sea air on the wide proms during the day and even that could lead to terror. The police had men on bikes, but they rode in silence under the stony stares of the whacked out, who simply faced the sea with the expression of dry concrete whenever a two-wheeled officer came by. The place was going bad very quickly and yet it remained a lethal sweet magnet, a Piccadilly Circus with surf. Well, a brown swell that was as toxic as it was ugly. It was not, as Ray was sick of hearing from London luvvies, a kitsch resort. There was nothing fucking ironic about Blackpool.

It had been a total shock when Manchester had won the right to build the first British super-casino. Blackpool still wanted to build an enormous gambling pit, of course, and Ray could see the logic behind the decision, but the place had some serious social problems and they were not going away.

Too many people who made money from the tourists withdrew their gelt at night, shuttering down their businesses and climbing behind the wheel of a Mercedes for a drive home and a night behind safety gates. It was flight through fear and that is never good wherever you are in the world.

People were turning a blind eye to the drug problem because the rooms were still full and piss-poor ventriloquists could still make a nice few quid on the pier with their arm elbow-deep inside a fluffy animal. The annual Illuminations trebled the balance and added to the council's positive mantra: *It's good, clean family fun at Blackpool*. Is it, bollocks!

But there was still good money in Blackpool: old-fashioned, saved-up holiday money. Thousands of decent people escaped to Blackpool each summer. Hundreds of kids cried when they left. They were working-class people and their heavy bags spilled from trains all day long all summer. They were good people with holiday clothes. Ray remembered being on holidays like that, when a fiver was suddenly worth much more than a fiver at home. It was holiday money. Year after year at Bognor Regis it had felt big and good in his pocket.

The problem was that the men and women of old Blackpool had been reversing the dough out of the city for too long. They created property portfolios and shook their heads at what their 'beloved Blackpool' had become and failed to invest on their doorstep. But it was not the fresh puke from the latest hen night that had forced Blackpool's best, brightest and richest to make their money and run; they left each night because the place was dangerous with desperate people looking for dirty money and the fix that soothed the craving. It was easier to just get in a car and drive to safety. They call it petty crime. That's what junk does, my friend.

It was obvious that 'Las Vegas by the Sea' was going to shit, but if the cash registers were still ringing all day and most of the night, and doubles and trebles were bringing back decent people year after year, then the problem would remain ignored. *What problem?* The takings were up (so were the drug-related crime figures and deaths).

Ray still laughed at the sight of ten birds from Nottingham all pissing on the pavement outside a kebab shop at 3 a.m. Sure, it made a nice picture, but only in Blackpool could such an act boost the reputation of a fast-food gaff. Blackpool was not retro. It wasn't the Raleigh Chopper of seaside resorts. Even the chairman of the football club had been sent to prison for raping a teenage beauty. He still maintained he was innocent and kept popping up all over the place, the sleazy old fucker.

Blackpool was a junk palace with enough porn to make it respectable in that area. Children were sucked along for peanuts. Each day and each night balding comics in velvet coats told jokes about darkies. Laughs? Right. Every night in a dozen rooms a comedian made people laugh. Funny? Not really, but that was Blackpool.

Ray walked towards some kids. They asked him for money. One from Liverpool, the other from Glasgow. They were 16 at best and that was allowing for what the shit does to a child. Greasy skin, greasy hair and filthy nails. Fingers dark and burnt from boosting the flame, chasing the high. Eyes that had been swallowed by the endless nights. It was not a joke in any way. Did you hear the one about the spade, the junkie and the rapist?

The poster outside Kebab King was falling off. It looked like the Moscow Circus had been in town. In the alleys between shops, nets to keep the pigeons out were stretched above the bins. The alleys were dark. The Red Bar had double vodka and Red Bull for 99p.

It had been a year or two since Ray had walked the streets in Blackpool and as he crossed, keeping his head a bit lower than normal, he looked for any of his three travelling companions. Down Market Street he went, in the slipstream of late shoppers. The lights suddenly came on above the Superbowl. It was daytime. In Blackpool, lights were king and queen in the desperate scrap for glamour. Then more tattoo and piercing parlours. He remembered a conversation he'd had with Billy Eden one night in the steakhouse at Mile End where the waiters always let you know that it is inconvenient to deliver food at any time of day and night. Ray was never there before midnight and they hated the sight of him. Eden had him crying that night with his own version of an age test. It was an easy test, Billy had insisted, and it was always right.

'OK, then, clever bollocks, let me ask you this. Think about this: how many ugly, fat birds over the age of 45 have you given one to, and – hold on, hold on, I'm getting there, you got that number in your head? . . . Now, answer me this: how many of those old slappers had a tattoo on the top of their arse? How many times has that happened? I'll tell ya how many times. *None!* You know why? Because you're old. Simple. If you were younger, trust me, the bird would have a tattoo. You know I'm right. It's the test of age. If you get your leg over with a tattooed bird, then you're still young. That's Eden's Rule. I'm sure there are exceptions in places like Blackpool, with big old birds with sailor's tattoos. Borstal tatts on their nipples. Fucking place is rough.'

Nobody at the table could dispute the logic of Eden's theory. Roy had been there and he admitted to never having kipped down with a bird with a single tattoo, unless he'd been paying. In Spain, all the Russian brasses had a tattoo. Every single one. Ray held his hands up and went along with the story, just to please little Billy, who sat there with a grin on his face. The dangerous little crank only saved skinny, vulnerable, multi-tattooed young mums. Roy had been right when he'd once said: 'Billy only fucks 'em if they've got a pushchair.' A pushchair and a deranged boyfriend or husband with a fondness for giving the women a whack! If the girl had a double buggy and a toddler, she was Billy's dream girl. Ray could have done with little Billy right now to keep an eye on his back. The thought had crossed his mind when he'd been at the Eagle, then he'd remembered Billy had called in need of a brief, which meant he'd clumped or kidnapped somebody.

A year or so earlier, he'd cut a man's toe off. The guy, according to Billy, was a kicker. He was always kicking his girlfriend. Billy had met the little bird one sunny afternoon and she came with the obligatory two kids. Ray had also met her. She was a terrific but damaged kid of about 22. Billy put her up in the flat and one day a geezer arrived at Billy's tidy but tiny flat. That was a mistake. He liked things neat. Billy met him at the door, hit him with a spanner in the ribs and dragged him back to his car. It was not the first time. He told the man's pal, who was sitting in the car, to drive. Many of the so-called pals ran; this driver stayed. Billy sat in the back with the bully as the petrified driver was directed to Homerton Hospital. In the car park, Billy pulled out a pair of nips and took off the big toe of the big boy's right foot. He then opened the car door and walked away. A few months later Billy helped to get the girl a little maisonette on a nice estate in Ilford. He never heard from the toeless man again. Billy checked and thankfully she'd never heard from him either.

There was time for Ray to sort out Billy Eden when the present mess was cleaned away.

The sea looked calm, but Ray was not interested in going anywhere near that side of the road. He'd spotted the casino. It was called the Victoria. Chalky had been right about the location. It was where Ray had seen it before and it was exactly where Chalky had said it would be. The entrance was exposed, but he knew later he'd be able to get in quickly without attracting attention.

He walked down Victoria Street by the side of the Tower and turned left on the front. He knew where he was going, knew it was a good place to put his face for a few hours. The palm-reading booths were closed – wrong time of year for that type of point-blank truth. Romany Tara and Romany Pearl and Gypsy Petulengro (who was, by the way, a big boxing fan): the travelling franchise of mystical girls. They told you the bad and the good. The bad was never quite as shocking as the good. Still, these girls were kosher compared with the women in Atlantic City and their palm jobs behind the blankets.

On either side of the palm booths, and stretching a long, long way into the distance, were the souvenir shops, almost as famous in Blackpool as its Tower. They were the first and last resorts for everybody when the rain and wind forced the punters indoors. Most bloody days, in other words.

The souvenir shops on the front had been transformed over the years and it wasn't just from touring queens looking for a way to delay an orgasm. Blackpool was very gay and the pink pound provided perhaps its single legal thriving business. *Funny Girls* was the best show in town and had been for a long time.

A man could buy twenty bars of rock for a nicker and a woman could get nine inches of vibrator for just a few quid more. Whatever happened to selling Kojak heads, plastic cushions that farted when you sat on them and fake turds? Kiss Me Quick hats had not yet been replaced with a 'Will Ream for Cocaine' version, but surely the day was not far away. The saucy postcards were nearly obsolete. Instead, poppers, arse oil, cunt juice, vibrators and dildos filled the shelves. Poppers and pipes and legal highs were everywhere. The souvenir shops were merciless in meeting demand. They moved so many sex objects that it was a wonder under-18s were not banned.

Ray kept on walking. Coral Island. Lineker's Bar. Klubb DNA. Mr T's Amusements. Palace Discotheque. Only in Blackpool and Accra and Mumbai were clubs still called 'discotheque'. And possibly Switzerland. There were more tanning parlours than Ray remembered and, to be honest, there were more tanned people.

He turned up off the front just before the Big Dipper's shadow came down across the pavement. It was less than a block before he saw the first skin parlour and knew that he was heading in the right direction for an anonymous few hours. The sex business in Blackpool had always been a busy old scene. The city by the sea had once been the blue movie capital of Britain. Blue movies . . . *how innocent did that sound?* There remained a legacy of velvet fuck films out there somewhere in Super 8 colour glory and silence. Sin City some even tried to call it. Anyway, it was no longer the capital and the films were no longer blue. Still, Blackpool was a final stop for desperate kids searching for the bright lights at the end of their personal rainbows. Same story, same ending. Naked girls, fat men and cheap drugs. A traditional triangle to satisfy the trade. There were also plenty of rent boys, too. Forget the image of Blackpool as simply a meat and two potatoes holiday centre. Kiss me quick, my arse. Or slow, for that matter.

Ray kept walking close to the walls of the buildings and every so often stopped, moved into a gloomy doorway and looked back.

Nobody was walking with him and nobody would search for him where he was going.

He was looking for Zito's. He liked it there. Zito's: A Touch of Turkey. Most people thought it was a Greek. Ray had factored in that Zito had only been in town five years and his place was never crawling with loose-tongued fringe players. *Men, by the way, who seldom came forward to pay in a hurry.* Zito's was a genuine place to eat authentic Turkish food. Well, Turkish-style food. The owner, which was another variation on the truth – a bit like the oregano-infused Istanbul lamb shank stew – was from Manchester. He was a nice fella. He kept his head down and never made any problems and that meant he went under the radar of the bullyboys and cardboard cut-outs. He was ignored by the Blackpool boys and allowed to get on with his business, but he was known elsewhere.

A man called the Snowman had given him a green card when he had first set up the restaurant and there had not been one single problem since that opening night. Blackpool was an old-fashioned place where a word was enough; reputations and recommendations went a long, long way. It was stupidly dangerous at 2 a.m. in the kebab slums, but real danger, and the really dangerous men, just got rich and tried to keep a low profile from behind their iron gates ten miles away. They all had to go to work, so playing Cowboys and Indians and mixing with scumbag bandits was not a great idea. They got rich at a safe distance and avoided all types of High Noon moments. The petty crime, which didn't seem quite so petty if it was your 14-year-old daughter who had been mugged and assaulted, was left to the corner boys to resolve. They acted quickly because the last thing the dealers wanted was common criminality on the streets after dark. The bottom-feeder dealers had their own workers and by about 3 a.m. everybody was in Doner Kebab Valley with a high and an attitude problem. The dumbest and most annoying pains in the arse had ended up in a dumpster on the edge of town and Ray knew that in Blackpool only the guilty suffered from that type of pain. It was, all things considered, a long, long way from the killing fields.

The Scouse invasion of other seaside resorts (where confessed junkies lived and roamed at the state's expense) had been turned back in Blackpool. It had caused one or two extra bodies to vanish, but a full-scale war had been avoided. The Mickey Mousers were having it bang off in Great Yarmouth and Scarborough and a few other coastal havens, where they had simply walked in unopposed to begin their trade. But Blackpool had turned out to be a sand-and-pier resort too far for the Scousers: there were rumours of a sit-down involving the men from Manchester, the vicious twins from Bolton and a voice or two from Liverpool. There was also some old Blackpool money involved, and old money was trouble. It meant the police and respectable accusations. It was touch-and-go for a bit.

The sit-down had happened; Ray knew it was more than a rumour. A man called Big Dom had been drafted in as back-up from his home in Essex. Big Dom was a bit like a supermodel: he never went to work unless there was a nice few quid on the table. Ray had heard that two different factions at the sit-down had called Big Dom and he never heard the rumour denied. It ended without blood, which was always nice. Liverpool was less than an hour away and it had certainly been a bit tense for a few months until a compromise had been sorted out. It was a poor man's version of the limo wars in Atlantic City. Ray had picked up bits and pieces, but his friends in the north were more interested in buying up land and creating small cities of four- and five-bedroom houses. They were all, as far as Ray could tell, having a fine old time. Their cash was just getting cleaner and cleaner, as they created mini-New Towns for like-minded men and women. They built gated communities on the outskirts of towns to keep the criminals in. It was a nice business.

On Zito's opening night, the city of Blackpool sent out its ancient and most-loved faces. It was like a reunion of *Opportunity Knocks'* winners from the '70s, a gathering of the pier's finest entertainers, with their syrups and nasty ties to prove it. Even bad comedians had been making a good living in Blackpool for 40 years with the same routine, the same spiel. It had been cash-in-hand during the '70s and a few grand was enough to buy a house back then, and that is what a lot of the funny men did. So, when Zito opened his doors, Blackpool royalty showed up and the real owners of the town arrived in search of a baby kebab and a bubbly freebie or two. It was not a shock: the Snowman carried weight, and a vicious legacy from his beloved Manchester, and was treated with a lot of respect because of a couple of land deals. Whenever he was in town, the people came out. Ray had missed the opening because of Bernard

Hopkins against Felix Trinidad. That had been a fight worth missing a birth for.

Ray was getting closer as the darkness fell. The neon strips at Pleasure Beach were clicking on, one at a time, when Ray started down a seemingly endless stretch of bed-and-breakfast flops. He could see, on the other side of the road, that the lights were out in Zito's, but he knew the door would be open, and he knew Lucky, who was Zito, would be there. There was no Zito and there never had been.

He crossed the street and pushed the door. It took his eyes a second to adjust. Lucky was at the last table, studying form and smoking. It was an obvious nickname. He loved to spend, offer odds and take on the ponies. It had cost him many things, but he claimed it kept him sane. Josephine, his wife, let him slide. She loved him and they had never had kids and under those circumstances it is easy to let vices slide.

Ray and Lucky had met at the Chris Eubank and Nigel Benn fight at the Theatre of Dreams in 1993. He was running his old man's restaurant at the time and running it very badly. However, he was minting it by laying off bets; he killed everybody at that fight because nobody had the draw. People get ugly when they lose and one of Ray's close old friends was not impressed. Stepney Ian, as he was known, had taken a lot of calming down that night. He had also dropped about five grand on a Benn win on points. For some reason, Ray had been the chosen negotiator and he had saved Lucky a death by somehow persuading Ian and his pals to get back on their private helicopter and put down their weaponry. Lucky had realised Ray's pal was serious – it's not hard when a man arrives in a private helicopter wearing a Zoot suit and delivers about ten ounces of coke to the party, then makes a show of taking out his sword. As a rule, that type of fella is a player. A crank, but a crank player. Sadly, Ian was shot a year later in Spain. The funeral was just a celebration that the fucking nutcase and his 14-inch sword were no longer on planet earth.

A nice fella called Armed and Dangerous led the eulogy, which concluded with, 'He will be sorely missed . . . Will he, bollocks!' It was a tremendous party.

Lucky knew just what Ray had done for him after the fight and it was a huge debt. In Turkish bullshit, it meant Lucky would be loyal to Ray until the debt was paid off in some way. From that point, they could both continue to try to fuck each other if ever the occasion arose, Lucky being an illegal bookie and Ray being an occasional punter. But their mutual friendship was solid and they both knew the Snowman. Well, Lucky worked for him and Ray knew him, which were most definitely two very distinct things.

Oddly, it had been Ray's idea to move the business out of Manchester to a place where it was possible to make a few quid legal, which is very different to making a few quid legally. Ray was the first to admit that his brain seldom worked in a criminal way, but he had come up with the Blackpool idea. Anyway, the Snowman saw the sense and the rest is, well, just a greasier version of kleftiko . . . the Turkish version, arriving in a bowl with the lamb half-hidden in flavoured sizzling oil. The money was pouring in and out, lots of stuff moving in and out of the kitchen, and it was all cash. By the time it had gone in and out of Lucky's modest little Turkish taverna, it was nice and clean.

Lucky was also the main reason Ray was no longer sticking anything up his hooter. Their regular calls were essential. He was Ray's sponsor in a way that was about as believable as Lucky being a chef. Lucky stopped the coke the day he opened in Blackpool and that was for a simple reason: he was planning a bunk. Ray knew Lucky had been skimming off the top since day one; his only concern was that Lucky wouldn't be content with vanishing: he would leave behind some incriminating details for the tax man and the Old Bill when they inevitably stepped in. For some reason, things like that often happened. Ray ignored the topic whenever they hooked up, but they each knew what the other was thinking.

'I said you'd be here by six and you're forty minutes early! Raymondo, how are you? You've been a busy boy, son.'

Lucky stood, all five foot of him, and walked towards Ray, but he swerved to the side before the obligatory embrace and locked the front door.

'Let's go into the kitchen.'

They walked round the bar, pushed the swing door and entered the kitchen. Lucky had a phone out. He lightly touched a button, grinned, and at the same time lit a Marlboro. He was a talent.

'Snow. Yeah, he's here now. I will. Lovely. See you soon.'

Ray thought Lucky looked fantastic. His eyes were clear and the smile on his face was genuine. He realised he'd been naive to think that he could bowl up at Zito's and expect Lucky to be surprised. Ray wondered if he could ever go anywhere and surprise anybody ever again. Everybody seemed to be expecting him – he was like a Mormon in the suburbs.

Lucky read his mind.

'The Snowman called me a couple of hours ago. He figured you were coming and asked for me to call him when you arrived. He's annoyed you never made the call.'

Ray was annoyed that he'd not called the Snowman. It was not the first time he had been a call or two behind since Eddie Lights had fallen from the neon sky into his life. Jay would be pissed off for a long time.

'How did Snow know? Was it Boydy?'

'He never said. He just called and told me to look out for you. That a few people were looking for you and that you were on your way to Blackpool, for some reason, and the people looking for you were on their way, too. Whatever. It makes no difference to me. You hungry?'

Lucky served his unique meze. It was his version and not the punter's version. It was vintage Taverna Blackpool style. Not quite deep-fried whelk, but it was certainly different: houmous, fresh börek with cheese and spinach, three types of olives, flat bread and octopus with chilli. And add in about a gallon of extra virgin olive oil and about a dozen sliced lemons. 'It's not a strict Turkish meze, but it's closer than most and I refuse to have curry sauce in the building.'

The conversation was general and it was half seven before the place started to fill. Lucky had been busy organising waiters and waitresses and the chef and at eight he called Ray into the kitchen again. They went out the back door. Ray saw the Snowman's Range Rover, the front window down and a hand waving. It would get even crazier now.

The kitchen's exit door closed. Ray looked back, but Lucky was gone. It was him and Snowman now. And a hired killer or two, a devious little blonde bird with about $2 million in a bag and a

Bentley somewhere in the night with a boxing promoter behind the wheel. It was a fascinating line-up for a night out in any town and by Blackpool standards it was positively Hollywood.

All the lights on the resort's front were on, but the Snowman drove away from Blackpool. He followed the road, as it turned first left, then right, with the sea dark and silent and present all the time. On the left was Pontin's, the ancient holiday village. Ray had spent many nights inside the compound back in the '70s during his first visits to Blackpool, when the holiday homes and chalets had been packed with young amateur boxers for the annual Schoolboy championship finals.

But 1977 had been a special year – and not just because so much had happened in the world and Britain during those 12 months. Britain was like a bombsite at that time. Pictures of the Silver Jubilee look tinted and treated. It's like looking at pictures from the '50s, not the late '70s. Everybody looks poor and the streets are dirty. Take away the tank tops and the scruffy hair and the kids look like they are playing in the streets after the war. The adults look ancient. Men of thirty look sixty. And, remember, this was about ten years after the whole Swinging Sixties crap was supposed to have changed the nation. Did it, cobblers! The recent retro movement missed the poverty and laughed at Chopper bikes, cap-sleeve T-shirts and the first punks. People still ate like it was the '30s in the '70s. The fondue nation was a load of old shit. Spaghetti bolognese came in a can. A fucking can! In 1977, the Schoolboy boxing finals were truly extraordinary. Some of the fighters from that day went on and left a permanent footprint. Ray had been there, sharing a chalet with about ten other kids, bunking in and out of the complex.

In 1977, Justin Fashanu lost in one of the finals to a kid from Sheffield. It was Justin's last year as a boxer. He went on to become the first million-pound black player and the first openly gay professional footballer. He was found hanged one morning in a garage lock-up in Shoreditch. Dead and gone. The papers said he was under suspicion at the time for an assault in the USA, but the charges had been dropped long before he jumped off a table into thin air and death. He was innocent, but that was overlooked. There was a rumour that he had ten grand on him when he died.

Ray still had the programme of fights from the night in 1977. Big

Fash was not the only suicide in the yellowed pages of the battered little document. Rudi Pika and sweet Dudley McKenzie had also taken their own lives. Great fighters. Chris Pyatt went on to win a world title but is perhaps best known for falling asleep in the back of a car during a robbery at a jeweller's shop. He was charged but got off because of his timely little kip. He runs a gym in Leicester now, like so many other amateur fighters from the '70s. Little pug-faced Jeff Geggus grew up real quick. He was about thirteen in 1977 when he lost, but only two years later he was on *Top of the Pops* as the lead singer in the Cockney Rejects. The band had a few top-ten hits, but their fame was out on the street. They remain arguably the hardest band in history. Banned in most cities, including London, because of their West Ham following, the Rejects ripped the scene to bits and made fools of the plastic punks. They had bands scared to move. Sting would have shit his leather pants if he'd found out the Rejects were in the area. The love affair between *Top of the Pops* and the Rejects came to an end when they were kicked out of BBC Television Centre in Shepherd's Bush after properly putting it on Legs & Co before a live recording. The girls seemed happy, according to Jeff, but the producers panicked and they were booted off the show and out of the building. As they left, they met West Ham boy David Essex getting out of his Rolls-Royce. They pleaded Hammer to Hammer, but there was nothing David of Essex could do.

Over 20 years later, Ray had found out exactly what had happened. The floor manager of *Top of the Pops* was sorting out one of the Legs & Co dancers and the fella was not impressed when he found out that the Rejects had been in the girls' changing-room. The situation deteriorated when he learned that his personal dancer had been involved in a bit of leotard fumbling in the khazi with Mick the guitarist. Mick, who had barely started shaving, understandably thought it was a love job. A simple mistake. The Rejects were escorted off BBC property and jumped on a Central Line train back to the East End. At about the same time as they were meant to be performing in front of eight million people, they were doing a runner at Bethnal Green Tube because they were skint. Jeff, the lead singer, who was always known – and is still – as Stinky Turner, was 16 and about to burn out.

Ray had spent many hours with Stinky at the Eagle gym and after fights talking about the nights and days in Blackpool. Stinky knew what many of the boys from 1977 were doing. He had a record of the dead ones, the live ones, the lost ones and the rich ones. There had been some tremendously successful people in Blackpool that cold afternoon in March 1977 and one of the best was the Snowman. Back then, he was just little Tony Langley from the Farnsworth Amateur Boxing Club. He was the winner by points of the Junior A under 42-kilo title that afternoon. Now, he was known as the Snowman to his friends and people feared him. He was a multimillionaire businessman – a legitimate one, of sorts. Ray couldn't remember meeting the Snowman then, but they were both inside the walls.

The Snowman turned off the front road and pulled down the side of Pontin's. He stopped the car. It was dark and quiet and they were alone.

Silence.

'So, Raymondo, what's the story here?'

'It's long, Snow. You'd struggle to believe it. I'm struggling to take it all in. And, to be honest, it's OK now. Well, nearly.'

If Ray could just keep it simple, then he could possibly, just possibly, get rid of the Snowman before he dragged him into the middle of things.

'So, there's no problem. That right? The story I heard has some American nutters trying to kill you. That a lie? I didn't think so. Do you need me to do anything? You need some money? What can I do?'

'There is a fella, a septic, with an anger problem, but he's not the reason why I'm here. I'm here to meet another fella. As I said, it's complicated.'

'This would be Eddie Lights, right? Hey, don't look so surprised. You introduced me to him when Lennox was stitched up in New York. I heard his name today when I spoke to somebody. Is Eddie cool with you? See, my problem here is that I like you, we go back a long, long way. I know this ain't your life. But what I'm hearing is that you're acting like a gangster for the day. You know what I mean? You're doing the Roberto Duran thing: everything you touch is falling to bits.'

'Snow, I'm telling you, this is all a big misunderstanding. Thanks for driving over, but it's going to be fine. Honest, trust me.'

'Whatever you say. But you know if there's anything I can do, you have to let me know right now. Anything?'

Ray shook his head in the gloom of the front seat of the Range Rover. The car was dark enough to blend into the wall of the Pontin's chalets. They had been inside the walls when they were kids and possibly in the same line for breakfast. So long ago and now so close.

'Fine, I'm going to drop you back with Lucky. I've got a couple of things to do and then I reckon I'll be back there about ten. You need me, get me there, and be careful.'

The car reversed at speed to the street.

Ten minutes later Ray was outside the restaurant. He waited for the Snowman to pull away, then looked at his watch. It was just before nine: that meant he had to shift a bit. He needed to visit the casino, just in case the woman was still there, and make sure he was in Crow's bar for ten to meet with Eddie. Earlier Lucky had told him where the bar was. He knew it was a risk sharing his dubious plans, but he needed to trust somebody. It was a bit late to care about a loose tongue. Also, there was a chance he would not be coming back. Lucky knew enough to let Snow seek revenge.

It was a night when death was a possibility, with odds no longer than evens. Some bookies would probably have been less kind.

He should have asked Lucky for odds.

BLACKPOOL: CASINO LIFE OF SORTS

He was not really a doorman and not really a greeter; he obviously just filled in when the regular guys were still drinking coffee or working out in the gym or talking cobblers to the female croupiers. The apprentice smiled nicely and held the door for Ray. He got that part right.

Inside, it was purple and purple. The small reception desk formed a wall between the street punters and the two lifts, which Ray imagined took all the other punters to the casino floor. It was a solid obstacle and behind it, sitting on a high seat with a smile that had surely once moved, was a woman of about 30. Well, close to thirty from ten feet away. She was ageing fast as he covered the carpet. It was lucky it was only a short walk. The smile started to shift down her cheek and when he was close enough to read her badge he realised that she was a well-preserved 50. Not pickled but pampered, and put together slowly over the years.

Shirley, the badge said. In homage to Vegas, it added that she was from London. That was both good and bad. The men who own clubs, bars and casinos like to have old London birds ramped up behind the jumps. It was a nightmare in Spain, where dozens of hard-faced cockney women glared at everybody. In fact, it was more like a squint because of the combined ravages of bad botox and too much sun. This one had that hard look, even under her beauty work. Ray noted the sun damage – she had served her apprenticeship in Spain during the heyday of the cockney Costa del Crime, guaranteed.

'Hello, sir, can we help you tonight?'

'Well, I'm hoping that you can, Shirl.'

The smile relaxed, her shoulders came down and it looked like being familiar had worked. Ray was going for the 'educated wideboy working in the media somewhere' approach. A producer at large. It was an easy role, one of his favourites, but it so often went tits-up. It was getting harder to read whether lies and charm were necessary in the business of blagging. It seemed that just a few lies were enough on most occasions. After the charm and lies came money and Ray was ready for all three before Shirley started talking and continued smiling. It was a good start by the hard-faced old bird.

'And what is it that we can do for you? I don't think you are a member, but your face is somehow familiar.'

Bingo. Lovely, lovely, lovely.

'Well, Shirley, I'm doing some filming at Pontin's. It's a special. We've got this celebrity chef feeding 800 holidaymakers. It's a new show. *X Feeds the Fast-Food Nation*. It's going to be terrific. Well, this chef we've got, he loves a punt – roulette, craps. Shirl, I don't want to mention his name. He loves it and, well, I was thinking about bringing him over for a relaxing night. But I need to have a look, just to understand the landscape, so I was wondering if I could get a tour? It won't take long, just ten minutes. Will that be possible?'

'Not a problem. Just one second.'

Shirley picked up the phone, pushed a number or two and spoke very quietly. Ray heard the magic words: 'film' and 'big gambler'. She was smiling, Ray was smiling and a few seconds after she put the phone down a door behind her arse opened. Ray took a second to look at her bum. She was a good old sort and she knew it.

A chubby little man of about 50 had come through the door. He didn't have a badge, but his face said Manager. He shook Ray's hand and they walked to the lifts. There was just the one button, just the one floor, and when the doors opened it was like walking out onto a stage with a casino on it. It was all a bit too tight and too tiny. It looked like all the other British casino floors; they all resembled pictures of Vegas from 30 years ago.

'Where would you like to start?' asked the guide.

'Let's give the poker tables a spin and from there I'm in your hands. Thanks for this. He will really appreciate it.'

The tables and the restaurant and the bars were busy enough. Plenty of young blondes with badges, names and home towns on their chests. The woman who had called on Ray was not there. He was looking for Carol of Blackpool.

It was pointless and dangerous asking the manager about the blonde. He was giving a tour with no holds barred. The guy was moist. Ray knew that even using the name Carol was unlikely to get him anywhere, but it was likely to make the man remember him. There was, as Ray kept telling himself, a dead blonde in a hotel room in London and just a few weeks earlier she had knocked on his door looking for her dad. It was likely when she was still breathing she worked here, served wonderfully off the arm and smiled. It was best to keep his eyes open and his mouth shut and make sure nobody remembered him if anybody came calling. And Ray was sure they'd come calling.

When the police started to put together the life of the shot girl, Ray knew he would wander into the frame. He was a jigsaw piece the Old Bill would find with ease; his number was on her phone! Ray really didn't need reminding.

Ray was in one of the bars with the manager. He was sipping on a vodka and cranberry and running over ideas in his head. None of them offered a solution, so he had another vodka or two. They worked, and he realised that there must be a changing-room and staff area. Perhaps there would be a name on a list or on a wall or a locker. There would also be a staff entrance and exit. It was a shot in a dark place, but that is where Ray was.

'There is just one other little thing. I was wondering, do you have a staff entrance? You know what I mean? Somewhere he could get in and out without too many people seeing him. I think it would be best for everybody.'

Ray followed the manager. They went through a door near the lifts. It led to a landing with grey walls and dirty grey lino flooring. They walked down the steps to the ground level. Ray kept his eyes on the noticeboards on the walls, looking for something linking Carol with Blackpool and making sense of Ray's role. There was what looked like a staff room to the left and two toilet doors on the right. At the end of the hall, there was a security guard sitting behind another desk. He waved at the manager.

Ray was stuffed. He had done the grand tour and he was no nearer the money or the girl or the truth. He looked at one of the boards on the wall: it was just safety notices and other warnings about the workplace. There seemed to be something similar near the security guard by the door. He would look at that on the way out. *She had to be here somewhere. Chalky couldn't be wrong.*

A buzzer sounded. Ray looked up to see a blonde walk through the staff door, smile and show her pass to the guard. It was another perfect fit, in many ways, but it was not his blonde. She walked in front of Ray and the manager and smiled again before entering the staff room. Ray followed her, watching as she walked through a door at the end of the room. It was probably a changing-room. The manager caught Ray looking and laughed.

'Like that?'

Ray nodded and pointed with his eyes in the direction of the door the girl had gone through. The manager followed his eyes and walked into the room. Ray saw the kettle, the microwave, a few old sofas and a television. There was a smell of old and dark and bad coffee and Ray spotted the machine. It was under another message board. This time it was personal. Flats for rent, rooms for rent. A scooter for sale. A card from a make-up artist. The number for Gamblers Anonymous. And a picture. One picture of two blondes.

'Lovely girls, Carol and Jane. They're not working tonight. I think they're in Spain on holiday. They are inseparable. We call 'em the Twins.'

'I can see why you'd make that mistake.'

'Sorry?'

'I mean, yeah, they look like twins. Are they?'

The manager shook his head. Ray had slipped up, but he'd got away with it. He looked at the picture. The women were laughing at the lens, their faces close enough to be sisters, certainly. Ray knew the one on the left. She was Eddie's daughter. She was now in a police mortuary in London and not anywhere near the sun in Spain. Ray needed the picture.

The manager was standing next to Ray, looking at the two blondes. There was a buzz again at the staff door. Ray could hear somebody talking and laughing. Another woman, an older woman this time, entered the staff room. The manager turned to her and said hello. It was enough time. Ray had the picture off the wall, in his palm and in his jacket pocket. It was slick. Before the manager had time to notice it was gone, Ray was walking and shaking hands. It was an old hoister's trick to pull somebody to a con, or away from a con. Walk, talk and shake. Keep moving. A few seconds later, they were at the staff door. Five seconds later, Ray was outside.

It was 10.30 and starting to rain. Blackpool had never been more inviting and for the first time in the Eddie Lights affair Ray had something solid to hold. He had a picture of a dead blonde and a blonde who had $2 million in a bag. It was only a picture, but their two smiling faces could save him somehow.

Ray quickly got his bearings and, ten minutes later, was opposite the doorway to Crow's bar. Lucky had told him to cross over at the side of the Winter Gardens and look for a small side street. Ray had been at fights inside the Winter Gardens. He was going over winners and losers from nights at the Winter when he saw Crow's at the end on the left.

It was at the Winter Gardens that John Conteh had done his first after-dinner speaking gig about 15 years earlier. John had been boozing and was close to losing everything he had fought for just months before the gig. He pulled back and with AA had battled the bottle. He needed to stay busy, needed to make a few quid. He had run into Bernard Manning one day and the dead comic had helped him with a script. He had helped him put his life back together. Manning had also booked him for his first show. Ray had not been there, but John had told him the story, told him it with tears filling his eyes one afternoon in Camden. John had called his sponsor, something he often had to do when he was reminiscing. It had been a nice day before John had told the story of Manning and the Winter Gardens.

According to John, 2,000 people were packed into the venue for some type of business conference. All pissed and all happy. Manning gave John an incredible build-up and as John walked through the crowd, heading for the stage, he was shaking hands and backslapping. It took forever to get to the top table. Standing ovation. He was greeted by Manning, who hugged him. He took the microphone. He was nervous, but the crowd loved it, loved the jokes. Loved the jokes about stupid, poor black drug dealers in Liverpool. The place was going bananas when he finished. Another embrace from Manning and then the walk back to his table through 2,000 white people. According to John, it was like leaving the ring after a great win.

Manning had the microphone: 'Gentlemen, please. Please, gentlemen, let's hear it for John Conteh, great fighter and . . . my favourite coon.'

Conteh told Ray that he froze. The place erupted with even more laughter.

'What could I do?' Conteh had asked Ray once. There had been a look of total sadness in his eyes.

On the night, with the laughter still heavy in the air, he simply went back to his seat, but as soon as it was over he went looking for Manning. The comic had gone. Manning was safe now.

Finding Crow's had thankfully been easy enough. Too many people in Blackpool had seen his face and spoken to him. He had lied in the casino and that could come back to bite him in the arse. Ray moved down the street from Crow's doors. He watched for a bit. Somewhere in the dark, cold night he could hear sirens. A lot of them. He could also hear karaoke in a bar just a few doors down from Crow's. He remained in the doorway a little bit longer. The sirens intensified. Ray watched several people come and go. Men, mostly in small groups. Three women came out of Crow's to have a cigarette. It reminded Ray of the night in Las Vegas waiting for Stacey. In another dark doorway, waiting, with no idea what was going to happen next. No change there then. It had been cold that night, too. What had he been thinking? It seemed like months ago, but it was only Wednesday night and that had been last Friday. Just five nights ago.

Ray struggled to get the nights straight in his mind. He had been in Vegas and Atlantic City and had spent a night in Philadelphia. He had been attacked in the room in Vegas, there had been the chaotic departure from Atlantic City, and the meal the previous night in London. Just five days. There was a dead blonde and $2 million now out there in the night. No wonder Ray was doubting his innocence.

Ray leaned back in the shadow and wondered why he was still standing. He should be exhausted and weary from the week, but he was glowing. He had stepped off the plane yesterday and the force of the chaos he was stumbling through had overtaken his jet lag. He held out his hands. They were solid in the cool air, which had just the tiniest drop of sea in it. Ray felt ready for the endgame. It surely had to be over soon.

Ray tried to imagine what was waiting for him, but it was hard. The police sirens were going crazy, but they weren't Ray's problem. It was Blackpool and the police were busy all the time. He had to go through the door and find out what was waiting for him. Ray started to walk.

It was 11 when he entered the bar. Tony Christie was playing on the jukebox. A long bar stretched the full length of the place. It was an old-fashioned pub. It was then that he realised he was inside the legendary Scarecrow. He could see the stage at the far end. It was the original club. It was where Eddie Lights had first started to sing. It was his pub back then. Ray had heard the stories: Tom Jones one night, Cilla Black the next, Solomon Burke for a weekend. All favours and all for Eddie before he switched neon cities. Les Savoire and Rumping Bear. Tony B was hugging his pillow. He had hugged the pillow a good few times on the little stage at the end of the bar. In Vegas, the boys had called one particular khazi Crow Number Two. Crow's was one of the original places for rhythm and blues, a hotbed of British blues singers and original rock and soul men. Even the miserable little sod Van Morrison had played there with Them round about 1965.

Ray looked over the punters, searching for familiar or unfriendly faces. No Little Sal – the groomed dwarf would stand out like a turd in a jacuzzi. The three women from the doorstep snout gathering were at a table with three other women. Still laughing. A few fellas sat and joked at different tables, and along the bar enough people were crowded to keep it busy. No Boyd, no Sal and nobody who looked like they had been sent to find Ray.

There were two behind the bar, a girl who looked about 11 and a boy of about the same age, and they looked like brother and sister. No Eddie. Ray walked to the bar. Nobody was watching. The girl got to him first. He went for another vodka. *A double this time and find some Stoli.* She was quick and she listened. He paid and stayed. Brook Benton came on the jukebox. The girl caught Ray's reaction. What was happening? He went for another double and there was another Benton song. He called her over and slipped the picture from his pocket to her eyes. It was a risk, but it was getting closer to midnight than safety. Ray would collapse at some point; he needed answers and needed something now. If she panicked, he could pull off the big brother looking for little sister twist, or the mysterious private-eye routine. It was graft, but the barmaid was a kid and would surely buy into whatever he tried. She looked at the picture for a second and a gorgeous smile broke her face. Great teeth, great eyes.

'I knew it was you. Come on, follow me.'

She walked down the bar, with Ray shadowing her from the other side. At the end, she stopped, lifted the chute and called to the boy, 'I'm going up for a second, Tommy. I'll be right back.' She came to Ray and smiled again. 'Come on, then. Stop gawping.'

They went through the main toilet door and, faced with signs for Men, Women and Private on three more doors, opted for Private. She tapped in a number on the mini security pad. The heavy door slowly opened into a small hall at the bottom of some stairs.

She motioned for Ray to go in. He did. She waited. Ray turned to her. The thought went through his head that he was back inside an endless series of events that were out of his control. Somebody else was doing his thinking and planning and he was just part of the mission. Somewhere outside the room and the bar he could still hear the distant echoes of faraway sirens.

Before he could move, he heard a noise at the top of the steps. A big man appeared and his bulk blocked out most of the light. He was smiling – the glow from his teeth illuminated the rest of his thick face. The sirens, blondes and Tommy Smiles – it was clearly a Blackpool hat-trick.

'Ray! Great to see you, son.'

It was old Smiles. Ray had napped it an hour or so earlier. Once again, a door closed behind Ray. He didn't have to look: he knew the girl was gone. It had become a pattern during Ray's short time hunting Eddie Lights: just as somebody appeared through one door, he or she would disappear through another just as quickly. Ray was not in control. He was a pawn again. It was the iron-jawed Blackpool heavyweight Brian London who'd famously declared that he felt like a prawn in the game after a dispute before his fight with Muhammad Ali. In the ring, it was ruthless business from Ali. London ended up battered. It was a bad after-dinner joke, but it always worked.

'Tommy, nice to see you. Unusual circumstances, but always a pleasure.'

Smiles stayed at the top of the stairs and Ray walked up.

'You met me grandchildren, Little Tommy and the beautiful

Tammy. Smart kids. Apple of their grandma's eye. They've got their mother's looks, thank fuck, but my fucking money!'

Ray joined Tommy on the landing and shook his enormous hand.

'They seem very nice. I'd expect that.'

Smiles was about twenty stone, six foot four and big everywhere. He wore a sovereign ring on every finger. Ray had seen the rings many times. He knew that each fat golden digit complemented the necklaces and diamond tie-pins. Diamond and gold to the max was our Mr Tommy Smiles. Diamond and Gold was his cab company name. D&G Cars, for short.

They stood on the landing and Ray could smell him. It was like an aftershave fart. It filled the space on the landing not occupied by Jabba the Smiling Hut and his bulk.

'You OK, kid? You like the gold? I love it. You do know that fucking dickhead Bobby George nicked that from me? I had him at the club once and the next time I saw him on TV he were covered in fucking gold. Bobby Dazzler, my fucking arse. I'd dazzle that cockney prick if I ever had the chance.'

Tommy turned and walked the six feet to a door that was covered in green velvet paper. There was a star in the middle of the door and 'Smiles' was written in the middle of the star. Sweet big Tommy had an ego to go with his girth. There were two possibilities for the occupant or occupants of the room beyond the door. Both, it had to be said, posed a serious risk to Ray's sanity. He was moving in slow motion and was exhausted. He wanted to fall to the floor and sleep. If Sal and Boydy were sitting there, then it was a safe bet Ray would not see dawn. He had betrayed the pair of them by fleeing and clearly making one with Eddie over and against them. It would be hopeless trying to explain that he was still somehow not involved. He was, after all, in a private room in a club that was formerly owned by Eddie Lights. He was expecting to meet Eddie. In his pocket, he had a picture of Eddie's daughter and another blonde. The girl he was meant to meet with them was dead and, to make matters worse, they had found her. It was like Ray was taking the piss out of them. She had been shot in the eye and that was not good. Boydy and Smiles were also pals and Ray was now trapped with the flatulent one at the top of a narrow set of stairs. There was a triple locked door at the bottom. It was a lost cause. That was the Boyd and Sal ending. Zero hope of being part of dawn. His innocence was blown.

There was also the hope that Eddie was on the other side of the door. Another killer, but he was, in theory, on Ray's side. It was just a chance. What would Eddie make of the picture? Would Eddie think that he had been busy on his own, chasing down the $2 million bag? He *would* and, in all fairness, Ray *had* been busy chasing it down. Not good. Though he was helping Eddie to find it. People like Eddie and Sal and Boydy would laugh at his integrity.

What if Eddie had found Sal but not the bag? It was possible. And what if Ray had found the blonde and the bag and avoided Sal? That would, by Ray's calculation, make him very rich and very wanted. Eddie would surely be making the same type of calculation in his head. They thought the same thoughts.

The door was closed. He stood in front of it and all he could think of was walking in and declaring, 'Hello, I'm Johnny Cash.' It made Ray laugh. Smiles looked at him and, for a second, his lips concealed the smile. This was nuts.

'Let's go in.' It was Ray's voice, which surprised him. Somebody in the last few days had accused him of having an attack of the superheroes and perhaps it was true. Ray had another flash of Johnny Cash walking out from behind a glaring light and standing there, before uttering his legendary opening lines. He was laughing again. He could feel a tear on his cheeks. He was near collapse.

It was never going to be simple. The room was always going to shock. Ray knew that, as he walked in. He stopped and looked on, stunned. The hunt for Eddie Lights hadn't been easy, but now it was getting very, very strange. Odd and deadly. These people were not right. All of them had some serious issues that needed dealing with.

On a chair in front of a desk sat Mickey Boyd. He was wearing what looked like a pair of underpants. He also had what looked like duct tape wrapped all the way around his mouth and head. His wrists were tied together and his entire body was taped to the chair in taut overlapping loops that made his flesh bulge in purple splendour. His tits were encased in brown tape. His gut was connected to the chair the same way. His knees and ankles were also taped to the legs of the chair. Ray noticed that he was wearing gold socks with brown

Gucci loafers. Ray tried to avoid looking in Mickey's eyes, but when he did look up he wished he'd tried a bit harder to ignore the man's stare. He held the gaze and hoped he was sending back pity – he doubted that was the look in his eyes.

Ray wanted to turn away, to put Boydy's stare of sickening fright out of his mind, but it was hopeless to even try to make out this wasn't happening. Michael James Boyd of Fulham, London, knew he was about to be killed. Ray knew it, too. He had seen it in the depth of utter fear and dread in the taped man's eyes. Boydy's lights had gone out. He was half-naked. As soon as he got down to his kecks, he'd have known change was coming from the barrel of a gun. There was only total despair and resignation in his eyes now. They belonged to a dead man. Boydy was going to die like a proper person.

Ray was stuck in the door.

'Well, I think he looks awright. I do.'

The words came with a hefty ring-laden slap on Ray's shoulders. He staggered forward. He simply couldn't look away from Boydy's eyes. Boyd flashed a look over Ray's left shoulder and when Ray turned he saw Eddie Lights. He was smart and shaven and smiling. He was also holding what looked like a Latvian pistol, one of the many that had flooded the streets. The guns were cheap and unreliable, but they were responsible for more and more needless deaths. The pistol had an attachment on the end that looked more like part of a hairdryer than a silencer. Eddie looked a lot younger and fresher: that's what being in control and holding a gun can do for a powerful man.

'Evening, Raymondo. We've been waiting for you to join the party. Tommy, get the kid a drink.'

The big fat man moved towards a minibar that Ray hadn't noticed when he'd walked through the door.

'A fucking drink? Are you two mad? Eddie, what the fuck's happening? The gun? Come on, man. This is lunacy. You've got to let him go. He's not involved and, even if somehow he is, surely it doesn't mean . . .'

Ray couldn't say what he had seen in those eyes. He couldn't finish the sentence.

'No, no, Ray. He is involved. Trust me. I told you that already.

He's not innocent. What about the dead girl? You think he's totally innocent? You think he pleaded for her like you're pleading for his life? No, that didn't happen. There was nobody there to plead for her, to lie for her.'

Boydy was trying to kick and move in his chair. He was glaring at both of them. His Gucci loafers were digging into the carpet. His taped flesh was turning an even darker shade of purple.

'Oi! Fucking behave, you.'

Smiles whacked Boyd on the back of the head with his sovereign weapon hand. The force of the slap nearly sent Boyd crashing face first onto the floor at Ray's feet. Smiles and his golden fingers grabbed Boyd by the shoulder and pulled him back. He gave him another slap with the rings and drew blood on Boyd's exposed shoulder.

'Tommy, tell Ray what happened earlier today.'

'I'd love to. Right, Ray, sit down over there and get this down you, son.'

Ray sat in the chair by the bar and took the drink Tommy gave him. It was a malt whisky. Boyd's eyes were glazed from the effect of the cuff from Tommy. Eddie had not moved and had not taken his eyes off the captive. The DIY gun hovered like it was floating by his side.

'Well, well, well. At about ten this morning, I had a call from Boydy. He wanted to know if I knew Eddie and if I knew where he was. I played dumb, which is fucking easy for me. Eddie had already spoken to me and warned me that this slimy cockney arsehole – no disrespects, Ray – would come crawling, looking for a favour. Now, I got no particular problem with him, but I've known Eddie a long, long time. That still counts for something in my book.'

Smiles took Ray's glass and went and filled it. Ray couldn't take his eyes off Boyd's shrunken body.

The Smiles monster handed another tumbler to Ray.

Ray sipped at his drink this time. Smooth. It started to slide down inside and he finally felt the exhaustion that takes control at the end of a long night. Fiends and gamblers know the feeling well. He was in a losing room. In odds, he knew they were stacked against his surviving, but that no longer mattered. This situation, this search for Eddie Lights would not go away. If he walked out now, it would be a problem for a long, long time. He had seen too much, met too many people on the road to this little room of horror, and that was never good. Did Eddie trust him enough to let him watch an execution and then walk away? If Ray was being honest, he knew the answer was probably no. If that was the case, he was getting the second one in the head and would be joining Boydy in the exit business.

'Anyway, Boyd called. We made a meet. The Hilton down on the front. The car park. Fucking lovely Bentley. Oh, a fucking beauty, it was. It's not now and that's for fucking sure! I sat with the pair of them. Him and the most obnoxious little cunt I've ever fucking met. A pipsqueak little shit of an excuse for a fucking man. It was horrible just being near that American twat. I wanted to strangle the little prick. It was a great relief when Eddie came over and put an end to proceedings. Boyd was fucking covered in blood and other stuff. It were gruesome. That's why he's naked. I left those fucking poof shoes on him, though. How the fuck can a grown-up man wear shoes like that?'

'Ray.' It was Eddie and his voice made Ray jump. 'Ray, I want to let you know that Boyd was in on the whole thing. He wanted a cut of the money. He didn't care what happened. And, I've gotta tell you, if Boyd and Sal were here now, you would be quickly dead. That's a fact. Am I right, Tommy?'

The fat man nodded and Eddie continued to talk.

'We left the car and Sal behind. You probably heard the sirens. According to a pal of Tommy's at the station, the police are all over the place. If you're wondering why I never left two men in the car, well, I couldn't get a clean shot on Boydy because he was on the floor squirming in all of Sal's blood. So I just grabbed him, and that's why he's here now. I also thought it would be nice for you to say goodbye. I was getting a bit concerned when you never showed. You did a good job of keeping your head down. We were looking for you. We wanted to get a message to you that it was all over. I'm very impressed, Raymondo, because we couldn't find you anywhere. Let me do this and then I want you to meet somebody.'

Eddie stepped forward.

'Wait. Are you sure? Ed, this is not a joke. Boydy's a player, he's got people. He's connected. This could come back. Think about it. Please, give it some thought.'

'I understand what you're saying, but this time tomorrow I'll be long gone. I'll be off and this whole thing will be behind me. Also, Ray, if he lives, he'll have me killed. And you, and Tommy, and Tommy's grandkids. All dead, if he lives. As you said, he's connected and he's never going to take this, is he? Come on, look. He's in his underpants, taped to a chair with his nipples turning white. You know it, he knows it and I know it. You see what I'm saying? There's no romance here. I told you last night people would die. I'm a pragmatic man. This is the only way. Trust me. You can piss off downstairs, if you like. I don't need an audience.'

'Oh, for fuck's sake. It's getting late, you two.'

Thud, thud, thud. It's nothing like a fucking melon falling off the back of a truck; the sound of flesh being torn is a lot duller. Three shots. Eddie started to laugh. Ray looked over at Tommy Smiles. He was laughing, too. The King of Cabs had the same gun in his left hand. It was a converted Latvian special with the same hairdryer silencer. It was three bullets lighter and smoking like a cheap cigar. The bullets were in Boydy's head and chest.

Ray looked away and reached for the door as his stomach looked for a way out. He fell onto the landing. They were still laughing in the killing room. Ray sat down on the carpet, dropped his head and closed his eyes. The smoke was strong in his nostrils. Three confirmed dead and his name was far, far too close to all three. Dozens of people could match his name and face to the two dead men. Diners, fight people. This was hopeless. With Boydy gone, there would be a backlash. People knew Ray had been running away and avoiding him. Boydy was a well-connected man and it would get serious when his people found out about the death. And they would find out. He would even get some heat over the Sal killing. Surely, it would only be a matter of time before his name was linked with the dead killer.

Then there was his message on the phone in the murdered blonde's hotel room. This was just getting worse. Old Bill and old friends of dead men – dead men who knew too many people that killed people. Ray knew he would be linked with the series of deaths. Too many people had listened to him asking about Eddie Lights. Now Eddie's little girl was dead. Now Boyd was dead. Dead, dead, dead and not a thing he could do. Ray was fucked and still they laughed inside the room.

The green velvet door opened and Eddie walked out.

'You OK?'

Eddie helped him to his feet. They walked down the stairs, through the bar and out the front door. The bar was busy with late punters. It was gone one when they reached the street. The stars were out and the air was as fresh as Ray could ever remember it being. He stood and gulped it down, trying to clear his mind and get rid of a few seconds that would live with him forever. He was stuck with the image of the eyes of a man waiting for his death. They walked in silence to a car parked outside a bookie's. It was an invisible little motor.

'Do me a favour and drive. That OK with you, Ray? You sure you're OK to drive? Don't get all fucking crazy on me. Forget it all now. They're all gone. Washed away. History. We have to move on, my friend, and that's why I need you to drive me somewhere now. It's a beautiful night, Raymondo. Let's not ruin it by acting stupid.'

Ray turned the key and waited for instructions from a man who was having a beautiful night. He'd killed one, laughed as another was killed, and all just 12 or so hours after finding out his daughter was dead. He was most definitely not right and now Ray was his chauffeur in the cool, cool night. The sirens were gone from the hopeless evening. There was nothing.

BLACKPOOL, STILL: A LAST SHORT DRIVE

It was a 15-minute drive and Eddie wanted to go the long way. He wanted to see the pier and the lights and the Tower. It was going to be his last time, his last time on the front in Blackpool, and he made that clear to Ray. When the car stopped outside a semi-detached house, the silence was shocking. Ray looked at the homes; there was not one single light on. It was always like that outside of a city. In London, houses had lights on all night, but away from the big cities there was silence and darkness in the empty streets. It was dark on the lost street. Ray sat with his hands on the wheel and watched as Eddie peered up and down. Old habits never die.

'You know something, Ray. I remember the silence. When I used to get back after playing, I would just sit and listen. I was surrounded by noise all night long at the clubs and then I would pull up here at about four in the morning and just listen to absolutely nothing. The silence. I love it. I did the same in Vegas. I loved the night, the quiet, you know that? Think about nights out at the house under the stars. They are long gone now. Come on, Ray. Let's go and sort all this out. I want an end to all this now. You'll like this. Trust me.'

At the door, Eddie produced a key and laughed. 'She never changed the locks and I never threw away the key. Come in. Come on, Ray. Welcome to my Blackpool house. No jacuzzi here, no pool. No shitters leaning over glass. This is a nice house. Welcome.'

Eddie turned on a light in the hall and closed the door. Three suitcases were in the way, jammed behind the back of the door and covering most of the carpet in the hallway to the stairs. They were big and pink and each had a small red ribbon tied to the handle. Ray looked in the mirror and saw the reflection of a picture on the opposite wall. He turned and was looking at Eddie on his wedding day. It was in black and white. The blonde on his arm looked like the same blonde in the picture in Ray's pocket. She was very beautiful and elegant. Mum and daughter. Wife and daddy's girl. Ray knew the wife was dead now and he wondered if Eddie knew. He would know. They were both dead, mum and daughter. Eddie had his own Blackpool losses to deal with. The killings he was responsible for would not bother him.

'It's upstairs. Come on.'

Eddie stepped over one of the bags and walked up. Ray followed. Eddie turned a light on when they reached the landing. Four doors. Bathroom and three bedrooms and no noise. Not good. Ray studied the lines of Eddie's jacket. Was the Latvian special in there somewhere? Was this finally to be the death door? He waited.

'This one.' It was the room at the back.

The door opened and Eddie stepped aside to let Ray walk in.

'After you, Raymondo. You deserve this. You've been through a lot, son.'

The room was a typical box bedroom. Small windows, a wardrobe, a covered radiator and a tiny desk with a laptop on it. Clothes were piled on the back of a chair. Women's clothes. There was also a double bed.

Fantastic. There was a woman taped to the bed. The mattress had been stripped and Ray noticed the bed linen was on the floor. The woman's head, mouth and throat were taped. It was the same brown duct tape that had gripped Boydy during the last hour or so of his life. She had on a bra and knickers, but the taping continued in loops and partially obscured her underwear. She was a blonde. She was one of the blondes in the picture in Ray's pocket. She was the image of the blonde in the black-and-white wedding picture. Ray had only ever seen her in the picture because she wasn't Eddie's daughter; she wasn't the woman who had come crying to his door. That woman had been crying for her daddy. The manager at the casino had called the women twins. Ray could see it, but who the hell was this blonde?

'Ray, I would like you to meet Carol Edwina Lights. Well, it's Cooke really, but she kept the name. She's my girl. My daughter and a more conniving, scheming piece of shit I've never met, and I've met some whore shit bastard dirty evil sluts in my time, as you know. This is the girl who nearly got you killed. She played you and tried to play me. She didn't give a fuck about anybody. She had her eyes on the money. She's got balls, I'll give her that. She lied about her mum. Told me her mum was going to die. I told you that. But, wait for it, my wife, God bless her, died a few years ago. I was at the grave today. It's fucking unbelievable.'

The woman was trying to move. Ray had seen this once already tonight and felt like telling her that it was a waste of time, that there was nothing anybody could do. He had been here before. The smell of the kill was still in his nostrils. She was waiting for death, Ray was convinced of that, and it would be quick if the business earlier was any indication.

'Eddie, it's not the right woman. This isn't the one that came to me. This isn't your daughter. The sort that came to my door looked like her, but it's not her. Look, I've got this picture. I got it at the casino. It's your daughter and this woman.'

Ray pulled out the picture and handed it to Eddie, who took it.

'Ray, you are a fucking dark horse. Good work. I was at the casino today and I never saw the picture. You were a step in front of me. Well done. I'm very impressed. But let me tell you why you're confused and clear up a little matter for you.'

Eddie walked to the end of the bed and sat down next to the woman's head. He crossed his legs and stroked her hair with his left hand. She tried to turn her stuck head, but there wasn't a centimetre of give in the tape. Her eyes were bulging, but it was not with fear – she was raging. There was no pleading in her eyes. She did have some guts.

'Argh, yes. Well, the girl you met is dead. She's the one from the Ibis and she was most definitely not my daughter. Blonde and good-looking, but not mine.'

The bed nearly lifted when the taped girl heard that her friend was dead. She was crying now. It had all changed. The snot was bubbling in her nose. She was trying to buck up and get free, but Eddie just continued stroking her hair. He stopped to look at her.

'Ray, tell her I didn't do anything to her friend.'

Eddie was smiling, but Ray was not saying a word. He never would.

'This is what I think happened. My lovely little girl here got a bit greedy. She decided to look me up and see if she could tap me for a few dollars. I still don't know why after all these years she thought I was worth looking up. Perhaps her mum told her I was worth a fortune. Billy Big Bollocks out in Las Vegas. Remember, a lot of people come through Vegas. Perhaps somebody saw me and told her, I don't know. I still don't know the link. Why, after 25 years, did she suddenly decide to track me down? You have any idea?

'So, her and her friend, the blonde actress who blubbed all over you, got their two tiny brains together and came up with a sob story. I still don't know how your name came into the frame, but it did, and they set about finding you to help them find me. I had vanished, by this time. You know now why I had to walk away. Once I had the money, I had no other option. You know that much about my life. Also, Ray, and I'm telling you this now because I missed it out earlier, I knew my wife was dead. Tommy told me. Did you think I was that much of a sentimental old bastard? I paid for the fucking funeral! Perhaps I'm getting a bit a sentimental in my old age.'

The woman on the bed tried to move again. Eddie reached across and grabbed her jaw and turned her face to his.

'What made you do it all? Tell me it wasn't just the money. You lied about your mother, you tried to take my money. You ran out on your friend. What kind of person are you? Sadly, I think I know. You're too much like me.'

Eddie stopped talking, released her jaw, and stood up and went to the door. He walked out into the hall and opened another door. The only noise Ray could hear was the girl's breathing. She was looking at Ray. Her eyes were begging him to help her, but Ray was thinking the same thing. Eddie came back in.

'So, where was I? Oh, yeah. I dropped under the radar. She used you to find me – you came close to biting it, I don't mind telling you. A lot of people don't believe you. Anyway, I finally made contact with her and that's when I dropped the money off. Then I waited and that's when I first saw my lovely daughter. I knew the moment she walked into the hotel lobby it was her. She looks just like her mother. She's got her looks and my ways, poor cow. It all fell into place for me. I knew when I crossed the road and followed her to the train; I knew she'd come back here.

'I decorated this room before she was born. I bet if you peeled this paper off, you'd find Noddy paper underneath. Her mum went mad with Noddy. I did it from top to bottom before I fucked off. Long time ago.'

Eddie stopped and looked around the room and down at his

daughter. She had stopped struggling and, for possibly the first time, they looked like Dad and daughter. Daddy's girl was listening. Eddie Lights was crying.

'So, I called Tommy. I met with you. I came here. They followed. And, I almost forgot – you will love this, Romeo – why did the other girl, whose name was Jane, by the way, wait in London? This woman, my daughter, claims it was because she wanted to see you. You were going to get your leg over, Raymondo! But, I gotta tell you, I don't believe a fucking word she says. I think – and this is what I would have done – she told Jane, poor dead Jane, to stay in the hotel and wait. Tommy said Jane was a lovely kid, just a bit simple in the common-sense department. I think she told her to sit tight. I think she betrayed her and left her cold. Poor Jane was probably waiting with her bag packed for a big trip. All rubbish. Bullshit. I would imagine there are only clothes for my beloved daughter in those bags downstairs. I would say that in the next bedroom, where Jane slept, there's not one piece of missing clothing. This fucker was walking out on her best friend with $2 million in the bag. My $2 million! It's beautiful. And she was walking away from her dad. Now, that is a liberty!'

The woman had stopped struggling and had closed her eyes, but Ray could see a vein by her left eye popping madly. She was not sleeping. Eddie reached across and opened the wardrobe. He pulled out a brown holdall bag. He flopped it onto the bed. Ray knew what it was.

'Ray, do me a favour and count out 100 grand. It's in bundles of $10,000.'

The money was cold. Ray piled ten packets on top of the desk and put the bag back on the bed.

'We're done here.'

Eddie stood up and looked down at his daughter. Ray could see the tears rolling down his cheeks. Eddie made no attempt to wipe them. He just stood and wept. She was looking up at him. Her tears had formed a puddle inside the lines of the tape holding her head down. Her body was shaking. It was fear, Ray thought. Ray could hear the suffering in the room, in the hearts of both of them. A killer and his little girl. They were both evil, capable of easy killing. Ray knew it right then and could hear it in their tears.

'Carol, there's 100 grand on the table. I'm going now. Somebody will be here in a few hours to let you loose. I want you out of your mother's house in seven days. If you stay, I'll kill you. If you speak to anybody about what has happened, I'll kill you. If you ever try and find me again, I'll kill you. If Ray has a problem with any of this, I'll kill you. Bye, darling, I love you.'

Eddie turned and was out of the door. Ray closed his eyes and followed. He had seen and heard enough and he had no reason to look at the woman on the bed. Fuck her eyes, Ray thought, as he went down the steps.

Outside, Eddie looked up and down his old street, taking it all in once again in a final painful embrace of memory. He had looked at the wedding picture one last time. Touched his wife's face with his palm and turned through the door. It was nearly light when they emerged and Ray could smell the sea.

On the street Eddie grabbed Ray in a tear-drenched hug. His cheeks were still wet when a car pulled up. It was a big silver Lexus and Tommy was driving. Eddie kissed Ray on the lips and looked into his eyes. He spoke from about six inches.

'I never told you this before, but that thing, that problem you had, well, there was nothing you could do to stop it. You made the play and it unfolded the way it does. A lot of things go to shit and you should know that. You lost people who you loved. It's that simple. Nobody could stop it. And she left because she wanted to. People tell me you're still going over it. Well, don't. Trust me.'

Ray tried to drop his eyes, but Eddie lifted his chin. They were eye to eye.

'I'll be watching you. Don't fuck up on me. You're clear, Ray. Don't worry. I love you. You're a good kid.'

Eddie started to get into the Lexus.

'How did you know I wasn't involved?' Ray had not wanted to ask, but he had to. He needed to know how he'd managed to walk through the death and the torture. He needed to know why he was free when others who knew far less than him were dead. He wanted an assurance that he wouldn't have to spend the rest of his life looking in mirrors and over his shoulder.

Eddie pulled the door fully open and held it a second before falling into the leather seat. 'I don't know for sure. How could I?

It's my fucking heart, Ray. I just hope I'm right. You deserve a break, kid. Adios, Raymondo.'

It was all he needed to hear.

Ray would live and Eddie was gone.

Ray had walked to the station and waited for the first Preston train. It had been cold and he was hungry and shattered. He was heading back into another mess. It would be dangerous, but he knew at least Eddie was gone. He had Eddie's word.

Back at the flat things were tidy. Eddie had straightened up before leaving. There was a note on the table: 'The steaks in the freezer are fantastic.' Ray knew there were no steaks in the freezer.

Ray opened it and saw the plastic bag amidst the half-eaten ice-cream cartons, some salmon pieces and the bag of peas he'd given to Peter Close before the whole thing had started. It was the night before the dead girl called Jane had knocked on his door in tears. Closey had sat at the table holding the peas on his bruises, trying to talk through the pain and the stitches. It had been an innocent time. A long time ago, when a bit of death and adventure gets in the way.

He took the plastic bag out and put it on the table. He knew from the weight it wasn't steak. There was a white towel inside the bag. He lifted it out. It was from a hotel. Then he saw the Ibis logo. The plastic bag floated off the table as Ray stepped back. He stood and looked at the little white bundle. He flipped one corner of the towel and saw a mobile phone. He unrolled it some more and saw a 9 mm handgun with a silencer. This was a real gun. He pulled back the final piece and saw five bundles of dollars. *That's fifty grand!* The towel was open in front of him. He knew his number and message would be on the phone. He knew the gun had been used to kill the girl. And he knew the money was his blood money. It was Eddie's safety hand. He also knew there would not be any prints on the gun or the phone. He ran a finger over both. The gun's blue was dark with frost and it resisted his fingers.

The exhaustion was sudden and heavy, like a short hook to the liver at the end of ten hard rounds. He dropped like a sniper had taken him out and tears fell onto the towel as he bent over. He had them all in his lap, as he slumped to the floor. Money, gun and phone. His toll, his pay, his penance for a good deed. His hands looked clean, but that was deceptive. The tears fell. He held his trophies from the long journey.

He had some terrible memories. And he had found Eddie Lights. But now he needed to sleep.

He had some fights to fix for Saturday.